HUNTER

THE UNWOVEN TAPESTRY
BOOK TWO

MORGAN CHALUT

Published by Water Dragon Publishing
waterdragonpublishing.com

ISBN 978-1-957146-42-3 (Trade Paperback)

10 9 8 7 6 5 4 3 2 1

FIRST EDITION

To creativity. To perseverance. To the excited spark that blooms from a word or an image or a song and becomes systems of magic and entire worlds, and manages to touch even the deep complexity of humanity. To the discovery of self. To interpretation. To knowledge shared and fitfully searched for. To curiosity. To the 'forever new' that weaves in a dance with 'always existed'. To belly laughs and shouts of outrage. To tears. To fine lines in the sand and hills of "here will I stand". To celebration and fear and trial and passion. To writing. To reading. To stories.

1

ON HANDS AND HEELS, the girl descended the riverbank. At the water's edge, heedless of the mud and stones, she scrubbed vigorously at the blood, dried, but still sticky, on her hands and clothes, picking it meticulously, compulsively, from under her nails. She was desperately thirsty, but could not comprehend drinking until the blood was gone. Her breath came in tense jolts, but she kept her face as neutral as she could manage. She dunked her head under the water to wash the gore from her hair and face, and finally took gulps of the clear water to sate the dehydration that pounded and throbbed at the back of her skull.

When she surfaced, she saw the young man doing the same. There was a child-like enjoyment on his face from the simple pleasure, as if he'd never dunked in a river before. He looked at her and grinned, splashed water in her direction. It fell short. She hadn't bothered to dodge.

"You're a serious little beast, aren't you?" he asked.

She didn't answer.

"Does anything in this world make you smile?"

Images came to mind, of an infectious grin, verbal fencing, solving puzzles, writing music.

"Ah .... your brother," the young man said.

"Stay out of my head," she ordered.

He shrugged carelessly. "Protect it. I don't tend to bother waiting for others to tell me what they're thinking. It's easier to look."

"Don't. Don't do that."

"Stop me, then."

Her lip curled in distaste, and he grinned again.

"A contract, then." He walked toward her through the knee-high water, and she saw that his balance appeared uncompromised, even across the slippery stones. "I'll teach you to protect your mind from any who would attempt to breach it, and to use your thievery magic, and anything else you wish to learn."

"The price?"

"You do what I say. Stay with me, learn from me, work with me."

"Doing what?"

"Whatever I choose."

"Why?"

"Because you seem clever. I like you."

"I hurt you."

His eye twitched above his smile, once liquid and genuine, but now frozen and feral. "Trust me, little beast. You've come nowhere near to hurting me." His nostrils flared.

She considered his terms. "I want to learn magic — all kinds, even if I can't do them."

"Why?" He cocked his head at her, his feral smile thawing.

"Why learn anything?"

"To have power over others," he answered easily.

"I'm going to escape you one day."

"You haven't tried even once."

"When the time is right."

He laughed. "Stay until I've taught you all I can, until you have a true chance at escape. But do as I say, and I'll make you powerful."

"You like that I'm clever. You want to teach me. You want a challenge," she decided.

"And you are familiar with the feeling."

"Yes."

She looked at the water and saw no trace of the blood she'd fed it. Even so young, she knew the river was her superior in this way; she'd be stained with blood again, no doubt. But what she'd seen him do, and what he offered ...

"Agreed, then."

He jumped to his feet and clapped his hands. "Ha! Good!"

"What do I call you, then?"

"Hm," he mused, and looked around. "How about ... Forest?"

"That's not your name."

"Does it matter?"

"It should."

"Maybe someday I'll find one better. Beast." He winked.

* * *

"For the crime of associating with blood mages and rendering them aid, we find you guilty. For the crime of being, yourself, a blood mage, we find you guilty." The council of judges sealed the judgment with a startling staccato of striking gavels.

The condemned man slumped in his chair. Chains rattled on his wrists as he shook with fear and horror at the proclamation of his fate.

Donovan took a deep breath and sat back in his seat to make a note in his journal. Whitman already had someone in place to interrogate those condemned of blood magic before they were executed, but Donovan wanted to keep his own records to reference, in case one of them knew something about Ruben's whereabouts.

The guards came to collect their manacled charge and led him through the door at the front of the courtroom. There, prisoners waited for transport to and from their cells in the holding wing of the Judgment Hall.

With the trial concluded, Donovan saw no reason to linger, so he made his way through the crowd of people with apparent interest in the day's cases. Their delays, due mostly to the infiltration of the Order, had caused more stir than they warranted and, when it was discovered that the now famous Donovan Rudd, the magus's mentor and master Seeker, discoverer of lost talents and all those idiot titles they insisted on trading around, was also visiting trials of blood mages, the Judgment Hall found itself practically flooded with gossipers and the suddenly curious general public.

Donovan ignored their stares and mumbled comments, even using magic to lower his hearing until he was clear of the crowds and out of the Hall.

Outside, the weather was perfectly pleasant and warm, despite summer approaching its end. Judges, scribes, guards, students, the occasional escorted prisoner, and anyone with interest in law, traveled around the courtyard and along pathways leading from one wing to another of the great buildings. With much of his life spent in the relative luxury of the Order, Donovan had been surprised to see how much grander everything was in the capital city, which housed the King's Palace, the Judgment Hall, the Great Market, the Great Bank, and many other places of note besides.

As he slowly raised his hearing to normal, Donovan meandered back toward the palace main, enjoying the warm breeze and distant view of the mountains. They weren't visible from the Order, though it was only a few days difference of travel. Even now, the range looked hazy in the distance, but plenty of nobles held lands closer to the peaks in which they stayed when trade was slower and social gatherings were few. So far, Donovan had been yet unable to determine when those two situations coincided.

Ordered to the palace four months ago, he'd since been dragged about by his friend, Annette Kraemer — occupational spy and sister to the queen — to dozens of balls and gatherings of various sizes. She seemed far more enthusiastic about attending these than he ever would have guessed, but he knew she was engaged in more than showing off the newest fashions and tasting expensive foods. A spy surely reveled in the chance to obtain the kinds of gossip spread about in a place like this, and she had a ready-made reason for being there, even into the most elite circles.

All the politicking quickly frustrated Donovan, who much preferred walking the grounds, teaching New Seeking to the young noble children, or busying himself with his project in the enormous library. He itched to get back to his research, but knew Annette would be expecting him to bring word of the verdict. She could find out for herself, and probably faster, but Donovan appreciated her attempts to keep him from isolating in this place, so easily overwhelming.

He passed the ornamental palace gardens to the training grounds where nobles trained in the 'art' of war. Annette had told him when they had arrived that it used to be practically empty, but these days dozens of young lords and ladies trained in the sword, bow, spear, and in hand-to-hand combat. A separate yard, much farther away from the main path, had space for practice in combative magic. Donovan could make out an Elementalist's fiery, explosive efforts even from where he stood.

The archery butts were crowded with classes, but there were private lanes for those who did not need or want tutelage, which was where he knew he would find Annette. Most of her free time was spent there. She'd been approached by no less than five high-ranking military officers seeking her assistance in their classes, but she'd declined each of them. Time and again she had said how little patience she had for teaching, though his experience with her had been otherwise.

Annette didn't see him arrive, engrossed as she was with her sport, sending arrow after arrow into her mark fifty meters away, all of them clustered in the center of the target.

When she'd emptied her quiver, she stood quietly, clearly thinking hard. Her arms were shaking from the strain of repeatedly drawing her heavy bow. Finally, she stretched her neck and spotted him, smiled, and beckoned him over with a jerk of her chin. Sweat soaked the fringes of her scalp. She cleared it from her brow with an impatient swipe.

They walked to the end of her lane to collect the spent ammunition and she examined her target, lamenting, "I lean left again. I fixed that years ago."

"Perhaps you should give yourself some more time to recover," he said pointedly, looking at her arms.

"Yes, well, I've never claimed to be a patient woman. Often the opposite."

Her hands were far more dexterous than the Healers and surgeons had expected them to be after a Hunter had nearly killed her, but she was still not as capable as she had been, and seemed to take it personally. Now, long, wicked scars traced up, along her forearms like thin, white serpents, and she occasionally struggled with tasks requiring fine dexterity. She'd bemoaned the loss of her fine handwriting, for one, but could at least feed herself now, which the surgeons had explained was accomplishment enough. Anything further was extraordinary.

"So?" she asked.

"Nearly all were guilty on both charges," he answered.

"Execution. Or hard labor. That's what we expected, yes?" Donovan nodded. "And nothing about Ruben?"

"We won't know until Whitman questions him, but I don't get the feeling any today were high-ranking. They won't know anything."

"And your project?"

He raised an eyebrow. "You read my journal every day. You're required to. No need to change the subject to make me feel better."

She grinned. "You caught me. Still, that seems to keep your mind off your irritation with being here."

"That obvious?"

"Everyone knows, Donovan. It's practically all my sister talks about, and I can tell you King Braun and I are a little tired of it."

"Sorry."

"Psh." She waved his comment away. "She complains about me, too, though more privately. I'm used to it. She didn't want you here at all, and Braun knows it. He thinks you're wonderful, however, and he generally wins those arguments."

"The king likes me?" Donovan's eyes widened and then rolled. "Great ..."

Annette laughed and clapped him on the back. "He's not so bad."

"No, it's not that. The last conversation I had with your sister was her accusing me of surrounding myself with powerful people. That's why she didn't want me at court."

"And that's why you avoid the more powerful nobles. Clever."

"I figure she can't hate me more than she already does if I don't let her perceptions of me come true."

"Of course, you might be doing more harm than good," Annette said lightly.

Donovan stopped walking and stared at her until she explained.

"You've a growing reputation as a modest man — a man of the people. Your time in the library hasn't gone unnoticed, and those who already revere you are fantasizing stories as to what you are doing there: namely, working to find a way to stop the Hunters. It *is* funny how often rumors are correct, isn't it?"

Donovan groaned and threw his head back, continuing their walk to the palace proper. "Do I have to get publicly drunk and make a spectacle of myself? Is that what it would take for the nobility to think less of me?" he demanded.

Annette shrugged. "Might do you well. Drunken spectacles here tend to end with people sent to their estates, reputations in ruins." At Donovan's teasingly thoughtful silence, she added, "Elliott needs you here training the children, Don."

He sighed theatrically. "More's the pity."

"Where are you off to now?" she asked, adjusting her bow against her shoulder.

"The library."

"As usual." Her tone was serious, but she winked when he looked at her.

He shrugged, "They shipped all those books here for me, and I get a secret room and everything. It's only fair that I should be diligent in my work, don't you think?"

"Very fair. I look forward to reading your journal entries. More about your state of mind, please, Don," she reminded him. "Your work is very interesting, but the point of the journal is tracking your mental state — blood magic being what it is."

"I haven't even attempted any yet!" He sighed. "I can hardly be addicted to something I've never done."

"Write to Elliott if you wish to register a complaint." She gave him a pointed look and he groaned childishly.

They reached the corridor that would send them different directions and stopped.

"Remember to eat."

"Don't make any new enemies."

"You're a harsh master." She poked his forehead and sauntered off in the direction of her rooms, whistling a simple tune.

Donovan rubbed the spot ruefully and turned the other way.

The Palace Library was at least as big as the one the Order boasted, and, while they held many redundant texts, each had their specialties. The palace possessed more books on politics, etiquette, lineage, census reports, and, Donovan had accidentally discovered, erotica. The Order held far more texts on weather patterns tracked back hundreds of years, trade tariffs more than ten years old, and, of course, magic.

Due to the recent infiltration of the Order, and young Ruben's kidnapping, many nobles were newly unwilling to send their children away for the training of their Talents. This allowed Elliot, the Head of the Order, to send Donovan to the palace under the pretense of training the young noble mages in New Seeking. The discovery of additional abilities to all Seekers had rippled through the kingdom, and Donovan did his best to bear the weight of his new recognition. The finding had nearly claimed his life, and he never could decide if he was more irritated when people did know that part, or didn't.

After Ruben's kidnapping by their elusive enemy, known to them only as the Smiling Man, Donovan had demanded to be allowed to study blood magic, the power of their enemies, hoping to find a weakness, or strength to use against them. Elliott had been persuaded, and seen to the transport of dozens of Order texts, hidden in various caravans and meticulously accounted for on arrival. Due to the seemingly addictive nature of blood magic, the texts were not allowed to be accessed by anyone without the Head of the Order's express permission, verified by the Head Librarian. Because of that, the only known books on blood magic were cataloged by physical description, and sometimes title, but that did little to help him find the passages most useful to his task.

Now, Donovan possessed the only key to a hidden room in which the books were kept, and only he, the palace librarians, Order Head Librarian, Annette, and Whitman knew of its existence. The king and queen knew Donovan was studying some project for the Order, but nothing of the details, and they did not know about the new store of books under their roof.

Elliott's stipulation for allowing Donovan's study to assist in their war against the blood mages was that he was to keep a detailed journal describing not only his studies, but his mental state to ensure it didn't render him unstable. So little was known of blood magic, after all. Annette read the journal daily, and was in regular correspondence with Whitman Acres, the bard — and Spymaster — who reported back to Elliott. The circuitous communication ensured that those who needed to know did, and those who didn't had a more difficult time of discovering the start and end of anything they might find.

Despite being the one to initially insist on the precautions, Donovan found them now to be more than a little irksome.

"Malena, Ireni, Markus, good morning."

The librarians returned his warm greeting. They were well-used to the sight of him by now and, while they knew of his use of the secret study room, none of them had access to it, and so did not know the subject of his study. Nor would they ask — their job was to preserve knowledge, and so knew well the danger that knowledge could possess. He was sure at least a few of the librarians had guessed, but they were wise enough to make no mention of it.

"Any news?" he asked.

Ireni tilted her head at him. "So much time in the courtrooms and I would think you know more than we."

He liked Ireni. "But you are so much better at sifting fact from fiction," he said, batting his eyes at her in an exaggerated fashion. They all stifled their laughter.

Markus said, "As I have heard it, some small Hunter groups have been found, but they offered nothing of value to the Mentalists' interrogations."

"Plenty of Order mages have come to raid our city plans and topography maps," Malena added. "Since the last Hunter training ground was found in caverns, they are starting with cave structures, but as Markus said," she shrugged, "little success in information gathered."

"And nothing, no word, whisper, or rumor on your little magus," Ireni said.

Donovan felt, rather than saw, the deflation in them all. He knew that if any information was gleaned, he and Annette would be sent immediately after it, along with half of the Order, to bring Ruben back under the Order's protection. But the continued silence kept him as tense as a bowstring, and he wished desperately to be loosed on his target.

If not for his own method of helping, Donovan would have been driven mad by impotency — he was not made for sitting about. He wanted to help, but had no realistic way to do so, other than what was already being done.

"You know I appreciate you all," he assured them. "Every allied eye in the kingdom is looking for Ruben. Your insights, and your company, keep me sane." He rapped his knuckles on the counter and turned away into the shelf-crowded space.

The key around his neck unlocked his study room. The entrance sat hidden behind a functional bookshelf that pulled outward from the wall to reveal a small doorway behind. The trick to this was that you had to stand in front of the shelf *next* to the one you were pulling on, or else a clever contraption in the floor stopped the shelf from coming away from the wall. Something to do with pulleys and weight distribution, the Head Librarian had explained. He'd been assured it had remained hidden for centuries, so Donovan wasn't worried about his store of books being discovered. He did occasionally worry about getting trapped inside, in case the door was blocked, on purpose or by accident, but that was the price for his secrecy.

The study room was about fifteen feet square with floor-to-ceiling shelves on every wall, two shelves deep. The front shelves, overlapping those behind, sat on clever little wheels so they could be moved about; most were loaded with texts, front and back so as to not waste the limited space. One entire shelf held supplies for notes, light, comfort, and sustenance.

Vents in the top of the room on all four sides kept the room full of breathable air, but keen engineering and thick walls kept it nearly soundproofed. Shouting would be heard easily enough, but a casual conversation would go unnoticed.

A large desk sulked in the corner, weighted down and marred by countless ink spills and frustrated pen-stabbings. A carefully measured hourglass hung mounted on one of the walls, giving the occupant the ability to keep track of time, which had come in very handy to Donovan more than once. He was diligent about keeping it turned.

With a sigh, Donovan collapsed into the surprisingly comfortable desk chair and stared at the books and papers arrayed in front of him. He let his mind turn and shift until it recalled where he'd left off the day before.

Several of the texts, including a precious four volumes from before the Cataclysm, referred to the blood magic he knew as 'living magic' or 'life magic'. The 'blood' terminology had been introduced sometime later, overtaking the common language shortly after the

Cataclysm. Probably. His timeline was terribly vague, and he'd had to redo it several times because of lack of detail.

So far, his reading had brought little insight. There was plenty of rambling and tangents and stories of heroes and villains, many of them with no clear ending, but, for the most part, the early histories he'd read showed no animosity between those who were born with magic, and those who spilled blood for it. Only in the last two or three centuries had that changed — and it was frustrating that he could not find a reason for the split. Besides which, he couldn't find a good reason for anyone to be so willing to befriend anyone who needed blood for power. He knew his bias was skewing the research, but was willing to acknowledge that he didn't care.

He did note that the few works from before the Cataclysm were the ones that showed the born and blood mages as a single people with little to no animosity, and the more numerous works that came after were the ones where the divide was more pronounced. Not for the first time, he wondered if the Cataclysm was the reason for the rift and subsequent warring, but there were so few histories from that time.

The Order as it had been, and most of the palace, had been destroyed with half of the royal family. Dozens of towns and villages, thousands of people had instantly died from an unknown magic, some kind of concussive explosion, resulting in decades of chaos and recovery. Closest to where the event originated, those scholars and mages who occupied the Order as it was had turned to dust, scattered to the wind, and so all of the records and histories of magic were lost in the same fashion.

Beliefs differed beyond that, and it was a favorite topic for fireside conversations, filling the shadows with ghosts and unknown horrors.

Donovan got to work in his journal and marked book passages with strips of colored yarn for reference. He was eager to begin practicing actual blood magic, but had found only bare references to the mumbling and hand gestures he'd heard from each of those he'd encountered. It seemed every writer expected the reader to have the basic understanding of how to wield the power already, and saw no need to provide detail.

Several passages made reference to speaking to cast the magic, but none of them identified what should be said — be it mantra, direction, or Words of Power. Donovan hoped to come across some kind of teaching primer in his sources, instead of the world histories and fables, while still interesting, that appeared to make up most of the collection.

Several hours passed before he made his last notes, filling the journal he carried with his general state of mind and more of his research progress. Since he was the only one using this room, he left the books and notes as they were and opened the inside door. The external door/shelf pushed outward slightly, unobstructed, but that didn't mean no one was in the aisle, so he opened the door a crack and used New Seeking to raise his hearing enough to perceive another person's heartbeat.

His own heartbeat, breathing, and the blood pounding in his veins were suddenly nauseatingly loud, but he'd learned by now to differentiate those when searching for another. Hearing no one, he slipped out quickly and left the library.

Marbled halls full of portraits, sculptures, and various priceless works of art had grown less daunting each time he passed them, but he still felt like an intruder until he came to his classroom. Larger and brighter than the one he'd used at the Order, the room had a large glass window to the outside that he could open along a sliding rail inset into the window frame. He'd been so impressed when first seeing it that he'd played with the sliding rail for longer than he'd ever admit.

Being that it was a Seeker's training room, the delightful window had several layers of thick black curtains that could completely block out the light and dampen all but the loudest sounds the palace was likely to make. He had requested, and been supplied with, candles and various perfumes, message boards and chalk, and a variable plethora of other supplies useful to his teaching. Despite the odd requests, nothing had been questioned or denied.

Almost all the students could raise or dampen their senses with a measured degree of control now, but concentration proved difficult for many of them, especially over a longer period of time when they might be assailed by so many sensations.

Donovan occasionally felt guilty about his own ease with manipulating his senses after such a short period, but then, Annette hadn't had any trouble after the first couple of weeks either. They'd had years of practice with at least *some* kind of Talent, while these children were brand new to it all. More than that, children were not exactly famous for their ability to concentrate for prolonged periods. They weren't supposed to: they were children.

Donovan sat behind his desk and stared out the window into the courtyard to calm and clear his mind. He liked to be present and ready to instruct before the students arrived and had found it was best to let them lead. As children of nobility, they'd had access to tutors for as long as they could remember, and didn't need as much of the classroom structure the common-born children received. Besides which, they were more focused when making decisions about what they wanted to learn.

Children, most of them chattering with friends, appeared and took their seats, all with expressions of curiosity, excitement, or boredom. He greeted each by name and their manners held true as they acknowledged his position. He'd been warned that the children of nobles might be unwilling to be taught by a commoner, but so far, he'd experienced no struggles. Likely, it was his reputation that helped in that regard, and they built respect together, for the most part. Either way, he had always loved children, and had found that he loved teaching, too.

When the students were settled, Donovan clapped his hands together for their attention. "Students! Where shall we begin today?"

*   *   *

"Agatha, please practice your sense of smell — I feel you're disregarding it over the others. Come ready to demonstrate next time." The girl made a face, but bowed, braids swinging, and trotted after her friends.

Donovan put away the candles and jars of scents they had used in the day's practice. He always felt accomplished after a successful class, and some of the students had experienced their own breakthroughs, which kept morale high.

A knock on the doorframe turned him away from his storage cabinet, and he waved Annette in.

"How goes it all?" She sauntered through the room to perch on his desk.

He smiled, but felt the pressure of sadness in his chest. "They're doing very well. Most everyone is motivated — which is nice until you realize that they're driven because we're at war. Half of them have soldiers for siblings and they all expect to find glory on a battlefield. Tell me about your day."

"Oh, you know, this and that." She smiled crookedly. "I have a letter from Whitman for you, but it's surprisingly short — only twelve pages."

"The pigeon who brought that is probably missing its leg, poor thing."

Annette laughed and handed the fat envelope over. Donovan glanced at the seal and set it on his desk.

"Got any journal entries for me?" Annette asked.

Donovan handed over the small book. "Minor things; a bit more on the existence of a spoken component, but no actual text for it. I wonder if there's a dictionary or something. A lost language, perhaps?"

"A bit complex if tens of thousands of people have passed it down in families and to strangers, and we've never come across pieces of it, hmm?"

Donovan nodded pensively. "Could be that the mere act of speaking, making sound, somehow helps call the magic. It does go on about a person's willpower, and strength of mind ..."

Annette flipped to the last entry and read dutifully. Donovan waited for her to finish and took the time to muse about his latest theory. If blood magic was about strength of will more than anything else, that would explain how it could be so natural to learn and teach.

Although, it would be counter-intuitive for a magic based around self-control to be so addictive. No one seemed to know how addictive, or in what way — everything so far was hearsay, and he had yet to find mention of such dangers in his reading. Was the magic itself addictive? Was the act of murder addictive? Perhaps it was the feeling of power when you used it? He was simultaneously repulsed and intrigued at the thought.

"Excitement abounds." Annette returned the journal with a wink. "I have a friend for you to meet if you would dine with me tonight. We've written for ages, though never met in person. She arrived here a couple of months before we did; I've only had a chance for a few short chats since then, and still haven't found opportunity to meet the children. I imagine you would enjoy the company, and you're far better with the younger generation than I."

Donovan agreed. "I'll find something suitable to wear, I suppose."

"Nothing too fancy; it's a casual affair."

"The clothing for what this place considers a 'casual affair' would have fed my entire town twice over for a year."

"As life can be, darling." She slid off the desk and waved over her shoulder, not turning around when she called, "Seven of the clock, and don't be late!"

Donovan made a noise like assent and turned to the letter from Whitman, excited to hear from his friend. Most of the letters were social — he couldn't trust important information in a letter to be stolen and put to nefarious use by the enemy — but he hinted at progress, and that was enough to put Donovan in a good mood. Whitman was ever optimistic, but never naïve, and wouldn't waste paper on anything that wasn't sure to pan out in some way.

He mentioned, too, that poor Kina was finally awake, though still unable to communicate. After her assigned mission with Donovan and Annette to track a Hunter with potentially important information, the young Mentalist had been magically damaged by the same Hunter who'd injured Annette's arms so badly. They suspected her of the same Talent Kina possessed, much as Donovan's partner Lucas had been bested when he'd come face-to-face with a Healer/Hunter hybrid nearly a year ago.

Kina had lived, but would not wake for the last several months, despite all the efforts the Order could bring to bear. The Mentalists and surgeons were still trying to solve her issue, but they had no timeline, or promise, of a full recovery. Whitman was visiting her every day, his letter assured him.

Donovan was glad to hear of Kina's progress, but his heart still dropped to hear about the newest predicament. The woman was young, but had been an incredibly capable Mentalist, and performed her job as well as any twice her age. He should have been seen through the façade the Hunter had presented, and his negligence had resulted in Kina's mental injury.

Despite the letter's mostly positive tone, Donovan's mood was dark. He put the papers away and left his classroom, making sure to close and lock the door behind him. His personal rooms in the palace were far larger than those he held at the Order. A man of simple tastes, he preferred the one room and one closet he occupied in the Retriever Hall, but nonetheless found himself here with an enormous bedroom, a closet the size of his old room, a study, and a sitting area.

The study was as yet unused, except for the filching of a few interesting-looking books. He did all of his research in the library, which took up most of his recreational reading time anyway, so he'd barely touched those. The sitting room was to entertain guests, but the furniture was mostly unused since his arrival. During Annette's occasional visits, she perched in a comfortable, high-backed, blue chair, and he rested on the couch now and then, but otherwise was not often found in the oversized rooms.

Still, he had to keep his clothes somewhere. Even in this, his world was newly complicated. Within the first week after he arrived, a room servant often attempted to help him dress until Donovan had to ask him to stop. Now the man only came by twice a day to clean and tidy, and occasionally provide food if Donovan missed a meal, but he could still be summoned with a pull-bell that somehow alerted the man to his need.

Donovan never bothered to lock the room when he wasn't in it, knowing full well that if anyone wanted to get inside, they would. Instead, he kept anything of importance in his hidden library room and let the potential burglars wonder. Because of that, and despite the months during which he had resided there, his rooms had a distinctly un-lived in feel.

From the closet, he removed a hanger with a complete outfit in a light brown color that he enjoyed. It was accented with rich maroon, he noticed as he pulled on the trousers, hooking the loop and lacing them tight. There was even a modesty flap that he could button on to hide the laces.

The shirt was high-collared and stiff, with buttons all the way up, including on the equally stiff cuffs. He tucked in the tails and added the jacket. It was too warm for a real jacket, but this one was made for style rather than warmth, of some thin material that breathed well and had fashionable slits in the side and back that showed his shirt beneath. A scarf hung looped around the hook of the hanger, so he tossed it about his neck. It felt awkward with the high collar of the shirt, but when did fashion ever wholly make sense?

He admired himself in the long mirror for a moment, and laughed ruefully. He could never be vain — it was too much effort. Still, he dampened his hair and fingered a moisturizing balm throughout it. It was scented more strongly than the one his father had taught him to make, but wasn't unpleasant. He used the fancy pick the servant had provided, and finally left it all behind. The jacket had two inside breast pockets, one of which now held Whitman's letter, and the trousers had sizable front pockets for him to carry his journal. He never took the library key from around his neck, so once again, there was nothing for anyone to find in his room. Those poor, thieving spies.

He grinned at the thought and reflected on whether he was actually a spy. He was friends with the Spymaster, and friends with one of his quietly-admitted best, Annette, and had been sent on several missions, but primarily as a bodyguard or guide. Had he received a pay increase? He made a mental note to ask.

Annette's rooms were not far from his own, but across the threshold to another wing of the palace. She was royalty, after all, even if she preferred to live what she considered to be a common lifestyle at the Order. He shook his head at the thought of all her extravagance somehow fitting into the small town where he'd spent almost all of his sixty-four years.

At the change of wings, marked by a wide archway and stripe of darker marble the width of the hall, a servant greeted him with a short bow and turned to lead him to Annette's abode. He knew the way, but one mustn't announce oneself, he knew. Donovan looked back and, sure enough, out of a subtle door secreted into the wall another servant emerged to hold that post. The efficiency boggled his mind.

The servant stopped at Annette's doorway and bowed again. "Would you like me to announce you, Master Rudd?"

"She said it was a casual affair; I don't think that's necessary," Donovan answered.

The servant nodded politely and walked back to his post. Donovan tugged down on his jacket to make sure that it hung properly and adjusted the scarf before rapping on the door.

It opened smoothly and another servant bowed and gestured for him to enter.

"Welcome, Master Rudd. Her Highness the Lady Kraemer is awaiting your presence in the formal dining room, and the other guests have yet to arrive." She waited a moment to see if he had any questions or requests before closing the door and leading him through.

Annette's rooms were enormous. This front sitting area was for entertaining and was approximately the size of Donovan's rooms in total. Stylish seating was positioned around the wall. A large and beautiful rug with geometric embroidery, probably from beyond Manazia, dominated the floor space. There were no windows, but a smaller socializing room led off straight ahead with a balcony view.

The servant led Donovan to the right instead, to the formal dining area. It boasted a long table with tall-backed chairs lined around it, capable of seating twenty. A chandelier overhead shone and sparkled reflected light around the space. Two servants waited by another door in the corner of this room where a small kitchen, stocked from the main kitchens in this wing, held the food to keep warm, or chilled, and ready to serve. Donovan could smell lamb and his stomach growled.

Annette sat at the head of the table with a book in hand, frowning at its words. She looked up when Donovan's boots touched the hardwood floors, and smiled brightly. Her smile dipped for a moment and then grew playful as she rose to greet him. A subtle gesture brought one of the servants forward to take her book away before returning to their post a few moments later.

"You look marvelous, Don!" Annette praised him. She touched the scarf around his neck and asked, "A new style?"

He hesitated and then asked, "I'm wearing it wrong, aren't I?"

She shrugged. "A confident man can never wear his style incorrectly."

"How's it supposed to be?"

She drew the scarf off of his neck to loop it deftly around his hips, just below the cut of the jacket, and knotted it at his side so the ends laid down the side of his thigh. "That's generally the agreed-upon fashion."

"Ah." He felt a flush rise in his cheeks. "Oh well, at least I wasn't late."

"True! You are right on time!" She gestured to the seat on her left.

"Who is it that you want me to meet?" He sat as she did.

"My incredibly good friend: Baroness Lasturn. She's the wife of an old acquaintance: Baron Holm Lasturn, her husband. They've been on the estate for ages, though we've managed to keep in touch. I started writing with her instead of him quite a few years ago, but we only just met, as I said earlier. The baron and I have little love lost. Honestly, I only stayed in touch because he always wrote back, and it's the proper thing to do. His wife is darling, though, and I'll finally get to meet the children tonight, she promised."

They made light conversation until the servant brought in three well-dressed children from the hall. Annette beamed and rose to greet the guests while Donovan followed suit. They shook hands politely with identical twin girls, about fifteen or sixteen years old, and a younger, stern-faced boy in the uniform of a military recruit without rank insignia.

"We apologize, mother is running a bit late. She said she would be only a few minutes behind, but insisted we come ahead," one of the girls said politely.

"No trouble at all!" Annette answered breezily. "It's a pleasure to finally meet you! Your mother has been telling me all about you as you've grown. Lizette, yes?"

"Luanne," the first twin said with a forgiving smile. "She's Lizette."

Lizette grinned wickedly. "She's a spoil-sport. I like to keep people guessing."

Annette laughed. "I can't blame you in the slightest. I'd do the same if I had a twin."

"Excuse me for being so forward," Luanne said. "But are you the Donovan Rudd who discovered New Seeking?"

"Yes, I am," he said, smiling awkwardly. He never knew how to respond to these increasingly common questions.

"Brilliant. Thank you for your contribution to the knowledge of magic!"

Lizette looked like she'd eaten a lemon, and Donovan assumed she was trying not to roll her eyes at her sister's flourified language.

"Well, you're very welcome. Are you a Seeker? Or mage of some kind?"

"Yes, I am a Seeker actually, and Lizette is a Healer. We're enrolled in classes. Arrived mid-semester, but we've had tutors on our family estate. I prefer group-setting to learn; it gives me more time to comprehend the lesson and see examples."

"Luanne plans to discover a new magic of her own," Lizette said, another wicked grin lighting her face. "All she talks about is theories of magic, honestly."

"I'd love to hear them," Donovan told her sincerely. "Lizette, are you trained in Healing, or have you only just begun?"

"Hardly. I plan to race to top of the class and graduate early, though. Then I'll take off, hunting monsters or something." They all laughed.

The young man scanned the room's layout and eyed the adults cautiously.

"Hugh, you said?" Donovan asked.

Nod.

"I apologize for my lack of knowledge: you're not yet ranked?"

"Too young."

"When will you be able to formally join the ranks?"

"Four years, but I aim to receive special dispensation. I've been taking practice tests, and all the instructors agree there's no reason to put off the inevitable, even if I'm not promoted to officer right away."

Donovan opened his mouth to ask another question, but the door opened again and the servant showed in a bustling, breathless woman. "I'm so sorry I'm late, I had to catch up on estate business before the messenger left, and I knew you wouldn't mind me sending the children ahead!"

"Not at all!" Annette answered in kind, gathering the woman's hands in her own and kissing each cheek. "Now, deep breath and come meet my friend, Donovan."

He stepped forward to give his best courtly bow to the Lady Lasturn. "It's a pleasure to mee—" The words died on his lips as he finally took in her features: lines and curves he knew as well as his own, despite the time so far separated. She, too, was frozen, her warm and familiar smile of greeting melting into one of shock, then fear, and confusion.

"Don, this is Cara Lasturn. Cara, Donovan Rudd."

Donovan barely heard her, as if she was far away, or he was under water. He couldn't take his eyes from Cara's.

Annette nudged his shoulder. "Something the matter? Cara?"

Lady Lasturn took a deep, shuddering breath. Her pale blue eyes didn't leave Donovan's brown ones when she answered, "Um, I thought I'd seen a ghost, is all."

"You've met before?"

Donovan cleared a suddenly dry throat, but did not answer.

Lady Lasturn turned to Annette and found a bright smile for her features. She said, "My friend, may I have a moment with Master Rudd?"

"Of course." The children went wordlessly into the dining room while Annette followed behind, giving Donovan a concerned look, which he did not soothe.

Long moments passed before Donovan cleared his throat again and said, "I suppose I know you're alive now."

Cara Rudd, now Lasturn, did not answer, but some of her tension relaxed.

"It's been a while." He felt like his brain had turned to a buzzing, stinging beehive.

"I couldn't stay there, Don," Cara whispered.

"I know."

"She was everywhere I looked, in everything I did."

"I know."

They fell into silence until Donovan managed, on the second attempt, to ask, "Are you happy?"

Cara nodded slowly. "I am. The baron, Holm, he's a good man. He loves the children, loves me."

She bit her lip in an expression so familiar that Donovan's arms physically ached to hold and comfort her, but he didn't allow himself to move, instead standing as frozen as any sculpture.

"Did you know each other long? Before marriage?"

Cara gave him a sharp look. "Do you mean —"

"I don't mean anything, Cara. Pull papers tomorrow and I'll sign to officially nullify our union. No one needs to know the rest."

Cara's eyes welled, but her voice didn't shake. "Thank you, Donny. Um. Don. Donovan."

They stood in silence for a tense minute.

"Your children are mages?"

She nodded. "Just the girls. That's partly why we're here, for their lessons. Lizette is a Healer and Luanne is —" she hesitated.

"Luanne is a Seeker."

"Yes."

"They have," his voice broke and he cleared it quickly before continuing, "They have your eyes."

Cara didn't answer, but he could read her expression like his own.

His mind spun. He felt lightheaded and claustrophobic; like he was buried alive and stiflingly hot as the air ran out around him. He was sweating.

"I should go."

"We haven't eaten ..."

He looked away and squeezed his eyes shut. "I don't know that I can. Right now."

"All right." She pulled drooping shoulders back into place. "I'm sorry, Donny. For ... you know."

"Yeah. Me, too."

Annette seemed to sense that their conversation was over and returned. She looked no less curious, but a glance at their faces killed any flippant comment she might have made.

"Everything sorted?" she asked gently.

He managed a brief, strained smile and said, "I find myself feeling too ill for dinner. I've work to catch up. I'll have an early night. It was a pleasure meeting everyone." He bowed politely and turned to march stiffly away.

Annette was speaking behind him, but he didn't wait for her, instead speeding through the massive rooms to the hallway, seeking escape like a hare at a hunt.

"Don. Donovan! DONOVAN!" Annette shouted behind him.

He swayed to a stop in the middle of the hall, breath catching in his throat. He didn't know if his legs would support him for much longer. Annette caught up in a rush and tried to meet his eyes.

"I don't want to talk about it."

"I'm sure you don't."

"Then *what?*"

"Do you want to talk about it?"

Donovan growled with irritation and turned away.

"What is it?" she asked earnestly. "Don, let me help you."

"Did you know?"

"Know what?" she asked exasperatedly. "That's what I'm asking you!"

"Annette, did you set this up?"

"I invited two good friends to dinner, Donovan Rudd, what else?"

He glared into her eyes, searching for a lie, but finding none. He scoffed at himself. How would he find a lie in the eyes of Annette Kraemer, professional spy?

"I'm going to bed."

"You won't eat anything?"

"I can't go back in there. Not right now," he whispered, suddenly feeling very vulnerable.

Annette nodded. She looked like she wanted to put her arms around him, but he prayed she didn't. The walls, fifteen feet away, already felt very close.

"I —" Annette hesitated and then said, "Those girls ..."

"Don't."

"They look just like —"

"Don't."

"Don, you told me your wife's name was Cara."

"Annette. *Stop.*" He knew there were tears in his eyes, but he refused to let them drop.

"What are you going to do?"

"I'm not going to do anything. I don't want *anyone* to do *anything*. Move."

He returned her hard gaze with one cast of iron until she gracefully stepped out of his path and let him go. He knew she was watching, but refused to turn back. He pushed open the door to his rooms and fumbled to lock it behind him, leaned on the wooden portal and stared at nothing while his mind whirled with memories, good and awful. Emotion rose in his chest until he thought it would burst.

He felt the tears well and fall while he gasped for breath through his sobs. His heart ached with loss, discovery, and the loss all over again. Three young faces hovered in his vision until they were all he could see. He clambered to his feet to pace like a caged beast, unable to contain the energy crackling through his veins. He wanted to run, run, run until he fell and *fight* and scream. But the walls had ears.

He lowered his vision and hearing and taste and smell and touch until he felt numb — numb to everything around him and the world was dark, silent, invisible, but even so, those faces hovered, one far more distant than the other two, but so, *so* alike to them. He pressed unfeeling hands to deaf ears, feeling only a deep, hot pressure within, but he still heard their voices, their laughs. He felt tiny hands wrapped around his fingers and saw tiny bodies learn to crawl and walk and speak.

Too much.

Too much.

Donovan brought back all of his senses in a mad rush as the pressure built too high to contain, and he gasped with pain at the burning sensitivity of it all. He wrenched a pillow from the chair and held it tight to his face, bellowing and screaming until his voice was raw and hoarse. He flung it across the room and paced again while achingly silent sobs wracked his frame. His hand ached and bled — the flesh was bruised and torn where he'd struck the brick of his room, knowing it would reveal no sign of his actions.

No one would know, no one would guess, no one would ever connect the two beautiful twins to the tired, old man that missed them without ever even knowing them.

*   *   *

Donovan woke some hours later, salt all over his face and his eyes gummed shut. He was exhausted and ached all over, but managed to stumble to the basin, staring blearily at the clear liquid before he could find the strength to rinse and wash his face. The water was cool and refreshing on his over-warm skin, and the cloth was cloud-soft. It took several steadying, deep breaths before he could walk into the sitting room.

The chair Annette usually occupied lay across the room, on its side from one of his enraged kicks. Cushions and his nice clothes from the night before were flung all about. He looked down at his loose cotton breeches and the faded shirt he'd brought from the Order; he hadn't worn the clothes in months and felt strangely out of place in the comfortable outfit, in this space.

He lethargically righted the chair and began to pick up cushions and clothing, grateful that his mind was an emotionally drained blank for now. Someone knocked at his door, and he growled in irritation as he went to answer it.

"Yes?" he snapped.

Lady Lasturn stood waiting.

"Am I catching you with poor timing, Master Rudd?" she asked softly.

Donovan felt a blush crawling across his face and his stomach dropped several stories. "No, of course not. I'm just — I," he glanced into the room. "Now's not — a good time."

"Would you mind if I spoke with you? Please?"

Donovan hesitated.

"Please, Donny," she whispered.

He stepped aside and closed the door to quickly explain, "I'm sorry for the mess. I was just cleaning up. Misplaced my journal."

He saw Cara's eyes dart from the cushions on the floor and the papers swept off the table, but said nothing. She held a folder of documents, and set them carefully on his desk, skewed from its original position.

"I brought you the divorce paperwork."

"Thank you."

Her bob of the head was so familiar that he shook as a shudder passed down his spine.

"You look well," she continued, "I heard you were a Retriever now. That's difficult work."

He agreed. "Rewarding, though."

"Did you — uh."

He waited, but she didn't finish.

"Did I decide to save other children because I couldn't save my own?"

She looked away. "That isn't what I meant."

"I know, I'm sorry." Donovan tugged on an ear. "Not at the start, not on purpose. But I think that's part of why I wanted to do it."

"The girls," she said suddenly. "They're yours."

His throat closed too tight to speak.

"I haven't told Holm," Cara said, "but I will. I think he suspects; I'm sure he does, but he dotes on them, Donny. He's a good man."

"I'm glad. That's good."

"Look, can we please talk? I — I can't stand this."

He gestured to the sitting room and quickly put cushions back on the couch. His movements were jerky, tense. Cara sat in the middle of the couch. Donovan took Annette's usual seat in the high-backed chair across from her.

She stared at her clasped hands. "I left, I didn't tell you, and I have never regretted anything in my life so much as I do that decision. Not leaving — I had to leave. But I'm sorry I didn't say anything to you. I was going insane there, Donny. We tried for so long, so much heartbreak, and when she ..." Cara squeezed her eyes closed for a moment. "When Kelsa was born, it was like the world was new. You remember, I know you do. Colors were brighter, and ... But when she died ..."

"When she was murdered," Donovan corrected tenderly.

Cara's eyes flicked to his. "When she was murdered, that new world was ... tainted. Everywhere. Everything was dark, like I was looking through fog, and I couldn't stand it. I remember I was looking for herbs and the farther I got from home, it was like I could breathe. It was all I could do to come back and you were still covered in the day's labor and we hadn't said two words in weeks. I knew we wanted to, but what could we possibly say? I took another walk the next day, and the less familiar things were ... I just kept going. I didn't take anything — I didn't have a plan. I never planned to leave you."

Donovan tasted copper and realized he'd bitten into his cheek. "I looked for you, but not hard. I knew you wanted to leave. I only hoped you'd left me and not fallen off a cliff, or been eaten by a bear."

She smiled. "You hate bears."

"Always have."

"And cats."

He managed a wry chuckle. "Damn things make me sneeze."

"What did you do? After I left?"

"I didn't have anything else. I blamed myself and so did your brother — he'd always hated me. I think he took up a soldiering post far east, toward Manazia, but haven't heard anything since. The rest of the town just moved on and I drank, did some odd jobs here and there. Marcus —" he sighed. "Marcus Sauls gave me some work and helped me through the worst of it. After a few months, someone asked me to help their child with magic. Seeking, of course. I refused. I knew I was too drunk to help anyone, but when the Retriever came to get them, I went along. Retriever training was hard, but it kept my mind focused on something outside of my misery, and I stayed busy enough to sleep, at least. After a while ... The pain hasn't stopped, but I ... manage it better. I miss her."

Drops fell from Cara's eyes and she smiled. "Me, too," she whispered.

They gave space to the shared grief.

"How did you come to be here?" Cara finally asked.

"That ..." he huffed ruefully, rubbing at his face. "That is a long story. I'm not even sure I can follow half of it."

"Donny, can you forgive me?"

He bit back the immediate assurance, knowing it wasn't true. When his jaw relaxed, he said, "I want to. I'd like that. Will you forgive me?"

She nodded stiffly. "Gladly. Will we be friends again?"

He put hands out. "We were children, Cara. We grew up together and I saw you every day. Everything has changed. I feel like I'm finally where I should be. Well, I was. This is all ..." he gestured vaguely and grimaced.

She laughed. "Let's start again, as friends."

He went to his desk. The paperwork wasn't complicated, but he couldn't read the words until he wiped his eyes discreetly. His scribbled signature completed their part of the document and handed the discreet folder to her.

"Your father's ring is back at the Order with my personal belongings. Vale has them in a box somewhere."

"I want you to meet the girls," she told him.

"I — don't know if I should. I met them last night."

"I want you to really meet them, though."

Donovan took a deep breath. "Cara, I don't know if I can. They're not mine, not really. I'm not the man they know to be their father and the last thing they need is that kind of complication."

"I want to tell them the truth. They need to know it."

They sat again, silence filling the space like foam — soft and gentle, but overwhelming, stifling, nonetheless.

"I will never tell you the right thing to do," he said carefully, "because I will never know what that is in a situation like this. But please take your time on this decision. I'm not … my work these days isn't the safest, and I don't …" His hands trembled and he clenched them together to hide it.

She noticed, as she always did. "I'll write to Holm, and see what he says. He's a good man."

Desperate to change the subject, he asked, "Why couldn't he be here? With you?"

"The estate always has to be managed, and he prefers to be hands-on," she replied, leaning back against the cushions. "He has guests sometimes, and trade deals to manage. There's lots to do."

"I thought you were supposed to hire people for that."

"His family is only recently elevated to nobility. He brought on a new steward, but still believes in working the fields, leading the fight, marking the ledgers with his own hands. He's teaching the children to do the same. He's a good man, good with them."

"I'm sure he is." He rubbed his palms together. "How long are you staying at court, then?"

"Several more months, at least. Long enough for the children to get some decent schooling. Lizette is a handful and Hugh …" she gave an exasperated sigh and looked heavenward.

Donovan smirked. "He seemed pretty reserved."

"He always does at first, but he's just like any other twelve-year-old. He's very … focused on one goal. Holm is keen on planning ahead, and Hugh wants to be just like him."

"A noble goal."

Cara gave him a look. "Was that a pun?"

"Possibly."

"Have you …" she cleared her throat. "Have you found anyone? Anyone else?"

"No. I had different priorities for a long time and Retrievers can't marry, so I'd have to retire. I like my work — it consumes my time and attention."

"Not to mention your rise to fame, I expect."

"You heard about that?"

"I didn't put the pieces together until I saw you, and then it hit me like a mountain of stone last night."

"It was an accident."

"A lucky accident."

He remembered the sizzle of lightning, the crack of his nose and skull on the stone corridor, and the blood pooling in his throat. "A very lucky accident."

"But now you're here, so tell me about it?"

"All right." He cleared his throat. "My partner Lucas and I were told of a magus ..."

2

THE YOUNG MAN, FOREST, SLEPT. His breathing was soft and his young face deceptively innocent. She stared and wondered what had made him so inhuman. Two weeks of travel through woods unfamiliar to her brought them only another day from a town he hadn't named for her. She knew they'd passed others, and wanted to know why this one was special, but she hated asking questions. A flaw, she knew, but she preferred to come by answers without needing to ask. It made her feel smarter. She liked to be smarter than those around her. Her brother had always understood, though he hid that better in himself than she ever managed.

Her eyes traced along Forest's features. She wasn't smarter than this one. He had answers that she craved, answers to questions she hadn't known existed, but she didn't dare expose the depth of her ignorance. He craved teaching as much as she did learning, so the answers would come. Patience.

As if he'd felt her gaze, his eyes opened. There was no sleepiness, no leftover disorientation that she could see.

He waited, unblinking.

"Teach me to use my magic," she said finally.

"It's late."

"It's been two weeks."

"I've taught you other things."

It was true. He'd wasted no time in educating her on the different edible and poisonous plants they passed, far surpassing the knowledge she'd gained with her mother. When it rained, he taught her to make a shelter, how to build a fire, how to navigate in day or night. He'd shown her constellations, though his were different from those her father had known, and he'd begun to teach her how to move as quietly as he did, how to pay attention to her surroundings, notice everything.

It wasn't enough.

It wasn't magic.

He sat up in a smooth motion, crossed his legs, posture perfect. "You know how to access your magic, how to Draw?"

She nodded.

"Pull life from that log."

She put her hand on it without looking, eyes squinted in concentration, searching. Soon enough, she felt the faint shudder of life outside of her own. It was dim, but she Drew it and felt the small bit of energy merge with her own.

"Slow, but acceptable," he said. "Now put it back."

Lips a thin line, she Pushed, her energy now sapping as she transferred the life from herself back into the log.

He shook his head. "Sloppy. Never give what you don't have to."

"I pulled its energy, and gave it back," she retorted.

"Why weaken yourself?" he answered.

She frowned at him.

"Touch is the only way to access your power?" He spoke like an aged man, not a young one — like how she supposed the professors in the Order might lecture.

"The only way that I've seen," she said slowly.

"And so, is it the only option available to you?"

"No."

"No. Do you feel the wind on your skin?"

She nodded.

"What else does it touch?"

"Everything," she whispered.

"Everything. What else might do that?"

She didn't answer, nothing coming to mind. What else touched everything around her?

He grinned toothily at her silence. "I think I will skip across the fundamentals with you and dance straight into the dangerous and complex. I'd warn you to be careful, but really, I want to know what you do with this knowledge."

Wren removed her hand from the log, seeing it anew — the wood was dead, but the lichen had grown, accepting her gift without hesitation or pride, and putting it to immediate use. She closed her eyes and touched the wind as it blew past her. She sought that shudder of life she'd found in so many other things, but it wasn't there. Patience.

She pushed her senses outward, looking for the life of the wind, or anything else she might use to transfer her magic without touch.

"Are you asleep?" Forest asked.

She opened her eyes and was surprised to see the sunrise.

"I thought not. Defeated?" he asked.

"Never," she growled.

"Do you want a hint?"

"No."

He laughed merrily, rolled to his feet and whistled while he strolled away.

* * *

Whitman limped, crutch under one arm and a pile of books under the other. Almost no one was awake at this hour, but he had ever been a night owl. The peace of the evening was a boon to his productivity. His best poems had come from sleepless nights, and tales told in the wee hours of the morning were by far the most honest and divulging.

A rare few other night owls passed, and he gave them warm greetings. "Good evening, Vijay." "Davis, lovely to see you again." "Leigh, looking well."

They each replied back, except for Leigh, who always waved and smirked good-naturedly, and never said anything.

Whitman hobbled to his door, juggling his books and crutch and keys for a moment before he managed to enter as quietly as he could. The lamp left burning on his desk gave plenty of light to see by, but the other rooms were dark and still.

He set the books on his desk and propped his crutch by the door, teetering as quietly as he could to the bedroom where a slender form disturbed the level of the quilts on his bed.

Perched on the edge of the bed, relief to his tired legs, he rubbed the form's shoulder, leaned down, and planted a tender kiss on the soft, bearded cheek.

"Are you new awake, or not come to bed yet?" the sleepy form mumbled.

Whitman smiled. "I thought it a decidedly brilliant idea to keep awake all night." *In the hopes that this newest bunch of stories would render my hunt unnecessary beyond tonight. My hopes are high. Never for a moment do I think I will so easily find that which I search for, for what is victory without the journey? Still, a tickling in the back of my mind suggests I grow closer to my quarry —*

"You need your sleep, my love."

"Soon, I promise." *And a promise made in earnest echoes through time, once broken, forever tarnished and made to dismantle the trust in which it was made, reflections cast by future promises already cracked at their birth. A promise is a sacred thing and I will always honor my word when I —*

"Don't be too long."

Whitman kissed his lover's cheek again, and then his lips, winning himself a sleepy smile. "I will be by your side before you can miss me." *Never miss me, my love, and I shall give you no reason to feel that you must. My place is in your arms, as you are made to fit in mine, now and forever —*

"I love you, Whitman."

"And I, you, Oslan. Now and forever."

And ever and ever and ever and ever ...

* * *

"Get up, sleep-about."

Whitman groaned and pulled the pillow more tightly around his head. He knew the curtains would be open and hatefully bright light would be streaming in through the window. How long had he slept? Four hours, five? Surely it wasn't yet time to —"

His husband's body landed roughly atop his own, eliciting a pained groan, and a hand snaked under the pillow to pat his face and pull at his cheek annoyingly. "If you hadn't stayed up so late, you'd be in better form now."

"I had *work* to do," he grumbled through the pillow. His whole body ached. Was this age? Was he old now?

"What? You're muffled. I should take your pillow," came Oslan's impish and hateful reply. Whitman griped it more tightly, *but sleepy fingers were no match for the scribe-hands Oslan possessed. Years of note-taking and speedy transcribing and skilled musical play had turned the muscles there to steel and even a practiced swordsman would find himself impressed at the young scrivener's grip.*

The pillow was wrenched mercilessly away and Whitman was forced to scrunch up his face to keep the light from blinding him through his eyelids, *the thin barrier determinedly working to keep those sighted orbs from losing their —*

"I will never understand how you can rise so quickly whilst on the road, but fight so hard to stay abed while home," Oslan laughed, now methodically stripping away the bedcovers.

Whitman conceded at last, flopping to his back and blinking rapidly against the harsh late-morning rays. "Because, my tender darling, the trials of the road do not allow for these delectably comfortable beds, and instead I am so often forced to drop wearily upon the needles and nettles and twiggy nests that carpet the forest floor." *Alas, 'twas a hard life, but truly I miss it, rising with the sun and running the rocky and mudded trails in pursuit of some knowledge or escape from those who would harm me and mine, and you are truly mine, most gorgeous creature my eyes have ever beheld in the light of—*

"You can't have been a very good traveler if you were sleeping on needles and nettles, darling. You always exaggerate in the morning. Come on. I had a page bring breakfast since I knew you'd want to lay abed this morning."

Glorious fiend, thou knowst my most dire of weaknesses! "I love breakfast." *And you know that, which makes my love for you burn ever brighter, soon to —*

"If anything was going to get you out of bed, it'd be ham."

"Or turnips." *The most delightful of palate pleasers, tickling the tongue and filling the belly with an unmatchable and glorious —*

"Come on, then." Oslan put a hand out and Whitman accepted. He slid out of bed to balance on his good leg, towering nearly a foot over his slender and wiry husband.

They moved together with practiced gait, Whitman's meaty arm about Oslan's lean shoulders, into the front room where Whitman fell into his desk chair with a heavy sigh.

"You can always bring your crutch to the bedroom, you know. It might make your mornings a little easier." Oslan folded onto a couch cushion, legs crossed beneath him.

Such heartbreak has no place in our shared space. "I know."

Whitman dug eagerly into the stacked plate of food that Oslan had thoughtfully requested for him: eggs, ham, toast and butter, dried strawberries and apricots ... Oslan had his own, much smaller breakfast of sweetened oats and milk, which he ate leisurely while reading through his work schedule and notes.

Whitman scanned his own notes from the previous night, as his mind woke and thoughts came together.

"More stories?" Oslan asked.

Whitman grunted assent. "If they were seen as too fantastical to deem worthy of the history books, I have no other method to determine what magi of the past could do, and therefore what they are now capable of, exceeding all previously considered boundaries. I know all of these pieces, but even my memory can fail, and so I research."

I must find what the deviant can do and how then to counter him. Even as a student, surely Ruben will not benefit from our Smiling Man's teaching in full measure, for what creature of evil would give all of his knowledge to one he does not trust? Ailen the Immeasurable was said to have extraordinary Healing abilities, but how does one calculate such a thing? Doren Belu is rumored to have killed with a single touch, but she was brought low in only three years. Such a young thing. What brought her to so early a grave? They were all so young.

Whitman frowned and pulled out his biography reference to mark a note to find out what he could about Doren Belu.

Was it Elementalism or Healing or some forgotten power that she wielded? Subtle, one would believe, else a description of its effects would have been recorded somewhere. Wait, what was I doing? Of course, the battles of Great Kell and Ferren Far-Sight ...

Whitman checked the hourglass on desk and said, "You have a meeting today, yes?" *A recalculation on the numbers submitted by the Guild of Merchants compared to recent influx of fish sales to confirm skimming on the part of Dikal Weathering: starts in twenty minutes.*

Oslan jumped to his feet. "Bah! I'm late!"

"You have twenty minutes." *Ten to get dressed and ten to reach the —*

"How do you keep my schedule in that crowded head of yours?" Oslan kissed Whitman on the forehead.

Whitman smiled. "I find room for worthwhile things." *And you are the most while that I worth, my darling love, with your strawberry mark splayed across your ribs like the caress of some long-forgotten fire-god, and the pale skin that shows me every line of your gentle frame, lithe even so, and your blue-black hair trailing into your depthless —*

"I adore you. Even when you aren't waxing poetic." Oslan kissed him again and went to their room to change. He emerged in his usual, boring clothes. Oslan held to the belief that scribes were not meant to be seen, but how he could ever fade into the background, Whitman had never figured.

"Don't forget to eat today," Oslan called as he walked out the door.

Whitman didn't answer, but smiled and made a note about the paragraph he'd finally translated. He had business of his own to attend, though less scheduled than he preferred. His meeting with Elliott would likely be postponed, depending on whether or not the reports from the western fires resulted in a meeting, and if he'd managed to schedule time with the Master Chronicler who was recently returned with several new books and tomes for the Order's library. Whitman was eager to get his hands on those, whatever they were. He'd send a page to find out.

Translations set aside, he hobbled to get dressed, smiling to see the outfit that Oslan had laid out for him on their bed. Whitman dressed in the bright color — various shades of blue today — as the scribe couldn't be colorful himself, he made sure that Whitman was always dressed brightly for them both. Whitman had never had an eye or care for clothing, so it was a sweet activity of Oslan's to take care of that part of Whitman's morning most days.

He gathered notes and a couple of books into his satchel and planted his crutch under his arm, locking the door securely when he left. He'd considered extra security measures after the Smiling Man had come calling, but had ultimately felt pointless. Still, there was no need for those of simpler means to get their hands on his things, even if he did write in various ciphers for anything important. Their loss would set him back weeks or months.

The medical wing stood on the other side of the Order from his rooms. He concentrated as much of his attention as he could spare on walking the way he'd been directed by the surgeons. *Not too much weight, careful application from heel to toe in a rolling motion, I have to get this damn thing healed, or my reputation will be in ruins, travel made impossible — horses certainly, why not horses? Of course they have very little to lend in the realm of subtlety. The right horse and I present myself as a lord of some notable influence, and another shows me to be a simple merchanting man, but what of the lowly beggar? Surely a limp would speak truly to a difficult life on the streets, but better to fake that which would slow you, lest your enemies catch whiff of their prey. Speed is the gopher's friend. He grimaced. Stoat? Weasel? Otter? Otters are sleek, yes but generally considered water creatures, very well, serpent? Haha, some would consider me a snake —*

"Good morning, Vant, James, anyone of note today?"

The two guards barring entrance to the medical wing smiled warmly at him. "Bloody bards know everything, don't they, m'lord? And you know we can't say such a thing."

"Not a word," Whitman winked as he crutched through the doors they held open.

The ward was quiet, though with the usual sounds of a room holding those with small injuries or illnesses. Nurses triaged those in need, making notes and assurances. An ill-looking Healer conversed with the nurses and asked quiet questions of the small group of waiting patients. Occasionally, he would touch someone, taking on their symptoms or injury, and they thanked him profusely before leaving. Whitman saw he bore two broken fingers at the very least from this morning ministrations, to be later passed on to some plants or nearly-dead animals.

Never could such as I bear the hardship of a Healer's life — so much give and so very little gain, unless one could slough off the societal expectations and take to a life of cruelty, refusing to give except to gain. Broken fingers? Certainly, but only if you give me a week of your eyesight in exchange ... no thank you. Of course, personal injuries thrown aside to any living thing would be a welcome benefit, bloody knee —

"Hello, Bard Acres," the newly-promoted head surgeon greeted.

She was impressively young for her position, and not a mage, which spoke of incredible skill. Whitman hoped to bring her into his network — a person of her ability indicated an incredible mind, and he needed more people who could be found anywhere without casting suspicion on their actions. Found in the slums? Aiding the poor. Found with some noble or another? Healing an embarrassing ailment, or teaching, or any number of excuses.

Still, he had to be wary with his recruiting, lest they find the offer unappetizing and turn him away, but now with the knowledge of his position.

"Lady Pennison! A joy it is to find myself under your gaze, so like the sun it is: warming, life-bringing ..." He grinned and she rolled her eyes playfully. "Ah, yes, there is the burn," he finished, and she laughed.

"Come to see Kina again?" They walked toward the rooms where patients with lasting conditions were given constant care.

Her pace slowed to his own limping speed without obvious impatience, which he appreciated. Of course, he exaggerated somewhat — it was never wise to give away your every advantage.

"Of course! Our conversations are illuminating despite their puzzles, and I would never miss the chance to alleviate some of her boredom."

Lady Pennison gave him a sideways glance to check that he wasn't being facetious. "Have you had any luck communicating with her?"

Whitman grimaced. "I apologize for insinuating that I had. The trick of that eludes me as so yourself, my lady. However, I do think the company helps her disposition, which could easily turn to the dreary. Barely-sixteen-year-olds are not meant to be cooped up inside, after all."

"Very true." She tugged on an earlobe thoughtfully. "She's been awake two weeks already and not been outside for any length of time.

We have considered an outing for her if only I could find an assistant with time." They both rolled their eyes at the idea of a surgeon with available time. "Ah, well. I'll make it happen," she smiled. They stopped at the doorway to the girl's room. "This is where I leave you."

"Our conversation, though brief, was as pleasant as ever. Thank you for your time." He bowed over her hand.

"Always, Bard Acres. I strive to learn, and you are a puzzle I have yet to conquer."

He grinned wickedly. "The best puzzles are impossible."

"I've yet to find one of those."

"I expect you will in time."

"Of which I have very little." She smiled again. "Duty calls."

She turned back the way they'd come and Whitman wondered if she already suspected. His rank and injury had granted him her personal attention eight months ago, and he knew it was possible that he'd said something revealing whilst unconscious, drugged and under her knife. He'd heard no rumor or whisper, but that didn't mean anything. He cleared his mind. Duty called.

Whitman pushed open her door and took on a grandiose pose. "Kina!"

She spun and grinned at him, "Bird imagery —" she stopped short and gestured for him to come in, which he did.

Lacking a window, Kina had covered the walls with art, in which she was quite talented. Paint and pastels, charcoal, even colorful wax surrounded her. Each view, however lovely, was from the day of her injury. Whitman knew that it wasn't by choice, however, just as the jumbled words that she could speak were tangentially related to her planned report, the translation for it lost somewhere deep in her mind.

A picture of Donovan in profile, crouched and concentrating, showed exquisite detail even to each gray hair and the glint of his eye.

Kina shook Whitman's hand politely.

"Any progress?" he asked.

Kina wiggled her hand back and grimaced.

"Truly. I imagine you are tired of the mental intrusions, but I also know you want to move past that day more than we do. Together, we will figure out why you can't communicate."

She nodded and wiggled her fingers.

"Yes, including through sign language." He paused and she pointed to her desk. "Thank you." he sat and pulled a notepad from his satchel, scratching down his thoughts before they faded.

When he slowed, she tapped his notepad.

"I wonder what the difference is in the small ways you do manage to communicate, versus when your speech is tangled."

Kina said, "Populous interspersed unknown —" and then stopped, lips pinched and eyes shut.

She took a deep breath and looked him in the eye, pointed to her temple, then held out her hands. She closed her eyes and looked away and wiggled her fingers. When she opened them, she once again looked Whitman firmly in the eye.

He stared back. *Her mind, I asked what the difference was in how she managed to communicate and she tried to answer, then showed her mind, her hands, and looked away from their motion. That in itself is the conundrum, and she demonstrates it once again.*

Dammit, she is clearly thinking without issue, and comprehending everything we say and do — the Mentalists are wrong to demand that we only bring one or two issues to her at a time. Focus: she pointed at her mind and then showed her hands to give me the answer to my question.

What is the difference between spoken language and signed language? She can learn the signs, indeed very quickly, but they are as unconnected as her words. What is the difference between sign language, and what she is doing? Gesturing, but the line between gesture and sign is slim enough — it must be something else. Head, mind, think, hands, eyes, closed eyes, blind, cannot see, cannot see hands, yes ... that is something. Cannot see hands with ... eyes? Head, cannot see hands — OOH — she cannot see her hands in her mind? How then does she — ah!

"You are not thinking words when you answer, are you? Is it, what, muscle memory? No, thinking one thing and saying or doing another?"

Kina clapped her hands, her face radiant with relief.

Whitman laughed aloud. "All we need then is a solution!"

Kina rolled her eyes. "Numerous branches —" She stopped herself with another grimace and then forced a smile she did not feel.

"I *will* think of something," he assured her. "Look how quickly we were able to discover this! You have only been awake for two weeks, Kina. I know that is a thousand years right now, but I am pouring as many of my resources into your recovery as I can, I promise."

A couple of unexpected tears raced down her cheeks and she hurriedly brushed them away.

Whitman hopped up to grab her in a tight hug, her head tucked under his chin. "I have no idea what you are going through, but I know you *will* get through it."

She bawled into his chest and he held tight. His leg ached from holding all of the weight off of his damaged knee, but he ignored it, determined to be the pillar of support for as long as she needed.

After a few minutes, she calmed enough to find steady breaths. When she stepped away, he let her go with a comforting smile. She brushed at his vest where her tears had soaked through, cleared her throat and blushed.

"Oh, that is nothing," he assured her. "I have nowhere important to go: only a meeting with the Head of the Order."

She made a face at him, and squeezed his hand in thanks.

"I will work on your problem and come back in the next day or so, as soon as I can. And I will tell the Mentalists what we learned."

She seemed to realize something and rushed to her desk, sorting through a stack of drawings until she revealed a drawing and delivered it to him.

Whitman studied the image, but did not recognize the features. A young woman, probably in her mid-to-late thirties, stared at him from a heart-shaped face. Her eyes were green, prematurely aged with crow's feet, and her smile bore more of a sardonic arrogance than any kind of mirth. Her curly, sandy-blond hair was braided tightly out of the way, and she held herself with unquestionable authority.

"Is this the Hunter who attacked you?"

Kina pointed at another picture on her wall of a different woman, her eyes wild and eager, with hands framing the page as though the viewer's face was held in her grip.

"Ah, right. Hmm." He stared at the woman's features a moment longer, sure he didn't recognize her. "Thank you. We will speak again."

Kina nodded, staring at the picture in his hand, dejected.

No reason to fret over it; we will have a solution for Kina's condition and she will be filling us in in no time. I expect she will never stop talking! Poor dear ...

*   *   *

"Bard Acres, a pleasure to see you," Bruno greeted him warmly, signing off on the receipt a page had handed him. "He's waiting; you can go right in."

"Thank you, Bruno. Hello, Arthur."

The page grinned at him and ran off.

Bright boy — Elementalist if I remember, of course I remember, ha! I will have him recruited in no time — half in my pocket already, I simply need to take more of a hand in his orders and see how he does. Fifth-generation Order-dweller, he would be excellent as a hand-for-hire in any village I sent him to, brothers and sisters are all builders —

Whitman went through the office door Bruno guarded. "Elliott."

The Head of the Order looked up from his paperwork and gave a tired smile. "Acres."

"Did you sleep?" Whitman helped himself to a seat in the sunken conversation pit, settling with a sigh, and massaging his tired leg muscles.

"I don't remember the last time I had a full night of sleep. And too much to do these days. With the aches and pains of getting older, it's a miracle I catch any night-bees at all. What do you have for me?"

Whitman handed over a portfolio from his satchel. Elliott took it with a sigh and adjusted his reading glasses to scan the first page.

"In the last few months, I have traced travel patterns and, at the risk of sounding paranoid: our blood mages have disappeared. Certainly not all together — the numbers I last had suggested that they would be hard to move *en masse*, but other than some possible distribution to a few towns here and there, the rest are gone.

"That said, the ones that we did manage to pin, point us vaguely in the direction they might be headed. I put trackers in those woods, and they agree some large group came through there, but the way that they disbanded in the first place suggests that we will never track them all down. They might be under timed orders, and we could all be attacked with little warning. Like the last insurgence I waylaid."

"You always bring me such heartwarming news ..."

"Yes, well, you never demand the impossible of me, do you?"

"I gave you more people."

"Untrained and unready. I need *time*, Elliott, to gather information, and time is the last thing we have. No matter what, this war will cost us dearly." *And more than it already has, impossible as it might seem —*

"This war will cost everyone dearly. Our goal is to make their cost the higher."

"If it lasts for too much longer, we will never recover." Whitman knew the frankness of his words would not keep him in Elliott's favor, but he was only human.

"We have to know what their plans are before we can prepare for anything. Is Kina speaking yet?" Elliott's change of subject was not unwelcome.

"Nothing but broken pieces. We have put together what little we can make of it, and efforts continue. Mentalists struggle to learn what was done to her so as to undo it, but in the meantime, we have to make do with meager sips."

Elliott sighed and rubbed his eyes. "All right, continue."

Whitman gave a bitter smile. "Still no sign of Ruben. Not a peep, which means either he has been killed and they do not want to brag until the timing suits them, or whoever is guarding him is impressively tight-lipped. It would speak well of their discipline.

"Nobles migrate to the palace from their estates for news and to find safety in numbers. There have been reports of four raids for supplies and fear mongering, the latter working perfectly well. Attacks have resulted in small injuries, only a few of them serious — deaths have been rare in these encounters. Dire threats appear reserved only to those who fight back, which makes the rest hesitate all the more.

"However, with the information we have from those raids, we have drawn a vague idea of the numbers they might be feeding, which fits roughly into my calculations. We can assume their base is within a close distance. The numbers are there for you, at the bottom."

Whitman took a breath and went on, "My trackers are searching for cave structures as the blood mages used before, but I imagine that our discovery of their previous location will keep them shy of such structures unless they have a quick escape to the surface that we know nothing of."

"How populated are these areas here?" Elliott asked, pointing to the map Whitman had provided.

"With the nobles out of residence and most of their staff with them, I imagine their stewards will be running those households with a skeleton staff — perhaps twenty to forty in each?"

"How many manors are there?"

"Twelve, based on census reports from the palace. A few towns and villages are peppered in the area. I have people in many of those, but not all. Recruitment has increased, but —"

"Good. I expect their reports to come in soon."

Whitman released the tension in his jaw. "Four new ciphers have gone out *this month*. With the number of people aware of them, I need new ones created and distributed every three weeks. As often as not, I expect reports in any of the updated ciphers, which means we will have to translate them in each. It will be confusion."

"That many? That often?"

"*And* we must be prepared for those to be intercepted and interrupted with more frequency than before. My rapid recruitment means that I have dozens more eyes and ears and hands, but also dozens more mouths — and neither my people nor I are infallible."

Elliott nodded. "It will be worth it."

Whitman shrugged a stiff shoulder. "One can hope." He pulled Kina's drawing from his satchel and showed Elliott. "Do you know this woman?"

The Head took it and studied her face. "No. Should I?"

"One of Kina's. She is important, but until we can communicate properly, we will not know why."

"How close are we to that?"

"The Mentalists have asked us not to overtax her with questions. They struggle to explain their magic to me, so I cannot make suggestions on that front. Too, the surgeons are determined to ensure she is well-rested, and so I have little time for my own attempts to hack at the root. We had a breakthrough a moment ago, however, creating its own problems, but I know I can find a solution. Soon, I hope."

"I will speak to the surgeons and Mentalists to give you more time."

"I doubt I could use the time you find for me," Whitman smiled wryly. "I am already going to be late for a meeting with one of my contacts. He will wait, but I need to receive what he has to tell me."

"I'll let you go, then. Thank you for this," Elliott gestured with the portfolio.

"I wish it was more," Whitman rose to his good leg with a suppressed groan.

"Standing shouldn't be that difficult at your age," Elliott smiled, clapping him on the shoulder and going back to his desk.

Whitman received the comment without one of his own. Elliott was lost in paperwork before the spymaster reached the door.

* * *

Whitman stepped into a servants' hallway, about half as wide as a regular one, meant to pass between rooms to save time when the passages were bogged down with people who didn't need to be there. The pages used them, and occasionally students, but generally only servants were allowed to. Doors on either side of him opened to other corridors, or rooms of the wealthy in this part of the Order.

He opened the door into one such room, the size of a closet. Inside it sat a tall stool and a door that locked from the inside, with a hatch that Whitman could open. The last was covered in a thick cloth that couldn't be seen through. He'd had Annette check it when Donovan's magical discovery had been made, in case a person could increase their vision to see through. The cloth, she had determined, allowed his voice to pierce, but would keep his identity hidden. Whitman set his crutch aside and perched on the stool, resting his legs with a quiet exhale of relief.

Ready, he opened the door's hatch and said, in a voice deeper and more gravely than his own, "I apologize for keepin' you waitin'.

Other business 'eld me. What information do you 'ave for our employer?" His accent was strong, and he was careful not to use it anywhere except in situations like these in case he was ever overheard and recognized.

Whitman's contact hurried over to the door and leaned against the wall beside it, clearly worried about being overheard, despite the room being soundproof. Though, of course, he wouldn't know about that.

"What kept you? I've been waiting!" he hissed.

"Yeah, we covered that. Never you mind — I said business. Now speak up!"

"It took me a bloody age to get in here. The security's been doubled and *Mentalists* are roaming the halls looking for reasons ... This is the last job I do for you."

"I doubt that, mate. I have some choice ruse for you to fulfill and a mummer like you would think twice to pass it up."

"Oh yeah? Mummer, aye, but coward as well. There are jobs even I can't fool, mark me."

"I mark you well, friend, and we'll get to that. But first, my information."

The man sighed sharply. "I gave that page of yours my report."

"With drawings, I 'ope."

"What I could put together."

"Good. Tell me."

The contact cleared his throat and seemed to straighten. Then, in a tone clearly practiced, much clearer and calmer than before, said, "The butcher gave a package twice the size as the cut of meat requested, so I followed, and after a *winding* route through the city, I finally came upon a rundown house. The gentleman's glance was enough to give it away, so I waited there for him. Sure enough, after traversing the streets for another twenty minutes, he showed, package in hand."

"You're sure it were the same package, mate? I told you *follow*. What if he passed it off?"

"It was the same package. Trust me."

Whitman did. Theil's memory was near perfect, better than Whitman's own.

"*If* you don't mind?" Theil said, sniffing at the interruption.

"Move on, then."

"I shimmied up the roof and watched through a hole. The package was passed, unopened. The gentleman went on his way, and my new friend started off on his own path. They didn't talk and seemed to hold no love for one another. I followed this bloke, and he was far and away superior at avoiding notice than my previous friend. He even had hats to change, and his cloak was reversible. He stopped for tea at one stand, and cheese at another, searching for a tail. Saw me, lost me. I had to switch to rooftops to find him again — luckily he's missing a toe or three."

"Aye?"

"A limp, but he's practiced moving — must have something shoved in his boot to keep his foot from sliding, but when he hurried, it showed, and I picked up his gait from above."

"Keen."

"Yes. And difficult. If he sees me again, I'm dead. Mentalist trash — I know his kind."

"Where'd 'e lead you?"

"Did you hear me? He saw my damn face!"

"If I know you, you was wearin' some kind of disguise, aye?"

"Of course I was, I'm not a fool. But if he recognizes me ..."

"We'll deal with 'im, all right? Where'd 'e lead you?"

Theil gathered his thoughts. "Eventually to the backdoor of an inn. It has a cellar that I couldn't get into."

"So 'ow'd you 'ear what they said?"

"Vent pipe. Barely noticeable, but I'd seen it years ago when I was drunk behind that same inn and thought it odd. They were quiet, but not expecting listeners."

"Blood mages?"

"A *pack* of them. Going on about recruitments and cursing their leadership. Apparently a new player took the field a few years ago and they don't like this person's methods. Says she's burning through resources, pushing people too hard."

"She?"

"Definitely, but no name — they were clever enough for that. I waited outside and counted seventeen exiting, with another four waiting inside to leave until they thought no one would connect them."

"Big meetin'."

"Bigger than I expected, certainly."

"Did they do any magic while in th' cellar?"

"None that I heard but, as my contact was late, and judging by the fact that they only traded off the package once, I don't imagine it was a particularly important meeting. I would have had at least six trades. Or four with two fakes."

"Which is why we're glad you're on our side. Did yeh find out what were in th' package?"

Theil's voice was shaky now. "I went back to the butcher's and poked around after he locked up. I knew you'd ask."

"Kind of you. What'd yeh find?"

"A dead street urchin and half a dozen jars of his blood. Th-the butcher came back while I was there and I barely got out without him seeing. *Barely.* He — he chopped the boy into pieces. I vomited on the street over; I won't eat for a month. Screw your next job, I'm — I'm not doing anything like that again."

Whitman sat for half a moment while his mind processed the information. "The boss wants yeh t'join them."

"No he doesn't, you damn fool, what would he want that for?"

"He needs yeh to join th'crew, be one o'them, a new recruit. We 'ave no one else so close inside and you're perfec' fer th' job. You know that was comin'."

Theil paced jerkily around the small room, muttering angrily under his breath. When he came back to the hatch he snarled, "I tell you about a plot of more than *twenty* Hunters right under your *nose* with a murdered boy and you want me to *join* them? What kind of sick, twisted —"

Whitman interrupted with shushing sounds. "Theil, now Theil ... You're the best we 'ave. Yeh learn language and body motion like a babe learns t'breathe. Yeh put on characters like a new shirt. If you don' do this, there's no one else."

"They'll make me kill for them."

"Aye, probably."

"You're a bastard."

"I'll get yeh a knight'ood."

"A barony. Somewhere far in the mountains where I never have to hear your stupid, fake accent again."

Whitman sighed. The accent was good, but he couldn't fool Theil's ear. "If yeh tell me wot I need t'know, I'll send yeh on your way with a smile."

"Who are you, really?"

"Why would yeh want t'know? Issa dangerous thing."

"You're sending me to my death. What danger could I be?"

Whitman didn't answer, but silence was answer enough.

Theil was quiet for a long moment and then laughed ruefully. "A wicked tongue earns no allies."

"Can we trust yeh?"

"You can never trust someone like me."

"Will yeh do this?"

"How do I inform you? They'll be watching me; I won't send letters."

"I'll find yeh. You'll 'ave notes a'fore you go, contacts."

"Make sure it's someone clever you send. If they give me away, I'll make sure they don't survive my escape."

"I believe yeh."

"Right."

"Keep your eye out fer th'magus boy."

"Right."

"Theil, are we losin' yeh?"

"I'm wondering how they'll do it. Because they'll want the blood ... My — father taught me how to drain hogs when we hunted and you string them by the ankles ..."

Whitman sighed again, pity welling up in his breast. Against his better judgment, he said, "If yeh don' think yeh can do th'job ..." He pinched his ear in frustration, but continued, "... we will find someone else."

"No, you won't."

"No, we won'. You're the best we 'ave. If we 'ave you."

"You have me."

"Not f'much longer."

"As long as it takes. Some sins don't fade."

Whitman knew, even without seeing him, that the man was staring at his wife's locket.

"Our boss is not th'one who can grant forgiveness. He's th'one who causes th'need of it."

Theil scoffed. "Don't tell me who you are. When they torture me, I don't want to give you away. I have guesses, anyway. I will demand one thing of you, though, and I'll have your word on it."

"All right ..."

"When they do capture me," he took a breath. "You send someone to kill me. Don't let them torture me? If they keep me alive, you send someone, and you see it done quickly."

Whitman nodded gravely. "I'll see it done."

Theil took another shuddering breath and then choked out a laugh. "I always knew I'd die a poor actor. Drunkards die young, but curses live forever. And they take the living with them." He started crying softly.

Whitman listened, torn between himself and his duty. Duty meant sacrifice. Sacrifice of the few meant life for the rest. Whitman looked at his wounded knee and focused on the ache that never went away. Everyone made sacrifices. Some were worse than others.

Listening to Theil's sobs, he was horribly grateful for his injury. He knew with absolute certainty that if he was whole, it would not be Theil trying to infiltrate the blood mages' inner circle.

3

WREN WAS UNIMPRESSED with the squat building. Large, single-storied, it displayed many obvious signs of disrepair — the roof certainly leaked; the paint, once attempting joviality with splashes of different colors, had all faded into a vagueness of what once was, now peeling and torn. The door, while large and imposing, looked as though it would grant splinters before entry. Glass still remained in a few of the windows; most of the panes were at least cracked, but they only made more pronounced the fact that so many frames were empty and relied on patched and waxed canvas to keep out the weather. One flapped loose in the breeze that tugged at her braid.

"This is where we part," Forest told her.

She frowned at him and looked back at the building, deliciously attractive to termites, perhaps, but not so to her.

"No," she answered with finality. "I'm staying with you."

Forest grinned. "You haven't a choice, Beast. Try not to be yourself."

"Where are you going, then?"

"To make friends."

"Where, I said, not what."

"If I say, you'll try to follow."

"I might try to follow anyway, and risk my life for it."

Forest shrugged one shoulder.

"How long will you be?" she asked when it was clear he wouldn't change his mind.

"That depends on how long my new friends take to see my way of things. I expect I'll want your help eventually."

"I can't just go off on my own until you call for me? I have to be here?" She wondered what lesson she was supposed to learn this time.

"Until you learn your basics and figure out where I am."

She raised an eyebrow and he grinned again.

"Do you remember when you asked for a taste of my memories, little Beast?"

She nodded hesitantly.

"A parting gift." He put out a hand. Remembering his harsh lesson on how he didn't like to be touched, she wavered, hand hovering. "Go on, Beast," he ordered.

Magic at the ready, she laid her hand gently on his and prepared to Draw from his memories. Instead, a wave of disorientation washed over her. Drowning, she sputtered and flailed, the torrential downpour and flood of mental images threatening to overwhelm her, forcing her to capsize and whirlpool down to the depths of the sea. She retched and felt arms around her, motion, sound, but was unable to concentrate enough to ground herself.

A momentary break in the overwhelming sensation of years and years by dozens pouring through her mind was a kiss on the forehead and a whisper, "Come find me soon, Beast. Don't do anything I wouldn't do."

* * *

Ruben woke with a start, unnamed dread coursing through him. With scant thought or effort, he brought lightning into his hands, crackling and popping. His eyes watered from the sudden brightness, and he traded the lightning in favor of a low-banked fire in his palms instead. Sweat had soaked through his clothes and left him clammy, and all of the hairs on his body stood on end. His stomach roiled with fear, but he couldn't remember the dream that had caused such a rude awakening.

Sometimes his nightmares featured the Smiling Man, standing over him or murdering his way through Ruben's friends. Sometimes he was back in Philipa, working the horses until Hunters would attack the city, and he'd try to bring his magic to bear, only to find that it had abandoned him. Most of the time, he simply woke with a vague sense of anxiety that stayed for hours and made him feel watched.

He'd never been afraid of the dark before, but with no light but that which he created, his fear grew day by day. What might happen if he couldn't create his own light?

Ruben ate a piece of dried meat from the small food basket, relishing the sensation of salt burning on his tongue. He hadn't been starved yet, but with no sense of time in this prison, he didn't want to risk it - he rationed as much as he could.

Sleep destroyed any count of hours he might have had. Was he tired because it was always dark, or had he been awake for sixteen hours? Did he sleep for eight hours? Five? Twelve? In the beginning he'd raged and screamed himself hoarse, scarred his hands and knuckles on the rough stone walls of his prison, bruised his body by throwing himself at the wooden door, but no one had come.

The only times he saw another person was when they brought his food and water, never with any regularity that he could tell, and they never spoke to him, or even made eye contact. It was like he didn't exist. He'd tried to starve himself at first, but gave in quickly. Sick after gorging himself, he had thrown up several times before he'd adjusted again. Now he could only try to keep himself occupied until the Smiling Man chose to release him.

Magic was the only outlet for his mental stimulation — that and exercising when he wasn't too depressed to be active, which was often enough to concern him. With the nightmare still in mind, he knew that he wouldn't fall asleep again soon, so he closed his hands around the fire he'd called to bear. He changed it once more to lightning and watched as it popped and crackled unpredictably. Something about it calmed him, even while it made his heart race with excitement.

He anchored one end of the lightning above the iron-crossed door in his cell and lined the ceiling with the natural light. The ends connected and he fed it from afar to keep the magic energized. It had taken him a while to discover that useful trick.

Done, he adjusted his seated position and took a deep breath, hands held out in front of him. As before, he slowly brought fire to life in his palms, banked low, then pushed it to build higher, burn hotter, the flame passing through red and orange to white and blue, as high as his head and back down to his palms.

He'd tried to burn through the door in the first few … days? Shortly after he started, Hunters had come through the door with some kind of invisible shield around them that his magic bounced off of, and they threw buckets of water at him until he felt like he might drown. He'd tried a second time a few sleeps later — they responded the same way, except the water was hot, near to boiling. It had taken him longer, then, to build the courage to try again, but when he did, the Hunters opened the small hatch in the door and poured buckets into the room, one after another, until nearly two feet of standing water covered the floor. They didn't drain it for days, and he'd nearly drowned half a dozen times trying to sleep.

He hadn't tried since then, but wondered morbidly what they'd do to him. His magical abilities included the control of water — he'd seen other users in the Order demonstrate the power in passing, but had never been able to find it in himself. Maybe when he did, he would try the door again. However long before that might be …

Without magic, he was positive he'd have gone mad already. As it was, he could only practice so much. Healing was off the table since he had no subject to work with. He'd removed his shirt and boots to practice Displacement and had greatly improved — past even what he remembered of the demonstrated abilities of his friend and roommate Frin.

Seeking allowed him some measure of peace — he could leave his body and cell to spread shapelessly through the country, counting points of light and aligning his breathing with the heartbeat of the trees — but he was afraid something would happen while he was away.

He imagined someone might come speak to him, or hurt him, and, besides, he didn't know the area where they were keeping him, no matter how hard he tried to picture the maps he'd looked at. He just hadn't paid enough attention, thinking his other magics to be more important to train. Still, he could now raise his hearing whenever he wanted to tell when someone was bringing his day's food and exchanging his waste bucket, and he had counted as many as forty-six dots of light — people — in the building of his imprisonment. He had lost count a few times, but was pretty sure he was right. Or close enough.

Ruben continued with his magic training regimen. He drove himself to manipulate the magic he could access, searching for his limits and then pushing beyond them, learning what he could do. He liked Displacing things and could send his waste bucket and shirt and boots flying all over the room — twisting and turning through the air, dancing around one another in intricate dance. He practiced tying his shirt into half a dozen different knots, which required fierce concentration. When he failed a self-appointed task, he was unforgiving, and his frustration often sent him into unexpected and violent rages. He didn't like this side of himself.

When he ran out of ideas, or grew bored with his limited magic options, he exercised. During his time at the Order, and a bit before with the guards of his town, he'd had a chance to watch some of the soldiers training, especially after the Order's infiltration when he'd been reassigned from caring for horses to running supplies for the various soldier companies and troops.

He wasn't sure exactly what to do, but he was getting stronger, which was all that mattered to him. He stretched and practiced various kicks and punches against the walls of his cell, fighting imagined enemies until he dripped with sweat anew. He kept going. And going. He pushed, doing more than he ever thought he was capable of.

Wheezing for breath, he finally began his cooling routine, jogging and walking in circles around the cell. He stretched again, more vigorously, now. He was far more flexible than he'd ever been, too, setting goals for himself and reaching them; he hurt himself less now, too.

The air felt humid and, while he was mostly past feeling disgusted with his unwashed body, he did long for a bath. They came in once in a while to clean his prison and leave a bucket of soapy water and sponge, but it had been a while since the last time.

If he'd ever learned how fast hair grew ... He shoved his shaggy locks out of his face, retying them with the bootlace he'd sacrificed to the cause. His boots and shirt lay discarded in a corner after his Displacement practice. The soles of his feet had become callused and leathery from the rough stone. His shirt was relegated to the status of a sweat rag and occasionally used for a brace if he overtaxed a joint in his exercises.

When his heartbeat had returned to normal, he drank from his water ration, slowly, carefully, and ate a piece of fruit. His food and water were low enough that he guessed they'd be coming soon.

Hopefully.

Their games were working. Ruben knew if he was given the opportunity to leave his cell, he would do whatever they wanted, at least for a while. Sometimes he found himself talking aloud or laughing or crying without even realizing he'd started, and it took him some time to regain his composure. Can madmen track their madness?

Ruben sat in his usual corner and lowered his senses until they were tiny drips of water on the surface of his mind, letting the isolation flow over and through him. Then he increased his hearing until his heartbeat was a war drum and his blood was the ocean. The silence of his cell was a benefit as it let him focus and listen for a long while.

He was rewarded for his patience: he heard boots, two sets. He wanted to say one had a militant stride, but he was kidding himself if he knew why. Guesswork was all he had, but it made his time feel less dull. He tracked the sound of the boots all the way to his cell door, then lowered his hearing to normal and raised his other senses at the same time. If nothing else, he'd become a master manipulator in that branch of his abilities. Terror was a motivating teacher.

Ruben did not finish his water, but set the pitcher aside. He hadn't heard the telltale slosh that indicated they were refilling his ration. The lightning flashing around the room kept his eyes fresh, but he dismissed it before they arrived — no need for them to think he was prepared to attack; he didn't want to be punished with a longer sentence. By the time they opened the door, he was as prepared as he could be. His stomach rolled with nerves, and sweat beaded around his hairline.

The door swung outward and gentle light advanced inside from the torch-lit hallway. A man and woman stood outlined in his doorway. He could make out the vague shimmer in the air that suggested one of their shields — his magic wouldn't affect them, so he didn't try. If he didn't try enough times, maybe one day they would let their guard down.

Don't wish for too much, Ruben.

He didn't speak, waited for them to say something, anything. He was trembling with the desire to hear another's voice.

Please, he thought. *Just a few words, another human voice; it's been so long.*

"Ruben," the man said.

His heart started pounding and he felt a sob welling up in his chest.

"Yes?" he tried to answer. His voice was a whisper of disuse.

"Do you remember me at all?"

What?

Ruben squinted his eyes and studied the man's plain features. He was of average height, athletic build, brown hair and eyes ... Perhaps there was a vague recognition, but he had a very average face.

Ruben shook his head and the man shrugged. "No matter. I've been instructed to ask if you're yet ready to listen."

Ruben's hands shook and he had to press them to his sides to keep them still. He nodded joltingly, afraid this glimmer of hope was going to be ripped away from him.

"We're going to keep you shielded, so please don't try anything. If you do, I've been instructed to move you to a different cell. This one's standards are generous in comparison. Do you understand?"

Ruben nodded again, swallowing a hard lump in his throat.

"Come on, then."

Ruben walked jerkily forward to stand in the doorway of the cell. He could see an expanse of hallway to either side of him, and torches in brackets down the wall into a distance he hadn't seen in some time. It made him momentarily dizzy. Too, he could see the total blackness of his cell, the close walls, his waste bucket, food bucket, water pitcher, boots, shirt. Why was he suddenly afraid to leave? It was all he'd thought about for ... however long it had been.

Ruben took a deep, shuddering breath and stepped into the light.

Pressure built steadily around him, and fear rippled through his body as he shrank his head down toward his shoulders.

"It's just the shield sealing around you," the man said. "You'll have enough air for a while." He didn't smile.

The old woman controlling the magic mumbled and muttered, weaving her fingers in and out of each other. In between some of her mutterings, she spit impressively. Ruben knew she was using blood magic — Talents couldn't do things like this.

Finished, she gave the man a curt nod and they all walked down the hall, passing other closed doors, cells. They were probably identical to the one Ruben had left behind, but he hadn't Seen anyone inside them when he'd gone Seeking. That didn't mean they were empty; perhaps the occupants were dead.

They didn't pass anyone else during the walk, but the initial hallway led to stairs, which brought them to more hallways, and doors which required keys, and then more hallways and more stairs. The temperature was colder now, less humid, and Ruben shivered. The scent of the air had taken on a different flavor, and he considered raising his sense of smell, but stopped, afraid.

What if they think I'm casting magic against them? What if they send me back?

When the floor changed from stone to polished wood, he realized they were in a very large house — a mansion judging by the casual grandeur.

They stopped in front of a door like any other. The average-looking man knocked politely and opened it at an answer from within. The woman didn't enter, but continued on her way.

Ruben's knees went weak. Straight ahead stood a set of double-doors that led to a balcony.

And the outside.

He trembled. Tears rolled down his face. The sky was so, so blue and the clouds were blinding white. It was daytime, morning, and the wind was billowing a set of thin curtains.

Someone spoke nearby. Ruben couldn't draw his attention away. Another sobbing fit wracked his body. His senses were overwhelmed by that window, the fresh air streaming through it, the feel of the wind across his bare skin picking at hairs that had felt nearly nothing for what might have been a lifetime. It was too much, and, even thinking that, he realized how little it was — a window. He was brought to tears by the sight of a window, but knew he'd remember this feeling for the rest of his life.

A face interrupted his line of sight and a screaming rage rose in his mind, but he did not voice it, instead bringing his eyes to focus.

It was the Smiling Man.

"Ruben, welcome. I hope you're ready for our conversation."

The Smiling Man dismissed the average-looking man and the shield around the boy, clearly confident in his own abilities to contain Ruben, should the need arise. He walked them through the halls of his mansion, seeming unimpressed or uninterested in the lacquered wood that floored the place and the various artwork they passed. Very few windows now, as they weren't on any outside walls, but Ruben felt a hunger in his soul to see the outside again.

As they walked, the Smiling Man lectured, "You and I are unique in all the world, Ruben. I've waited a very long time to find someone like you and I think we can benefit one another."

Ruben tried to listen and keep his attention on the house, its layout; if he needed to run, he wanted to know which way to go. But after so long alone, he was finding it hard to stay focused on anything.

"These mages suit my purposes," the Smiling Man continued. Ruben had lost the thread of the sentence. "They hate me, because they hate anyone born to magic, as their theology teaches them to, but they tolerate my presence and recognize the benefit I bring them to keep me not only present, but satisfied."

He grinned at Ruben and the boy flinched. Ruben hated himself for it, even as he justified his reaction internally.

The Smiling Man was still talking, "We are not like other people. We have powers they only dream of, write stories of — and what you were shown at the Order merely ripples the surface of your gifts. I am very old, Ruben, and I know so much. I want to be your teacher."

"I had teachers," Ruben croaked. He didn't recognize his own voice anymore.

The Smiling Man gave a patronizing smile. "Uneducated, the lot of them. They would rather sit in darkness and hold to familiar teachings than face the truth of their incomplete knowledge. Following the treaded path is easier, but the one who went first had the greater adventure, and reaped the benefit of the rewards." He grinned toothily.

Ruben didn't miss the reference to his darkness, but held his tongue.

"I am a poor teacher, however, if I do not give examples of my knowledge. Tell me Ruben, what do they teach Healers in the Order about personal Healing?"

Ruben rubbed sweaty hands on his trousers as he tried to recall, "That it — um, cannot be done without — um, a, um, a — a — transfer?"

"Yes. And what do they teach about Displacing that cannot be done?"

"You, um, you cannot move yourself except by, um, pushing against a force greater than, um, that which you create," Ruben half-quoted.

The Smiling Man grinned. "Yes, and Empathy?"

The words came to him slowly, "You cannot create an emotion, only increase or decrease those already present."

"What if I told you I can do all of those things they claim to be impossible?"

Ruben shrugged again, feeling helpless. He was tired. He didn't care about any of this and only wanted to sleep, to be alone again, even so soon after craving companionship. Before he realized what was happening, the Smiling Man pulled a knife out of the back of his belt.

Ruben's heart sped and his breath caught, but the blade was offered to him hilt-first.

His hands didn't twitch from his sides.

"No?" the Smiling Man asked. "I would have thought you'd jump at the opportunity. Well, perhaps next time." Without hesitation, he pulled the blade deep through the meat of his forearm. Nothing happened for a long, astonishing moment. Then blood welled and fell, waterfalling to the floor as if desperate to escape its prison. Ruben stared, terrified, but curiosity gnawed at his insides now.

"I should fear a wound of this nature," the Smiling Man said without rush. "A wound of this depth will surely fester and the blood I lose will leave me weak and helpless. My arm, if it survives the infection, will never be the same, never work quite as well, the muscles and tendons broken beyond repair." He wiggled his fingers half-heartedly, and with difficulty.

The blood spread in an ever-widening puddle at their feet, staining the polished wood floor, marring its surface like a morbid painter preparing his palette.

The Smiling Man seemed to savor Ruben's horrified reaction before he took a deep breath and let it out in a long, controlled hiss. Ruben's eyes flitted from the blood on the floor to the Smiling Man's face, and then to the wound, which began to knit and mend before his eyes, its edges pulling together and sealing with no scar.

It was the work of moments.

"What is my cost?" he asked when the wound was gone. He showed Ruben the unbroken flesh, the unmarred surface beneath the blood he smeared carelessly. Ruben stared uncomprehendingly.

The Smiling Man repeated, "Those born with magic feel illness, dizziness, sickness, headaches when they access it. What is the cost a magus pays?"

"Nothing," Ruben whispered. "We pay nothing."

The Smiling Man smirked. "I'll teach you the truth to that falsehood. Our cost is a dangerous one, but I know how to mint the coins."

He grinned at his wordplay and continued walking, leaving his blood behind like so much garbage, even in this house of blood mages. Ruben was drawn into his wake, his thoughts spinning so fast he felt dizzy. The walls whirled and he realized he couldn't find his balance.

It was only a moment before he fell, the ground rising to meet him like a long absent friend, and he was slowed only by the wall he struck before landing.

The darkness closed in on his vision and his mind screamed, desperate not to return there. The Smiling Man's features swam in his vision and his voice echoed in Ruben's ears, but the words were ... too far away ...

*   *   *

Ruben jerked awake to find bindings tight around his arms and legs. He thrashed and they didn't come free, instead seeming to wind tighter and tighter. His eyes burst open and he screamed incoherently, trying to escape, *escape, ESCAPE.*

Someone was speaking soothingly, but it didn't help, didn't quiet the fear. He told himself to calm down, but it took a long time for his body to obey.

Soon after, he realized he wasn't bound, but covered in a heavy blanket which had twined around his limbs. He untangled them quickly and took in the rest of his surroundings with wide, sun-blind eyes.

A bedroom. An actual bedroom with tapestries of battles on the walls and bookshelves with leather bound books, some cracked with age. A small desk stood between two of the shelves. Above it, a window with its curtains open and shutters secured, back to let in the breeze.

The thickly carpeted floor was woven with bright colors to match the quilt he lay under. Beside a standing chest of drawers against the opposite wall stood a mirror. Next to that, a door stood half-open. A middle-aged man stood there with his hand on its knob and a sympathetic smile on his face.

Ruben's heart raced as he tried to catch his breath. He panted and shook, fear making him grip the sheets in sweaty hands.

"I was told you might have nightmares," the man explained in a westerly accent, not unlike that of Ruben's former master, the horse trader, Garth. It was too familiar. Ruben hurriedly sent the thought away before he cried.

"Was it nightmares, lad?" the man offered kindly.

Ruben nodded, his breathing still not returned to normal.

The man nodded back sympathetically. He had salt and pepper hair, no beard, pockmarked skin, and a bit of a paunch.

"Nightmares'll bring you to day far faster than any man would wish to be woken, aye?"

Ruben didn't answer.

"Difference between you and most folks is most others don't magic the room around or bring fire into their hands when they're nightmarin'. Not that I saw such, mind, but the lass before me swore it." He smiled benevolently again. "I don't figure you're a bad sort, and a man can't help his birth. 'course I haven't met you yet."

"You were watching me?" Ruben asked warily.

"In shifts." The man's face grew serious. "In case you tried to make trouble or part from our company. His Lordship came to check on you once or twice, but seemed never worried, lest you fret."

Ruben frowned. "He checked on me?"

"Aye. You were lying there in sleep, or something near it, for 'bout two days. I'd best report you're up. Hold a mo'." He spoke over his shoulder into the hallway, which seemed to receive the news well enough, because Ruben heard someone walk away a moment later.

Ruben was about to increase his hearing to follow the footsteps, but stopped.

What if they send me back?

"I imagine you're hungry. Lads always are."

Ruben shook his head. He felt like he had a lead ball in his stomach, but as he considered his body's needs, he hesitated and said, "I really have to pee."

The man laughed. "Of course you do. Come on, then."

Ruben slid out of bed and then stopped. "I'm naked."

"You couldn't expect to be wearing the clothes you came in with, could you? Those weren't fit for rags. I expect they've been burned. Take the robe there and I'll bring you to the baths — like as not'll be empty this time o'day."

The corridors were plain, but rich, with doorways, open now, showing into unoccupied bedrooms, offices, or sitting rooms. The walls bore numerous portraits and paintings of famous events Ruben didn't recognize and couldn't be bothered to wonder about.

Glazed ceramic tiles patterned across the entire floor of the bathing room at the end of the hall, except for a large pool at ground level. Shelves held bathing supplies — it was much as the Order had kept its own rooms.

It seemed convenience was convenience, no matter who you demonized.

The man gestured to everything with a kind smile and left Ruben alone. *Alone.* The silence was loud and the slightest sound rang loud in his ears. Ruben's hands shook and a shiver rocked his spine, but he ordered his legs to move. He dropped the robe at the edge of the pool and descended the shallow steps into the hot water, wincing and taking his time to let his body adjust to the change of temperature in stages. It didn't take long for the heat to soak relief into his muscles.

Ruben took deep, calming breaths to let the water reach into him and draw out the poison of stress. How long had it been since he'd soaked in a pool? How could he have taken such a thing for granted? If they hadn't taken him back to his cell yet, maybe they wouldn't. If he kept in line long enough to gather knowledge, could he escape? Or maybe get something out to Whitman and Donovan — a letter, perhaps. No, he couldn't do anything without information. With the blood mages keeping him, he had to know more before he could simply leave. And they would surely come after him. The Smiling Man would certainly find him.

His thoughts flashed to the Smiling Man's knitted wound, gone without a trace of a scar. He had said he wanted to be a teacher, to pass on his knowledge ...

Ruben took the soap and scrubbed until his skin was pink and tender. His hair was long, but he didn't see any scissors or a knife with which to trim it. The bootlace had fallen out or been taken, so he had to keep pushing it out of his face, but that, too, he washed, very thoroughly, scouring his scalp. There was a nail-trimming tool, but his were chewed to the quick already; he tried the tool on his hair, but gave up immediately.

He wanted to soak forever, but imagined they'd come for him soon. Regretfully, he climbed out of the pool and used two towels to dry off, leaving them in the laundry hamper before donning his robe again, feeling like a different person.

When he opened the door to leave, the man from earlier was gone, but an older woman stood waiting for him. She gave him a critical look and said, "Come on then, let's have you clothed and shod." Her tone brooked no nonsense, and Ruben followed her docilely.

"I swore I'd never treat poorly them as treated me so, but that bile rises and cannot be helped, only borne." Ruben listened, confused, as she continued, "I see critters such as you and it's all clear to me that you'd best treat as you'd be treated, but injustice sits caged in my breast, boy."

She led him out of the mansion wing and downstairs to another. They had yet to pass anyone else, which made Ruben more nervous than he could understand.

They came to a sort of meeting room or study hall, furnished with tables and bookshelves. A few people stood in a small group, talking quietly. The woman beckoned impatiently to the group and a silent old man took Ruben's measurements with practiced speed before leaving without a backward glance. A short, gray-haired woman took tracings of his feet with measurements of his legs and hands, and she also disappeared, almost running, either to catch up with the man, or to escape Ruben's presence.

Last was an elderly couple, both with arms crossed. Their attention burned. Ruben shrank back, but his firm guide said, "The lord said he's to be shorn however he likes. Don't make trouble."

They glanced at each other and the wife left, spearing Ruben with a foul look before disappearing into another attached room. The husband gestured impatiently to one of the chairs and pulled a brush and set of scissors from his back pocket.

"Well?" he asked briskly.

"Um, very short, please."

He set to work and Ruben was relieved that he'd washed his hair so thoroughly as the damp locks fell to the floor in a heap. His head felt pounds lighter, but the sound of scissors slicing so close to his neck and ears, held by a man who seemed to despise him, made for the most uncomfortable cut he'd ever had. Still, he said nothing, and didn't move.

After a few minutes, the cut finished, Ruben was gestured away. The haircutter had tears on his cheeks, though Ruben hadn't heard him crying. Dread filled Ruben's stomach, but he didn't know why.

The stern woman took him back the way they'd come, but even so, the uniformity and neatness of the place made it hard for him to get his bearings, and he pushed his mind to remember, *remember.* This tapestry, that sculpture, here the stairs ...

Back in the room in which he'd woken, the strict lady stopped him. "Stay in there until you're sent for. You'll be taken for food soon, and clothes will be provided, so be dressed when you're gathered. I'm sure his lordship will be along shortly."

The bed was still a mess from his thrashing and the window was still open to the refreshing breeze. He wandered around until he heard the tell-tale thump of fabric outside his door. He looked out hesitantly — no one was waiting — and brought in the stack of clothing.

He found two sets of loose breaches that stopped mid-calf, but had a drawstring he could pull tight, and two wrap-shirts. The sleeves went to mid-forearm and he took a few moments figuring out how to tuck one side across his body and the other over so that the front closed and buttoned. Once he figured it out, he decided it was a very comfortable outfit, if unlike anything he'd worn before. His mind flashed to the tailor's face and Ruben wondered what he'd done to be so hated.

He went to the window and looked out on a far-reaching vineyard. He knew from his Seeking that the land continued for miles and miles before other groupings of life, indicating a small town or similar, were visible. He saw several fields with sheds placed for access to tools and probably water — at least one shed for each field. He could see people working the fields, but even so, there were not nearly enough of them out there to fill this place. The edge of the vineyard was fenced by a tall wooden barrier. He supposed it encompassed the entire, immense property — nothing he couldn't get over with relative ease, but a moment of watching showed guard dogs trotting along the perimeter with handlers walking slowly behind them. Dogs trained like those probably couldn't — or shouldn't — be trifled with.

Hang on, Ruben thought. *I do have magic.* What if they sent him back? He trembled at the thought. *I'd best not be caught, then.*

*   *   *

Someone knocked on Ruben's door and he spun away from the window in time to see it open. The young man who'd let him out of his cell — who'd asked if he looked familiar — examined him for a moment and then said, "Do I need to be worried about you?"

Ruben shook his head. "I'll go back to the cell if I use any magic?" His voice was still hoarse in his ears and he cleared his throat pointlessly.

The man nodded. "And you don't recognize me, you said?"

Ruben shook his head, perplexed.

"Come on."

Ruben followed him out of the room and through the corridors to a huge dining room, nearly half the size of the one in the Order. It was full of benches and tables with food laid out on the occupied ones. Dozens of people sat, but most of the tables were empty. The press of humanity, even this few, was claustrophobic after his isolation. Where had all these people been the last time he'd been escorted through the halls? They couldn't all have been waiting in here, could they?

The noise in the room noticeably dropped when Ruben appeared, and people turned to stare at him. He stayed on the heels of his guide and kept his eyes averted while discomfort caused the hairs on his arms to rise.

His guide ignored everyone and led Ruben to a table of five. As soon as they made to sit, the five stood with their plates and relocated. Ruben's guide didn't comment.

"Eat."

Ruben took a plate from the depleted stack on the table and served himself a small share of the beef and noodles that was the main course. He took a slice of sharp cheese and a small tear of bread and ate in shy silence. The volume rose in the room, as did the number of stares aimed in his direction.

"You should take more food than that." His guide spoke in a dull monotone while he carelessly shredded a bread roll.

"Why do they hate me?" Ruben asked.

"Because you're a costless, ungrateful, uneducated little shit who, by the luck of your birth, ended up with an obscene amount of easy power that you don't even understand, but take for granted that you should get to use however you want." He chewed and watched Ruben's face with a sneer glued on his features.

"Costless?"

"Yes." He didn't elaborate.

Ruben decided that he hated this man.

"Why should I recognize you?" he asked.

The man scoffed and pushed brown bangs out of his eyes. "It really doesn't matter."

"It mattered enough that you asked twice."

"And now it doesn't."

"Well make up your mind sooner next time."

"Watch your tongue," the man snarled, pointing a violent finger at him.

Ruben clenched his jaw, shaking and afraid, but his rising temper betrayed the wisdom of his previous silence. "Why should I? If you could do anything to me, you'd have done it already. If *they* could do anything, they certainly would." He gestured with his head to the rest of the room.

Ruben served himself another helping of the food when his guide failed to answer, hunger coming to him more heavily the more he ate, it seemed. He knew he'd lost weight in his prison, but didn't think he'd been too underfed; the variety was what he craved.

The guide found his tongue and muttered, "You arrogant ass, you have no idea what kind of ruin you've brought here."

"No. I don't. Because I was kidnapped and kept in a dark prison cell for … how long?"

The guide shook his head. "Your kind makes me sick."

"My kind? I'm surrounded by blood mages and I make *you* sick? You kill people. At least my magic only harms me."

"You don't know what you're talking about. Shut your mouth."

"You first."

"You upset the balance. You take it for granted."

"Sure, but killing people and then being sorry about it — that's definitely better."

They stared at each other furiously until Ruben rolled his eyes and shoved another bite of food into his mouth. The confrontation left him shaking on the inside — *what if they send me back?* — but he had more information now than he had before. It seemed that his only rule was avoiding magic. Who was this man, though?

"What do I call you?"

"What?"

"What's your name?"

"Why?"

Ruben put his hands out in supplication. "Seriously?"

After a moment of suspicious consideration, as though checking for possible traps, his guide said, "Oats. Thomas Oats."

"Your accent isn't as harsh as some. Are you from around here?"

Oats narrowed his eyes. "Shut up. Are you finished?"

"No." Ruben picked at the rest of the food on his plate. He regretted his second serving as the richness made him nauseous. People still stared at him, but he put a passive look on his face and stared back until they looked away. Mostly they did; those who didn't, he ignored.

"Whose mansion is this?" he asked around a mouthful.

"Some useless lord," Oats answered, poking at his plate. He looked up quickly, and continued, "But now it's ours."

"And they don't know you're here? How many people do you have, I wonder? This isn't your army — there aren't any young people." Ruben looked at him. "Except you."

It was true. Thomas Oats was the only person that Ruben could see who was less than fifty. A table across the room had a dozen babies and children as old as perhaps fourteen, but everyone else bore obvious signs of age. Oats had turned red, flushed through his ears, but didn't say anything else.

"I'm finished," Ruben decided at last.

Oats led him to a stack of dirty dishes at the other end of the room. Ruben followed with his plate, the hairs on the back of his neck standing up as the rest of the room continued to stare. He did a better job of ignoring it this time.

They left the cafeteria and Oats kept a fast pace that Ruben could barely keep up with. The man really didn't like him.

"Did I do something to you? Is that why I should remember you?" Ruben asked breathlessly, hoping his meal didn't rebel.

Oats shook his head and didn't answer.

"Then I'm going to stop caring, because I have no idea what answer you're looking for."

"Here." Oats stopped in front of the same door as yesterday — the Smiling Man's door.

Ruben ran a hand through his newly short hair, nervousness bunching him up with tension.

Oats noticed his discomfort and said, "At least if he kills you, you won't have to worry about what all the people here would happily do to you."

"I'll remember that," Ruben answered.

He wasn't sure how he meant it, but Oats seemed to take it as a threat.

Oats put his shoulders back and glared. "One day ..."

"You'll tell me what you want? I look forward to it. Go away." Ruben was shocked at his own audacity, but there was no going back now.

Oats's eyes widened and then narrowed. He took a step forward, but the door opened to reveal a man whose reactions neither of them was certain of, judging by the way Oats quickly sobered. He glanced at the Smiling Man, glared at Ruben, turned on his heel and strode quickly away.

The Smiling Man watched him go with a thoughtful expression. "Welcome, Ruben. I hope you're feeling better?"

Ruben didn't reply. The Smiling Man had changed little from when he'd seen him at the Order, attempting to kidnap him the first time and nearly killing Donovan. His blond hair was cut short now, much as Ruben's own, and patches of gray were visible over his ears, despite his apparent youth. His skin was darker, as though he'd been longer in the sun, but his eyes remained the same bright blue, and he moved like a monstrous cat. They wore similar clothes, but he had thick cloth slippers while Ruben remained barefoot.

The Smiling Man stood aside from the doorway and beckoned for Ruben to enter, which he did warily. His eyes swept left and right, alighting on the window that showed him the outside. Last time, freshly out of his cell, and seeing day for the first time in ages, he'd been reduced to tears. This time, he only felt a sense of longing so fierce he thought he would lose his lunch until he ripped his eyes away.

Otherwise, the room was much the same in style as the one in which he'd woken, but on a larger scale. There was also a sitting room and bedroom that Ruben could see through open doorways — but more than that, the space felt homey, cozy. The wood in this room was dark and rich, and the couch and chairs were upholstered in rich plum. Bookshelves on the far wall shared the area with a neatly organized desk and a rug bearing geometrical shapes covered much of the floor.

"I hope you like my room," the Smiling Man said.

"Why?"

The Smiling Man laughed. "Found your tongue, I see. Or are you still afraid of me?"

"Yes."

"No, no, NO!" he barked.

Ruben jumped back.

"You're supposed to make some quip about how nothing could scare you as much as that hole in which I kept you."

The Smiling Man sighed theatrically and threw himself down onto the couch, gesturing impatiently to one of the chairs. Ruben sat gingerly.

"You've been Seeking."

"What?"

"Do you know where we are?"

"No."

"I can tell when people lie. It's a boon of the Empathy magic you'll learn."

"Then you'll know I'm not lying," Ruben's confusion morphed to irritation.

"I can't tell if you *think* you aren't lying. Mentalism and Empathy aren't exact arts." The Smiling Man smiled widely, showing his very white teeth. "I wanted to know how much security to keep. Drawing rosters is quite the chore, even when delegated. Not that they could stop you if you really applied yourself."

Ruben didn't answer.

"What do you remember from our last conversation?"

The image of a spreading puddle of blood and wound knitting itself together flashed into Ruben's mind. "Everything, I think."

"Good. I always worry about head injuries, but it doesn't appear you struck the wall too hard."

He smiled warmly and Ruben's stomach rolled. He didn't want sympathy or warmth from this man.

"Ask your questions, Ruben. You can't get away with any surety, and I wasn't lying when I said I wanted you as my student. I encourage questions, curiosity — it's how I came to be as powerful as I am, after all." His smirk was arrogant, but probably deserved.

"I don't have any questions."

"Lie."

"Where are Whitman and Donovan?"

"Boring!" The Smiling Man rolled suddenly and switched sides of the couch with an irritated groan. "Magic! Ask me about magic!"

"How can you tell when someone's lying?"

"GOOD!"

The yell startled Ruben and he pushed away, rocking his seat, and gripped the arm rests in terror.

The Smiling Man laughed cheerfully and tapped his chin as he thought. "Empathy magic is all colors and textures, and of course no one perceives those the same way. With practice, you can shape them how you want, view them however you wish, but that is more of a preference than need." His voice, his tone seemed to change when he spoke this way — like the youth of his face was a façade. "The mind is a joyous toy, and I find regular play only enhances its abilities. Empathy! Excellent tool. At the first tier, you can sense the emotions of others. If they are angry, they might be colored a hot yellow. If they are sad, perhaps a discordant blue. There's more to it of course, but which emotions might one feel if they are lying?"

Ruben was surprised by the question. "Um, fear?"

"Of being caught? Certainly, fear might be expressed. What else?"

"I — maybe ... maybe jealousy?"

"Jealousy? Hm. Depending on the subject of their lie, that would definitely contribute. How about the thrill of excitement? Or a rush of betrayal?"

"Betrayal isn't an emotion ..."

"Of course it is!" The Smiling Man bounced in his seat for a moment, like an excited little boy. "That, too, has its own cocktail, however. But learn the scent, and you can find it wherever you go."

"So lying is just a combination of other emotions?"

"Precisely. Just as some colors are combinations of others."

"How do you know which is which?"

"Every mage is different. I don't choose to express anger in a discernible color or smell or texture — that is for the Empath to decide and interpret. Your magic allows you to sense the change, and your mind brings it to bear in a specific, interpretable, way. Most of those I've questioned seem to *see* it in some way, but a few claim they hear or even feel it in some way instead. Harder to teach if everyone is sensing it differently, so they get pushed to the wayside, consider themselves broken or damaged, and work to express their magic in the acceptable, predictable way."

Ruben's eyes widened as he listened.

What else?"

Ruben frowned. "What else?"

"Yes, what else? What other questions?"

"Um." Ruben hesitated. How much should he give away? He couldn't lie apparently, and he didn't want to lose any edge about his practice that he could keep.

The Smiling Man sighed and rolled his eyes playfully. "Come now, Ruben. Do you think I won't be testing your knowledge? Tell me the truth. What can you do? Brag a little."

"Some. I've been practicing," Ruben admitted finally.

"Yes?"

"I can make fire and lightning, I can Displace things, and I can speak into others' minds if I know them. I can Seek — both kinds."

"Can you read a person's thoughts?"

"Sometimes. If I know them."

"You can read all of the thoughts?"

Ruben frowned, confused.

"Surface, or deeper?" the Smiling Man explained.

"I — I think just surface thoughts?"

"You know a Mentalist can be lied to, if a skilled enough person is being questioned?"

"They spoke about it in class."

"In passing, I suppose." The Smiling Man rolled his eyes. "Can you Heal?"

Ruben shook his head.

"You Healed Donovan when I tried to kill him."

"That was the only time I could. I've tried but ..."

"Well, I seem to have caught you at a beautiful moment, where you are as yet unaware of your limitations, except those imposed upon you by our lessers, and yet you have very few bad habits for me to break." He finished the word with an especially hard k sound and Ruben winced.

"Show me your fire."

Ruben dried his hands on his legs and gathered his mental image, felt the heat grow in his hands, slowly at first, and then with more vigor. It didn't burn, but he felt the energy growing, like he wanted to run, but all contained in his palms. He used the energy to build the flame until it filled both of his cupped hands, burning a merry orange.

"I see," the Smiling Man stated. "It takes you a while."

Ruben didn't answer. He thought he'd gotten faster.

The Smiling Man held out an upturned fist and, as he opened his palm, fire blossomed. In the barest second, it grew to twice the size of Ruben's and, where the base overflowed from the Smiling Man's hand, it curled upward, bowl-shaped.

"Why do you build an image of what you want to create?" he asked. "Do you picture each step before you walk?"

"No ..."

"No. Because you have learned the basics of the process so thoroughly that you do not need to concentrate. Even a more complicated maneuver, jumping or skipping or running, does not require all of your attention. You must build the memory into your magic as you would any muscle. Again."

Ruben opened his hands to build fire. It was unexpectedly smothered.

"Again," the Smiling Man ordered.

Ruben tried to obey but, once more, his fire was extinguished by an outside force. He growled in irritation.

The Smiling Man laughed as Ruben's shame grew.

"Stop *thinking!*" the Smiling Man bellowed. He stood and loomed over the boy.

Ruben launched backward in the chair, shouting as his legs rolled over his shoulders. He found his feet quickly and let lightning pop and crack around his fists while the chair hovered in front of him like a mobile shield.

The Smiling Man didn't look surprised. He crossed his arms and eyed the chair with interest. "It's not fire, but it's something," he shrugged.

Ruben sobbed as he gasped for breath and let the tears run down his cheeks.

The Smiling Man quirked a smirk. "Ready to continue?"

Ruben released the chair and it landed with a rocking *thunk*. "I just want to go home," he whispered as the lightning faded from his hands.

The Smiling Man smiled tenderly. "I understand. I do. However, recognizing that is not going to happen, what can you do while you are here instead?"

Ruben wiped his eyes and tried to calm down. He wanted to curl into a ball and disappear.

The Smiling Man stepped closer. "I want to teach you, Ruben. You have so much to offer the world, so much power, and I can teach you to control it. You can harness the world to your will. Let me show you how important you are — teach you what you need to know."

Through his tears and ragged breathing, Ruben's mind churned. He wanted to run, but he wanted to learn, too. This man was the enemy, he knew that. But if he couldn't escape, why shouldn't he learn? They'd find him — they had to find him, to come get him, but ... if they didn't, he had to save himself, and he could do that better if he was trained ...

Ruben looked up at the Smiling Man, standing over him with an anticipatory smirk dancing hungrily across his features.

Ruben nodded.

The Smiling Man put his head back and laughed, clapping his hands like an excited child. "Yes! I have so many things to teach you!"

They practiced the basics of magic for hours. The Smiling Man was a surprisingly good teacher, if unpredictable. Ruben finally felt that he was coming to understand how magic worked, not just how to make it work. Mostly, he watched the Smiling Man perform feats of magic while he asked Ruben theoretical questions that he struggled to answer.

When his mind was full to bursting, and his answers were worse from the mental fatigue, he was sent to do chores. He scoured cooking pans and buckets of dishes with sand and soap stones. Thomas Oats, his ever-present shadow, alternated between irritation, anger, and boredom. The chores helped Ruben's disposition as the familiar tasks let his mind wander and take in more of his surroundings.

Most people avoided him, while a few threw him angry looks or occasionally made rude gestures. Some rare few showed sympathy or pity. He was still confused by their reactions, but more by the occasional bits of magic he saw.

The cook started her fire with hand motions and a word, "*Pah!*" He almost missed it when another woman used more gibberish to help steady and lift a load she wasn't quite strong enough for. A man pulled spits from the fire with his bare hands, no burns to be seen. All of them used nonsense words or small gestures. The man spat into the flames, too.

When Oats saw Ruben looking, he interposed himself between Ruben and the workers. As he did, Ruben was struck again by the fact that Thomas Oats, barely in his twenties, was the only young person he'd seen, aside from children. And the Smiling Man.

"What are you doing here?" Ruben asked him while he wiped down the tables in the cafeteria with a damp rag.

Oats, sitting on the opposite bench, looked up at Ruben's words, but didn't answer.

Ruben continued, "It can't be only to guard me. There's got to be a dozen others who can do that, right?"

Oats shook his head. "I don't know what information you're trying to gather, but you won't get it from me."

"Uh-huh. Thomas, I'm fourteen. I'm bored. I'm curious. Why are you the only young person here? I'm not asking where your army is, come on."

He didn't answer.

"Are you a particularly good jailer? Can you not run? Do you lack some skill —"

Without warning, Oats grabbed Ruben's wrist and yanked him into the table edge. Ruben winced — he'd have a sharp bruise on his ribs — but he met Oats's furious eyes.

"You stop questioning me, all right? I don't like you, and I'm not afraid of you. You disgust me. There's nothing wrong with me. *Nothing.*"

Ruben felt a roaring anger build in his stomach. Oats yelped and dropped his wrist as Ruben sent lightning arcing through his body. Still crackling with the energy, Ruben Displaced the table sharply into Oats and tripped him over the bench, causing him to sprawl roughly across the floor. Fire bloomed into life around his prone figure and licked hungrily inward until he rolled disjointedly to his feet.

Oats started to come over the table, but Ruben knocked his feet out from under him with more Displacement. The young man tripped and sprawled into the next table, grimacing with pain as his ribs and back struck the edge.

Ruben let the fire on the floor die away. It left no trace. The lightning cracking across his skin faded. He glared at Oats, seeing red, and then a whole array of other colors, before they started to fade away. He blinked rapidly to realize that this was his Empathy magic finally revealing itself.

The cafeteria doors burst open and four people advanced inside with their hands held in threatening positions, but without a weapon in sight. Ruben raised his own empty hands in defense. A man on the end started muttering, but before he finished more than a syllable, he cut off with a grimace.

The Smiling Man strode in behind them, eyeing the scene. His stance was easy, his hands folded behind his back. "Well done, Ruben. Oats set you off?"

Ruben glanced sideways. Oats had returned to the bench, no longer sprawled against the table, but holding his ribs as though they pained him.

"Yes, I imagine so," the Smiling Man answered his own question. "You four can go."

Dismissed without a glance, the blood mages glared at him and then at Ruben, but did as they were bidden.

The Smiling Man looked at Oats and a small smile curled his lip. "Mind your tongue. You're a minder, not a soldier. Your life would be a small loss the next time my protégé *really* loses his temper." He gestured to the tables with his chin. "Get back to your chores."

He left the room as he had entered, hands folded behind his back, his stride unhurried. Ruben Displaced the tables and benches back into place, horrified by Oats's wince of fear. He hadn't meant to do that; he hadn't meant to do anything. He picked up his rag, dipped it into the soapy bucket beside him, somehow undisturbed in all the madness, and continued to silently wipe down tables while worry and shame gnawed at his insides.

*　　*　　*

Ruben lay curled up on the bed they'd given him with the blankets pulled stiflingly over his head. The day had stretched forever, and he felt like he hadn't experienced any of it — like it had all been a dream. Or a nightmare. He blinked in the near dark. Light from the full moon filtered through his window and against the blanket. His tent grew warmer with every exhaled breath until he was forced to throw off the covering.

Tired and sore from the chores, he felt satisfied nonetheless. Physical activity, more than just exercise, was something he'd missed desperately. He'd been kept away from the outside, of course, and he'd swept, mopped, scrubbed, dusted, and cleaned just about everything they could find for him, but he liked it. He'd liked the work, and the feeling of accomplishment it brought to him.

The fight in the cafeteria, though ... His mind kept going back there and he saw clearly Oats's wince of pain, and the Smiling Man's look of satisfaction.

Donovan's voice came to his mind, a memory, *"I think you've learned that using magic dishonestly, taking advantage of those without, is more disgraceful than I can express to you."*

Ruben took several deep breaths and rested his head on his knees. He felt sick. His rage had been terrifying enough, but then what he'd done with it ... he could easily have killed Thomas Oats. He'd *wanted* to.

Never again. He had to keep control, keep his mind sharp. He'd lost focus, but now he would find it again. His only goal had to be escape.

*　　*　　*

"Do you think someone should be forgiven for murder?"

Ruben slowly surfaced from sleep, the words echoing about in his mind until his eyes allowed him to see blearily through the darkness.

"Wha...?" he grunted, passing a hand lethargically across his face. A shape was at the foot of his bed — a person. His heart jumped in his chest and sleep dissolved like mist.

"What are you doing here?" he demanded as fear cracked his voice. He jerked upright and pushed himself away.

The Smiling Man shrugged a shoulder unenthusiastically and shifted to face him, crossing his legs. "Murder. What do you think?"

"I think it's ... wrong ...?"

A thoughtful nod.

Ruben wracked his brains. *What was the question?*

"I want to know if a person should be forgiven. For murder," the Smiling Man supplied.

"Oh ... ah. Maybe?"

"Care to elaborate on that haphazard conclusion?"

"Did something ... happen?" Ruben asked. The idea of murder populated his mind with terror and he gripped the blanket tightly. "Is-is something going to happen?"

"Not you, not yet." The man waved dismissively. "What if it's not your hand that strikes the murderous blow?"

"That's not murder, is it?" Ruben answered, pushing his own now-sweaty hands across the blanket. *What did he mean 'not yet'?*

"Is it not? What if you are the reason it occurred? Are not generals responsible for the actions of their soldiers?"

Ruben paused. "If they're giving the orders, sure. But if the soldiers are, say, visiting home and something happens, then no ... right? They're not a soldier then — they're just ... a person. Right? Or, they're a soldier, but not ... working ...?"

The Smiling Man looked amused. "An interesting point. One I've considered, but something in it simply doesn't strike true." He stood and wandered about the room, pacing carelessly. He brushed a hand across the top of the desk chair, down the wall, across the shelf of books. He caressed the windowsill and then gripped it tightly. "If I were to kill someone you loved, and you kill me in return, that's murder. But often it is believed that one is justified, while the other is not."

"I think murderers should all be punished," Ruben agreed. "And if the punishment fits the crime, that's better."

"You think that if I steal bread because I'm starving, I should have bread stolen from me?"

"Maybe, um, maybe not exactly. But you could work a bit to pay for it, or something like that? That's why there's laws."

"So if the murder is an accident, you should still pay for the crime? You trip, perhaps while cutting vegetables, and stab your assistant in the heart. You should be killed for that."

Ruben shook his head. With the immediate threat gone, his brain was trying to convince him to fall back asleep. "No, because that's an accident."

"But the assistant is still dead."

"But it was an accident."

"So you should pay for his life in some other way? What's the cost of a man's life?"

"I — I don't ..."

The Smiling Man scoffed. "The life mages will presume to tell you. They claim to know what life is worth, certainly." He paced again, arms crossed. Fire bloomed gently across his form. "Have you done this?" he asked with a sly smile, like a child at mischief.

"Set myself alight? No." Ruben leaned further away from him.

The light across the Smiling Man's shoulders and chest, flickering and sparking, brought a demonic glint to his features.

"It's a good way to warm yourself. And worry others. Fire behaves like any other magic: you build it in your hands and it doesn't burn you. Tell it to respect your clothes and it does the same."

Curious now, Ruben watched as the Smiling Man manipulated the fire up and down his arms, torso, legs, around his shoulders and face — an elated expression on his face all the while. The flames danced like ocean waves, rolling with the currents of his direction. It was beautiful.

"Go on," the Smiling Man encouraged.

Ruben brought fire to his palms, urging it up his arms. It was slow to move, but he soon figured out the knack. He was nowhere near as graceful, but he made it flow across his shoulders from palm to palm.

"Warm, but never hot. Like bathwater when you're late to wash," the Smiling Man laughed.

Lightning crackled in his mouth to outline his teeth in blue-white. It sparked across his fingertips and shot between them, filling his hands with the snapping, popping energy.

Ruben's fire died away as he watched this newest display. If fire rolled, lightning jumped. No acrobat had ever been so skilled as this: it filled the room, flashing from each corner of the ceiling to the edges of the desk, the corner of a shelf, the floor, ceiling, bedframe; nothing was safe. The room was alight with popping magic.

Ruben let out a laugh of wonder.

The Smiling Man echoed it. "Beautiful," the Smiling Man crowed.

Ruben realized his expression was a mirror of the Smiling Man's own and his face fell.

"Ah," the man said as he dismissed the lightning. "The fun's gone after all."

"Did you murder someone?" Ruben asked suddenly, the recent line of questioning still on his mind. "I mean, recently."

The Smiling Man smirked. "No."

"Then why were you asking?"

"Memories are a plague," he replied cryptically. "One cannot escape them all, and eventually you must succumb to their rot, whence is born the most vile of emotions: doubt. Doubt breeds questions, and they do enjoy company." He smiled with childish brightness. "Go back to sleep. I'll teach you more tomorrow."

The Smiling Man left on silent feet, magic closing the door behind him. Ruben slid down under the blanket and tried to fall back into whatever he'd been dreaming about, but every time he closed his eyes, he saw the spark of lightning and the roll of fire.

* * *

"No, no, *feel* it! Stop speaking to magic as though it were a stranger — it is a part of you! You're still thinking!"

Ruben took a breath and tried to ignore the beration, but the fire flickered and died anyway. He forced his fists to unclench. "Shouting at me won't help."

"No? It did last time," the Smiling Man taunted. "Again. Lightning and fire are easy — they want to play about. Stop *telling* it what to do and start *letting* it do what it wants."

"What if it wants to burn this damn place down?" Ruben grumbled.

The Smiling Man clapped his hands and laughed. "I certainly wouldn't stop you. I've considered it myself a time or two."

Ruben put his hands together and let out a slow breath as he drew them apart. Lightning crackled to life, growing in intensity as his hands separated. He started pushing his palms back together and the lightning shot back and forth, faster and faster until Ruben's palms touched and the lightning disappeared with a *snap*.

The Smiling Man was ginning again. "Much more fun than lighting candles, aye?"

Ruben managed to smile back, flush with success.

"What do you want to do when you're free of this place?" Once again, the Smiling Man's questions flitted from topic to topic without apparent aim, like summer bugs flying drunkenly through the air.

"What do you mean?"

The Smiling Man groaned, throwing himself dramatically backward over the arm of a couch. "I *mean*, what do you want to *do* when you're free of this place? It's not a trick question, Ruben."

He shrugged one shoulder and looked away. "I hadn't thought much about it."

"No? Never had dreams and desires and goals?" the Smiling Man asked scornfully.

Ruben's lip curled. "I did, but ... everything changed."

"Not had time to catch up, then?"

"Something like that."

"Well what *did* you want to do?"

"I wanted horses," he answered easily.

"To ride?"

"Most of all. But to trade, and breed, and care for. I like horses."

The Smiling Man righted himself on the couch. "If you don't know what you want, people will tell you what they think you *should* want. And they are always wrong."

Ruben blinked at him, unsure what to think.

The Smiling Man raised his arms dramatically. "One day very soon, the worlds of magic will collide. As often happens, it will be violent, and after a short period of recovery and reflection, the victors will get to decide what to do with the survivors." He gave Ruben a significant look.

"You think the Hunters will win the war?" Ruben asked.

The Smiling Man bobbed his head. "Truly, this upcoming encounter is surprisingly uncertain. If the born mages win, your rejoining their side will be seen as a victory of its own. If the life mages win, I guarantee that your continued survival will come into quick consideration. If they do not see you as a true ally — a believer of their cause — then why would they tolerate your presence in their world?"

"You ... you want me to join both sides?"

"Why not?"

"Because ... it's wrong ...?" Ruben struggled.

The Smiling Man laughed merrily, clapping his hands again. "Delightful! No, my young protégé, you must do away with such concepts. Wrong is what you make it to be. You still don't believe me?"

Ruben shrugged noncommittally. He didn't want this confrontation.

The Smiling Man steepled his fingers and gazed over them. He gestured for Ruben to sit, so the boy sat across from him, perched on the edge of his seat, hands clasped tightly.

"What is a rule that cannot be broken?"

Ruben licked his lips, "Um ..."

The Smiling Man raised a delicate eyebrow. "Um?" He cocked his head. "Are you still afraid of me?"

Ruben nodded slowly.

"All right. I promise not to kill you today. Better? No? Oh, well, participate anyway."

"Um ..."

"Good grief, boy, show some confidence." He flashed a cheeky grin. "Cannibalism!"

Ruben felt his face twist with disgust.

"Exactly! Our society has eschewed cannibalism in favor of the choices that make us stronger as a people. What else?"

"Murder comes to mind," Ruben said, thinking about the strange conversation last night.

The Smiling Man grinned. "Yes, murder, good. As you said last night, you cannot blame someone for doing something they had no intention of doing, yes? Despite the result? If the laws do not apply to all persons equally, to all actions equally, then how do you have civility? How do you build a community large enough to span each horizon?"

Ruben rubbed his cheek. "You have to ... make better laws. You have to make them for all situations, right? If you have a law for accidental murder, then you aren't treating anyone differently — you're treating them the way you should, for what they did."

"And if you leave your land and travel to another? The laws they've agreed upon have changed, no? The customs are different. Here, I may bow to a man of higher station, but in that land, it's seen as an insult, and they cut off my feet. Where is the consistency?"

"You think everyone should live under the same rule?"

"Laws ... they are beautiful and complicated. And magic is above them."

Ruben frowned at him.

"They say a law of the earth is gravity. What flies upward must fall downward." The Smiling Man demonstrated with his hands. "This is undeniable, and much the same is magic. How are those with magic then held to the same laws as those without?"

"You have to have self-control!" Ruben argued. "Otherwise, what's to stop me ... burning down this house?"

"Yes!" the Smiling Man barked excitedly. "Do you know what it is?"

Ruben shook his head.

"MORE MAGIC!" He fell back laughing. When Ruben didn't join in, he asked, "You're not amused. You disagree?"

"Do you think a magus should be king?"

"Shouldn't they?"

"I don't want to be a king."

"Why not? I've heard it's fun. But more than that, it isn't always about you, Ruben. Why shouldn't a magus rule? What country would dare send bandits and invaders to harass the people, knowing the ruler could snap his fingers and kill them all?" He demonstrated the snap with vigor. "What plague could harm your people, what drought could kill your crops, if you had only to wave a hand to cure all?"

Ruben licked his lips. "You can do that?"

"Oh yes. Yes I can."

"What if the magus is a bad sort, then?"

"Like me?" the Smiling Man grinned.

"How are they stopped, then? What if they kill everyone and can't be stopped?"

"Ah, so you want the ruler beholden to the people."

"It's right."

"It's lawful. And so we come round the circle."

"Magic or no, you have to be beholden. Mages more, because we're more dangerous."

"Why not then kill all the mages, like they do in Anago? Or enslave them to the state, as in Manazia? The problem goes away, certainly."

"Because you can't kill people!" Ruben groaned and threw himself back in the seat.

The Smiling Man grinned at his irritation. "I never agreed to obey these laws. I was born to this society; where is my choice?"

"But you live here," Rubeny pointed out. "So you have to. It's ... it's a promise, an oath, so everyone can live together."

"Does the ocean swear to gently carry sailors across the sea to get your spices and trinkets? No. It behaves as an ocean, sworn to no man, doing as it wishes. Does the wind swear to blow only cool breezes in the heat of summer? No. It brings storms and throws dirt in your eyes."

"I'm not an ocean. And neither are you."

The Smiling Man laughed. "I'm much more an ocean than a man. I may swear my allegiance to a person — or a people, or their cause — but I can never be held. Our objectives may align for a time, but when they no longer do ..." he dusted his hands gently, blowing across them.

Ruben shook his head. "You can't live that way forever. You have to have friends, to — to defend you and stand up for you, help you stand up for what's right. For what's lawful!"

The Smiling Man sneered serenely. "It's darling to see an idealist. I used to be like that." His face darkened suddenly. "Until I *grew up.*"

Ruben blushed, but refused to back down. "When are you going to betray these people?"

"Looking for information to share with your Order?"

Ruben shook his head, disgusted again. "You shouldn't abandon someone just because you feel like it."

The Smiling Man leaned back, stretching his arms across the couch. "These people are grateful that I haven't killed them all. Who says rewards only come at the end?"

"They hate you as much as they hate me, don't they? They know you'll turn on them. Do you think they aren't ready for that? I would be."

"I would be more afraid of you than a hundred of them. Once you're trained, of course."

"That's good to know."

The Smiling Man threw back his head and bellowed a laugh. "So fierce, so dangerous."

Ruben didn't respond to the bait.

"Yes, yes, all right. A certain amount of benefit is gained from having me as a benefactor of their cause. I provide a measure of security for their elders so that the youth may gallivant about various businesses for the plots and plans they enact, and I perform various duties of my own. What do I gain in return?"

Ruben wracked his brain before realizing the simplest answer, "Information."

"Exactly."

"You want to know what everyone knows so that you can betray them when you get the most of it."

"Spoken like the son of a merchant town."

"Am I wrong?"

"We're dealing in hypotheticals. I've never confirmed that I plan to betray anyone."

"People still sail on the ocean, and harness the wind."

"Eh?"

Ruben licked his lips. "I spoke to a sailor back home who told me about those storms, and those ocean waves. He said they hid below sometimes, when it was very bad, but otherwise they'd grab the wind in their sails and make it push them to other countries for those spices, and oranges, and glass, and all sorts of things. So, I guess they still work together, even if one of them doesn't like it."

"And ...?"

"And, maybe," Ruben struggled to find the words, "maybe you don't have to swear allegiance or keep your word, but that doesn't mean someone can't use you just the same as you use them."

The Smiling Man studied Ruben for a moment. "True enough, little magus. How's your skill at arms?"

The change of topic was jarring. "What? Um ..."

"Um," the Smiling Man mocked.

Ruben grit his teeth. "I haven't had any training."

"None at all?" he asked incredulously.

"I scrapped a bit with other children ..."

"Blazing sun, how do they manage anything with this measure of incompetence?" The Smiling Man rubbed his eyebrow. "I'll add that to your curriculum."

"Fighting? With weapons?"

"Eventually. Hands and feet first."

Despite himself, Ruben was interested. "When?"

"Not now. Go away."

4

"WELL?"

"He's quick to learn. Not the cleverest I've taught, but that might be what keeps him alive."

"Will he fight for us?"

"Not yet."

"How long?"

"It all depends. *I'm balancing a delicate edge: I push too quickly and he balks, breaks; I take too long and he learns the truth too soon and disappears. I must have time to bring him along."*

"People are nearly in position; pieces are in motion. You can't linger too long."

"If he has to go back into a pit, he has to remain long enough to ingrain the deep fear, the lasting terror that drives his decisions. Isolation has a way of turning to clay that which thought it was iron."

"I know."

"Hardly."

"And when do you want me to come into it?"

"When he finds strength enough to challenge, but is still afraid enough to seek comfort. Soon. He has conflict with himself: a love and hate of magic."

"I need him to learn living magic."

"Not yet. Don't get hasty; let his curiosity bloom. I've done this before."

"Unsuccessfully."

"If you trust nothing else of me, trust that I know the limits of human endurance. I'll bring him to you. This one, I can turn. And then maybe *you'll find your freedom in his cage."*

* * *

"Hullo."

It took a moment for Ruben to realize that the voice was directed at him — that hadn't happened since his first visit to the dining hall. He looked up from his plate to see a man in his early sixties, waiting patiently for permission to sit.

Ruben nodded and gestured politely, his movements twitchy with surprise.

The man settled himself and his plate and said, "Magic training, eh?"

"Um, yes?"

"It always takes it out of you: mental, if not physical."

"I guess so."

"Naught as you're familiar to, eh?"

"I guess not." Ruben considered for a moment. "You're the one I met the first day. Or when I woke up — the one who asked about my nightmares."

"Aye. Kind of you to remember, being it was *so* long ago." He grinned to take the sting from his words. "I'll join you most days as I'm able. People need company to keep they'selves sane. How's the ham?"

"Um, it's good. And — thank you." Ruben swallowed a lump of emotion.

"Name of Travis. You?"

"Ruben."

They shook hands. Ruben felt the lump grow in his throat at the contact, and took a bite of his lunch to swallow the sudden emotion into his belly.

"Got any plans, then?"

"For what?"

"For the day."

Ruben blinked rapidly at him. "I'm a prisoner. I don't get to make my own day's plans. I don't honestly even know why no one here likes me, but I assume it's because I do magic without blood, and that's hated for some reason."

"Interesting conclusion you've come to." Travis took a bite of his ham and chewed thoughtfully. "Kidnapped from the Order's belly?"

"Yeah."

"Notable."

"I suppose."

"The lord grabbed you, huh?"

"His people, I think. I don't remember. I was unconscious, but I remember there were lots of them."

"Ah. Might've been my daughter — she's with the army. An officer, and on the march to promotion."

"Um, good?"

Travis laughed with real mirth. "You know naught by my people *or* life magic, do you?"

"Is that the same as blood magic?"

"Only by relation."

"Then, no, not really. I know it's addictive and I suppose anyone can be taught to do it? And apparently you have to kill people to make it work," Ruben said darkly.

Travis clicked his tongue with disapproval. "Hold a temper, sir."

"Sorry."

"Not anyone can mess it, son. Blood magic and Hunters and all those cruelties is what those who don't understand our ways label life magic to be. It comes on as frightening, but the same is true of your people to us."

"So what is it really, then?"

"Are you done?" Thomas Oaks arrived at Ruben's elbow. He glared at Travis, who stared back, unintimidated and unimpressed.

"No, I'm not," Ruben told him sharply.

"Too bad. You've got chores assignments."

Ruben bit the inside of his cheek and rose to his feet. Oats had been cowed for a while after their fight, but appeared to have regained his bad attitude.

"I'll mind the plate, son," Travis said, "and we'll speak again."

Oats led Ruben downstairs, toward the room where he'd been measured for clothes and given his haircut. He hadn't returned since then and the area was unfamiliar.

"What am I doing today?"

"Laundry."

The end of the hall led to another door and more stairs down. Ruben shuddered in the dim light as the creeping darkness set his hairs to attention. Through another room, he felt a sudden rise in humidity. Oats let them into a brightly-lit space filled with steam and copper pipes. Water was everywhere, warm under his bare feet, cold dripping down the walls and from the ceiling. Men and women, all of them old, but hardy, conversed in loud voices as they agitated cloth and scrubbed in acrid soaps and bleach.

A man marched to bar their way and looked Ruben up and down. "What is it?" he demanded with a sneer.

"He's to do chores." Oats always seemed intimidated by these people — nearly as much as Ruben was.

"Not here."

"The lord says."

"He's not my *lord*."

Oats shifted from foot to foot, unsure of what to do. Ruben leaned to see past the man blocking the way. A dozen people were watching him through the steam, sleeves rolled up high, sweat on their faces. The cheerful mood had shifted abruptly.

"What's special about laundry?" he asked curiously. "I mean, why's it different from dishes, or sweeping?"

The man looked down at him distastefully. "We don't want you here."

"I don't want to be here either, but it's just chores, right?"

The man crossed his arms petulantly, without answer.

"Wilting trees and *flattened hills.*" Ruben half-turned around to see that Travis, from the dining room, had followed them and was now lounging in the doorway.

Oats was glaring at both him and the laundry-man now.

"Boy's got a merit in the question — you ever done laundry afore?" Travis asked him.

"I've done nearly everything, I think. Indentured since I was little," Ruben explained.

Travis chuckled and came forward to clap a hand on his shoulder. "Go on, everyone back to your tubs. Roll your sleeves up, boy. Parker, calm the storms — be out the way."

"I said we don't want him here," Parker sneered.

"Naught wants you here, yet still you stand," Travis retorted.

Parker snapped his fingers and snarled a gibberish sentence of consonants.

Travis slapped him straight across the face, startling the man from his fury. "Stop acting a fool."

Ruben, stunned by the actions around him, felt the pressure of two hands on his shoulders. They navigated him around the shocked and angry Parker and past the first several tubs surrounded by people, all giving him one nasty look or another. Travis deposited him at a tub near the back. The people around it quickly vacated to others, but Travis ignored them and joined Ruben at the work.

Travis didn't speak as he and Ruben soaped and scrubbed the clothes in the near-boiling water. As before, the chores were a nearly-pleasant familiarity in so hostile a place. Ruben set to the work with a will, unconcerned by the effort involved even while sweat dripped down his face and his arms and back ached.

He didn't know how long they worked, but, when Travis called a halt, the last of the clothes stewed and cleaned, the rest of the workers were gone. They drained and wiped down the tub, wringing and hanging the last sopping cloths to dry in the outer room where a clever system of piping let in fresh air and kept the humidity at bay. Then, with a small wave, Travis left.

Ruben looked around, saw no escort, and so made his slow way upstairs. He wondered where Oats was, but none of the few elders that he passed in the halls stopped him or said anything at all. He found his room and found another set of clothes waiting on his bed.

Relieved, he changed and dropped the wet set in the bathing room hamper. It wasn't yet time for dinner, not that he was especially hungry anyway. As he started back toward his room to wait, a realization stopped him.

He started walking again, let his feet lead the way, mind blank except for his jangling nerves providing horrible scenarios periodically.

With nowhere else to be, maybe he was allowed outside. Perhaps he could practice his magic, seeing as he was getting training from the Smiling Man himself ...

Ruben descended a set of stairs with stiff knees, and marveled again at the size of the mansion. Who did it belong to? Were they still alive? If they were, and they were clearly rich, they'd be close to the royal family ... Ruben was deeply uncomfortable to realize someone supporting the blood mages might be so close to the leaders of his country.

Unless the king *did* know. He stopped that thought in its tracks; the idea too abhorrent. His mind was spinning at the possibility, but came to sudden attention when he heard a door open behind him — Thomas Oats stepped into the hall and looked his way. It took Oats a moment to realize who he was seeing, and then his face turned a dark red.

"Where are you going?" he demanded.

Seeing no reason to lie, Ruben answered, "Outside."

"You're not allowed."

"Are you sure?"

Oats looked away, the question clearly catching him off-guard. Ruben was surprised to realize that Oats's eyes were wet, his nose red.

"Were you crying?" he asked.

Oats's face snapped back to him and his hands curled into fists. Ruben saw a burst of color materialize in his vision to surround the now clearly furious man. Oats advanced and Ruben retreated in near-equal measure.

"What does it matter to you?" Oats snarled.

"It — it doesn't. I was just asking."

"Why do you care?"

Ruben took another step back. "I'm sorry. I didn't mean anything by it."

"I'm *sure*. You couldn't understand. You were born with magic — more than anyone could ever want or need. What makes you better than me?"

"Nothing."

Oats advanced again. "Nothing," he agreed. "Nothing, but here you stand. You and your costless magic — you ruin everything! I should kill you where you stand."

Ruben bumped painfully into a wall and Oats continued forward. Trapped and afraid, Ruben put his hands up and felt the familiar warmth of fire build in his palms.

Oats stopped and sneered despite the obvious fear in his eyes, and the yellow staining his aura. "You'd never stand up to me without that."

"Probably not," Ruben agreed as anger boiled once more in his stomach. His face felt warm. "But I thought anyone could learn blood magic, so use that. No? What's wrong with you, then? Face me if you want to try."

The red in Oats's face turned purple and spittle flew from his lips as he snarled, "You don't know anything about me!"

"You don't know anything about me, either!" Ruben put his fear and fury into the flames, let them build as they wanted.

The angry young man looked terrified, but stood his ground. Lightning cracked through the air over Oat's head. He flinched and staggered backward.

Ruben advanced on him. "I haven't done anything to you! Just leave me alone!"

Oats roared with promised violence, but couldn't come forward. A wall of snapping flames and twisting lightning had built across the floor and up the walls, rolling hungrily toward him.

Ruben snarled, a small part of him reveling in the man's fear, even as the rest of him hated it and hated himself. The walls shook and groaned with strain. Loud cracks ran across short sections of the floor and Oats tripped.

Ruben studied the young man's Empathic aura — a mix of colors swirling around him like steam. He reached out and grasped at the yellow, so thick and viscous, and drew it toward him. He saw it expand and grow. Oats's eyes widened in horror. Ruben blew low on the cloud, like feeding a campfire. The color grew thicker, denser, vivid.

Oats screamed as the yellow fear won out over his indigo anger. He scrambled backward and tried to gain his feet as the fire and lightning closed toward him. The walls and floor tilted and shifted and made balance a chore. Except where Ruben stood, in an island of raging calm.

As Oats staggered and sprinted and finally disappeared down the hall, Ruben released the magic to fade away. The energy coursing through him drained at the same time, but he still wanted to run after his tormentor and pound his face into a bloody mess with his bare fists. He wanted outside, to sprint and keep sprinting until he couldn't breathe and collapsed in the dirt. He wanted to scream and pound the ground with his fists and feet until they refused to obey him.

Instead, he sank to the floor, the once endless well of emotion replaced by numbness. He welcomed it even as it scared him.

It didn't take long for a dozen elders to appear in the hall, all of them with expressions of worry or anger. They kept at a distance from him, too afraid to get close.

He managed to look up at them and, in their faces, saw the people of his own town: people who had raised him, punished him for foolishness, encouraged his efforts, trained him in his trade, even bullied him. Just people.

Tears finally fell and he buried his face in his hands as sobs wracked his small frame. His knees drew up to his chest and he wrapped his arms around them, weeping shamefully. He wanted to go home. He wanted to just disappear. He wanted his mother — no, he wanted Donovan.

Arms closed around him and he jerked away, afraid they were taking him back to the hated cell, or worse. It took him a moment to recognize the embrace — how long had it been since someone had held him? When he stopped the instinctive struggle to get away, the arms gathered him tighter and held him close. His tears flowed harder and his stomach heaved to bring them up from the unplumbed depths.

Another set of hands rubbed his back tenderly, encouragingly, and someone murmured motherly things in his ear. Ever so slowly, he began to calm. The tears subsided, leaving him with hiccups. He groaned and a woman chuckled into his hair. Her weathered hands helped him to his feet. Someone else pressed a handkerchief into his hands. He scrubbed at his face and held his breath until the hiccups stopped.

"You all right now, love?"

He started to nod and then shrugged helplessly. When he finally managed to look up, he saw that the crowd had gone, leaving him with only a couple of older women, one with her arm still around his shoulders.

She gave him another squeeze. "Thomas acting a prat?"

Ruben winced.

"Sore, that one. Not his fault, not your fault. You're both young and he's anger itself — you were bound not to get along."

"I didn't mean to," Ruben whispered.

"All right, darling. We'll have words. Keep your chin up."

"Oh," the other woman said, distracted.

Ruben looked toward the doorway and saw the Smiling Man lounging against the wall, as though enjoying a play. His evident amusement cheapened the moment and Ruben felt his face flush as embarrassment took root once more. The women took a step away from him.

The Smiling Man laughed once and strolled away, humming.

A shudder shook Ruben's frame. "I'm sorry if you're in trouble," he whispered.

"He's not our leader," the first woman said angrily, though she kept her voice low. "We tolerate his presence because our lady says he's necessary. Were he not ... k-k-k-k-k!" She shook her fists at her sides.

"Shush," the second lady snapped. "None of that. You should go back to your room," she told Ruben. "I'll send someone with a plate for you. I imagine some word will skip about, avoiding every puddle of truth, and it might best be if you weren't standing the brunt of it until reason and calm reigns anew."

Ruben nodded tiredly. They walked together to his room, an awkward silence lingering until they reached his door.

"Laren," the first woman said, gesturing at herself. Her hair still had a tinge of brown amongst the gray.

The second woman, shorter, named herself, "Beth."

"Thanks. I'm Ruben." He blushed, "I guess you already knew that."

Laren smiled. "Get some rest, son."

He went to the window and looked out over the fields, aching to walk through the tall and distant grass, swaying in a light breeze.

The fight played through his head. He'd sworn he wouldn't overreact like that again, but barely a day had gone by before he'd broken that promise. He couldn't stop using magic, could he? How would he learn? How would he get free? What would the Smiling Man do if he refused? What would Ruben do next?

Ruben laid his head against the cool sill. He'd shaken the walls, the floor, for the first time. There'd been a vague and confusing connection to the stone in the hall — a sort of ancient heaviness through his bones — but now there was nothing. The idea of digging his fingers through the stone wall and climbing to the ground flitted through his mind, but it was pushed aside by the image of the Smiling Man's knitting wound.

Ruben wanted to learn to do that. He wanted to learn proper control and abilities that could change the course of the war — if only he could master it quickly enough.

Then he saw the cloud of emotion again — saw it billow and heard Oats scream. He'd never heard a sound like that before. And he'd liked the feeling that had come with it — never in his life had he felt so powerful. But remembering it now made him sick. Was there truly no cost to his magic?

* * *

"What happened?"

"Exactly what was needed. Bubble the pot, let him shy away from what bit him, then kindness extended from those who previously hated him ... I couldn't have planned it better. He doesn't know it, but he's bringing them to his side, creating bonds of allegiance."

"And now?"

"Now comes rebellion. Now he decides to stand strong, find his iron. He's too scared to lash out, but that same fear will push him to look for control over his surroundings — try to fit in, find peace in routine. When he remembers that we aren't his friends, but he can no longer see us as his enemies, we'll renew his hope and his anger will grow. That is when we give him something to be truly angry about, and he will want to fight. Time, Beast, and I'll bend him to our side."

"Mind you don't break him."

"Certainly not. Anger is simple to create, simple to quench. I'll temper before you sharpen."

"Don't expect more from him than he has — he's only a boy, still."

"*Don't* get in my way. You'll ruin what I'm creating."

"I only plead caution. It is too late to change the course of things now. We have mere weeks, after years of planning, and all of it balanced on this knife's edge you are creating."

"Fear suits no one."

"The coward lives longer than the hero; the scholar longer than the soldier."

"You'd turn the world to peaceful little grazers, no motivation to drive them."

"And you'd see it all burn before its time, just because you like the screams in the flame."

* * *

Ruben felt calmer. As though his mind had been working through all of the events of the last few days and come to some subtle conclusion. As though all of the Smiling Man's conversations with him made more sense now than they had.

He ignored his new guard, a tall and wrinkled man he didn't recognize, while he bathed and dressed, and went to breakfast. He joined the end of a nearly empty table, and no one moved away from him this time, though several gave him sidelong looks.

After a few minutes, Travis sat across from him with the same groan Ruben had heard thousand times from Dnovan. The thought made him smile, but he quickly stifled it. Travis heaped his plate and dug into it greedily. Ruben felt lighter with the man's presence; they might not be friends, but Travis didn't seem like his enemy.

A few bites into the meal, the older man said, "The lord wants you in the training room."

"Training room?"

"For teaching little lordlings the art of combat."

"Oh."

"Probably top rank not to fill your belly."

"Right." The prospect of learning to fight had been exciting, but now he was worried. "Is Oats all right?" Ruben asked.

Someone at the end of the table looked at him.

Travis swallowed thickly and said, "Aye, he's passable. Scared, bit sore, but you've not hurt him."

Ruben nodded, relieved. "When do I have to go to the training room?"

"Snappish."

"Where is it?"

Travis pointed at his plate and shoveled more food into his mouth, chewing with furious speed. It was an impressive skill, the way he didn't choke despite the size of his mouthfuls. It reminded Ruben of Whitman's ability to clear a plate. In moments, Travis was standing to put his empty dish away and Ruben hurried to do the same, following in his wake.

Travis left him, with a bow and a wink, in front of a set of double doors, returning the way they'd come. Ruben watched until he turned a corner and disappeared and only then did he open one of the doors and take a look inside.

The room was large — about a third the size of the dining hall. The high ceiling, with large glass windows at the tops of the walls, allowed in plenty of light. Thickly cushioned mats lay secured to the floor, soft to walk across, but not so thick as to impede his forward motion. Two of the walls were similarly cushioned, but the two with doors were not — those held racks of practice weapons and cabinets of training gear.

The Smiling Man watched Ruben's examination with a bored and amused expression. With no rebuke, Ruben wandered. He ran a gentle finger over the shields, swords, axes, bows, spears, daggers — all with dull or padded edges. He eyed a set of boiled leather armor — his time learning to make saddles and other gear for horses showed him its fine quality. His bare feet liked the cushioned floor, and he dug in his toes as he walked. Finally, he went to the center of the room to face his trainer.

The Smiling Man grinned down at him in anticipation. "In this room, I give you permission to strike me, to try to inflict whatever damage you can. Magical prowess is one thing; physical another.

Having the ability to rip someone apart without touching them lends one a certain reputation, and choosing not to do so builds upon it. Why kill you with my hands when I can use my magic? But why waste my magic when I can kill you with my hands?"

Ruben kept his face blank, but the Smiling Man asked, "You have something to add?"

"We can't exactly waste our magic when we can't run out of it."

The Smiling Man sneered. "So they teach, but we know the lie of it. Patience, and I'll teach you the truth. You're angry because I withhold so much? I know you plan to run away — I see it plainly every time you count another new face or memorize another pathway through the halls."

Terror seized Ruben's stomach in an iron grip.

The Smiling Man leaned toward him, "Know this: if I wanted to stop you, it would be simplicity itself. I could have you blinded and led through the halls by rope. Or just break all of your toes. I could layer the doors with so much Empathy that you would be paralyzed at the very idea of leaving. I could root around in your little mind and pull loose the threads of those thoughts so that you could never follow them to completion, always searching for the conclusion to your ideas ..."

Ruben knew his face betrayed nausea at the threats as the horror of it all sank in.

"But! Instead, you agreed to learn from me, widen your horizons, hone your skills. Imagine taking all of my knowledge and destroying me with it. Use what I teach you against me." A hungry look filled his eyes.

Ruben didn't like that look. "You'll never teach me everything you know." He was surprised at the bitterness in his voice.

The Smiling Man bobbed his head. "You don't understand what I've been telling you. Why would I ever want to stop you from mastering your gifts? You —" he laughed and turned away to pace. "You have *no idea* what it is to crave a *challenge*. I have nothing to fear in this or any lifetime. There is no purpose to life without barriers. Immortality is tedious without stimulation. A student who could match and surpass me in wit and power is all I want. Why bother conditioning you to fail, when I could groom you to greatness? *Listen* to me, Ruben. Don't be a child."

Ruben didn't answer right away. He could sense the Smiling Man's amusement morphing into a more dangerous emotion. Thomas Oats's scream echoed in Ruben's mind again.

He took a deep breath. "I don't want anything from you. I don't want to learn from you. I don't want to be *molded* by you, made into your likeness. You are a plague, an unending rain, a fool who wants what he can't have because someone told you *no*. You are a child more than I ever am."

The Smiling Man was no longer smiling. His eyes had narrowed. "Perhaps I came for you too late," he hissed. "An open mind can be so easily bricked in the halls of those who could crush it closed, blind it to any ideas but their own."

Ruben threw his arms in the air. "I could build bridges!" he seemed to take the Smiling Man by momentary surprise. "I could move rubble; I could heal the sick and dying. I could save homes from fire or bring peace to warring nations! One in generations — in *centuries* — and you've decided that *your* want for a peer is greater than the thousands of other uses I could have to *all* the people of our world! There is no word for the selfishness that — that —" he broke off as words failed him.

Ruben pulled his hands down his cheeks. "Just kill me. You'll put me back in that pit, I know, but I won't learn from you, I won't bow to you. My allegiance is to those who told me I could be great and showed me what greatness was. What —" he shook his head. "No one's heard of you. You live in the shadows, afraid to even lift a finger to help anyone. But why? What use are your great powers if you only use them for yourself?"

The Smiling Man clapped slowly, tainting Ruben's words with sarcasm. "Very eloquent. How much of that did you rehearse, I wonder?"

Ruben gritted his teeth and held his tongue.

The Smiling Man's eyes were bright and furious, though his face was still jovial.

"I *will* put you back in the pit I took you from."

Ruben's heart sank to his stomach.

"Not for long, though time loses meaning in places such as those, I know. You are not the first I've turned to my cause — yes, *my* cause. But I had high hopes for you. My cruelty comes from what I was made to be by the people you claim hold your *allegiance*. I knew nothing else, and so I used what I had and made myself powerful."

"You're powerful because you have magic," Ruben spat. "Without that, you'd be nothing, like anyone else, held to the *laws* you hate so much."

The Smiling Man sneered. "I'm very aware of what I was without magic. I was less than nothing." He advanced on Ruben. "I was *enslaved* by the very creatures you hold in such high regard. Their way of life, their teachings are a *perversion* of truth. You could build bridges, you say? How noble. How worthless. Bridges fall. I can move the earth to my will. You could heal the sick and dying? I could destroy the disease that claims them. You could stop wars? I could destroy an entire race of people and raze their country into never — was *if I desired it*. You are enslaved, Ruben. Your chains are silk, and their whips are encouraging words, but you are a slave all the same."

His advancements had pushed them halfway across the room and Ruben was trying not to trip on the soft flooring. He'd gone too far. The Smiling Man was going to kill him, and slowly — he could see the madness in the creature's eyes.

"Enough."

A new voice, authoritative. Ruben wanted to turn and see who could command even this beast in his temper, but the Smiling Man was still very close, and he hadn't looked away. Rage and power rippled through him and his tongue darted out to wet his lips. He twitched a smirk, his eyes never blinking.

The mad magus took an obedient step back and Ruben started to relax. He never saw the kick that cracked into the side of his head, and he was unconscious before he hit the ground.

* * *

Ruben opened his eyes, closed them again, and felt his body start shaking. He took several deep breaths and tried to relax. He opened his eyes once again to a darkness so complete that he couldn't see his own hand.

I survived before; I can survive again.

He sat up and put his hand out, bumping immediately into the wall and scratching his knuckles on the rough stone. He felt his way up the barrier and stood on shaky legs to move forward. In only a few steps he reached the second wall. A corner, then. Good.

Movement helped. His head ached, but he pressed on. After only six paces he met the next wall, jamming his fingers painfully, unexpectedly.

Before, the cell had been fifteen paces from wall to wall. This one was six. To confirm it, he continued faster than he should have, scraping his finger pads over the stone, and sure enough — six paces later — he met the last wall. This cell was less than half the size of the last one.

Worse, he had felt no door.

Ruben laid his back against the stone and summoned fire into his palm, wincing and blinking at the bright light, even banked low. His eyes watered as they adjusted, and he looked around the tiny prison, convulsively trying to swallow his rising panic.

In the middle of the floor was a hole the size of his fist, which led to sewers from the faint smell wafting up. There was a wooden hatch in the ceiling that had no hinges that he could see, and it was banded with iron.

Nothing else.

A hatch in the ceiling, a hole in the floor, with stone and darkness surrounding him. He sank to the floor and sobbed, the fire in his hands fading until he held nothing.

5

She screamed, throat raw from the numerous times the sound had ripped through her, seeing horrors in every shadow. She felt blood, sticky on her hands, and rubbed them desperately down her clothes and the floor and the wall to make it stop, stop, *but the blood only welled thicker, welling, dripping, pooling. She saw herself kill again and again, revulsion turning to indifference, turning to enjoyment and back again as the sensations echoed through her bones like a song that would never stop.*

Day and night, pleading voices overlapped, all of them screaming in her ears and nothing would block them out. When she tried to use the wall to silence them, she found herself restrained, and that was the worst — helplessness at the hands of those meant to protect her.

Confinement and starvation and pain — her body burned and bruised as she saw it take a thousand lashes, ten thousand beatings with anything that was within reach. Her feet bled from cold and blistered in heat. She ached and cried and pled and bargained and tried time and again to escape, but was always caught and thrown back in the hell she knew as dearly as any close friend, and loved like the wash of pain across her skin, because at least she was still alive.

After all, the dead can't take vengeance.

She blinked. Took a deep breath. Stared at the ceiling. She was hungry. And tired, though she'd been sleeping only moments ago. She tried to sit up, but found that she had been secured to the table — not tightly, but with the clear intention of ensuring that she couldn't free herself. Never claustrophobic before, now the sight of the ropes and bindings pulled a heavy dread from the pit of her stomach and she tasted the bile of fear.

Warped hinges squeaked in protest as a woman entered the room, beautiful but for a cruel and disfiguring burn scarring her cheek. It was still fresh, judging by the redness of it. She was only two decades Wren's senior, but looked weary for her years. Her hair was a tight bun at the back of her head and she walked with an air of confidence and purpose.

She glanced at Wren and then paused. "Are you awake?" Her voice was surprisingly vibrant and musical.

"Yes." Wren's own voice was scratchy and painful.

"Are you really?" The woman approached cautiously.

"Should I not be?"

"Do you know where you are?"

Wren glanced around to see the dilapidated state of the place and nodded. "I came here ... yesterday." She decided to feign confidence, but realized with a pang that she couldn't remember. "It's a home for children."

"It is, but you didn't come yesterday." The woman's deft but scarred fingers untied the knots that kept Wren in place.

"When, then?" Wren rolled her wrists and sat up.

"Been three months."

Wren felt her world shudder, crack. "Three months," she repeated.

The woman nodded sympathetically.

"Wh— but I — ..."

"You've been sick." The woman's voice was a symphony of compassion. "Screaming, ranting, thrashing about. We had to bind you up so you wouldn't hurt yourself or anyone else. You've had a few clear days, but this is the first time I've seen sanity in your eyes, girl. Whatever happened, you might be through the worst of it."

Wren took another deep breath. "I very much doubt that."

*   *   *

The music was beautiful, lively, and inspired many of the attendees to grace their way across the enormous dance floor, polished to a high shine. They spun and twisted — some with more skill than others — but most with evident enjoyment, switching partners as they swirled through complicated steps, and executing perfect bows when the music changed, nearly seamlessly, from piece to piece.

Despite the high windows showing it to be full dark outside, the room stayed as bright as day. No timepiece confessed the hours, suggesting time need not to exist at all, except when exhaustion forced tired bodies to rest.

Sculptures graced the edges of the room — glass, metal, stone, or ceramic — each with a plaque describing the piece, the process, the artist. Three sets of double doors led to outside balconies where guests wandered for a cool breeze or quiet conversation. The last corner of the room held a colossal staircase that led to the upstairs of the enormous mansion. Plenty of viewers stood there to look down at the patterns the nobility danced through, enjoying private discussions above the noise. Around the floor, regularly spaced tables were accompanied by comfortable chairs and couches to allow guests to sit and rest in conversation.

Opposite the staircase, a buffet table stood with servants standing ready to offer small plates of delicate foods, sweet, savory, and exotic. Beverages were served, most of them alcoholic, but Donovan found a tart punch he preferred.

"You can't stare at the food forever," Annette said from behind him.

Donovan didn't look at her, but asked, "How do they get the punch this color?"

The noblewoman took Donovan's shoulders and led him gently, but firmly, away from the buffet and across the room to a circle of her noble friends.

"You said he was here, my lady, and we didn't believe you!" one man cried in jest.

"A prime diplomat to lure Master Rudd from his library and into a gathering of this size," said another.

Donovan smiled ruefully and added, "She didn't give me much choice, threatening to write to the Order with tales of my ailing health due to overwork."

"I do what I must, for the good of the people," Annette placed a hand on her heart and a look of mock seriousness on her features.

"Master Rudd, do tell us what project has you so locked away? Surely you've not discovered *another* lost magic?"

Donovan laughed, despite the churning in his stomach. He hated lying, but couldn't rightly tell the truth. Which of the gathered mass of rich humanity here was a spy for the opposition who would gladly take his information and use it to further their means?

"Lord Altin, do you really think I could do two such marvelous things in my lifetime? Besides, how would I know? I am only a Seeker, not a magus to test and challenge every piece of magic at our disposal! I lay no claim to any marvelous scholarship. Luck found me and I took her hand."

The assembled men and women nodded agreeably.

"If a wallop on the head is what it takes luck to show, I expect I would be willing to join the line!" Lord Cervates added.

"If only it were so simple, our age would be one of wonders," Donovan agreed, toasting.

The others joined with their own drinks.

The wallop laid me unconscious for two weeks, you pompous ass, and I still have nightmares about it.

Annette took Donovan's arm gracefully and told the gathered crowd, "I cannot let you monopolize our man's time, ladies, gentlemen. I expect we'll see more of our friend in the future, so plan to catch his attention again!"

Annette once again steered Donovan across the room. "You kept your temper," she said softly.

"My temper was less in doubt than my tongue," Donovan retorted, sipping on his punch.

"Garvis is an idiot of the richest class and has never learned to consider his words before spitting them. He has friends the way a lump of rotted meat has maggots, and were his money to dry up, so too would the maggots."

"Thank you for the imagery."

"I have to keep you from skulking around the buffet somehow."

They wandered from group to group until Annette was pulled away to discuss business dealings she thought the crown might or might not support. Donovan was forced to hold his own, rehearsed dialogues scrolling through his mind. At least this small group of younger nobility seemed much more willing to leave his personal life alone.

"I'm simply saying that we need to build a stronger defense here — the palace holds irreplaceable records and almost every governmental peer in the kingdom, especially this time of year. If the Order's wall can keep out any attack, as they boast it can, then the palace should have one as well, to protect the king and his assets." The young man finished with a decisive gesture and settled back to receive the argument.

None was immediately forthcoming, so Donovan added, "The wall around the Order has stood and been enhanced for some hundreds of years. Recreating it now would take funds and skilled workers, not to mention magic that cannot be spared."

"The young mages in the Order are training to defend us anyway. Why should this make a difference?"

"Because the majority of them are already assigned to important positions and withdrawing them would cause gaps and holes in an already shaky defense of a different sort. Elliott is stretching his forces thin to seek out the Hunters we can and take the enemy before they're ready to engage, but that takes time, and isn't readily noticeable to an outsider."

"The students, then."

"They're children." Donovan frowned. "Magic is dangerous to master, and children would not be worth the risk."

The lordling shrugged in clear disagreement, but held his tongue.

"What kind of defense does the wall boast, then, that would be dangerous and difficult to recreate?" another asked. This man appeared to be in his mid-thirties, with a scholarly look about him. His brown hair, shiny and clean, kept falling across his brow. He pushed it back and looked at Donovan with a clear and interested gaze.

Donovan didn't trust him and didn't know why.

"I'm not sure. It was never my realm of study, but magic is innately dangerous. The toll it takes can be brutal if overused. Especially for a child."

"But the wall itself is secure enough that you believe the cost and time involved in recreating it would be too much?"

"For this war, certainly. Besides which, the palace grounds are more expansive than the Order's if you wish to include the Market and Justice and the Bank. Even excluding the town surrounding, as the Order does, your wall would need to cover half again the distance."

"Why is the town excluded?" a young woman asked.

"It grew outside after the wall was built," Donovan answered easily. "I'm not sure exactly when."

The aggressive lordling shook his head. "There was an Order and a city long before the Cataclysm destroyed them both, and most of the palace at the time. Thairnsdale was rebuilt and has grown massive, expanding a hundredfold since. I hear they're building again, out and up. It's an expensive place to live — much as it is here."

Donovan acknowledged his contribution with a grateful nod as two ladies joined their circle.

"Master Rudd, I thought I spotted you!" one of the pair exclaimed.

Donovan laughed and bowed politely. *I have no idea who you are.*

Her straight blond hair was cut at a severely straight line along her jaw, bright colors on her eyes and lips accentuated her unfamiliar features.

"I brought Lady Lasturn to meet the nobility as she's been away so long, and I decided she would enjoy your company. Master Rudd is the gentleman who discovered New Seeking."

"We've met." Cara met his gaze. "Through a mutual friend."

Donovan dropped his eyes in another polite bow as his heart started to race. Her springy salt and pepper coils framed her face in a stormy cloud that nonetheless could not shadow her beauty. Unlike her companion, she used the barest amount of color on her features, and he found her to be the most stunning woman in the room.

"Are you enjoying the festivities, my lady?"

"Very much so," she smoothed a hand down her green velvet gown. "Our estate does not see entertainment on this scale, but I think a bit of wildness now and again is necessary to a worthwhile life."

Donovan looked at the 'wildness' and sighed inwardly. The twice-yearly celebrations their hometown of Weston had held were much more exciting than this, if less opulent. The entire town participated, donated goods and services, and the party could last for days. Despite his preference for the peace of the Order, he had very fond memories of those parties. He blinked to remember that he'd first courted her at one of those parties. She'd been wearing green, then, too. Cotton, not velvet.

"Master Rudd, do you dance?" the unknown lady interrupted his nostalgia.

"I was not raised to court life, and so never mastered the steps." Donovan was grateful for the line Annette had helped him practice. "Besides which, my age encourages me to not be so lively so late in the evening." He smiled sheepishly and held up his beverage. It was the same one he'd been nursing all night, and non-alcoholic, but plenty of others were approaching drunk on their multiple servings.

"A shame!" she struck his arm playfully.

"I dance, lady, if you've an interest in a second choice," the untrustworthy lordling suggested.

The woman accepted and they strode off together.

"What was that gentleman's name?" Donovan asked. "I didn't catch it when I arrived."

"He's a country baron's son. Sir Anthony Ghiel, I believe," Sir Jameson answered.

"I hope my counter-stance didn't upset you, Sir Jameson," Donovan said.

The previously aggressive youth shrugged. "Please, Master Rudd, in a setting as this, you must call me Hartford. I worry for my people. When the enemy wears the face of a friend, it's difficult to know where to strike, and so I look to defense. I imagine my father will keep me from doing anything rash, but I plan to invest in the stonemasons when I gain my inheritance. Once this war is won, I'll have my wall." He smiled ruefully.

Donovan clapped him on the shoulder. "Wise words, Hartford. I'm sorry to excuse myself, but I've grown warm and hear my name on the wind."

He shook hands and bowed all around, avoiding Cara's eye, and strode away. He finished his drink and handed the glass to a passing servant with thanks. Donovan made his way across the carpeted floor and around the side of the dancing section, excusing himself from several requested conversations with empty promises to return. The main balcony held a crowd of people and the second almost as many. The third, the smallest, held only a few, however, and he stood near the door, away from the groupings, to take deep breaths of the fresher air.

Below lay a sprawling garden where high hedges and carefully tended plants provided a cool space to walk. It allowed city-dwellers to enjoy the outdoors without risking any pesky stinging plants or feral animals. Couples strolled through together and he briefly entertained the idea of jumping over the balcony to curl up under some of the bushes, but argued himself down. He rubbed the back of his neck and sighed deeply.

For years Donovan had believed that all he wanted was to have Cara back, to carry on their loving marriage as it had been before. Then all he had wanted was to be around her, even if their marriage couldn't last. Now he had that, but seeing her was a thorn in his heel — a reminder of things that were and could no longer be. Their conversation had cleared the air, expunged some of the poison, but now it was almost worse. He hadn't been so aware of the poison before and, despite there being less of it, he felt as though it was killing him faster.

He lowered his hearing and sense of touch and closed his eyes until he felt like he was floating, his thoughts drifting away on the breeze he could no longer feel. He breathed deeply in the silence. Only for a moment, but when he raised his senses again, he felt nearly cleansed.

Knowing that Annette would scold him if he stayed too much longer out of the public eye, he started back for the festivities, but stopped sharply in the doorway, blocked by none other than Lady Cara Lasturn.

"So soon? You used to take an age to calm down after something riled you." She glanced at the small crowd behind him.

"Old age has sobered me," Donovan joked in kind. "I wasn't riled. Just ..."

They stood awkwardly for a moment.

"You look good. In that outfit."

"Annette chose it." Donovan smoothed the front of the coat. Much in the style of what he'd worn to dinner weeks ago, this sash was tied correctly, and the golden-brown tone suited his dark features. He liked dressing up these days, but was positive that if he had to wear these kinds of clothes every day, he'd go mad. A man couldn't relax in a suit.

"Heading back to the party?" she asked.

He nodded. "Annette insists I be seen."

She smiled and his face warmed. "You said you weren't much of a dancer, and I almost argued."

"Not these kinds of dances," he shrugged.

"You're not drunk, either."

"No. Not anymore."

"I see Annette taught you how to lie."

"I hate doing it." The silence stretched. "I'm not sure how to respond."

Cara pulled on one of the jewels in her earlobe. "I miss the honesty of our small town sometimes. Sure, there were cheats and pettiness, but it was never like this. Annette and Holm both know how to lie. They were raised to politics. Holm ... he never lies to me, nor to our children, but I see him floating around in a room like this ... He's a good man, but I'm glad I don't have to watch him tonight. It's just sometimes he wears a mask."

"Everyone wears masks."

"Not everyone." She gave him a hard look.

"Excuse me." An irritated voice from the doorway made them jump and Cara stepped aside.

Sir Anthony Giehl, the young noble that Donovan mistrusted from earlier, stood impatiently, waiting for them to clear the doorway.

"Thank you," he said irritably as he passed by Donovan in the small space.

"I should get back —" they both said, smiling ruefully.

Donovan took her hand and bowed, pressing his lips to the soft skin on the back of her hand.

"My Lady, it was a pleasure."

She curtsied. "My Lord, the same."

"Not a lord," he smiled.

"All the same."

Cara glided away and to a group of women, all at least her age, and none of them nearly as stunning. Donovan watched her converse with the noblewomen, his thoughts twisting and tumbling around one another.

"Put your mask on, dear, lest they interpret your frown into something telling."

Donovan jumped and fixed the practiced look of vague amusement on his features. Annette brushed imaginary dust from his shoulder. "Much better. Did Cara say something upsetting?"

"She doesn't have to say anything." Donovan graced her with a deep bow, appropriate for royalty.

Annette accepted it with a shallow curtsey, and they linked arms to take a slow stroll toward the sculptures. She looked magnificent tonight in royal blue, her dress clinging to her curves with what she would claim was a modest slit cut halfway up her thigh. Her shoulders were bare, her neckline bold. She wore sapphires around her neck and down her ears and her thick, blond hair was bound up in a style that defied gravity, braided through with silver chain and more sapphires.

The queen, Annette's sister, was similarly styled, but in red to match the king's maroon, and gold accents. Donovan had been avoiding them all night, but more than once he had looked over to see the queen's eyes on him — as they were now.

"Upsetting her royal majesty again?" Annette gave him a sly wink.

"Not on purpose."

"With whom have you been mingling while I was otherwise engaged?"

"Everyone. You've been dragging me from one group to another — all the names and faces are a blur now. I'm too old for these games. And my knees and back hurt — how have you not sat down yet?"

"Poor darling, having to socialize. How horrible." She squeezed his arm and laughed at him.

Donovan let her laughter calm before he asked, "Your evening is going the way you want?"

"It has been very productive!" Her eyes lit, but she didn't continue.

"For selective ears only?"

"Unfortunately, so. You're too visible right now, else you'd know more."

"Wonderful. Nothing about Ruben?"

Annette looked sincerely sad before her pleasant expression returned. "No, no word yet. I'm still listening."

Donovan nodded and swallowed his disappointment. "Do you know Giehl? Anthony Giehl?"

"Hm. Yes — he's one of Holm Lasturn's merchant friends, or his father is. Wool, fat, things like that, why?"

"I'm not sure. I just don't like him."

"We can keep an eye on him. And your classes?"

Donovan was getting used to the rapid subject changes. "Good. The children are a joy to teach. Full of curiosity."

"You're wasted in the field; you're a good teacher."

"I like teaching."

"How are your — the girls? I know Cara's daughters have joined the classes in your hall. And you've been getting to know the other instructors?"

Donovan took a breath, even as he felt like the air was squeezed out of his lungs. "Sometimes I wonder if you do that on purpose."

Annette didn't answer.

"Luanne and Lizette are doing very well. I'm told that both are excelling in their studies."

"Lovely to hear."

They rounded a larger statue, this one studied by another couple, and continued along until they were out of earshot.

"Do you gain anything from this situation?" Donovan asked.

"Such as?" Annette's tone was pleasant, but he knew her well enough to detect the iciness.

"You seem very interested, is all."

Annette looked at him, head tilted. "If nothing else, it is an interesting set of circumstances, and I am incredibly nosy. More, I consider you a good friend. I realize that I may seem a different person since we arrived here, but I do value your companionship and hope that you'll realize that you can trust me."

Donovan shook his head with somber amusement and said very softly. "Annette, you're a spy. You're a member of the royal family. You were raised to intrigue and politics and I'm a man born and raised to the speed of growing potatoes. I don't lie, I don't cheat.

I'm a trusting sort. But I'm wise enough to see there are some things that make that a liability to myself. I value our friendship, but I know I'm near the bottom of a long list of your loyalties."

They rounded two more statues in silence and then stopped as a man waved to Annette and started toward them.

"I can see why my sister is afraid of you, Don." Before he could answer she released his arm and said, "Lord Baron General Ost! How are you?"

"Your Highness!" The military man executed a perfect bow. The gray in his hair and beard suggested an experienced age that didn't hinder his actions. Donovan envied him — he was positive he would fall over if he tried anything more than a stroll right now.

"This must be your man, Rudd, yes?"

The general bowed politely, Donovan matched it, and then the general put out a hand to shake. His palm was dry and calloused and strong, but he didn't test Donovan's strength like so many others.

"Excellent to meet you, sir!" The general's voice was loud, but not painful.

"What brings you in from the field?" Annette asked him. "We haven't seen you in ages. I thought you had planned to stay with your army while they were put through their paces."

"True, my lady, truly I was there with them until the king called me to return for his party. I have also decided to take the opportunity to escort his newest batch of recruits and graduates personally — they include my daughter, at last."

"Already? She's just turned four, hasn't she?" Annette wore an expression of mock surprise.

Ost beamed. "Certainly not! Sixteen and already the head of every class. Hasn't chosen a specialty yet, of course, but there's time — she'll have her pick when she's ready."

"And who watches the other children while their father is away?"

The general had a pleasant laugh. "I've a good crowd of officers to mind my soldiers, my lady, you know well."

"I do," Annette agreed, joining his laughter.

"One day, I'll have you in my army. I'll give you however many you want so long as you lead them in the bow."

"And if I want them all?" Annette's eyes twinkled dangerously.

The general bowed. "I know when my match has met me, my lady. Master Rudd!"

Donovan raised his eyebrows at the sudden attention, but smiled. This man was growing on him. "Yes, General?"

"You're a military man?"

"Not in the slightest."

"Donovan is too modest. He holds his own in a fight — he's faced Hunters before." Annette tilted her chin at him — a warning not to try and slip away through self-deprecation.

"One-to-one, perhaps, my lady, but an army is far more cohesive than I have ever managed to be. My strengths are not in the sword."

"No, they're in the kick, I hear."

Donovan cocked his head.

"I keep the records of all of our trained fighters," the general explained. "Even those stationed with the Order, as they're still under my command if I call — it's tricky politically, but Elliott and I have always got on well. As I recall, you received high marks for your class of Retrievers. Not a popular fighting style, but you did well enough to graduate, and your strengths were in other aspects of the job, I believe."

"Oh. Thank you. Yes." Donovan felt tongue-tied. He hadn't known the Retrievers fell under military command — or maybe just the records. Retrievers were specialists, after all.

"I'm a Seeker myself," the general was saying.

Donovan smiled. "Are you?"

"It's damned useful in my career so long as I can rest after, or have a willing Healer on hand. Troop movements are far easiest to coordinate from above, and the advantage in Seeing the enemy's position is worth a few headaches."

"Of course," Donovan agreed.

"If you've ever an interest in assisting, you're more than welcome." He looked thoughtful, as if an idea was occurring to him then. "You should come to my lands when I take these recruits — they're all mages, probably some of yours among them."

"My students are far from graduating." Donovan smiled politely, ready to refuse, but hesitated.

Ost continued, "My land is only an overnight from here with a wagon train. You can educate my Seekers while you're there — give them a rousing talk and be scholarly. Not all of my people have skulls fit for wall-breaking." He laughed at his joke.

Annette looked at Donovan with raised eyebrows, seemingly as surprised as he was.

"I ... will strongly consider your offer." He was surprised to realize he meant it, too.

The general shook his hand. "Well enough, I suppose. I'll send a page to remind you in the morning. We'll leave the day after tomorrow. Dawn, of course."

"Of course."

General Ost bowed deeply again to Annette and strode off, catching the attention of another noblewoman to engage in conversation.

"That was unexpected," Annette said when he'd gone.

"Was it?"

"I love the man, but he's not one of mine. He and King Braun were boyhood friends — a worry throughout the court when he was elevated — but he's the best general the army has had in two decades. I've known him since I was a child."

"He seems a nice man."

"I wonder if he has other motivations for inviting you." Annette took his arm again as they continued their slow stroll.

"Of course he does." Donovan forced the tension out of his shoulders. "He had the chance to speak with you all night. I imagine he didn't want me cornered and scared off, so he approached you *with* me, and now I'm seriously considering going with him. He has something to tell me, and I would like to know what it is."

"You're not too old for the game after all. But be careful. I can't go; I've too much to do here."

"I figured as much."

She gave him a sideways look, "You are going, right?"

"I have to now, don't I? You would make me, even if I hadn't already decided."

Annette laughed. "I should mingle. And you should mingle, too. Stay away from the buffet." She offered her hand and he bowed low, brushing his lips over the royal seal on her finger.

When she had disappeared into a crowd of admirers, he turned straight toward the buffet, despite her warning. How late was it that he was so hungry? Certainly later than he would normally have been awake. If he went with General Ost, he would have to transfer his classes to another teacher. But if he *was* going to travel with the general, he wanted to make sure his project was in a good stopping place, possibly bring some kind of work with him to study away from the prying eyes of the nobility.

Donovan blinked and then grunted with frustration. "Am I not allowed to sustain myself at all?"

Annette, somehow now standing in his way, laughed. "Grab a few bites, then."

"You've come to drag me about again," Donovan guessed, accepting a plate of small sandwiches from a server and immediately shoving one into his mouth, whole.

"Aren't you enjoying yourself even a little?" Annette asked.

"You're enjoying yourself enough for the both of us," he answered thickly.

"Perhaps," Annette conceded. "I've been away from court for a much longer time than I was previously. I was born to be busy." She looked across the room filled with nobility and servants and a predatory grin stalked across her face.

She turned her smile on Donovan. "Ready?"

* * *

Donovan gave a start and rolled to his feet, then sat back down heavily on the bed as his world spun. He moaned and rubbed his eyes while he tried to ignore the throbbing and pinching of his aching joints. He made another attempt to stand and stumbled to the door. Another knock came in that time, far too loud in the quiet space.

He opened the door and croaked, "Yes?" A young military recruit in uniform stood, ramrod straight, before him.

The girl put out a folded piece of paper and said, "From the Lord General, *sir*. He ordered that I put the note in your hand. I've also been ordered to wait for a return message."

"All right, give me a moment." He cleared the frog from his throat. The girl stood in an at-ease position, exuding the willingness to stand in this doorway all day if required.

Donovan yawned while he unfolded the letter, opening his eyes wide and blinking to try and focus.

Msr. Donovan Rudd

I expect this letter to wake you, so I sent it at noon.

In case our conversation fled from your mind, please remember your offer to train my soldiers in New Seeking. I expect not to keep you for more than a couple of days. Please send your response with my recruit so that I can have preparations made for your company.

All the best,

Lord Baron General Vernon Ost

Donovan yawned again. "Please tell the general I would be delighted to join him."

The recruit nodded abruptly. "With that answer, I was instructed to tell you that he will be leaving from the eastern stables at dawn and not a moment past."

"Thank you."

"Of course, *sir*. Have an excellent day, *sir*." She turned on her heel and marched her way down the hall.

Donovan went back to his bedroom and pulled aside the curtains. He winced and lowered his vision until he was nearly blind, then allowed it to slowly return until the burning light of noon was tolerable.

For the third time since his arrival, Donovan pulled on the cord by his closet to summon his room servant. A few minutes passed before the man arrived.

"You summoned me, sir?"

"Could you please bring me a breakfast tray, Peter? I'm not feeling up to the Dining Hall this morning."

"Of course, sir. The time being what it is, would you prefer a lunch tray?"

"Yes, of course. That. Thank you."

"I'll return momentarily, sir." Peter left quickly.

Donovan sat heavily in one of his padded chairs and dozed off again, awakened again by a knock, but the visitors didn't wait for him to answer — Annette and Cara opened the portal, sauntered in, and made themselves comfortable. They both looked far livelier than they had any right to as they settled together on the couch opposite his chair.

"'Morning, Donovan." Annette grinned wickedly.

"Afternoon," Cara reminded her with a gentle touch. "Be nice to the poor man. He's not used to staying up until all hours, and some of us need more than four hours of sleep a night."

Annette smiled at Cara and adjusted her skirt across the couch. "We passed your man in the hall and sent him to fetch lunch for us, as well — easier to handle business over a full stomach."

"Business?" Donovan asked wearily.

"Are you hung over?" Annette asked in turn.

"I drank punch all night. I need a moment to wake, is all."

Cara rose to fetch a glass of water from the basin in Donovan's room and handed it over.

Donovan drank gratefully, willing himself to wake. He cleared his throat. "What business did you want to discuss?"

Annette folded her hands in her lap and grew serious. "Have you heard anything from Whitman?"

"Not since the last letter you gave me. I don't expect to receive much from him, though, why?"

"That was my last message as well. I need to send someone to check on him, and I cannot send you."

Worry lent Donovan energy and he found himself on the edge of his seat. "I'll cancel my visit with General Ost. Easily done."

"He has something he wants from you, we agreed. Ost is a clever man, and he had reason to speak with you. He can be a bit eccentric, but I would trust him with my life."

"Who, then?" Donovan asked.

"Obviously I'm speaking of Cara."

Donovan blinked at her, then at Cara, who gave a small wave from where her hands were clasped in her lap, like a proper lady.

For a moment, he saw her as she was when they were children together, covered in mud and wrestling a young sheep. He smothered a smile.

She arched an eyebrow at him, so alike to Annette's. "You don't think I'm suited for the task?"

"No, no," Donovan assured her. "It's not that. I just — I didn't ... Um."

Annette, braiding a lock of her hair, grinned at his discomfort. "It's a new position, but yes, Cara is one of mine."

"Ah."

"I wouldn't have taken you for a spy, Donny."

"That's rather the point," Annette said dryly.

"I'm not actually sure I am one," Donovan remembered. "Annette, did I get a pay raise or anything for this change of duty?"

"You can take that up with Whitman." Annette waved dismissively. "Cara will leave with a caravan shortly, under the guise of considering the Order's classes for her children. In the meantime, I suggest we send no letters, in case Whitman has been compromised."

Peter returned to the room with a cart behind him, laden with a beautiful lunch. He set it out and left without a word, taking note of the privacy their silence implied, except for Donovan's thanks.

They helped themselves to food — the fare simple, but delicious. Donovan ate most of a third sandwich before he felt satisfied, and they spoke of simple things until then.

Feeling much more human, Donovan asked, "Do I need to do anything while I'm with the army? Look for anything? Speak to anyone?"

Annette considered the questions and decided, "No. Keep your eyes sharp, but otherwise flow with the river current."

"What ..." Donovan looked at Cara. "Who will take care of Lizette and Luann and Hugh?"

Cara smiled at him. "I'll leave the girls in charge of their brother, and put them all under the hand of my servants. I don't expect to be gone more than a week — there and back again, after all — I expect they'll do fine; they've been practically running the estate for a few years now."

"What are you going to do then, Don?" Annette asked.

"I expect to spend the rest of my time in the library before a week-long hiatus." Donovan shrugged.

"You'll go blind, you know."

"Not a problem for me, right?" Donovan winked at her, and Annette rolled her eyes.

They finished their meal with companionable conversation until Annette and Cara went about their business and Donovan his. He let himself into his secret room and took a deep, contented inhale.

The smell of the space was one he quite felt he was growing an addiction to. The aroma of the books, and ink and the faint scent of sealed away foodstuffs were comforting after so many hours of success and failure — more failure than success. He wouldn't mind so much if it wasn't his link to finding Ruben.

He sat behind his desk and picked up where he'd left off, scanning through his most recent text and making notes along the way. He was near the end of this one and meant to finish it today.

The book was another mythology about various heroes of either side and their battles. With little doubt of the magics mentioned, since his own discovery, he made careful notes about the various abilities either side boasted — no matter how strange and seemingly impossible. While it wasn't what he wanted, he knew it could all be useful, and so was happy enough to immerse himself in the stories.

A soft tap sounded against Donovan's door. That had never happened before, and it took him a moment to register that it was real, and then another to react beyond surprise. He went to the door and hesitated, increasing his hearing to beyond the threshold of pain to make sure that there was only one person on the other side of the portal. The effort left him sweating, and swearing with a headache, but he felt safer unlocking and opening the door a crack.

One of the librarians waited outside and, without a word, passed him a note and then pushed the shelf closed. He locked the door and opened his letter, only three short sentences, but it chilled his blood faster than would a winter night.

Elliott is dead.

Politics in motion.

Your plans do not change.

- A

Donovan stared at the words.

The Head of the Order was dead.

The leader of the magical society of which he'd found himself an unwilling, but motivated member ...

... had been murdered? What happened?

The note was frustratingly devoid of information.

He looked up at the hourglass. Hours had passed since he last spoke with Annette, but it wouldn't yet be dark. He blew out his lamps and left the room in a hurry, through the library and down the corridors, winding through servants and nobility alike until he came to Annette's wing.

The servant there stepped into his path. "She's already left, sir."

"What?" He stared at her.

The servant repeated, "I was informed to tell you that Her Highness the Lady Annette Kraemer has left the palace."

"Where's she gone?"

"I was not instructed to tell you, sir."

"Gone already?"

"Yes, sir."

Donovan swore and ran a hand across his hair. "Did she tell you anything else for me?"

"She said she sent a note, sir."

Donovan waved it vaguely, much crumpled after his hurried trip from the library.

"She's likely caught up by now."

Donovan gazed at the servant with confusion.

"To the caravan."

"Oh, right! Thank you."

He wandered slowly back the way he'd come, staring at the words as though they might change their meaning and give him more information, make more sense, anything. How could a blood mage get to Elliot? The same way they got to Ruben, of course. Donovan's face darkened.

"What do I do?" he whispered.

He was far beyond his abilities, and the weight of responsibility was pushing him under. Donovan took a breath and started toward his rooms, gripping the note tightly. He would go with the general and hear what the man had to say. He would handle everything as he could. He had to — people depended on him.

"I wouldn't mind if they trusted me a little less," he muttered to himself, pacing around the foot of his bed.

If Elliott was dead, what happened to Whitman? He felt chilled at the thought. "No, no," he told himself firmly. "We'll get through this. I just hate to see how we get there ..."

6

THE WOMAN INTRODUCED HERSELF as Valene and led Wren through the children's home, larger than it had originally seemed, but no less worn and rundown. Warped boards threatened to trip her steps and promised splinters if she was careless enough.

Valene's booted stride was fast despite her not-insignificant limp, but she kept her pace reined in for Wren's weakened state. It was the strange weakness and lack of balance that had convinced Wren that three months had truly gone without her.

They passed a number of other children — a mix of ages and birth places showing in their looks — all with curious eyes. Wren let them stare; she wanted to know what she might face before challenging. Valene listed off various rules, but Wren only half-listened while she memorized the layout, taking in what she could.

"What happened to this place?" she asked, interrupting something about eating hours.

Valene answered easily, "My mother takes in anyone who needs help and is often at odds with the king's rulings. In return, this place is denied tax relief and soldiers are often sent to harass and make trouble."

"Your mother rules here?"

"That's a good term for it," the woman laughed musically. "Yes. You're older than you look, aren't you?"

"That would depend on the eye."

The woman laughed again, like wind chimes, and said, "What was your name, little fox?"

"Wren."

"Ah, a little bird! A bird who dresses like a fox, I wonder?"

"The scent of the fur in my nest keeps larger birds away," Wren answered, delighted at the play of words and imagery. Her mind still felt sluggish and heavy, but Valene was easy to speak to.

"I see," the woman answered. "Best hope the scent doesn't draw more foxes, then. They're quick to spot their own and eat the rest." She opened the door to an office that appeared meticulously organized, but still faced the chaos born of being overwhelmingly busy. Heaviness pervaded the place — physical, emotional, mental — it was everywhere.

"Anja, this is Wren."

An older woman stood at a shelf, transferring neat stacks of documents from her arm. She glanced up and nodded. "Thank you, Valene, that will be all."

Valene winked at Wren and left.

"Healer, are you?" Anja, Valene's mother, asked.

Wren could see their family similarities in the shape of her face, the line of her jaw, and the tight bun of her hair, though the color had faded to silver and gray.

Wren ignored the question, instead looking at all the books. Many of them were damaged — like everything else in this place — but they looked interesting enough.

"You can read them if you like, but I'll ask you to tutor the other children. Too much to do and too little time. Everyone works."

"Are you going to send me to the Order?" Wren asked.

"Do you want to go to the Order?" Anja sat at her desk.

Wren didn't answer.

Anja rested her arms on the desk's scratched surface. "The Order is a place for children to learn to use their magic, and to learn ethics, and history, and reading, and mathematics, but it is not — should not be — the only place for such things to be learned. I don't think living far from home and learning information without application is healthy for young minds. They can tell you anything they want and you would never know to question it."

"So the King sends soldiers," Wren confirmed.

"That girl ..." Anja closed her eyes briefly, a flash of irritation showing. "Yes. The Order and the king send people to pester me, to urge me to change my ways."

"Why don't they burn this place down, then? It would only take a spark."

Anja's eyes narrowed. "It is not law that all children must be sent to the Order. It cannot become law, or else parents would fear the lack of choice and the Order would lose its power. One must choose the Order, and so it is made quite seductive. To those it wants to house."

"I don't want to go to the Order," Wren said. She wouldn't be able to find Forest.

"Good. You'll learn here."

"Will your daughter teach me?"

"No. Gods no. Valene has been here only to recover from injuries. She will leave soon."

"You don't like that," Wren guessed.

Anja tilted her head. "No, I don't. Do you know why?"

"Because she works for the Order?"

Anja smiled. "Clever little thing, aren't you? My daughter collects children from their families and deposits them within the very place that threatens our freedom."

Wren remembered a kindly, bearded man, and a pair of immobile boots, lit by firelight. She remembered the blood and rubbed her hands together.

"You'll be safe here, Wren," Anja said gently.

Wren looked up at her. "No, I won't. But it will do for now."

*　　*　　*

"Stuck?" Whitman asked with a frown.

The Mentalist nodded. An instructor of the advanced classes, she was one of the primary mages attempting to help Kina's recovery.

"This is a very basic concept that is taught on nearly the first day of classes. It's very useful, even for non-mages such as yourself."

Whitman smiled thinly. "Then I look forward to your excellent explanation."

"Imagine your mind as a mansion — some kind of building with many rooms. You can store any knowledge in such a place, hide it from view, or organize it so as to be readily available. It helps to avoid forgetting things, or keep your more private memories safe from other Mentalists."

"I see." Whitman didn't forget much, but he knew that others had more of a problem with that than he did. The bards had similar training, and the previous Spymaster had taught him yet more memorization methods, and ways to organize his mind.

Whitman said, "Kina is stuck wandering the mansion, unable to access most of the rooms, and unable to make the things therein available to anyone outside of it, yes?"

The Mentalist blinked. "Um, yes. Basically, yes."

Whitman leaned back against the wall. *All right now, this is the key to the answer, this mansion of rooms. If she cannot come out, then we must go to her. THINK!*

The Mentalist in front of him winced.

"What was that?" Whitman asked her.

"Um, I ..."

"You were listening to my thoughts?"

She looked guilty. "I just thought if I could maybe listen in ..."

"Do not do that. Ever. Can a person go into another's mansion?"

"Certainly," she said in a rush, chastised. "That's what we've been trying, but we've been unable to make much progress because of the risk of our Mentalists getting stuck, just as Kina is."

"Stuck — unable to communicate?"

The Mentalist looked confused again. "Not exactly ..."

"What?"

"Well, hers is a unique case. You see we've had others get stuck, but ..."

"Please stop hesitating, and explain to me what the confusion is." Whitman kept his temper in check, but his frustration was on the rise.

"I mean ... Um." She seemed struck by inspiration. "Have you ever had a dream you couldn't wake from?"

"No ..."

"Or, I mean, you're dreaming, but you know you're dreaming?"

"I suppose ..." Whitman almost never dreamed — though he had his share of nightmares — but Oslan often shared his own dreams when they woke together.

"Like that, but for an age. Maybe an hour, or a month, or forever."

"I would get stuck in the dream?"

"Right, in the image."

"But only mentally. What would my body do?"

She shrugged. "Depends, I guess. Some wither away and die, some can go about simple tasks."

"What is different about Kina's case, then?"

"It's too complicated. She's too complicated. She understands everything, and goes about her day, draws, eats, all of that with no guidance, no help. She just can't talk."

"She can talk."

"In gibberish."

"The words have meaning, but we lack a key. Hm. Can you Heal someone who is stuck?"

"Only if there is damage, but the Healer would be in a similar or sometimes worse position. Usually we have to wait for them to come out of it on their own. People who try to go into the memory with the patient can often find themselves stuck there as well, only it's not their memory, and the results are dangerous. Insanity, mostly, though there was a case of someone who could only speak backward ..."

"There is nothing else you can think to do?"

She pursed her lips. "There are a few cases of someone managing to draw the memory away. If they're stuck in it, a Talented Mentalist could remove the memory from the patient's mind. They'd lose the memory, the information, but they'd be free of their mind."

"If the memory is drawn away, what happens to it?"

"It's ... garbled. It's trash, nonsense, altered beyond recognition."

"I see ..." He understood now why Elliott wanted all other avenues attempted first.

"Sometimes, too, the patient could go the same way ... Memories are delicate things. Perhaps you have a new love of spinach when you hated it before, or you remember every word to every song you've ever heard. Or they're altered beyond recognition. Sometimes they die, or, again, they could go terribly mad." She looked on the verge of tears.

Whitman was horrified but said calmly, "Well, that is not what we want ... What do you need from me?"

The woman spread her hands appealingly. "We've never seen this before. Elliott is asking for the impossible."

"Not the impossible," Whitman said gently. "Merely the unheard of."

"That's what I was sent to ask — to see if you had any knowledge of something like this in tales and stories. The Librarian said you've been studying myths of Talent."

"Ah." It had been some time since a person had sincerely asked him anything to do with his bardic training. He almost laughed. "She has all of her memories, but the doors are locked. And you cannot unlock those doors," he mused. "What about new doors, new memories? What can you do with those?"

"I don't —" she looked on the verge of tears again. "We can't do anything with them."

"Not even something that happened a few moments before? She has new memories — you are saying they get locked away immediately?"

"What are you asking, exactly?"

"I am not sure yet."

"Let me pass through your mind, unblocked? I — I might be able to draw something out to help?"

"There are too many private things in my mind," Whitman argued apologetically.

"I can keep secrets. It's my job."

"Not a risk I am willing to take."

"A single memory? Surely that couldn't hurt?"

"How would that help you?"

"It would help me better understand the idea you're considering, if I got your pattern."

"My pattern?"

"Yes ..."

He waited.

She continued reluctantly, "Every person has a mental pattern. Like the lines on your hands — but far, far more complex. The more aligned to their pattern you become, the more easily they are ..."

"Manipulated?" Whitman suggested.

She winced, but nodded. "Family, friends, the better you know someone, the better attuned to them you are, the easier you find it to move through their minds. In this case, it would let me make more sense of the imagery you're trying to build for me."

Whitman rubbed the bridge of his nose. "Fine."

"Bring a memory to mind," she directed.

Whitman tugged on an earlobe. What could he possibly show? Something from his childhood, perhaps — that was as far from the Order's business as he could get.

"All right."

Her eyes lost focus and her hands fidgeted about, as if they played a musical instrument. Whitman wondered which and considered the sounds a variety might make with the patterns she made. There was a pressure in his mind, a slight tickling behind his eyes, and then she was back.

His heart thundered in his chest. "That was nothing like passing through the front gate."

"Their orders are to test for guilt, read surface thoughts, nothing probing." She looked thoughtful.

"Well?"

"All right, you showed me a man, your father, at practice. He's got a crossbow and a bucket of quarrels. As you saw, he shoots the quarrels every day until the bucket is empty. He never looks down and the quarrels go exactly where he points them. But imagine if one day, when he's loading the quarrel, it slips off the track and hits the dirt."

"That never happened."

"Exactly."

"Ah," he said slowly. "*That* is what I was thinking — the pattern would be broken. It would be wrong. Change the memory just a bit, in unimportant ways, and you find yourself free of the original." He chewed the inside of his lip.

"You can't be stuck if the stuck isn't there," she said excitedly.

"You have such a way with words."

She didn't answer, unsure if she was being complimented or insulted. Uncomfortable with his thoughtful silence, she said, "Your father was quite a marksman."

Whitman forced the tension in his jaw to release enough to say dryly, "He was a soldier. Wished the same for me and was not terribly thrilled when I chose poetry and travel over foot rot and diseased bread. Or vice versa."

"Ah. Um."

"What?"

"I didn't pry, but I do pick up background ..."

"What else did you see?" Whitman demanded.

"You learned the crossbow, too?"

"I was an obedient son, for a time." He took a cleansing breath, and changed the subject. "What resources do you need to help Kina with this new method?"

"We have to find the memory in which she is stuck," the woman said slowly, thinking hard.

"Would it not be when the Hunter woman mucked about in her head?"

"We would start there, but it could be in quite a few others — language and memory aren't always related the way you think — *oh!* It might be two places, hence the difficulty of her case! Let's see ... Something recent: her classmates haven't mentioned a change of personality, so she wouldn't stuck, stick, at a younger age. She definitely remembers the instance of her attack, so I would wager it's some loop she's been living from between the start of her mission to just after it. She certainly remembers you, and the mission ..."

Whitman thought of the pictures Kina had been drawing. "If that Hunter was looking for what Kina had found, the violence of the intrusion was perhaps put Kina in this loop."

"Possibly," the woman agreed. "It will still take time to be sure, and then we have to make the memory changes."

"How long?"

"At least a week. Too many minds on the task will blur her patterns. Her best chance of remaining herself will take time."

"Patience: my least favorite word," Whitman said with a practiced smile. "Please keep me notified of any changes. In case I can help further." He bowed and took his crutch under his arm, leaving the room without a further farewell. The Mentalist had started to grate on his nerves. He could tolerate few things less than those who did not look for answers, but gave up at the first sign of the unknown. He had some unexpected time on his hands, a meeting postponed, and decided he could use the comfort of his own room.

The halls were crowded, but people gave him space for the crutch. He kept a tight hand on his satchel, always nervous of pickpockets or Displacers. Everything he had for himself was in cipher, but encryptions could be broken. He'd broken a fair number in his time, after all.

Whitman set his crutch aside and groaned as he rubbed at his tired eyes.

"What's on your mind, love?" Oslan asked, coming out of the bedroom. He had changed from his working blacks into a pair of loose shorts and a loose gray shirt. Possibly one of Whitman's; it was huge on him.

"Much. I just came from a Mentalist's office, to help her understand how to use her own magic in a new and different way. Somehow it had never occurred to her to try something never tried before, simply because the tried and tested method worked *so well.*" He took a breath and harrumphed dramatically.

Oslan smiled and sat on the couch, beckoning. Whitman limped to the seat and tossed himself down, moving about until his head rested in Oslan's lap, his legs propped on the couch arm. Oslan stroked his hair and face, and Whitman closed his eyes. He felt the tension leak out of him.

"What's really bothering you? People don't get you this riled unless they're actively working against you."

"Felt like she was," he answered petulantly.

"And?"

Whitman pursed his lips. "I was trying to understand her magic well enough to find the right questions. Onto something, she could not grasp why I was asking what I was, and so she asked for a memory of my own to better understand my idea. I could not rightly give her anything recent, and so I gave her a memory of my past."

"Of your father?"

"Yes."

"Mmm," Oslan said. It had a sad tone.

"And now I have dredged up all of that again."

"I'm sorry, sweetheart."

"I work so damn hard to keep the present always 'now' in my mind with a healthy dose of the future. Looking back brings no one aid, but here I am, not five minutes later, and already torturing myself about something over which I had no control."

"Which memory did you give her to use?" Oslan asked.

"My father firing at that damn target."

"From before or after?"

"Before. I could not stand to see him stumbling about, waving the damn thing around ... He was not the same after she died, and I hated him for it."

Oslan leaned down and kissed Whitman's forehead, his breath and beard warm and tickling. "Can you take some time away? Rest here for a bit? Get your mind back together?"

"Probably not for long," Whitman answered sadly. He needed more time with his husband. They lived together, but Whitman missed Oslan desperately.

They sat in gentle silence for a bit, Oslan stroking Whitman's hair, Whitman seeking to drown himself in his lover's touch.

"I noticed you serviced your father's crossbow. After the attack."

His words were jarring. Whitman came back to the surface of wakefulness.

"Yes," he admitted shortly. "It saved me in a pinch; I found it only fitting." He sighed with frustration. "If I had kept it in better repair, it would have punched through the bastard's head instead of merely kissing the skull."

"It was a good shot."

"Of course it was. Perfectly on line. Would have taken his eye if not for the movement, and, even then, it was a killing blow. Had the string not been so slack."

Oslan smiled. "Your pride could hold the sun in the sky. It's a good tribute."

"I doubt he will care, being dead and all."

Oslan was silent.

"That was unkind. I am sorry."

"I know."

"I know you are trying to help. You are helping. I just ... I am angry."

"You always get angry when people give up."

"I think he was the first one to make me that way."

"He'd lost a child."

"I lost a sister. Donovan lost a child, and he is still carrying on."

"Yes, but I don't think he's carrying on quite so jovially as anyone else."

Whitman nodded, his hair mussing against Oslan's legs. "I wonder what Annette has him doing."

"I'd fear mutiny if we didn't trust Annette so much."

"Certainly. But I do. With my life and those of nearly every contact I possess. If something happens to Annette, I will lose quite a bit before gathering her notes, but our personal cipher is damn near impossible to break. If I did not get everything, no one else would either. And if anything happened to me, well ..." he shrugged.

"Well?"

"Anything she did not know, she could find in my notes and you would be able to pass along the day's work."

"There's so much in that busy head of yours that no notes can track."

"I do try."

"You write more than I do."

"I shall take that as a compliment."

"So long as you don't retire and turn to scribery," Oslan threatened playfully, holding up a pen-callused hand, faded ink stains like memories long forgotten all over his fingers and palm. The thick muscle there was as dire a threat as any axe or sword.

Whitman held up his own hands, begging for mercy even while he chuckled silently, his body shaking. "I would never dream of taking your work. Your penmanship puts mine to shame. They would fire me immediately."

"Only because you'd continue to correct their speech and translations."

"Yes, well. They should learn to speak more accurately. We have developed a complicated language for a purpose."

Oslan kissed Whitman's forehead again. "I have to go. The Forrester's guild is meeting."

"I love you."

"And I, you," Oslan said.

He rose and gathered his things, changing into his blacks. He winked at Whitman as he left.

The large man flopped his head down where his husband had previously been and sighed, closing his eyes. His thoughts still spun, as they always did, and an internal timer warned him that he had a meeting with Elliott in half an hour, but he tried to relax, and breathe out his frustration.

After a couple of minutes, he rose from the couch and went on his way. *Busy, busy, busy.*

* * *

"Have a drink, Whitman."

Elliott paced to his bottles and glasses, nearly spilling as he poured. Whitman saw his jaw tense as he wiped up the spill. Whitman sat back in his own seat and rubbed his leg; it ached more than usual today.

"I appear to have displeased you," Whitman said in a monotone. He stared ahead and let his eyes unfocus.

"I am not displeased," Elliott said over the sound of liquid pouring. The decanter clinked against the glass. "Merely as frustrated as I have been the last four months."

Whitman had no answer to give.

"How do we lose an entire army?" Elliott asked. "Better, how do we lose them and fail to find *any* useful sign of their passage? You say there's no sign at all. How is that possible? We estimated their numbers in the early thousands, and yet *no sign* can be found. Where are they? How did they disappear?"

Elliott handed Whitman a glass with a measure of peach-colored liquid, his own serving a good bit higher. Each of them sipped and Whitman licked his lips against the buzz and burn of the alcohol. He didn't often drink. In his line of work, it was an unwise habit, and he'd never enjoyed the flavor of alcohol besides. Whatever this was had a very sweet taste, but there was a spice that flowed behind it.

"We still have the group meeting in town."

"Any more murdered urchins?" Elliott asked.

"Not that we've discovered."

"Have you ordered the arrest of the butcher?"

"No."

"Have you arrested either of the package carriers?"

"No."

"And the rest of the members in the gathering?"

"No."

"I see."

"I have a man prepared to infiltrate their ranks."

"To become a Hunter?"

"To move amongst them. He will choose his time to gain trust, glean information, and then arrests can be made. It is my intention that the scare of capture moves the group away to meet with the brunt of the army."

"This is not the first attempt of this nature that you've made."

"No."

Elliott gave him a measuring stare. "Will your man be in regular contact with you?"

Whitman hesitated. "He ... is in a delicate role, and will certainly be watched, so unusual activity would be ... unwise."

"You're telling me that even with this man recruited, and you're sure he'll stay loyal, despite all, we still won't know where he goes with the rest of his new crew of blood mages."

"Likely."

"Whitman, I need something to help us *now*."

"I know, sir."

"The public is terrified. They need reassurances."

"You cannot make arrests without proof, Elliott. You cannot turn the city against itself. There will be riots."

"There will be riots anyway if we don't show *some measure of progress*."

"... I understand, sir."

Elliott rubbed his eyes. "I'm pushing you hard, Whitman, and I'm sorry for that. I'm pushing everyone hard, myself most of all.

We've been officially at war for nearly five months, and I have nothing to show for it except some terrified people, and the tension is building every day."

"It would be easier if they attacked, but they seem keen on waiting for our move."

"Which we struggle to make because of a lack of commitment on their part," Elliott agreed. "Stalemate." He drained his glass. "Please tell the guards to prepare cells and ready themselves for interrogations. I expect arrests to be made by tomorrow."

"I will inform your officers of the increased expectations." Whitman took a last polite sip of his beverage and rose to his feet.

"The knee seems to be doing better," Elliott said.

"Does it?" Whitman asked. He limped his way out. "Good afternoon, Bruno."

Bruno looked up from his busy desk and nodded distractedly. Whitman took a candy from the bowl and watched a page run in to trade a packet of documents for another before turning to run back out. Whitman whistled for his attention.

"Sir?" the boy spun to face him. He was probably twelve, dark-skinned and bright-eyed.

"You know the training grounds for the guardsmen?"

"Of course, sir."

"Do you know who is in charge at this time of day and where they can be found? Who their second is? Who the upcoming shift captain might be, or the one before them who might have signed previous orders?"

"Um, no sir. I can find out for you, though."

"You're twelve?"

"And a half."

"Plan on paging for much longer?"

"It helps my family's bills. I just got a new baby sister." He grinned broadly.

"That information is daily posted in the page's paper room. If you know everything, you are indispensable."

The lad nodded thoughtfully.

"On your way," Whitman shooed him and started on his own way at a much slower pace, stretching his knee and wincing. He hadn't recognized that boy; he must be new. The increase in the flow of instructions meant more slots for messengers — one of the Order's most valuable internal resources.

Soon enough, the change of wings was evident by the lack of civilians and the increased traffic of men and women in uniform. Many of them were in a hurry, jogging through the halls on their way to somewhere else, and several appeared to have just come off duty with their uniform jackets open, walking at a leisurely pace, exhausted.

The noise and smells were different, too. This part of the Order breathed far more the scent of boot polish, leather, and oil than of paper and ink. Whitman looked at the set of stairs before him with irritation. The next level up held offices, while this one gave access to the barracks, and outside to the training grounds.

"Bard Acres, sir!" someone called behind him.

Whitman turned about to find the source of the voice.

A uniformed woman jogged up to stop neatly in front of him. "Captain Gant saw you walk past and sent me to retrieve you."

"You are a wonderful person, Lieutenant, so save me from the horrors of unnecessary elevation."

Whitman followed her to the training grounds. The weather was warm with a slight breeze and Whitman took a deep breath, feeling it ruffle his shaggy hair and lighten his mood.

When was the last time I was outside? Even just with an open window? I really should get fresh air more often. I hear it can be good for you.

"Well, well, the bard Acres himself," came a hoarse and familiar voice.

Whitman followed the sound to its source in Captain Robert Gant, sitting with a handful of lower officers, all of them taking notes. Further out in the yard, soldiers were going through marching drills while other groups of various ranking guardsmen exercised or practiced with weapons. The calls and directions intermingled in a confusing jumble of shouted orders that the soldiers were nevertheless quick to obey.

As Whitman came close, the officers made space for him. Captain Gant put out a hand to shake and Whitman took it warmly, the soldier's scars still very rough against his palm. Those same scars showed themselves on the soldier's neck and face, marring his chin, lips, and left cheek. Most of his left ear was missing, and hair didn't grow on that side of his head. Luckily, both of his eyes and eyelids still functioned, though his left eyelid drooped in the corner. The burns were still very pink, and somewhat gruesome, but none of the officers were staring.

"I thought it was you I spotted wobbling through our hall."

"Doing well, I hope, Captain?"

"Exceptionally, Master Acres. Yourself?"

"Aching as always, but otherwise prime."

"What brings you to my yard?"

"Heralding the Head's orders, for your ears only."

"Would you excuse us?" the captain instructed the officers.

They all quickly dispersed, and Robert waved Whitman closer, gesturing to an area of benches used for large groups in outdoor classwork nearby. Robert straddled one and Whitman sat at a right angle to him.

"You look good," the spymaster said.

Robert ran a hand over his scalp and down his face. "The surgeons said it was as good as could be expected."

"At least you were saved a wobble."

Robert smirked. "I never did thank you for the promotion."

"You never did need to. Promotions do not come from bards."

"Right. What were the orders you're to deliver?"

Whitman kept his tone neutral. "Elliott wants public arrests, to make the town feel as though progress is being made. I will have a document drawn up of those people the Head has been watching. Not all of them are guaranteed blood magic users, but all of them need to be questioned."

"I see."

"The war is progressing, but it is quiet, and that makes people nervous."

Robert traced the nub of his left ear with a thumb. "This is going to turn the city against itself."

"The city has already turned against itself."

"Not like this. There will be more violence. People will feel justified in attacking their neighbors for suspicions and past wrongs, however thinly related."

"We will need double patrols."

"Triple. My guards understand the mood of the city. Echoes of it ripple throughout the ranks."

"If you need anything ..."

"I'll send word to the Head."

"Right."

"How's Donovan?"

"Doing well. I get little word, but he appears to be keeping his head in the land of haughty tempers."

"And Annette?"

"She thrives."

"I should write to them."

"They will be pleased to hear from you."

Robert's jaw tightened. "And the Smiling Man?"

"I promised to give any word I received on his whereabouts. As of yet, he has been silent."

"Not silent. Just quiet. You'll find him for me."

Whitman nodded. "And then you will know."

The two men shook hands again and Robert said, "I'll expect that list."

"I will have it delivered shortly."

Before Whitman could stand, a messenger burst through the doorway and into the yard to look around frantically. Robert frowned and stood, raising an arm. The messenger sprinted toward him, his eyes widening when he saw Whitman.

"Private message, Captain."

"Very well?"

The messenger handed over a hastily folded document, pacing from foot to foot. His breath was ragged from his sprint and sweat beaded his face. He kept glancing at Whitman who stared back, eyes narrowed, a dreadful thought forming in his mind.

Robert read the note with a carefully blank expression. Finished, he cleared his throat and tucked the note away into his breast pocket. "No return message."

"But sir —"

"It's Captain. Thank you. I'll see it dealt with."

The messenger's eyes darted toward Whitman again before he jogged off. Robert let the silence lengthen before he took the note out of his pocket again and read it a third time, the corner of his damaged lip between his teeth. Finally, he handed it to Whitman.

Hastily written, and blotched where it was not given enough time to dry, the note read:

Head of Order found dead
Main suspect Bard Whitman Acres
Take into custody immediately

Whitman felt the dreadful thought in his mind burst into a thousand painful shards as it finished forming and became shattering reality. His stomach fell into his bowels and his lungs seized. With shaking hands, he folded the note and returned it to Robert, who returned it to his jacket pocket.

"Well." Whitman cleared his throat and came to his feet, "I expect I should clear my schedule for the rest of the day."

*   *   *

Whitman blew gently across the page of text he'd been writing, urging it to dry faster. As he folded it, the door opened and Captain Gant entered with another guard, who stood respectfully at the door.

Whitman pushed the document into his hand. "Here is the list of possible suspects I mentioned for you."

Robert opened it and raised his eyebrows. "You wrote this by memory?"

"Yes."

He tucked the letter away and said, "I hope you're comfortable."

"As can be expected in the circumstances. Am I allowed to speak with a barrister?"

"Soon. We're still determining what could have happened."

"Gant, I am concerned."

"Yes?"

"Assuming the weapon was poison, please note that I drank from the same bottle as Elliott, but I feel no adverse effects. I want to make sure someone gets a hold of the correct alcohol and the glasses we used to check them for evidence."

Whitman handed him another note — this one with an intricately drawn floor plan of Elliott's room and writing at the bottom of the page.

"That is the best description of the alcohol and glasses used that I can come up with for you. My position in the room is marked there, and his movements are ... there. At the top is the list of everyone I saw on my way to and from his office, but of course there are back entrances to the place that servants and others would know of. I would be better able to gather that information for you were I to have access to my rooms."

"I appreciate that, Whitman. Unfortunately, we cannot let you leave just yet."

"Is the Order closing its gates? I did not hear the bell."

"We're keeping suspicion as low as possible, carrying on as normal."

"And while you do, the murderer is potentially getting away."

"We're hoping they carry on in their daily business as well, thinking that they got away clean."

"And at the end of the day, when they go home and never come back?"

"Whitman ..."

"Who is giving your orders? Do you know who has temporary rank in Elliott's absence? I do. Why have they not come to question me?"

"Question a bard?"

Whitman pursed his lips.

Gant said, "I get orders from my superior, as always."

"And you trust her?"

"Of course." He gritted his teeth and his lips twitched.

"Why am I in confinement? I cannot exactly run, and I would be much more useful in my office."

"You're suspected of murdering the Head of the Ord—"

"Suspected, not guilty. I need my barrister."

"One will be brought to you."

"Robert. You know I did not do this."

"I'm following the law, Whitman. Nothing more."

"And nothing less."

Captain Gant turned to leave.

"Stop," Whitman said. "I need my surgeon. My knee needs attending."

"I'll bring someone."

"Not someone — I need Lady Pennison."

"She's Head of Surgery, and likely very busy."

"I am aware of her position. As for her workload, has there been an influx of other injured persons, besides our recently deceased Head?"

"Whitman —"

"Bard Acres, thank you. Bring me Lady Pennison immediately. A delay could cause further damage to my injury, over which you would be held liable as soon as my barrister arrives."

Captain Gant gave him a long look and then nodded. "I'll ask her to come."

"Thank you, Captain."

Captain Gant and his guard left, locking the door behind them. Whitman stared at the stone walls surrounding him. The office was a small one, belonging to some junior officer of little note, and clearly few interests, judging by the lack of décor.

"Home sweet home ..." He drew a fresh piece of paper to him and wet his pen.

*   *   *

The gentle knock at the door was a call to battle. Whitman turned over the page of notes he was reviewing. Lady Pennison entered and closed the door behind her. Whitman saw a guard outside and guessed a second was less visible on the other side of the door.

The Head Surgeon looked at his knee, invisible behind the leg of his trousers, and said softly, "Looks to be everything is in order, Bard Acres. I hope you'll call on my services again in the future." She didn't move, however, and Whitman didn't answer.

They stared at each other in a stalemate of wills, but Whitman didn't mind. He knew she would speak first, and soon.

"You're my second patient of the day, Bard Acres."

"Yes."

"You know who my first was."

"Also yes."

"I assume you've a different facet to the story than that which I've heard."

"Not impossible, considering I have yet to hear the script and have only the truth in my possession."

"You poisoned the Head of the Order."

"Why?"

"Excuse me?"

"What would be my motive?"

Lady Pennison's hands twitched and tightened around each other. "I do not know you well enough to guess."

"Certainly. But there are others who believe they do. I would be interested to know what they assume my motivations to be in murdering a man I consider a great friend and have for many years." Emotion swelled in his breast. He closed his eyes and took a deep breath. His bardic theater training came to his aid in keeping his head clear, his eyes dry. Mostly.

"There is nothing more to be done about your knee at present, Bard Acres. Why else then would you request my presence?"

"I need your help with something incredibly important."

"I cannot promise anything to you, in the present circumstances."

"You are a woman of outstanding morality, and I do not doubt my request will fall to a willing heart."

She answered with a tilt of her head.

"I need you to find my husband, Oslan, and put him under your protection."

She frowned. "Why?"

"He is the single most important aspect of my life. Someone has seen fit to frame me for the murder of the Head of the Order, which means this person — or persons — has some specific hate for me. Easily deduced from that is the theory that they seek to hurt not only me, but those I love: my husband would be the next logical target. There has been one murder today. Do not allow there to be a second."

Her hands relaxed to her sides. "I will see what I can do."

Whitman held up a hand. "Please understand my next words very carefully. They are meant as a threat, and might substantially hurt your view of my innocence, but nevertheless must be said: If anything needlessly detrimental happens to Oslan, I will make it my mission in life to destroy not only those who hurt him, but those who failed to protect him. I would bring the Order to the ground. I would crush this kingdom and raze its fields if I believed for one single moment that it would bring me closer to taking the life of someone who dared breathe harm in his direction."

Lady Pennison's eyes widened and then narrowed as he spoke.

When he finished she said, "I understand. And thank you for telling me."

"Thank you for coming."

"It is my duty to see to all my patients."

Whitman suddenly thought to ask, "Would you be at all willing to continue keeping me updated on Kina's condition? I expect to be kept from her in the following days, and do not want to lose the opportunity to check her progress and consider more ideas for her improvement. Especially as a new plan was put into motion just a few hours ago."

Lady Pennison gave a vague smile. "I will do what I can."

"Thank you."

"Anything else?"

"What was the poison used?"

She froze. "I beg your pardon?"

"If Elliott was poisoned as suspected, what was the poison that was used to kill him?"

"We haven't yet determined."

"The symptoms then? Was there sweat? Froth? Blood? Are his pupils dilated? Is his tongue bloated or changed in color? Is his throat swollen?"

"I really couldn't say."

"Very well." Whitman leaned back in his chair, unimpressed with her unwillingness to share.

"You know poisons?"

"I'm a bard. I know everything. Second only to librarians, of course."

Lady Pennison smiled truly then, and let herself out without another word, the door locked behind her.

7

SHE SAW A RABBIT'S WARREN by one of the fence posts. Bending for a better look, a boy behind her said, "They left a month ago."

"Oh?"

"Aye. From my room, saw the babies hop away." He pointed at the side of the building where an unshuttered window gave a glimpse of a bunk room, nearly identical to her assignment. He stuck out his hand. "Dal."

She hesitated, but took it, "Wren."

"Newly woke, aye?"

She nodded.

"Saw you come with that blond bloke what left you," Dal said. "Wondered what happened 'til Valene said you weren't well."

Wren didn't have an answer, so she nodded again.

"Lotsa' folks have troubles when they come, but we mostly end up well enough." He crossed his eyes briefly and grinned.

She smiled.

"Making friends, Dal?" came an unwelcome voice.

"Aye." Dal suddenly became nervous.

Wren noticed then how slight he was and, as he reached for it, a faint red welt on his elbow, likely from an Elementalist's shock. Dal was prey here.

Wren stood and dusted her hands together. She eyed her surroundings and felt a flash of anger with herself — no adults in sight, an out-of-the-way area, and now seven lesser bullies with their leader surrounding her. And Dal. Prey.

"Who are you?" Wren asked the girl. She recognized her as the annoying one who tried to bully her earlier, but bullies didn't like to be forgotten.

Sure enough, the girl frowned with irritation. "Rowen," she snapped. "Don't bother with yours — you're nobody."

Wren smiled and raised an eyebrow. "The brave Rowen, here to bully nobody, fighter of nobody, winner of ... nothing."

A few of the children chuckled and Rowen turned red. Wren felt her own temper rising, but didn't know why. She wanted to fight, to hurt this girl, despite already having won with words.

"I hear you're an orphan. Killed your parents, freak? Or did they kill themselves for having birthed you?"

Wren laughed at the petty insult, but it sounded bitter in her own ears. "Better than being left unwanted," she shrugged.

Rowen grinned and Wren realized her mistake too late. She looked at Dal's sad, pale face. "I didn't know.

"You don't know anything," Rowen said, reaching for her elbow, lightning already crackling at her fingertips.

The shock burrowed up Wren's arm, stinging through her hand and shoulder. Her fury was immediate. She latched onto the girl's wrist, too large for her small hand to fully encompass, slender as it was.

All she needed was a touch.

She Drew on the bully's magic, so much less vast than Forest's — like a candle where his was a thousand stars on a moonless night. With little effort, lightning crackled at her own fingertips, buzzed through her frame. She gasped at the sudden energy. And anger.

Rowen fell to the ground, tears racing down her cheeks and fear in her eyes. Wren recognized the look. She flexed the magic, eager to explore it, and teach the others to leave her alone. Lightning was forefront to the earth, water, and the rest. She grew the arcs in her hands, letting it crackle from palm to palm. The circle of bullies spread away from her, children too afraid to run, but desperate to get away.

Her hands started shaking. Her eyes blinked rapidly. She felt dizzy.

Suddenly, the children were gone, adults in their place, all leering and shouting. She hated them, hated herself, but them more. In the crowd stood a tall man, bearded, with fearsome features, craggy and old, but she knew him to be far from human — he was like a storm, unpredictable and furious. Before she could lash out, something knocked into her, bearing her to the ground. The lightning coursed through her body, someone screamed, and her vision disappeared, reality taking its place.

Dal was on the ground beside her, hair all at end, eyes wide. He was crawling away — away from her. Rowen was running with so many other children — some throwing terrified looks over their shoulders. Most just ran.

Blackened grass surrounded her and showed in patches around, like she'd sent strikes of lightning out, attacking foes only she could see.

It still buzzed through her, but slower now. The anger was fading, leaving shame in its place, like cutting shards.

"What did you do?" Dal whispered.

"I — I don't know." The hated phrase.

The boy stood carefully and backed away, running to where the others had fled. An adult ran toward her now — a man with a worried expression.

"Get away," she said, rolling to her feet, magic readily burning in her palm.

The man skidded to a stop, his hands held placating before him. "Wren," he said. "Everything is safe here. You're fine."

"No ..."

She looked left and right, her vision blurry, like another picture was laid on top, trying to overtake her. She shook her head, then again more violently. The jeering and shouts were loud, overwhelming. She felt sick. The vision was spinning; she was spinning. Someone shrieked and she hit the ground again, gasping. She couldn't breathe, felt tears in her eyes. She clutched at the grass, felt it char in her hands. A sob escaped her.

"Let me have the lightning, Wren," the man said gently. "Can you give it to me?"

She opened her eyes and put out a limp hand, feeling numb, and yet full of overwhelming sensation all at once.

The man took her hand and she felt him Draw away the lightning like poison, but it left all the sensation in its wake.

"Better?" he asked kindly.

She shook her head, seeing the leering faces on her eyelids, her tears failing to blur them away.

* * *

The bare beginnings of Mentalist preparation had tried to teach him to compartmentalize his thoughts. Ruben had spent a week of classes picturing a stable where every stall, every bucket, every storage room and loft and bale of hay was a different category of thought. There, he kept his memories of his parents; there, his apprenticeship training; there, his childhood friendships.

He hadn't been very good, though the teacher had been kind. Still he'd sensed her frustration, impatience. She'd let him move on to using his magic, but he was sure she'd been pushed to do so by authority over her head — Whitman had suggested it was to have evidence of his progress for political reasons.

He wondered if he'd focused on that lesson, worked harder, pushed himself, if he'd be struggling as he did now.

He's an adept fighter even without magic.

He believes magi have a cost.

He was enslaved by people associated with the Order.

What else did he know, or believe, about the Smiling Man? He wracked his brain, patiently assembling his stable and organizing his thoughts. He had nothing but time.

He can do magic unheard of.

He will easily break oaths, turn on his allies if it suits him.

He craves challenge.

Ruben imagined Whitman's elation when he finally escaped and told the bard what he'd learned. He longed for his captivity to result in something useful for the Order, to help in the war.

Even as he thought that, he pictured Travis, and Laren, and Beth. He saw a nameless woman in the dining hall laughing at some joke, and another man stroking his sleeping child's hair. Did he want the Order to win the war, if it meant hardship to these people? They hated him, some did, but even in his town he'd known children to hate him for no other reason than because he was indentured.

It was a striking thought. If there had to be a war, who did he want to win? The Order, certainly — it was a place of learning, and had been filled with students and scholars and Healers. If the blood mages won, they'd tear it down, or teach their own magic instead, forcing those born mages into hiding — as they themselves now hid.

Ruben frowned. What was the difference? He pondered the Smiling Man's words: he'd claimed to have been enslaved by the Order. It was illegal to own slaves — the closest one could get to it was selling themselves or their children into contracts, as Ruben had been. There were rules around that, though, and if your master was breaking them, you could go to any guardsman and they would take your master to courts of the law — that's why they had those laws. Everyone knew that.

But he also knew the horror stories of indentured servants who hadn't fared well in the courts, and suffered for their trouble.

Ruben passed his fingers over the stone, playing with Seeking magic, increasing and decreasing his touch.

Out pain, in numb, out pain, in numb.

He'd said something about immortality, hadn't he? It was boring, apparently — what did he mean? Surely not true immortality ... he pictured the Smiling Man's odd flits between childish behavior and mature adult, pictured him switching to an aged fatigue between breaths. How old could he be? He set that aside, knowing he wasn't going to answer the question; he didn't know enough about history to begin to guess.

He changed tracks and once again pictured the Smiling Man's wound Healing, sealing, even after so much blood had spilled. So quickly! How was it possible? It was possible. If it was possible for the madman, it was possible for Ruben.

Out pain, in numb, out pain, in numb.

Other than Healing Donovan in the woods, he'd so far been unsuccessful in purposefully Drawing pain out of someone else — let alone getting rid of his own. This was different, though, wasn't it? This was Healing of a different *tier* — that was the word. Like Seeking and New Seeking. Vastly different, but similar at their root. The manipulation and control of senses, and the removing of self to Sense, to See surroundings ... It made sense then for Healing to have these tiers.

Out pain, in numb, out pain, in numb.

He had nothing but time ...

* * *

Ruben had been fed seven times, never enough to be filled, and only with bread and a vague mess of bland, stewed vegetables. He'd been watered ten times, and once again he was left in complete isolation. The hatch in the ceiling would open and a bucket on a leather strap would lower in on the end of a rope. He would unclip the strap and take the bucket and, after a few hours, they would lower the rope to take it back. The hatch was very quiet, greased, but he kept his hearing sensitive enough to know they were coming, and made sure that he wasn't practicing magic when they did. It meant that he couldn't do any Seeking to get away from his body and study the surroundings, but he could still practice plenty more.

He looked at the bucket in the light of the lightning he'd set around the room, floating it before him. It was wooden, sturdily made, but ultimately unable to withstand the pressure he used to Displace the pieces apart. He wasn't careful with the power, and shards burst in every direction, jagged edges whizzing past him, but he didn't blink. Simply let them all ricochet to the ground and chose one that fit his hand well.

He put his back to the wall and looked at his forearm, eyeing the soft flesh. It bore a few scars from his apprenticeship, and he could see the veins beneath the skin, like tiny rivers. He laid the jagged wooden edge to his arm and pressed, hesitated. He struggled to commit the violence against himself.

It shouldn't be difficult — skin was fragile. He'd bumped and scraped himself all over the walls of his cell, but had so far failed to Heal any of that. He'd injured himself many times in his few years, but this was the first time it was intentional, and that seemed to make all the difference. He pulled the makeshift knife away and again examined his arm. The Madman, as he'd taken to thinking of him, had dug his blade deep, but that had been with a knife, sharp and made for cutting. Ruben lacked any sort of tool in his cell.

What if he didn't succeed? What if he bled and they didn't find him in time? Worse, what if they were watching him now, waiting for him to show weakness? What might they do? He'd fallen asleep twice and each time suffered nightmares that brought him to horrible wakefulness, shaking and sweating, fearing a presence in the darkness, watching him.

He bared his teeth. That was no way to live.

Again, he laid the jagged wood to his arm and pressed firmly. Realizing his mistake, he quickly lowered his sense of touch to barely anything, allowing him to properly grip the wood and control his actions, to all but remove the sensation, and therefore fear, of pain.

It helped, but still he hesitated until, gritting his teeth, he forced himself to yank downward. It hurt, even without most of his sense of touch. It hurt in his mind, seeing that injury on his body. It hurt as though the idea of his arm had been offended, and his mind was imagining the sensation as he watched the torn and jagged skin stain red.

Blood welled around the wound. He tossed the wood aside and eyed the cut. If he couldn't Heal this, he would need help or risk infection and worse. He gripped his wrist and focused. He pictured the wound coming together, closing cleanly. Breathing slowly, measured, *concentrating,* he imagined the sensation: how wounds itched and tickled as they healed, the bruising, the scabs forming and falling away, the shiny pink skin revealed beneath the bandage.

Nothing happened.

Worry sped his heart and he imagined the blood was falling faster. He tried to keep his composure, grateful that he couldn't feel the punishment for his stupidity. He tried to pinch the slippery edges of the wound, willed them to close, to gather. Magic was the result of focused intention, right? Why wasn't it working?

Planning ahead, he'd torn his shirt into strips for a bandage and grasped for one now, trying to wrap it tightly with one hand. He was soon covered in blood, his hand and torso slick and the numbness doing nothing to help his coordination.

Hating himself for it, he nevertheless yelled, "Help! I've cut myself. It's very bad! Please help!"

No response.

"Please!" he tried again. "Please help me! I'm sorry, I've made a mistake!" He pressed the sodden bundle of cloth to his arm, applying pressure as fear grew in his belly. He slid down the wall as his knees started to give way. He wasn't yet light-headed, but he was sure it would come soon.

Finally, the hatch opened, and a woman glared down at him. He stood unsteadily and held his arm out for her to see. Her eyes widened and she slammed the trapdoor shut again. Ruben winced at the noise and stared upward impatiently, refusing to look at the injury in case it had gotten worse.

Only a few moments passed before it opened again. Two men, one burly and the other smaller, dropped down into his cell with another two people up above to watch. They had crossbows ready to lose in his direction

"What did you do?" the burly man asked angrily, grabbing Ruben's arm. He was sure he would have screamed if not for being numb.

"I — I was trying to practice Healing. I thought I could do it."

"With a wooden bucket, you made this injury?" the smaller man asked calmly.

Ruben nodded.

"This needs stitching, Dan — throw down my kit!" the burly man told the others above.

They did so and the second man, Dan, caught it deftly and handed it over.

"Sit," the first man told Ruben, joining him on the floor. "You've numbed your arm?"

Ruben nodded again.

"Good. That'll save time. Idiot boy."

Despite telling himself the same thing, the words stung, and he fought back tears as the man threaded a needle and started stitching. Ruben watched, more fascinated than disgusted, as the delicate thing popped into and out of his skin. Dan helped push the wound closed to keep the line as straight as possible. They didn't speak to Ruben except to give him instruction: relax, move this way, don't flinch.

When it was done, the burly surgeon cleaned the wound with water they passed down from above, and let Ruben clean his torso as well. Another bucket was poured over the floor to wash away what had spilled.

"*Don't* do that again. We'll let you pass out next time, hear me?"

Ruben looked at the tightly stitched injury and nodded.

"Leave those alone, too. Don't pick at them. If infection starts, I'll have to clean it out, and you won't like that. We'll bring soap and water to keep yourself clean, but don't think we'll be careless, right?"

A ladder lowered and the two ascended, pulling it up behind them. The door in the ceiling slammed again. Ruben sat on the ground, running numb fingers over the stitches. He let the lightning in the room fade, and let the darkness claim him. Despair was close. He fought it, but knew his resolve was trickling away, like blood in the drain.

*　　*　　*

He was fed and watered several more times and the soapy water was delivered as promised. He ate and drank mechanically, cleaned his wound, but otherwise laid and stared at the darkness. Sleep was easy. Once, he found himself staring at stars. It took him a while to realize he'd inadvertently been Seeking — his mind was searching for escape while his body was trapped.

After a few more sleeps, which could easily have been in a single day, the hatch opened and a ladder was lowered. He stared at it uncomprehendingly, waiting for a person to descend until someone above asked, "Are you coming?"

Surprised, but still slow to react, he found his feet and carefully climbed the ladder, checking that he placed each hand and foot securely, unable to feel the grip.

People were here, but he didn't look at them, wanting to lie down again. The light hurt his eyes and he winced away from it. He remembered the last time he'd been freed, and cried to see a window.

He was led out of the cells again and had to concentrate on where he placed his feet. People spoke to him, but he barely heard them, and didn't care enough to focus on the distant buzzing of their voices. He stood in a hall until someone came out and spoke. He made the effort to look up at her. She said something and it took him a moment to hear it, like he was deep under water.

"Wha'?" His tongue felt thick and hard to move. His eyes didn't want to focus.

She spoke again, but not to him, so he looked back at the floor. He was led in another direction. A woman led the group and he watched her thick curls bounce as she walked. The light made them shine.

The hallway shifted and he tilted his head, trying to understand and shake the fuzz from his mind. The ceiling was up. He must have fallen. But he was still moving — carried? It was easier to close his eyes and drift away.

"Ruben. *Ruben.*" The voice was coming from far away, and he swam lethargically toward it. Something was very wrong.

"Can you hear me?"

He moved his head in an approximation of a nod.

"I need you to stop your magic, Ruben."

"No' usn'."

"Yes you are, Ruben. You're Seeking, right?"

"Mmm."

"You need to stop."

"'s gun'hrt."

"No, see? You have ointment on your cut. See?"

He looked at his arm. The stitches had a thick layer of yellow balm on top.

"It's there to keep it from hurting. You don't need to Seek, Ruben."

"Mmm."

He tried to concentrate. He could vaguely remember when it hadn't been this difficult to adjust his senses however he pleased.

"Ruben?"

He blinked hard and scrunched his face. Slowly, ever so slowly, he felt the magic change and fade. As it did so, it allowed the sensation to flood back in and he gasped, increasing the shield of numbness again.

"No, no, Ruben. Let it go. You're all right, I promise."

"No …" he moaned.

"Yes. You need to let the numbness fade."

"It hurts."

"Not bad, though. Like an icy pool until you warm up, right?"

He tried to push the magic away again, writhing and twisting as feeling rushed back. Like a thousand pins stabbing at his nerves.

He cramped and ached and even the air stung his skin. His stomach rumbled and his head throbbed.

"Ow ..."

"All right, boy."

He looked at her as the fog in his mind started to finally burn away. He blinked a blurry film from his eyes. She appeared to be about two decades his senior, but still had freckles around her green eyes. He'd always liked freckles.

"Hello there," she said.

"Hi?"

"Do you know what happened?"

"I ..." He looked at the salve smeared on his wounded arm and winced as another wave of pins rolled through him. "I don't know."

"You can't Seek like that." Her tone was cool, not quite icy.

Ruben focused on her voice and struggled to keep from Seeking the pain away again.

"Stay numb for too long and you forget what sensation is. Stay blind for too long and you'll injure your eyes; stay deaf and you'll find it hard to hear again. Every magic has a cost."

"Not to me, though, right?" His tongue seemed to be obeying better.

She pursed her lips briefly. "Even you."

Realization struck him and Ruben sat up sharply to stare around. His head spun at the sudden movement, but the Smiling Man was nowhere to be seen. The room was full of beds and curtains. There was a desk and a few chairs and cabinets, but no Smiling Man sneering down at him.

"He's away," she told him.

"Where? He'll be back."

"Yes, he will, but not yet."

He looked back at her and blinked. "Who are you?"

"Feeling better?"

"Um, I think so. My arm hurts." He cradled it to his chest.

"Yes, I expect so. That happens when you cut a gash into it with a chunk of wood."

The embarrassment didn't come, and he offered no explanation. She didn't seem to expect one.

"I want to talk to you. Think you can focus enough to listen?"

Ruben nodded, curious what she wanted to say. She stood and checked the room, speaking to someone out of sight, and returned to sit beside the bed he'd been laid on.

"My name is Wren and I am in charge here."

"Oh?" He hadn't expected that. Her voice was familiar, though … that moment in the training room, before the cell. A voice, her voice, had ordered the Smiling Man to stop.

"I need your help." The words seemed unfamiliar to her mouth. She leaned forward conspiratorially.

He resisted the urge to lean away, but it was a near thing.

Wren whispered, "I need your help to end him."

The hairs on his neck and arms stood to attention and a shiver meandered down his spine. His hands grew warm as he unconsciously summoned fire to defend himself, but stopped the magic before he set the linens aflame.

She sat back, and looked him in the eye. "We have very little time."

* * *

They sat on the floor face-to-face. She hadn't said anything since her revelation, and he hadn't asked questions as she led him from the medical room to her office. The space was filled with books, mostly in neat piles or shelved, but occasionally stacked haphazardly, many laying open on top of others or used as markers themselves. A couple of the piles lay in the middle of a slow collapse and the desk was nearly invisible, hidden amongst the pages. A thick rug covered the floor and very little furniture was available, all shoved toward the walls and out of the way.

The remains of the pins threaded through his limbs and back and he shifted uncomfortably. Fear boiled his stomach as he wondered what the Smiling Man would do when he returned and found him out of his cell, planning mutiny with this woman.

She controls him, he reminded himself sternly. It didn't help.

"Before we go any further," she said, seemingly sensing his thoughts, "I have to teach you to protect your mind. He'll know I've done it, but he loves the contest. He's constantly challenging himself, especially with magic, and he sticks to his rules. He'll assume I've told you to kill him, to try, to take his place. I've done it before, and somehow he twists it about in his mind to believe I'm merely testing him. His madness works to our advantage in some very small, but significant ways.

"That said, you must master this technique, today, before I let you go from here."

Ruben hugged his knees to his chest, staring at her. "You don't think he has spies here, listening at your door?"

She smiled faintly. "You're wise to be suspicious, but you don't know him as I do. If you wish to leave, I can't stop you."

He pondered the words. "Can't ...?"

"You're a magus," she replied flatly. "I'll inflict damage, I imagine, but eventually I'll be overwhelmed."

"You're a life mage, though?"

"I know life magic. You'll learn more about that, but it would only prolong the combat, and likely still fail to defeat you."

"No, I — I mean," he stammered, "But you're the leader here. Why can't you just let me go?"

"Leaders are in charge because their followers believe they deserve to be. So?" She stared at him expectantly, green eyes piercing right through him with no resistance.

"So ... the people don't want me freed? They'd turn on you?"

"Good."

"Why do you want him dead?" Ruben rubbed his jaw as a wave of pins rolled through it. "He's your best advantage in the war, right?"

She closed her eyes for a long moment, then opened them, wearing a sad smile. "Do not expect me to take the time to explain the complexities of my years-long campaign to a prisoner — whatever his power and position otherwise might be. Will you learn what I have to teach you?"

Startled at her response he answered, "I'll learn, of course I'll learn."

"Good. This is Mentalist magic, and I have no way to show it to you, I can only describe it, so concentrate. It's one of their basic techniques, so you should pick it up fairly quickly."

He folded his legs and straightened his back. Her eyes were closed, and he followed suit.

"Mentalist magic is no more complex than any other. Their power lies in the mystery and fear and regard others hold for them. The complexity comes from walking a line of danger, and morality, which, of course, you will not need to consider. Imagine now ... your mind is a castle, a mansion. Brightly lit and littered with rooms — dozens, hundreds of rooms of every size."

Ruben's eyes popped open. "I have one of those: it's a stable. Like my Seeking room. I did take beginning Mentalist classes before you kidnapped me, you know."

Wren blinked at him. "Well, that makes things significantly easier."

Ruben bit his lip. "I'm not very good, but I've been practicing. I know what to do. In theory."

"Theory won't be enough. Work. Get it right."

He nodded urgently.

She continued, "Good. As for your worry of listeners at the door, he doesn't have friends or allies. Those require trust, and he doesn't trust anyone. The people here are loyal to me, so long as I don't ask of them more than they think themselves capable. They have learned that I am their best chance of surviving your people, and he has decided the same. For now, our goals align."

"Surviving my—" Ruben felt the anger brewing. "*Your* people kill mine! For no reason! You kill children!"

"The same can be said of your people, Ruben," she snapped. "Everyone who thinks they are just in their cause kills children — for the crime, the sin, of being the wrong sort of mage. Families are destroyed because they *might* be the cause of fear in the future. Open your eyes, boy!"

Something smacked into the back of his head, and he pitched forward, snapping back up to defend himself.

"Put those fires out. They won't help you read."

Ruben extinguished his flames in a moment, embarrassed, and then angry at his embarrassment. The object of his fury floated in front of him, pages slowly turning.

"Wha— you're ... you're a Displacer?" he said slowly.

She scoffed, prideful. "No. But an acceptable guess." The book floated toward him and he took it. The cover was blank.

"What is this?" he rubbed the back of his head now.

"He wants a student; I want a savior. We both want a weapon. Don't think my intentions are noble. Because I do expect you to kill him when you get the chance, just as he intends to have you kill your friends — and probably me — to show your loyalty to him. Hopefully, you'll see my side of things before those particular teachings take root."

Ruben's breath trembled in his lungs. "So far, I'm on your side of things."

"Good. I'll find someone to teach you life magery. In the meantime, read the book and consider a new perspective. You'll find that some are drawn to a path of righteousness, and others find that to be too much work. Some strive to make a better world, and the rest decide to take what they can, to go too far. Magic is free for everyone who wants it. Some are born to it, and have to decide what to do with their abilities. They can destroy, kill if they want, steal from those too weak to resist. Or they can create, improve humanity for everyone to enjoy.

"Those who aren't born to magic have the same choice. They can learn to harness the earth's powers, to make a better life for themselves and those around them, or they can go too far, and do too much, take too much. Seeing a pattern here?

"Choices are free. Sometimes you even escape from the consequences of your actions —

It's not fair, but that's life. The consequences always catch up to someone, and that someone might cause a lot of damage, depending on how much of your consequences they catch."

"You're ... very confusing."

"Yes, I expect so." Her lips thinned. "This war is nothing more than a stockpile of consequences. These prejudices are not your own, but side effects of long-held grudges from people you've never met."

She stood in a smooth motion and Ruben scrambled to his feet as well, clutching the book tight under his uninjured arm.

"I'll send someone to teach you soon. You don't have to learn, but I recommend you try to seize any advantage. *He's* done this before, and will do it again. Keep that in mind when you imagine you might know something he doesn't."

"Done this? Kidnapped people?"

"Kidnapped magi."

Ruben frowned. "How many?"

She shrugged one shoulder. "At least one, probably another. He's older than he looks, and his techniques are effective." She grimaced. "Lock your memories away. If he comes for me in earnest, I'll assume you failed. That's the cost of trust."

"I'll do it," he promised.

"Get some rest. Your teacher will come in the morning. I expect you to pay attention."

Ruben let himself out and walked slowly back to his above-ground room, his mind mulling over the conversation. He realized with a jolt that he was alone, without a guard, and without the Smiling Man in residence to confine him. He stopped short and looked up and down the corridor, then down at the book in his hands. It had no title, and smelled old.

He started to walk again as heaviness settled over his shoulders. He'd already decided once that he couldn't leave without answers, and now he was finally getting them. Time would tell if he was making the right choice, but there was nothing to do now except wait for the consequences to catch up with him.

8

"I see you found me after all."

She lay in the grass, utterly spent. This hill was the last of the miles she'd walked, run, staggered, knowing where to find him, and unable to stop until she did. Once she'd gotten through the memories he'd left her, she'd found this location buried at the end. She would have sobbed, but didn't have the energy.

"I expected more of you, frankly. You came in good time, but you fail within sight of your target." He tutted mockingly.

She pushed herself upright with trembling arms and saw his boots ten feet from her. She brought her knees up underneath and crawled haltingly to kneel within reach, to lay a finger on the brown leather tip of his boot. Her breath came hard in her aching chest and she barely had the strength to brush a piece of errant hair from her mouth.

"There. Don't you feel more accomplished now?" He crouched down before her, bouncing youthfully on his calves. He put a finger under her chin and lifted her heavy head. She didn't want to meet his eyes — she knew clearly now the horrors she would see reflected there.

"A bit," she admitted. "Because —" The knife was wickedly sharp. It went into his thigh with barely any resistance.

He grunted with fury and kept his balance with a hand in the grass. Their faces were very close now.

She hissed in his ear, "Don't ever, ever give me your horrible memories without my permission. I will kill you next time."

He returned the knife with an appreciative nod and she cleaned it while he Healed himself, sweating with the effort. When he helped her to stand, he kept an arm companionably around her shoulders. She cringed at his touch, but only inside, where it was harder for him to see.

"Behold, the glorious and all-powerful life mages, masters of ... well." His voice was heavy with derision. Tents and a few newer permanent buildings littered a valley below them. It wasn't a terribly small town, but it should be in a better state, considering the nearby river and number of hands to work the fields around the place. They must have only just settled, still organizing leadership.

"They think I'm but another poor, helpless follower of their beliefs, come to build anew and try, try again to survive. How long do you think they'll last when the born mages learn they're here?"

She shook her head wearily. "I just want to sleep. I'm too tired for your games."

"Never. Games are the point of living." He looked down at her and seemed to realize she wasn't jesting. A deft scoop of her legs and she was in his arms, head lolling against his chest.

"What did you do to me? It's like I can't think straight, and all of these images, these feelings are banging around in my head, confused and muddled ..." she trailed off, voice thick with emotion.

"Don't fall asleep yet, Beast. I want to tell you a story."

* * *

Donovan huddled deeper into his cloak and cursed the cold morning air. No one else seemed to mind it, all of them riding about as though they couldn't see their breath. It was getting warmer, turning into a perfect spring day, but until then, it was too cold for his bones.

This morning, he traveled with a group of one hundred-odd men and women, most of them very young, barely adults, and all of them in military training. The caravan of recruits would be on the road for several hours today and the formation rode in near silence except for the stomping of horse hooves. Officers rode through the ranks periodically to scold and threaten and correct. At the end of their group followed a supply train of ten wagons with food, clothing, weapons, armor, mail, and other goods. It was guarded by more recruits with several veteran soldiers assisting.

At the head of the train rode Lord Baron General Vernon Ost in his finery. Medals and markings decorated the shoulders and breasts of his crisp royal blue uniform, declaring his rank and bravery. Several high-ranking officers rode beside and behind him. Donovan rode behind them with the lower-ranking officers. He sat back in his saddle, patting his horse's neck. The creature was plenty patient, and more than willing to follow the others with little guidance. Ost had clearly seen that he wasn't a skilled horseman and had supplied him accordingly.

The miles went by slowly and he had nothing to do but worry vaguely about Whitman, and Annette, and Cara. He smiled thinly, imagining showing up at the Order to find Cara running the place. His smile fell when he remembered that, with Elliott murdered, the position was currently void. Poor man. What could have happened?

The young woman who had awakened Donovan the previous afternoon trotted outside of the train to catch up with him with infinitely more skill than he would ever possess. She came alongside him and said, "The Lord General requests your presence at the front."

Donovan thanked her and she wheeled her mount, racing further down the line, probably to deliver more messages. He urged his horse out of the formation and past the mass of officers ahead of him. A few nodded as he went by. Mostly he was ignored, which suited him just fine.

When he came within sight of General Ost, the nobleman waved off his other attendants. They had to speak loudly to be heard over the noise of the horses, but that meant that eavesdroppers would be easily spotted, hovering too close.

"How are you, Rudd?"

"Very well, General, thank you," Donovan answered. "A bit sore. I've not spent much time in the saddle."

"Not even out picking up children for the Order?" His eyebrows perked up into his hairline.

Donovan corrected himself, "Rather, I haven't spent much time recently. And even then, I was only passable. Depending on the distance, it was common enough for us to walk, General. Especially when you consider that most children we collected didn't know how to ride."

"Eh, seems a waste to walk most of the time," Ost mused to himself. "This trip is to teach my youngsters the basics of several things before joining the main army. It is not a trip for comfort, I'm afraid. We'll eat in the saddle at noon, jumping to a trot shortly after. Be sure to stay up front; they'll learn not to gorge themselves on the road pretty quickly. After the colorful festival, we'll dismount for an hour to give everyone a chance to clean up and get steady feet. And learn to tolerate a few hours' hunger."

"When do we make camp?" Donovan asked.

"About two hours before nightfall," came the ready answer. "A river passes through this edge of my land and I want the recruits to know how to use it before they arrive. Don't worry about camp; you're a visitor and will be treated as such. I have people assigned to you. They'll find you, or I'll beat their heads in."

"You're very kind, General," Donovan said.

"I'm no such thing. I want a proper army, is all, and sometimes that means readying camp for visiting dignitaries and suchlike. We'll ride at dawn tomorrow and be with the main army before noon."

"The trip could be made in a day, then?" Donovan asked.

Ost nodded. "Easily, for a single rider. More than one hundred people slows it down, some. The king has always wanted me on hand, and granted me lands with that in mind."

"Thank you for the information, sir."

"I'm sure you're wondering why I invited you here, Donovan," the general said.

"I was curious," he admitted. "I assumed you had reasons beyond teaching your Seekers."

"Indulge me for a moment. I appreciate the privacy the road brings, but if you wouldn't mind increasing your hearing, and I will do mine, we can virtually guarantee not to be overheard, even by accident."

Donovan did so, watching the man's lips to gauge how sensitive his hearing needed to be. His face froze in a grimace as the sound of the wind passing by, the breath of the horses, the creak of leather, and stamp of hooves grew increasingly louder.

Finally, Ost boomed a whisper, "My military has recently found itself with a host of deserters. I hope to use your skills to locate them and bring them back to the brotherhood of arms. Does that surprise you?" the general asked to Donovan's silence.

"Terribly," Donovan whispered in reply.

"I apologize for the subterfuge, but I could not trust this topic to notes or share them where others might overhear. The situation is mine to fix and not a thing for courtly gossip — seeing our ranks as weakened would only encourage the enemy."

"I expect that is a reasonable fear to maintain."

The general nodded. His expression was neutral, but a crinkling in the corners of his eyes revealed to Donovan that the volume was taking a toll on him as well.

"My apologies, General, but what exactly do you expect me to do to assist you while I am here?"

"I had hoped that your reputation would inspire some of these people to see that their cause is not justified, but merely a misunderstanding."

"You want me to endorse you," Donovan confirmed.

"I need a neutral party to locate them. Our training includes ways to hide from Seekers, and they are putting the skills we trained into them to use. I expect them to contact you in some way and allow me to call off the search, which has risked more deserters and rumors to fester."

"I'm to negotiate their return?"

"To be something of an ambassador."

"Forgive me, but these are dangerous people by trade. Have they not told you what their grievances are, and why they are leaving your ranks?"

"They lack leadership, and what we've heard has no substance. We hope in your ambassadorial duties that you could find out exactly what they want — solidify their cause, as it were. As for your concerns of safety, well. Most of the kingdom sees you as something of a celebrity, Master Rudd. Harming you would only harm themselves."

"I see."

"I believe they are operating out of a base camp on my land, near enough to my castle to spy in person, and not exclusively rely on the defectors left behind. If that is the case, we might have a lead on the whereabouts of the rest of them. I have no doubt that they are carefully watching us. Your arrival will not go unnoticed."

Donovan remained silent. He didn't know what to say, but he was irritated.

The general looked at him.

"Sir, I'm a teacher," Donovan explained. "What makes you believe I could be capable of tracking down deserters and negotiating their return?"

The general gave a wry smile. "How long have you worked for the Order, Rudd?"

"Sixteen years."

"How many children have you fetched and brought back?"

"Very many."

"How many times were you pursued by Hunters?"

"I had very capable partners." A lump came to his throat, which made it difficult to whisper.

"How many times did you have to convince a parent to part with their child, for the betterment of the child's future?"

"Many."

"You never lost a single child. All I need from you is to find them, understand their desires, and convince them to listen to reason."

"And if they decide I'm one of the enemy?"

The general closed his eyes for a moment. "Then I wouldn't put money on your chances. But Master Rudd, we are at war. I do not expect your obedience, but I expect your loyalty. If you cannot do this, tell me now."

"... I understand."

"Excellent. Lunch will be passed out soon."

The general's eyes relaxed, and Donovan lowered his hearing to normal, relief coursing through him. A vague headache and nausea had set in, but he was able to ignore them as he rode back to his original place in the line. The general's dismissal had been clear.

Soon enough, junior officers rode down the lines with baskets hanging off the sides of their saddles, passing out bread. Another came down the lines with cheese, another with some kind of fowl, and the last two with apples. It was basic fare, but smelled delicious. Donovan kept his at hand, waiting.

Sure enough, the order to speed to trot was trumpeted. The bouncing and jarring didn't bother Donovan much — his beast had as smooth a trot as he'd ever experienced, and he had plenty to think about since Ost's conversation. He scowled at the eventual sounds of puking behind them and looked distastefully at the officers' grimly amused expressions.

One saw his expression and said, "It's the water. Half of them have refilled their canteens more than once, which means their bellies are full. Add even this food to that, and the salt on the turkey makes them drink more ..." he shrugged. "You learn to be aware of your belly."

"I'm glad I was never in the military."

The officer smiled politely and rejoined his peers.

The signals for walking came at last and they all slowed their horses. Donovan ate his lunch, saved his apple, but shoved the meat and cheese into his bread for a sandwich. Ost's words bounced around in his mind now, and he wondered: how many deserters did the military experience in any given year? He knew the size of the kingdom's army was immense, but there was no draft — discharge was granted on request, though breaking contract did void any benefits you might otherwise receive. How many deserters would it take to cause this kind of worry? He found himself watching the tree lines, feeling new tension and discomfort in every step his horse took.

The stop that Ost had promised wasn't very long, but was welcome nonetheless. He'd spoken truthfully to Ost about a Retriever's time in the saddle, — it had been long enough that Donovan was experiencing soreness in unfortunate places.

Arrival at the river showed the camp set up at perfectly acceptable speed to his mind, but officers walking past kept *tsk*-ing and *tutt*-ing. Several walked up and down the rows of blooming tents to yell and order the recruits about. Near-screams of *"Is this what you call a straight line?"* and *"Do you want to see your squad trip over your ropes?"* and *"I have not seen a mess this incredible since my dog was shooting from both ends, soldier!"* came echoing through the air.

As Ost had promised, two recruits found him shortly after they had dismounted and whisked his horse away to be groomed and watered. Another two appeared a few moments after that to lead him to a small tent being erected with speed and skill. An officer looked on, but apparently found nothing to criticize. Poor thing. As soon as it was raised, they all disappeared to other tasks.

Donovan tossed his pack inside and laid out his bedroll to make the space comfortable. He wished he had someone to speak to. It had been a long time since he'd been alone, and loneliness wasn't an emotion he had expected to experience.

Even when Ost invited him to dine, the conversation stayed on the topic of duties, and he had little to contribute. Afterward, the camp quieted quickly, and, despite the silence, Donovan had trouble finding sleep. Nothing was comfortable. He had to get up and find a trench to pee in, he couldn't get warm ...

With no one nearby, he dug into his pack and pulled out a slim, unlabeled book. He'd barely glanced at the untitled cover before hiding it amongst his shirts, assuming, like most of the others had been, that it would be more stories and mythology and history, but nothing substantial. If he couldn't sleep, he might as well study.

It didn't take him long to realize this was something other than what he'd previously read. Every other page had drawings of a woman or just her hands or fingers moving in an attempt to explain motion on a page, several in each row giving a sequence to help clarify. The first picture was something mundane, and the last was a change to the mundane action: seed scattered for chickens, wood chopped, a pit filled in with dirt.

He flipped curiously through the pages. The book was old, and the pages were dry and stained; some of the drawings heavily faded where countless hands had passed over them. He was reminded of his childhood primer, used to teach him letters and numbers. It had been owned by his mother, her brother, their father, and beyond, carefully put away when the children no longer needed it, and brought out for use when the family had new additions.

He wondered vaguely what had happened to the primer. His daughter Kelsa had it last. Did Cara take it when she left? He forced his mind away from the thought with practiced familiarity, and back to the book at hand.

There were a dozen pages with motions and half a dozen more with word examples:

Soft sounds for soft actions, hard sounds for hard actions:
Clean has hard sounds — might this break the dish?
Wash has soft sounds — might this lather the dish?
Heavy words for heavy actions, light words for light actions:
Fly is a light word — might this ease the load?
Bear is a heavy word — might this increase the load?

He stared at the words, mind moving as though in syrup. The words and action examples were all of day-to-day tasks and chores, the pictures showing effects after the motions were taken ... This *was* a primer. This was a primer for blood magic. Seeing it presented this way, written for children, his mind presented him with gallows humor for the natural course of a blood mage:

Kill has hard sounds, maim has soft sounds ...

He continued to flip through the pages, hoping for more information. For its simplicity, this was far, far more information on blood magic itself than he'd previously found in all of the tomes and texts he'd spent the last several months reading. Still, there was little to it. It didn't explain anything else, only gave suggestions for words and motions to make for the desired effects. His lightened mood slowly sank. His treasure was on a higher shelf, but at least he knew he'd found the right room this time.

He silently berated himself for bringing the thing. What if it was lost, or damaged? It had seemed a good idea at the time, but now he cursed himself for a fool as he wrapped it back up and returned it to his bag.

As he tried to relax, he found sleep even harder to find now with the images of the pages flipping through his mind. More than that, a feeling of wrongness ticked in his mind. His neck hair stood on end. He lay still, eyes closed, and listened. The camp was still and quiet. His tent flaps moved slightly in a breeze. He raised his hearing to pick apart the noises he heard: horses on the other side of camp, the river a fair ways behind the tents, recruits snoring softly tents away. No wind shifted the grass outside. Nothing was wrong.

Hold. With no wind to shift it, how could his tent flaps move?

His eyes snapped open and he stared through the darkness. The tent material was too thick to see a shadow through but, with increased vision, he could see a pale hand slowly, *slowly* untying the flap from the inside.

Heart racing, Donovan pondered his options. If he attacked and didn't get through the tent flap fast enough, the person could escape, but if he let them enter, they might be able to act before Donovan could. A crossbow at this close of range didn't need much time or skill to aim, and a drawn sword could carve him to pieces before he'd cleared his blankets.

Before he'd decided on the action he wanted to take, the hand withdrew and the flap was eased open. A person stepped inside, and let the flap hang behind them. They took a careful step further in, probably to let their eyes adjust to the increased darkness.

Donovan let out a wordless shout as he threw off the blanket. He lunged to his feet, stumbling slightly across the bedding. The intruder swiped an empty hand at Donovan's face and Donovan twitched backward to trip over his bedding and land hard on the not-very-thick bedroll. The attacker came forward, leaning toward him. Donovan threw a boot from beside his pack, hitting the would-be-attacker square in the face. He soon had his Order knife in hand and the intruder was escaping out of the tent and into the night.

Donovan pursued in earnest. Either this was one of Ost's deserters, and he could get that task finished and out of the way to rejoin his companions, or this was a blood mage whose testimony could help bring more information about the war to Whitman's ears.

They might know where Ruben was.

Red colored his vision. Donovan leapt and caught the fleeing man around the knees, dragging him to the ground. With acrobatic grace, the man squirmed free and tried to flip to his feet, but Donovan had a grip on his leg that would leave bruises.

"ALL HANDS ALL HANDS RISE TO READINESS! ATTACK, ATTACK ON THE CAMP!" Donovan bellowed. He clambered to his feet as the intruder wriggled free of his grip.

The attacker drew his own knife and stabbed at Donovan. Donovan staggered backward and swiped his Order knife at the man's wrist as he withdrew. They traded slashes and stabs, each successfully dodging for now, but the attacker was getting desperate — he would soon be hopelessly outnumbered.

The camp was waking in earnest now as the sentries repeated Donovan's call. Officers called orders and recruits rose in barely-contained panic. Torches came to life all over the camp.

The attacker turned to run and Donovan pushed a skip-kick into the man's hip. He tripped over a tent rope and into a pole before he collapsed into a heap. Donovan threw himself bodily on top of the attacker, effectively pinning him. He put his knife to the man's throat.

"Stop it, STOP IT. You've failed; everyone is coming," Donovan wheezed as the man beneath him squirmed.

"You don't understand, get off, get *off*. Don you —" his words were cut off as aid finally arrived. Donovan was pulled gently but firmly away as the intruder was wrenched upright and manacled. Donovan stared at him — had he heard right? Damn or don't or Don ...?

The man was glaring at him, but his mouth was a tight thin line — a promise that he wouldn't speak willingly.

General Ost strode into the clearing, fully uniformed and with several senior offices close in his wake.

"Who are you?" the general demanded.

The man smiled thinly, but his lips trembled, and his breathing was nervous and quick.

General Ost stepped forward into the makeshift circle that had formed. He boomed, "Secure the perimeter of the camp. Officers, lead your squads in a grid pattern to check for others. I want you, you, you in my tent in five minutes. Master Rudd, please join us. You, and you, secure the prisoner and take him to my tent. *MOVE.*"

The world erupted in movement at his order and in moments the area was clear. Two soldiers came forward to grab the prisoner under his arms and drag him in the direction of the general's tent.

"Anything I need to know?" Ost asked when most of the crowd had disbursed. He frowned at Donovan's shirt. "You're injured."

Donovan looked down and saw blood. "Damn. No, I don't think it's serious."

"Keep pressure to it. My Healer will take a look. What happened?"

Donovan looked back at Ost. "He came into my tent. I wasn't sleeping well, but he woke me from a doze and I tried to stop him. Seemed more interested in getting away than finishing the job."

"Killing you?"

"I would assume." Now he felt uneasy with that assumption.

"He didn't say anything?"

"No. I don't think so."

"And you don't recognize him."

"No." Of that, he was certain.

"We should be ready to interrogate. With me."

The general turned on his heel and led the way through the neatly arranged tent lanes. They passed several jogging patrols, each with a high-held torch and a bell ready to ring in case of more trouble.

The general's tent was not far, and twice the size of any other they passed. They entered to find a thick ground-cover and a neat cot in the corner — the bedding appeared undisturbed. A desk with a camp chair was positioned next to it and had several candles burning. Documents were strewn across the desk surface. The men and women the general had ordered to his tent already waited inside. The infiltrator knelt in the center of the space, wrist manacles secured to a rope around his ankles. It looked uncomfortable. He wasn't gagged, but his lips were shut tight in a thin, fearful line. He appeared still and outwardly calm, but Donovan could see that he was sweating.

When they entered the tent, the infiltrator's eyes darted to each of them, back and forth, sizing them up, calculating. One of the officers passed a folded piece of cloth to Donovan, who thanked him and pressed it to his shallow cut.

The general stood in front of the prisoner for a long moment before he asked, "Who sent you?"

"I am not at liberty to say." The response was calm and steady and prepared.

The general looked at one of his officers who stared fixedly at the prisoner. She gave him a curt nod.

Ost continued, "Where did you obtain that uniform?"

"I am not at liberty to say."

"What is your name?"

"I am not at liberty to say."

"Are you associated with the Hunters, the blood mages?"

"I am not at liberty to say."

"Were you sent to kill this man?" Ost gestured to Donovan.

The prisoner's eyes flicked to Donovan and back to the general. "I am not at liberty to say."

"Are you a member of a military force, or civilian?"

"I am not at liberty to say."

"What *are* you at liberty to tell us?"

The man twitched an ironic smile. "I am not at liberty to say."

"Carter, Hothman, Dole, take this man and secure him out of range of hearing. We may have further questions."

"Yessir," the junior officers replied in unison before dragging him with them.

"Kelick?" Ost looked expectantly at the young woman who had nodded before.

She shook her head and took a deep breath, blowing it out. "Either he's practiced at avoiding scrutiny, or he is operating alone, General."

"Did you get anything?"

"He stole the uniform from someone at base camp. I doubt we'll be able to find out who it belonged to, but I'll put someone on it. He came from that direction as well, assuming my memories of the landmarks are correct. I would make a guess that he's associated with the Hunters, but I've got nothing except gut instinct backing that." She frowned.

"Excellent, Major. What else?" Ost asked.

"Just flashes of images, sir. I'll see if I can sort through them on my own and present my report, unless you want me to speak with him again tonight."

"See if you can find out how long he was waiting, how long he's been in camp. I want to know how he knew which tent was Master Rudd's, and how he knew to expect him."

"Yessir." She saluted and left quickly.

"Mik, see to it that the prisoner is secured properly and a guard is posted watch over him."

"Of course, General," Mik answered. He headed for the tent flap.

"Oh, and Mik," the general continued. He looked disgusted. "Get him out of my uniform."

"Yessir."

Mik disappeared, leaving Donovan once again alone with the Lord General Baron. The general took a massive breath and let it out very slowly before turning to sit behind his desk.

Donovan awkwardly moved to stand in front of it. He felt like he'd been called before the Dean for some miscalculated prank. He realized then that it was cold and lowered his sense of touch until the moving air didn't affect him, hoping that would do the trick until he could get back to the tent. He checked his cut: it had stopped bleeding, but stung. It really had been a graze.

"You say he likely came to kill you. Can you tell me why he might want to do that?"

"Not ... exactly."

"Because you don't know or because you are under orders not to say?" Ost's eyes narrowed.

Donovan considered telling him that he was under orders, but then reconsidered. If he did that, the general would want to know who gave him the orders, which technically no one had. Besides, Annette held no official office that he knew of, so any way he answered would be suspicious, and he would be immediately pegged as a spy. Which he was ... or wasn't ... He still wasn't sure, officially, and it would have to be verified, which only Whitman or Elliott could do, officially, and one of them was dead, the status of the other unknown.

"Rudd?" the general prompted.

"I'm sorry. Really I don't know. I would hazard to say it has something to do with the unnamed magus who leads the blood mages — works with them? We call him the Smiling Man. He seems to hate me. It's reciprocated."

"I see." The general steepled his fingers and pursed his lips. "Can we expect more of these attacks?"

"If he already knows I'm traveling with you, sir, I can't imagine that will be the last of them."

"That would have been good information to have much sooner, Master Rudd."

"I haven't been attacked since leaving the Order, sir, and it didn't occur to me to mention the possibility, since the Smiling Man ... got what he wanted." Donovan's face darkened.

The general didn't answer immediately.

Donovan continued, "To be fair, you brought me under false pretenses. If I'd known you wanted me as more than a simple teacher, I might have considered an attack."

Ost's eyes flashed, though with irritation or amusement, Donovan wasn't sure. "I —" The general appeared to want to say more, but stopped. "Thank you, Master Rudd."

The dismissal was clear. "Of course, sir."

He restored feeling to his chilled feet enough to keep from tripping and wished he'd had time to put on boots, instead of using one as a projectile. It had seemed reasonable at the time, but he realized now how idiotic that had been. The entire scene played out in his mind over and over and he felt more and more like an idiot. The dew had come in and now his feet were growing numb without his help.

He hurried past the tents, calmed in the time he'd been with Ost. Many of the lights had been extinguished, and he passed plenty of shadows on his way back. His heart raced and he considered running; he imagined another attacker everywhere he looked. He stumbled and gritted his teeth as his back gave a warning twinge and a knee threatened to revolt.

When Donovan finally reached his own tent, he saw it was now under guard. Two soldiers, older than most, but still putting them about forty years his juniors, were standing at attention.

"Sir, we are here for your protection."

"Oh. Thank you."

"Of course, sir. We'll be walking the perimeter of your tent until morning, so please do not worry to hear us striding past."

"All right. Good to know."

He ducked into the tent and grabbed his blanket. His teeth started chattering. Now that the excitement had died down, he realized how bruised he was. Besides the thin cut on his ribs, he had at some point bruised a shin and both his elbows. His knees were reading him a list of demands, and his back was considering suicide. Or murder. The cold didn't help. He groaned and sank onto his bedroll, trying to straighten out and stretch without making things worse.

He had expected to be unable to sleep during the few remaining hours of night, but unexpectedly found himself dozing off immediately. his last thoughts were the continued puzzle of the prisoner's words before capture.

*   *   *

Dawn was cold, but the dew was burning off quickly, promising another warm day. Donovan basked in the strengthening sunlight, eyes closed, as he let his horse lull him into a near-meditative state. The panic of last night seemed almost a dream, except for the colorful evidence it had left behind. His scratch was already scabbing over, but the bruises he'd collected would last a few days. He wanted to speak to the prisoner, ask him what was going on.

He rode ahead to catch Ost's eye. The general beckoned him closer and Donovan maneuvered his horse into talking distance. Ost had bags under his eyes, indicating little rest after the night's activities. His actions, however, betrayed no sign of fatigue.

"I wondered if I could speak with the prisoner," Donovan said.

Ost clicked his teeth together a few times behind closed lips. "Anything in particular you wish to say to him?"

"To ask him why he came for me, specifically. In case it's for better reasons that I suspect."

Ost's jaw moved as he thought. "No, I'm afraid not."

"I see." Donovan's face fell.

"The man tried to kill you once already. It wouldn't be prudent to give him a second chance."

"Even with guards?"

"Even so. We'll arrive in a few hours. When he's properly contained and questioned, you can make your inquiries. Another thing: when we pass through my gates, you will leave the company. Your quarters will be in the keep, not barracked with the soldiers. I'll have you down to the training fields once everything is settled."

"Thank you, General." Donovan rode back to his place behind the officers.

The messenger girl from the day before rode up a little while later. She didn't appear to have news, but rode by his side for a mile before speaking, "You brought down the prisoner."

Donovan nodded.

"I didn't expect you to be brave," she said.

"I'm sorry to disappoint," he answered, wondering what she wanted.

"I apologize, sir. That was rude of me. My father says you're a great man, but scholarly more than you are a fighter. I had not realized the two could coincide so drastically."

"Who's your father?" Donovan asked.

"The Lord General Baron."

"Ah. Your name?"

"Sir, this recruit's name is Private Camila Ost."

"You plan to take his place one day, Camila?"

She nodded firmly. "If I can show myself capable of leading, that is my goal." They rode another mile before she asked, "Do you have goals, sir?"

Donovan stared at the hazy, distant mountains. "I've never been a man of goals," he told her. "I only find myself here because I want to work, to stay busy. I never had a plan for myself."

"What about your scholarly work?" she asked. "You found New Seeking."

"That was an accident. Everything else I study is to ultimately find Ruben — the magus that the blood mages kidnapped. I have to do what I can to help find him, and, if I can't be out searching, I'll do whatever it is I *can* do to help. Finding him is my only goal."

She was quiet, but her young face betrayed the inner process of thought. "He must mean a great deal to you, for you to risk your life as you have done," Camila said.

Donovan smiled at her. "I always wanted to be a father — I love children. In some ways, I'm jealous of your father, because I see you're a capable young woman, with your goals in mind, and keen to work hard to achieve them. I never got to see my child — or any of the children I've Retrieved — do what you've done."

"You've no one at all?" she asked, affronted at the idea.

"Retrieving lets me be a part of a small family, I suppose. Family of circumstance. And I keep up with most of the little ones I've helped through the years when they want to stay in touch — I want to see them grow and develop into world-changing men and women, like you will someday. Or to see them live their lives in comfort and peace.

"With Ruben ... how many opportunities has he lost through no fault of his own, now? How many struggles will he be forced to endure that are beyond the strength of a fourteen-year-old? Or beyond what one should ever be asked to face. What are the depths he's been made to find in himself that he never should have had to develop?

"He's just a child, Camila, like you and all of the rest of these soldiers. I know you think you're grown, and you are in many ways, but take an old man's word for it: this war is going to mean something to the future we're leaving our children. If we can't protect someone like Ruben ..." Donovan shrugged. "Then it's only a matter of time."

"Only a matter of time?" Camila prompted.

"When you can't protect your children, what can you protect?"

* * *

The sun hadn't quite reached noon when their destination came into sight. A great stone wall, fifteen feet high and manned by archers, surrounded the keep itself, which was built on a rise. Trees were cleared for several miles around. When they could pass through the walls, six feet thick with a murder hole over the entrance, Donovan saw there was a ditch surrounding it all the way around, about twelve feet deep, and six feet wide.

The road that led to the base of the structure was maintained and wide enough for three wagons side-by-side, and lined with herbs Donovan recognized as various medicinal types. There were three switchbacks before they reached the iron drop-gate, which barred the thick, oaken double doors. Each of those had a four-foot door cut into it so they could let small groups or individuals through, but still keep them at a disadvantage. When the long line of recruits passed over the ditch, Donovan saw that it was filled with sharpened stakes, and the bottom was mud.

"Pity they've got no fortifications ..." he joked to himself.

The gates opened to calls and signal whistles. Their company passed through into a large courtyard. Stone stairs in each corner gave quick access to the wide walkway where guards above held a defensive position from which to watch for trouble.

In the courtyard, soldiers and servants hurried from the surrounding entryways to perform pre-arranged orders. Several high-ranking officers broke off from their positions with the general, who continued straight through the courtyard. The officers motioned to Donovan to exit the train as well.

He reined his horse and dismounted to watch the mass of recruits go by, working hard to keep in their neat rows. He waved at Camila and, though she didn't wave back, he saw a small smile cross her face.

At the end of the train came the supply wagons. Seven of them continued through the courtyard, but the last three creaked to a stop. The prisoner rode in the back with three guards to monitor him.

Several soldiers came forward to take custody. They lifted him down from the wagon so that his leg bindings didn't need to be removed. The ropes were tied in the crook of his knees so that they didn't slide around while he walked, but it meant he couldn't move very quickly. They, again, hadn't gagged him, but his lips were still in their tight, thin line. Donovan watched as he was led away.

With the wagons and horses, the courtyard had grown cramped.

A servant came to Donovan's side. "Master Rudd, I can take your beast for you," she said.

"Oh." He handed her the reins.

"Would you like to keep your bags, sir?" She had a slight twinkle in her eye.

He blushed and untied them from the saddle to pull the packs down onto his shoulder. She smiled at him and led the horse away, a second set of reins in her free hand, both creatures walking docilely behind her.

He found an out-of-the-way wall to stand against and wondered where he would be sent next. Recruits swarmed to unload the wagons, while others marked off an inventory list as each container was removed. A veteran officer supervised.

After a few minutes, he saw another servant waiting on the other side of the courtyard, watching him. He threaded through the crowd of workers like misplaced bees in the hive and hurried through a passageway on the other side of the wagons.

"Good afternoon, Master Rudd. I am the Head Steward. My name is Beal. The Lord General has bid me aid you during your stay, and has given me instruction on how you are to be kept whilst in his home. If you'll follow me."

Beal took him down the corridor and up a flight of stairs, further into the keep's second floor. A set of glass windows looked down on the bustling courtyard, but he was led away, down a narrower corridor. Beal had an odd stride — he favored his right leg with a very slight limp. As they walked, Donovan felt a faint pressure build in his head and then fade. He tugged at his ear and swallowed, but the sensation had gone. Beal stopped before a door at the end of the hall.

"For your stay." Beal opened the door and stood back.

Donovan nodded in thanks and deposited his saddlebags onto the bed. The room was small, but lavish, paneled in different types of wood, with a comfortable reading chair in the corner. A wine-red rug covered nearly the entire floor. Donovan was pleased by the décor — it reminded him of his room at the Order, and he was surprised to feel a pang of homesickness.

"Am I to remain here until the general calls?" Donovan asked.

"He made no such specification," Beal answered coolly. "I trust you will wish to bathe before touring the rest of the keep. I can have a bath drawn for you. Luncheon is a small affair here, but the Lord General wishes you to join him at the main table for dinner."

"I would appreciate that, thank you." Beal started away and Donovan followed. "I'd like to walk the ramparts, if we're allowed," Donovan added as they walked.

The servant pursed his lips and his nostrils flared, "I will see what can be done to accommodate your request, *Master* Rudd. This way to the bathing suite. It is not as excellent as that to which you are accustomed within the walls of the palace, of course, but we will strive to keep you thoroughly satisfied. Please do not hesitate to call on me for anything that you may want."

All of his monotone words were directed toward the walls, Donovan noticed. The man hadn't yet made eye contact. Technically, this steward was of higher rank than Donovan was, but he'd never been put in a position of having to consider his social standing, and it made him uncomfortable.

Beal led the way up another set of stairs to the top floor. When he stopped and opened the door, Donovan felt a wave of heat exhale from within. He blinked rapidly and peered through the fading steam.

The room had no paneling or rugs to cover the stone, but there were half a dozen man-sized bath-basins with pipes leading into them from above. The floor was covered in about half an inch of water. The only reason it stayed in the room was a six-inch-high ledge in the doorway that had to be stepped over to gain access. There were drains at the base of the far wall. A young man swept the water toward them.

One basin was filling and another was already full. As they watched, the second basin reached a black line marked on the side, and the servant watching the water, a young boy, banged on the pipe with a smaller length in hand. The water stopped flowing shortly after and the boy returned the little pipe to an apron pocket.

"Any remaining luggage will be brought to your room. When you are finished bathing, merely let an attendant know and clothing will be brought to you," Beal told the air.

Donovan stepped over the ledge, leaving his boots in the hallway where another young boy quickly claimed them and retreated to the corner with a pot of boot polish in hand.

Beal went on his way. The water on the floor was room-temperature, when Donovan expected it to be cold. He was pleasantly surprised not to have his feet freeze as he waded across the floor.

The two basins were identical, but the bath servants looked expectant. Donovan chose one at random and tested the water with a hand, wincing slightly.

"We have water to cool it, my lord." The servant waved the pipe-boy over. He jumped to action with two buckets from along the wall, all filled with the room temperature water, and poured them in while Donovan undressed.

A servant folded his clothes and put them away on a shelf while a second attendant appeared with a small end-tray for him, and put out an assortment of soaps, lathers, brushes, and razors for his use.

Donovan climbed into the basin, winced at the heat still, but adjusted quickly. He felt the tension begin to leach out of his aching and bruised muscles as they soaked, and he let out a great sigh of relief.

A servant came to his side and asked, "Would you like a shave, sir?"

Donovan ran a hand over his stubble and agreed. It was a unique experience, to be shaved by someone else. But once he the terror of having a razor so close to his throat in someone else's hand abated, it was relaxing and enjoyable.

"Scrub your back, sir?"

Donovan looked at his small desk of supplies and chose a mild soap, thanking the man again as he scrubbed the days of travel from the rest of his skin. He realized that a year ago he wouldn't have considered himself to be especially dirty — certainly not enough to need a whole bath — and he still didn't. But it felt nice. And places like this reminded him that he had to recognize the differences in the circles of culture that he was swimming in these days.

He didn't linger, much as he would have liked to continue soaking, and it was a short time before an attendant was sent for his fresh clothing. Dressed, he stepped out of the room and the youngest boy followed with towels to help dry his feet before the polishing lad helped him don his fresh socks and newly polished boots.

"Do ya' need 'elp back to yer rooms, sirs?" the boy asked.

"No, thank you," Donovan answered easily.

The boys looked surprised, but let him go. The route hadn't been difficult, and a lifetime of memorizing maps gave him the knack of learning a place's layout without much difficulty.

But he didn't want to go to his rooms; he wanted to see the ramparts and view the countryside from above. He considered the layout of the courtyard and set off upward another floor once he found the stairs. It didn't take long to find a door leading outside, and he let himself through it, careful to make sure the wind didn't pull it open behind him.

Donovan walked to the surrounding wall and studied the ground. It was high compared to anything other than the wall of the Order, where even the birds flew close, but a fall from this height was plenty deadly. He could see into the trench, full of stakes to impale unwary enemies, and far across the killing field cleared around the keep. Birds were turning in lazy circles over the forest. Their calls carried to him on the breeze and he smiled, calm and comfortable.

On the wall itself, he saw regularly placed barrels in sets of three: one held fresh water, another was full of arrows, and a third was filled with sand. The barrels were lidded and stored under cover that could protect about five friendly people from bad weather, as long as there was no wind, but canvas rain jackets hung on pegs next to the barrels for the inevitable spring and winter dousing.

He walked the length of the wall and enjoyed the fresh wind blowing across his face. He was sure it would be tiresome if he worked this duty every day, but he had always liked being up high. The courtyard below was still a beehive of activity, but it was less frantic now. Several of the wagons had been emptied and stowed away somewhere else. A guard walked past and gave him a cursory look, then dismissed him as a possible threat and scanned the area around for signs of anything amiss.

Donovan made his way down the walkway, past the looming wall of the keep, to the other side of the building, a mirror to this one. The courtyard they'd arrived into was one of two — the second another bustle of activity. He saw that the stables were through a large passage on this side, shaping the keep like a giant square cross. Traveling clockwise, you'd find a courtyard, stables, courtyard, storehouse, and all of the rooms were on the second and third floors. Outside the keep, but likely connected by underground tunnels, Donovan saw where they housed the livestock off of the stables. Goats, pigs, and chickens were tended to within safe distance of the protections of the keep, and beyond was the extension of the Lord General's lands.

Those lands housed soldiers. Barracks stood neatly built, row upon row upon row. Flags and painted marks showed the few differences between the otherwise identical buildings. A command structure stood on the other end of the enormous camp and after each group of six barracks, a larger building stood, probably for supplies or gatherings, Donovan decided.

A structure half again the size of the double-story command structure stood in the very middle of the camp. Donovan guessed it was for meals. His father loved to regale him with stories about rotating eating schedules, and having to get used to new ones depending on your shifts, or which squad you were assigned to. Every story had been full of misery that had somehow been pleasant enough to result in nostalgia.

Beyond the command tent lay a large, open field, across which soldiers were marching, running drills, and learning to obey, and give, commands. On a smaller field to the right, archers loosed into targets, and, to the left, soldiers practiced with swords and spears.

Donovan wondered where Lucas's siblings were — last he knew they had been posted here. He'd never received return letters from them, but didn't mind. He wasn't really family; his only connection had been his and Lucas's Retriever partnership, and his friendship with their mother, which had also come from that. Still, it would be good to see them. It had been ... two years? Nearly.

Looking around, he didn't see anyone to ask, and, after all, no one had specifically said he couldn't visit the training grounds. Ost had told him to leave the train of recruits so he could get settled into his room, which he had done ...

Without allowing thought to create doubt, he made his way down to the stables and borrowed a horse from the young woman who was mucking stalls. She looked like the rebellious sort, and didn't seem to care either way.

Donovan didn't see anyone else as he rode toward the training grounds. Two miles wasn't very far at all, especially on horseback. He stayed at a walk and shifted uncomfortably about to find a spot on his rear that wasn't bruised or chafed from the previous day of riding. He noticed that, even here — perhaps especially here — the grass and trees were kept trimmed back from the road. Visibility for the keep was a clear priority.

The noise level increased steadily as he approached while instructors yelled orders and recruits shouted responses. Synchronized boot steps were audible across the fields as they pounded past to learn marching, or running in a group. Flags over every barrack snapped in the wind, and loud laughter could be heard from those off duty, or slacking. Bells rang periodically to signal various things, and everyone was in uniform, most eyeing him curiously. Donovan smelled sweat, and oil, and the tang of steel.

Not sure exactly what he was looking for, he rode for the stable and found a class in progress. The officer leading the exercise glanced his way, but otherwise ignored him as she used a chalkboard diagram to teach the class about the different pieces of tack they'd be handling.

He wasn't standing idle for long, however, before a young man ran over with a grin. He bowed politely and waved him to follow, leading Donovan behind the class and out of hearing range.

He pointed to an empty stall in a mostly empty row and, when Donovan had settled his beast and removed the saddle and bridle, the young man said, "Can I help you, sir?"

"I'm looking for some soldiers," Donovan answered.

"Anyone in particular? We have a few options here …"

Donovan grinned at him. "Yes. Jannie Fain? Connor and Rennic Dolson, and Cameron Hardrick?"

The young man thought hard. "Pretty sure I know where one of them is, but for the rest, you'll need to go to Command and see if they'll check the records for you."

"Let's avoid Command for now." Donovan was still not sure he was allowed to be here.

The young man gave him a mischievous look, probably guessing Donovan's mind. He led the way out of the stable, avoiding the class again, and past a maze of buildings. Despite them all looking alike, the young man seemed confident he'd located the one he wanted and knocked loudly before he let himself in.

It smelled vaguely of oak and humanity with a tinge of feet and honey. The few people inside looked up curiously. "Anyone seen Corporal Fain?" the young man asked.

A woman lounging on her bunk called back, "Up at Raven with her brother."

"Aye," his guide replied, closing the door behind them. "Raven's this way," he said, taking off again.

It wasn't much farther on, twisting and turning down the paths. Raven had a woven doormat, dirty with use. He repeated the knock, and opened the door, "Anyone seen Corporal Fain?"

"Here," came the call. The young man stepped aside and Donovan entered alone.

"If you need me, it's Private Oats. I'll be at the stable." He grinned at the thanks and disappeared.

The brightly-lit barracks contained two dozen bunk beds taking up three quarters of the room. The remaining space was filled with two large round tables and wooden chairs. A group of people were seated at one of them, all looking his way.

"Don?"

"Jannie." He moved toward the table.

"Holy shit, it's Rudd," one of the men said, rising to his feet.

"Hey, Connor, you got bigger." Donovan smiled at him. Emotion tightened around his throat again.

Cards were laid down and the two of Lucas's siblings came to greet him with handshakes and back slaps.

"Budge up, assholes," Connor said roughly as he forced the group at the table to disburse with mutters and grumbles.

Donovan sat and passed a hand across the table, roughly made, but polished from years of use.

"Finally come to visit us folk in our lavish home," Connor grinned. He had an eighteen-year-old's cockiness. "You never did before, but I guess it makes sense, now you're famous."

Donovan shook his head, but didn't answer, eyes locked on Jannie's. "You got my letter?"

She nodded.

"I'm sorry."

She nodded again.

Connor glanced between them and said, "What it read, didn't look to me like it was much your fault, Don."

He didn't reply.

"Hey, you wanna play cards?" Connor asked.

"Conn," Jannie barked. "You wanna take a moment to shut the hell up?"

"Sure, Jann," he said, unfazed. "Sorry about Luke."

"Yeah, well, you didn't know him much."

"Nah. But I know you were close."

Eyes still on Donovan, the woman nodded minutely. "Taking down Hunters?"

"Right."

"How many?"

"Two the first day. Three the second."

Connor whistled. "Solo?"

Jannie nodded once. "Sounds like him."

"Serious?" Connor asked with surprise.

She turned to look him in the eye. "He could wrestle your fat head into the dirt nine bouts in ten, and he'd give you the tenth because he'd want you to feel good about yourself."

Connor grinned. "Damn. Wish I had a chance at him, now."

"Where's Rennic? And Cameron?" Donovan asked.

"Cameron's on assignment, officering somewhere, but Rennie's on the butts."

"Always practicing." Connor rolled his eyes.

"You want to get promoted past private, you'll put a single thought in your head and look toward practice, too."

"Nah." Connor leaned his chair back on two legs. "I'll stay a grunt forever and retire bored and alive."

Jannie rolled her eyes. "He's an incurable idiot," she told Donovan. "I've been trying to kick sense into him, but he's resistant."

"They always are at eighteen. You could write home ..."

Connor's chair slammed down on all four legs and he put his hands on the table, eyes wide at Donovan. "Don't do that."

"Worried Kail might have something to say?" he asked with false innocence.

"Don't. Don't tell ma."

"We're going after Renn," Jannie stood and straightened her uniform jacket. The front corner was folded down to show she was off duty. "Stay out of trouble."

"Not likely." Connor picked up the deck of cards and shuffled it quite skillfully. The displaced soldiers returned to their seats.

Jannie led Donovan outside and through another maze of buildings until they stopped with a clear view of the training part of the training grounds. They heard metal clashing, the *thud* of bodies hitting the ground, roars and shouted instructions as soldiers learned to fight and maintain their skills.

The archery butts were further out, aimed far away from any other structure. Crowds of people in various states of uniform walked to and from the place — some looked relaxed, others tense.

"Specialist tests are in a few days," Jannie told Donovan. "They're busy right now. She might not have time to socialize."

Veterans wandered all over, their keen eyes focused on safety protocols, and assisting where they were needed. A whistle blew and all shooting ceased immediately for people to reclaim arrows. It rang again and the *snap* of bowstrings on bracers echoed startlingly loud once more.

The last few lanes looked the least busy, and Jannie led them there. She scanned the people — children, really — learning to loose an arrow dozens of feet downrange at a tiny man-shaped target. Donovan thought about Annette trying to teach here and smirked. She'd lose her voice to shouting inside of three days.

"There she is." Jannie headed for the second-to-last lane. A woman half a head taller than her, slimmer and several years younger, stood to loose arrow after arrow into the target.

When her quiver was empty, Jannie called out, "Renn!"

The young woman looked around with an irritated expression. She saw her sister and opened her mouth to reply, then stopped as her eyes found Donovan. She stared for a moment in surprise and then called, "Hey!"

Donovan waved and smiled.

The whistle blew and she startled. She had to run to retrieve her arrows and come back.

"How much longer do you have?" Jannie called.

"Twenty minutes. Can you wait?"

"Sure!" Donovan called back.

They watched from behind the low fence marking the boundary for those not participating. Everyone on this end of the range was superb. He could tell they were the elite, even without being a bowman himself. There was no fumbling to pick out an arrow from the quiver, no hesitation about nocking it to string, only the economic motions working one after the other to devastate the target, already fatally wounded in a dozen different places.

When the twenty minutes was up, a bell rang out for the hour and everyone in the range gathered their equipment and traded spots with eager newcomers. Rennic unstrung her bow, stowed it in a waterproof bag, and looped the string around her neck. She put a lid on her quiver and shoved it to the back of her hip, then sprinted toward them and hurdled the fence without hesitation.

Immediately, her arms wrapped around Donovan. She squeezed him tightly, cracking his back with her muscular arms.

He replied in kind as best as he could, laughing at her enthusiasm.

"Donovan! Long time!"

"It's been a while!" he agreed. "I never knew how excellent you were."

"I'm hoping to get into the Archers. I failed last time."

Donovan's eyebrows rose, amazed she'd failed, considering her skill.

"She might have a shot this time," Jannie said. Her arms were crossed and she eyed the newest batch of bowmen with an officer's judgment.

"Why did you come?" Rennic asked as they returned toward the barracks.

"I was asked by the general," Donovan answered.

Both women straightened at that, looking at each other and then away.

Donovan continued, "He wants me to do some Seeker training, but I've wanted to come talk to you in person, since Lucas died."

"That's kind of you." Rennic's voice was soft and her fingers drummed a pattern on the lid of her quiver. "We got your letters. It was nice that you wrote them each separately."

"I thought it was only fair."

"Cameron cried. He thought we didn't see, but we did — he loved Lucas."

"So did I." Donovan let out a shaky breath.

"Shame Connor never got to know him that well. Just as kids, but Lucas was out training at the Order half the time and ma had Conn in classes as soon as she could. He's a handful."

"I got that impression."

"Military's good for him," Jannie said firmly. "He's competent, just lazy. And he falls in with bad sorts."

"Are you specializing in anything, Jannie?" Donovan asked curiously.

"Nope. Just walking up the promotion ladder. I want to train recruits eventually. Rennic's the Archer, Cameron's off studying tactics and strategy — he's angling for major, but is stuck at lieutenant for now. Too bad he'll miss you. I don't expect you're staying long?"

Donovan shook his head. "I'm teaching Seeking at the palace, so I can't stay more than a couple of days."

"What happened to Retrieving?" Jannie asked with a frown.

"I'm recovering. I got an arrow in the lung a few months ago. Unconscious for a week."

"No jest?" Jannie asked.

Rennic's face was concerned, but when Donovan didn't immediately fall over, she relaxed slightly. "Angry family members, or …?"

"No, nothing like that," he laughed. "We were sent for Ruben, suspected to be the magus, and the Hunters caught wind. After Lucas saved us from the ones on our trail, we were ambushed by a man working with the Hunters. It got a bit hairy, but the Order had people looking for us, and one of them was a field surgeon. She got me to the Order, and here I am."

"Sounds like you've been having adventures without us," Rennic grinned.

"You have no idea." Donovan sighed and rubbed the back of his neck.

"We heard about the magus," Rennic continued with a glance at Jannie. "He was kidnapped, yeah?"

Donovan nodded, throat tight as anger shivered through him. "By the same madman who shot me."

"Son of a bitch," Jannie spat. "Hunter trash."

"Something like that."

They reached the start of the barracks buildings and Rennic said, "There won't be anyone in mine; they're all on sentry duty. I was excused with special permission, so I'm free until night shifts."

She led them to a structure with a wind chime out front.

"That's not regulation," Jannie said.

"That's correct."

Inside was bright with light from the open windows, but as empty as Rennic had promised. While she put away her bow and quiver, Jannie and Donovan sat at the table.

"A bunch of us were sent to look for your magus." Rennic joined them with a bundle of sinew and a block of wax. She sat with a knee braced against the table and began to braid a new bowstring.

"No luck, of course," Jannie added angrily. "Then they had a bunch of Seekers out searching the wilderness with Mentalists and Empaths and any other sort they could possibly use to help flush them out."

"But not you?" Donovan asked.

Jannie shrugged. "Elementalists are useful, but not what they wanted, I guess."

"Someone pointed out the general might be putting on a show of power soon for someone over him, since he's been hoarding all of his mages at base, otherwise."

"Oh yeah?" Donovan asked. He hadn't heard any such rumor at the palace and wondered if Annette or Whitman knew anything about it.

"Yeah, Displacers, Elementalists, all those types — almost none of them are on orders, just slated for extra training and whatever while we're here."

"But you said the Seekers were out searching the wilderness for Ruben?"

Rennic glanced at Jannie again. "That's why we were curious," she said. "Most of them are gone, so the ones still here will probably appreciate the training, but I thought they'd all covered the basics weeks ago. Now they have time each day they're supposed to be practicing. But, like I said, I'm pretty sure they're mostly on duty all over the kingdom."

Donovan's mind raced. It made sense, considering the general's true purpose for having him here, but he couldn't share that information — much as he wanted to.

"Maybe he wants you to look for spies," Rennic said quietly.

Jannie snapped her fingers and the younger sister blushed, hands busy braiding.

"Did I miss something?" Donovan asked, looking at each of them.

Jannie shrugged. "It's all just rumors."

"Rumors, like spies in the ranks? That's pretty serious ..." Neither of them answered. "Jann. What aren't you two saying?"

She leaned forward, arms on the table. "Look, Don, it doesn't concern you, right? You're not military; you're not an Order specialist. You're a retired-Retriever-turned-teacher. Leave it alone, yeah?"

"No need for that, Jannie," Rennic said angrily. "It's not like you're talking to some know-nothing recruit — this is Donovan Rudd, all right? He's family."

Jannie leaned back and rolled her eyes.

Donovan looked to Rennic, who continued in a low tone, "There's a lot of talk about there being faces around that no one recognizes. And ... people are deserting because of it."

She paused, clearly waiting for Donovan's surprised outburst, which he forgot to utter.

Jannie uncrossed her arms and leaned forward. "What aren't *you* saying, Rudd?"

Donovan grit his teeth, not sure if he regretted the mistake or not.

"I — I'm not —"

"You're not here to teach Seekers. Why the hell would you be here, then?"

He laid his hands flat on the table. "The general thought my recent fame might make the deserters reconsider their actions."

"And you *agreed* to it?" Rennic asked, shocked.

"You wouldn't?" Jannie snapped back. "Renn, I swear to the Elements, if you're a deserter spy, you will tell me or I will drag you up on charges."

"How can you ask that?" Rennic cried back as her face blushed deep red.

Jannie stared at her for a long moment, eyes narrowed.

"I thought your problem was with me, not your sister," Donovan interjected.

"Maybe I can have a problem with both of you."

"You're being a child. Say what you have to say or get out."

Jannie stood abruptly. "I've said what I want." She stomped away and slammed the door behind her.

Donovan let out a long breath.

"Would you believe she's gotten better?" Rennic asked wryly.

"Truly?"

"She's different at home, Don. You should have realized that. Out here, she's on duty, even when she isn't, and everything she does has to show that she's on top, in charge, and ready for action. And she's loyal to a fault. Imagine her trying to pull that in front of ma ... Not that they don't fight all the time anyway."

"I thought we got along fine."

"You probably did, until she decided that you'd failed something. You should have seen her when I didn't make the Archers last year. We didn't talk for *three months* after. I just feel bad for Connor, who's in her direct command structure. It's better when Cameron's around. And Lucas." Rennic hesitated. "That's why she hates you, you know. She thinks you failed to save Lucas. I know you did your best."

Donovan let the silence stretch and then said, "I'm sorry to miss Cameron while I'm here."

Rennic nodded, focused on applying wax to her string.

"Renn."

"What?"

"You're the worst liar I've ever met. And coming from me ..."

"Only around people who know me," she whispered.

"Cameron's here, isn't he?"

"... yes."

"He doesn't want to see me?" Donovan prepared himself for the hurt feelings.

"No, that's not it at all — we didn't know you were coming."

"Then what's the problem?"

"He's ... he's one of the deserters," she whispered. "No, they haven't deserted, they just ... There's something going on around here, Don. Jannie will skin me ... you saw. She already suspects I know what they're planning. I'm amazed I haven't been brought up on charges already, but she knows there's no proof, and she knows she'd go down with me — she's waited too long already. Family, and all that." She realized she was rambling and stopped abruptly.

"She's not here now," Donovan pointed out.

"You already said I can't lie, and it's hard enough keeping the Mentalists out of my head when they come poking around!"

"Renn, please tell me?"

She took a deep breath. "The supplies we've been bringing in don't add up — like we're feeding another army. Everyone's being kept close by, even in patrols, like they want us all ready for something close, or they're afraid we'll see something. And half the officers don't understand their orders, either. Everything from Command just seems cryptic, like we're prepping for some big maneuver no one knows about.

"Cameron's always had plans, ideas for things far beyond him; he's been plotting and planning since I was born and before. He always makes sure he's in a position where those plans can be put to action, and I know he's brewing something, but I can't tell you what it is — don't ask me, I don't know. He's protective and won't let me in on any of it. Plus, he knows Jannie would find out. She's already having to choose between family and career. I honestly don't know what she'll choose. She's been questioned *three times* and I'm amazed she hasn't turned me in already."

"Sounds like she's chosen, then," Donovan said.

"Maybe ... but you said you're here to get the deserters back. No one talks about it, but we all know they're gone — how could we not? There's at least one person missing from just about every barrack, maybe closer to three, average, and we don't know where they're going. All of Bear is gone, *all of them*. I know some people still here are in on it, and occasionally they ask me to pass on word to Cameron, so I know he's in the thick of things, but I promise they're still loyal, Don, they shouldn't be punished, but they know something's not right and they're pushing back."

The torrential flood of words finally subsided and Donovan could tell that she'd been holding all of it in for quite some time.

He raised his hands and said soothingly. "All right, all right, please just be careful. Your mother would kill me if something happened to you while I was here."

Rennic let out a shrill laugh. "Yeah, she probably would. Mention her around here and the veterans just get quiet, like they're still afraid. Half the stories about famous soldiers doing daring things have come up around our dinner table and she corrects all the rumors."

"Can you tell Cameron I'd like to see him? That I miss him? And I'm sorry."

She nodded. "I'll do it."

"Thank you. What about these spies you mentioned? Are they and the deserters the same?"

Rennic shook her head. "No, those are the faces people have been seeing that no one recognizes. I haven't noticed anyone, but Cam said to keep an eye peeled, and others have told me they saw officers wearing uniforms wrong, or not knowing their barrack assignment. More than just greenstick recruit nonsense, Don. These people shouldn't be here, but they're usually dressed at higher rank or with an officer. Benson from Owl questioned one of them and wouldn't drop it. He was flogged for insubordination. *Ten lashes.* That's when the deserting really started. That's when Cam left."

"Who does he think they are? How many have there been?"

"Maybe a dozen in the last eight months? Not many, but enough to ask questions. As for who they are ..." Rennic shrugged. "Cam won't tell me anything. They probably don't know anything, but maybe they do, and can't say. They've kept command structure, but if they had proof of something, or even strong suspicions, you don't think they'd warn everyone?"

"I'm sure they would." Donovan's heart was racing anew at the thought of encountering these people and asking them to reconsider their reasons for leaving — the general really thought that Donovan was a good choice for something like this?

"Do you want to Seek while you're here? You could look for the spies, maybe? I have herbs for my Displacing that you can use."

Donovan shook his head. "That's not exactly how Seeking works. I really don't want to try until I'm sure of where to look."

"Still hate it, huh? New Seeking didn't help?"

"Not as much as we'd hoped."

"That's a shame."

"Connor doesn't know either, right?"

"Are you joking? Jannie didn't jest about him hanging about with bad sorts. Ma will whoop him something fierce when she finds out. And he couldn't keep quiet about a fart, let alone something like his big brother's secret mission or whatever it might be."

"Well, that's something of the pot calling the kettle —"

"Shut up, shut up! I did fine until you ... asked." Rennic threw her hair behind her with a practiced motion and set the finished bowstring aside to start another.

"You know, Connor's a lot smarter than people give him credit for."

"I was only teasing."

Donovan eyed the string she was working on. "Stocking up?"

Rennic nodded. "You can never have too many. I'd rather have a pack with more bowstrings than food, and, around here, you can trade them for just about anything."

"Renn, how does Cameron get in touch with you?" Donovan asked.

She hesitated. "Um, when I'm on sentry duty, he finds me. Or sends someone to me at the range."

"Even with the schedule changes?"

She nodded.

"Just curious."

"I heard you were attacked on the road?" she asked suddenly, remembering.

"An assassin came to kill me, we think."

"You think?"

"It's complicated."

"Is he dead?"

"No, he's in custody."

"Who is he?"

"No idea. I wasn't allowed to speak with him, but I'm hoping to have a chance."

"I guess the Hunters want to kill you pretty badly if they risked that."

He blinked at her.

"I mean, the road isn't a bad idea, but surrounded by soldiers? Even in training? That's risky."

"I was in the palace before that, or on my way here ..."

"Sure. But they said he came through the tent. Why not set a bunch on fire and kill you in the scuffle? Seems like there were other choices, and he chose poorly. Sloppy."

"Sloppy, huh?" Donovan thought about that. It was sloppy. The attacker couldn't have guaranteed that Donovan would be asleep, or that a scuffle would have gone unnoticed. And it would have been faster to cut through the tent wall, or even shoot a crossbow bolt through the fabric. Instead, he had untied the tent flap and come inside. "I should get back."

Rennic touched his arm. "Look, Don, I love Cameron, and I know he's loyal to the country, but I want this whole spy and deserter business stopped as much as anyone else. People aren't sleeping, and I'm one of them. Just ... do what you can, right? While you're here?"

"I'll see what I can find out. If there's anything I can do, I'll do it, and gladly."

"See you, Don."

"Take care, Rennie." She hugged him from her seat and he kissed the top of her head before letting himself out.

A group of soldiers next door were throwing axes at a target they'd painted on a section of tree trunk propped on its side. He let their voices wash over him while he thought about what he'd learned.

If there were Hunter spies here, what information were they looking for? And if it was bad enough that the 'deserters' had left their posts, who was stopping the spies from infiltrating further?

"Oy, you all right, mate?"

Donovan looked up, "What? I'm sorry, I was thinking. Got lost, I guess."

"You're Donovan Rudd, right? Like what came up with New Seeking?

"Can you throw axes, Rudd?"

"That's me, I'm afraid."

"Yeah, I heard of him. You."

"Look, can you throw or not?"

"Come here to find a new magic, Rudd?"

"Nah, he's looking for your mom!"

"Already found yours, I expect."

"Are you going to throw or what?"

"Pipe down, Allen, look at the man — couldn't throw a cat."

"I think an axe would be easier to throw than a cat," Donovan said.

They all laughed.

The first man continued unfazed, "My little sister's a Seeker. She always said how much it hurt, and this New Seeking of yours doesn't, so thanks for that."

Donovan gave a sheepish smile. "You're welcome."

"Come by when you like, Rudd. I'll spot you the first round."

"And you can learn to throw axes."

"Good grief, Allen, shut up and take your turn."

Donovan waved to them and headed back toward the stables. The soldier's look of sincere gratitude was one he would remember for a long time, deserved or not.

In the stables, the tack class from earlier was finished, but no one else was in sight.

"Hello?" Donovan called.

He walked toward his horse stall. Private Oats popped out of a tack room, straw in his hair and a book under his arm.

"Back again?" He grinned.

"Hiding in the tack room?" Donovan leaned to see into the small space.

"Not hiding. I was studying for exams." Private Oats held up the book for explanation. "I like being in the stables, and the library is far."

"What are you studying for?" Donovan asked.

"Specialist."

"Of?"

"Cavalry." The young man gestured around.

At Donovan's confused expression, the private continued, "I'm training to be a scouting officer. I get to go without armor and with few weapons to get as close to the enemy as possible, and then run away when they spot me."

"Sounds ... invigorating," Donovan replied.

"Eh. I also get to train the horses and riders eventually, so it has its perks."

"Grew up around horses, did you?" Donovan asked.

"Yessir."

"Whereabouts?"

"Philipa."

Donovan inhaled saliva and choked. He bent at the waist and coughed violently. His eyes watered and he wheezed on every inhale.

Private Oats patted him urgently on the back, startled but unable to do anything real to help. Donovan waved him off. When he was able to gather his wits for a moment, he pushed his sense of touch far down to almost nothing. He still struggled to breathe normally, but it was no longer painful, and he managed to calm down much faster. He managed a couple of deep breaths and cleared his throat awkwardly, and then increased his sense of touch slowly back to normal.

"Sorry about that," he croaked. "Nothing worse than failing to breathe."

"We've all done it," Oats assured him. "Need help with your tack or anything?"

"I think I can manage." Donovan cleared his throat again.

"I should get back to studying," the young man said. He pointed his thumb back at the store room.

"What was your name again?" Donovan asked hoarsely.

"Private Oats. Nathaniel Oats."

"Thank you for your assistance, Private."

"Of course, sir. Maybe I'll see you at the keep later. I'm posted for duty there tonight." He smiled and disappeared.

Donovan stared after him, worried after the talk about spies and conspiracies. Philipa wasn't a small town, and they were very well known for their horse breeding and trading.

It's just a coincidence, he told himself firmly as he mounted up.

"And now you get to try to interview an assassin," he muttered. Today was turning out to be far more interesting than he'd wanted.

* * *

"Ah, Master Rudd." Beal's oily voice came from ahead.

Donovan had easily navigated back to his room, and Beal apparently had anticipated his arrival. Donovan thought about the pressure behind his eyes when he'd first arrived at his room and took another look at Beal. There was no way to tell, short of asking, but if Beal was a Mentalist he would be firmly on Donovan's "Not To Be Trusted" list. He gave off an air that set Donovan on edge for reasons he couldn't quite label, other than his rude manner.

The steward was still unwilling to look Donovan in the eye and so spoke to the wall past him instead. "The Lord General wished for me to remind you that dinner will be served at six. If you require anything, you have only to ask. He wishes for his guests to be kept in comfort for the duration of their stay." He bowed shallowly at the waist and walked away. His movement was hampered only slightly by his limp.

Donovan watched him go, not fuming, not yet, but definitely left to boil. He entered his room and wondered what he should do until dinner. He wanted to speak with the would-be-assassin, the prisoner, but the general had told him not to. At least until he'd been questioned by Ost's people. Donovan wondered if someone was going to tell him when that had concluded. Probably not. What's to say they hadn't already finished?

He paced the room and thought about what Rennic had said about the assassination attempt being sloppy. Why not use magic of some kind? There had been plenty of other, better options, now that he stopped to consider it. And he'd only drawn his knife after Donovan had drawn his own ...

Where are the prison cells, anyway?

Donovan considered the layout of the keep and consulted his mental map. They'd be underground. The keep had too much security to overlook that obvious choice, so he would want stairs on the ground floor. Near the entrance, no doubt — escorts wouldn't want a prisoner to see too much of the building. You don't parade them past the kitchens or bedrooms, after all.

He opened the door and his heart jumped nearly out of his chest to see Beal waiting patiently outside.

"Yes?" Donovan asked sharply.

"I'm to escort you wherever you want to go," the steward explained to the door beside his head.

"I can find my way about," Donovan assured him.

"Nonetheless." He was clearly determined.

"Can I visit the prisons?"

"The prisons are out of bounds until you are given express permission."

"Fine," Donovan said rudely. "Let's see what else there is."

He chose a random direction and took any turn that stuck his fancy. A spark of cruelty flashed to life in his anger and he didn't change his usual stride to accommodate Beal's limp. It worsened as the steward kept pace, but he didn't complain. The only words he spoke were to explain the use of the rooms Donovan came across, or warn him of out of bounds places — such as guest quarters, or the general's study. Not that Donovan was entirely convinced that Beal was telling the whole truth each time, but his wandering did give him a chance to see more of the keep and fill in some of the blanks in his mental map.

Servants were everywhere, but much more often they found soldiers of various ranks performing innumerable duties: cleaning, polishing, dusting, sharpening, repairing — they were everywhere. He thought about what Rennic had said regarding Hunter spies and felt the hair on his neck stand up. If they were suspected in the ranks, why wouldn't they also be here as they'd been in the Order?

"How often do the soldiers change duties?"

"The upkeep of the general's keep is considered a position of honor and reward. The soldiers who perform the duties here are hand-picked from the ranks for exemplary service."

"Do they join the rest of the army for training?"

"Rarely more than the most necessary requirements. That is a storage room, Master Rudd."

Donovan tried to open it anyway, but it was locked.

"Do you wish to survey our supply of brooms and wash-buckets?"

"I might. Do you have a key?"

"What is it you are hoping to accomplish, Master Rudd? I might be better able to *assist* if I knew what you are looking for."

Beal came forward slowly. He was breathing harder than usual and Donovan felt a twinge of regret and shame. When the storage room door was unlocked, he gave the brooms and buckets and piles of rags a look, and felt like an idiot.

"Nothing in particular," he answered the steward.

Beal relocked the door.

"I like to get my bearings."

Beal stared past him, apathy clear in his posture.

"I'm sure you have more important duties to see to," Donovan tried again.

"Hardly, *Master* Rudd. The Baron Lord General personally directed me to see to your every need." His tone didn't conceal his feelings on the matter.

"You don't like me."

"Don't I?"

"Fine. I'm going to read in my quarters."

"Very well." Beal turned to lead the way, his pace slowed to suit his limp once more.

Donovan followed dejectedly and wondered how much of his stay would be spent cooped up inside.

"Please don't hesitate to call for me if you wish to *wander* again, Master Rudd." Beal deposited Donovan at his door and walked away without a backward glance.

Inside, Donovan felt the all-too-familiar itch in his mind, suggesting Beal was performing more of his duties than he had any right to. Disgusted at the thought of someone rooting about in his mind, Donovan threw himself into his chair and fumed like an adolescent.

When the itch faded, Donovan quickly jumped through the window of his mind with practiced ease. Now that he could control his senses, the passage through the window was more of a mounting pressure, like swimming too deep in a lake, rather than the stabbing, horrible, torture it once was.

As he spread out from his room, he struggled to See — it was hard to Seek through buildings, especially stone ones, but all of the materials were dead, with no life-light to them, so he could just barely make out the lights around his room with a sort of foggy, blurry vision. No one was in his corridor. Quickly returning to his body, he grinned and came to his feet, raising his senses to their proper place.

His head and body ached, and the familiar nausea returned, but he had been away for less than a minute, and could mostly ignore the discomfort after years of practice.

Donovan smiled politely at everyone he passed and fought to keep his pace unhurried. He wasn't sure he would even be able to get inside — Beal had probably told the guards to keep him out, but he wanted to try anyway. He felt like a youth attempting a stupid prank.

After passing through the courtyard and down a set of stairs, Donovan knew he'd come the right way. He passed two doors, one of them open to show a guard barrack, half empty, the occupants sleeping or playing cards. Only a couple of them glanced at him, but he passed the doorway quickly.

Glass lightning lit the way further down, but torches were placed strategically in case the magic failed. It was rare to see that kind of thinking and it surprised Donovan to realize it. Anywhere else he'd gone, when people had this kind of ready access to magical artifice, it was taken for granted. He saw ropes tied to mounted brackets, in an easy-to-loosen knot that would release the gates kept flat along the ceiling. The stairs deposited him at a wider landing and a closed gate where a guard watched him from the other side.

"Hello," he said.

The guard nodded.

"The general said I could speak to the assassin when your lot had finished interrogating him."

"Yessir, he said he'd send you. Didn't expect you to come so soon." He unlocked the gate.

"I have a few questions in mind and didn't want to wait." Donovan's heart was pounding.

"Straight through, sir, and you'll reach Major Kelick."

The corridor was constructed from the same stone as the rest of the building. He was surprised to look up and see a solid ceiling instead of the grating that the Order used to be able to track and manage prisoners, and visitors, from the halls above. He supposed there was only so much the general could have, despite his fortune.

The hall wasn't very long and he soon knocked on a thick wooden door, banded in iron. A hatch slid to identify him at a glance, and the door opened a moment later. The Mentalist from the night before greeted him with a smile.

"Major Kelick," she reminded him, shaking his hand.

"I thought I recognized the name," he smiled in return.

She had been the Mentalist in Ost's tent after the prisoner had attacked. He didn't feel her rooting about in his mind, which meant she was either more careful than Beal, or followed the laws governing her Talent. He liked her immediately.

She led him to a small table off to the side of the room and sat down. Curious, he joined her.

"Can you please empty your pockets, sir?"

He showed them to be empty. "I don't carry much."

"He's been a model prisoner, sir, but all the same, we prefer to be careful." The Major pulled a sealed pewter flask from her jacket and passed it across.

He held up a hand, "Thank you, but no."

She smiled. "Of course, sir. This is for the prisoner. Or rather, we hope you can use it to entice him into speaking."

"I see ..."

"When I reviewed what I had gleaned with my magic, I found a strong hunger for drink buried amongst the rest of the jumble. The general thought a friendlier tactic might not be a bad idea, and with you here ..."

Donovan put the flask in his pocket as he listened.

"We haven't gotten much from him, truth to tell. He isn't a Mentalist — or Talented at all — but he's had training to keep his thoughts private. It isn't complex to learn, but it does take quite a bit of determination, and strong control under stress. The general didn't give any further instruction, so I will remain up here. I'll hear if you holler, though, never fear — it's half a moment to get to you, and I'm quick. Please don't pass anything through the bars, except that flask if you think it's wise. Keep your body from the bars, too. No need to tempt any action we'll all regret, right?"

"Sure. Makes sense."

She smiled reassuringly. "Go ahead then, if you're ready."

Major Kelick unlocked and opened the door into the prison. He always expected a darker scene than he had ever witnessed entering a prison. Instead, the room was brightly lit with no screams or sounds of torture, no blood or gruesome images in sight — only cages for men and women, and basic amenities to keep them contained and reasonably comfortable, waiting for sentencing or time to flow by.

The only occupied cell was the third one from the door. He took time to calm his nerves as he walked. The assassin inside watched him approach from the far side of his prison, arms crossed, face unreadable.

Donovan stopped a few feet away and met his eyes. "I don't know you."

"No?"

"Should I?"

An almost imperceptible smile formed on his lips. "Alas."

"Why did you come to kill me?"

"Who said I came to kill you?"

Donovan rubbed the back of his neck. "Who sent you?"

"That's a more complicated answer than I think you'd expect."

"I'm glad not to hear that you aren't 'at liberty to say', but I was hoping for more than this."

"They sent you with alcohol to offer, didn't they?"

Donovan pulled out the flask, gave it a gentle shake to hear the liquid slosh, and then offered it up.

Identical to how Donovan had reacted minutes before, the man inside raised a hand and shook his head. "Thank you, but no."

Donovan put the flask away. "I don't drink either. Not anymore."

"Oh? Kill someone?"

"No, but I didn't like who I became."

"That's often the case."

"I stayed drunk for nearly a year before I figured out that it wasn't making anything better, and I still wanted to live after all. It was hard to say no after that, but every time I do, it gets easier."

"If you say yes, do you think you'll say no again?"

Donovan shrugged. "I'd rather not find out. Who'd you kill?"

"My wife."

"Ah." He hadn't meant the question seriously, and was rocked by the reply. "I'm sorry."

"I didn't expect they'd let you speak to me alone."

"I ..." Donovan's eyes shifted sideways.

The prisoner laughed. "You are a terrible liar."

"I've been told." They let the silence build. "If you weren't coming to kill me ..." Donovan said slowly.

"Yes?"

"What were you coming for?"

"Information."

"Like what?"

"About the Hunters."

"What do you want to know?" Donovan asked, confused.

The man in the cage shook his head. "To share, not to receive, friend." He smiled crookedly.

Donovan's mind spun. "Why not come in daylight?"

"Why do you think?"

Donovan thought. The man hadn't moved; he still leaned against the back of the prison, his arms crossed. He seemed more confident than he had the night before. As though his performance had been that: a performance.

"You're not a blood mage."

"Oh?"

"You're a spy. For the Order."

The prisoner nodded.

"For —"

He held up a hand. "If you're about to say his name, I'd rather you didn't. We have a private relationship, the Spymaster and I, and I'd hate to ruin the game so soon." The tight line of his lips was back. Not all of him was a performance, then.

"All right," Donovan conceded. "What's your name?"

"Theil."

"What have you risked death to tell me, Theil, that couldn't be delivered in a letter?"

The man finally came forward to the center of the cage. He licked dry lips and said, "The Hunters are not as you think they are. I will require a very open mind for this revelation because our friend didn't tell me how to proceed from here, which tells me that he had no idea what I would find."

Donovan took a step forward, intently interested.

"He did, however, tell me about you, and I need you to get this information to him quickly."

"All right ..."

Theil pressed his palms together. "The Hunters are split into two factions." He pulled his hands apart, palms up. "Faction A wants to kill all of your Order brats — anyone born with magic, and spread their mindset through the world. They're whom you're most used to encountering, I'd wager."

Donovan nodded.

"Faction B, however, would prefer *not* to kill the born Talented, and would like to see themselves not hunted down either — everyone living in harmony together. I see from your expression that this is somewhat surprising. You'll be more surprised to know that faction B is winning. Significantly. And has been for years."

Donovan searched for words, a question or comment, but he didn't know where to begin.

Theil continued. "This declared war is rightly against our dear A faction, but what you don't realize is that the B faction has already declared that war. Years ago. And they are fighting it right now, as they have been for, as best as I could gather, nearly two decades."

"That's where the army is," Donovan finally managed.

"Sorry?" Theil asked.

"General Ost, the Order, they've been wondering where the blood mage army is, why they wouldn't field a proper attack. Where the — B, no A's army is. The one attacking them, us. But it's already been attacking — Hunters versus Hunters. This is confusing." Donovan put his hands to his head.

"A bit, yes," Theil agreed. "Think of it this way: you have a family living in your town. They do magic of a kind different than your own. It doesn't require blood sacrifice, but it is one that is teachable, learnable, rather than inherited at birth. What would you think of them?"

Donovan shrugged. "I wouldn't think much of anything."

"And if someone in a nearby town was murdered and the culprit brought before the judge and found to be a sort that performs that same kind of magic as your quiet little family?"

"I see ..."

"That's what I know, Rudd. I have my orders, and I'll continue my job." A shiver shook his frame. "Or I'll die trying, I suppose."

"Do they know you're alive?"

"Absolutely. When I escape here and tell them you are too, though, they won't be happy. Tests of loyalty get complicated when you fail."

"Just stay here, then, under the general's protection. I'll tell him about this and he'll help."

"There's more going on than you know, Rudd. Like I said, I've got orders, and staying in this prison doesn't picture into them."

"Do you know how blood magic is performed, then?" Donovan took another step closer and put his hands on the bars. "Can you teach me?"

Theil smiled. "I can't, I'm sorry. My character is a difficult one to perform and I cannot ask too much for guidance, lest I be found out. Make sure our friend learns this? He'll know what to do with it."

"If Ost learns where it is, he'll attack your camp," Donovan said suddenly.

"Of course he will," Theil said. He waved the treasonous words away, unconcerned.

"Theil, if they catch you, you'll be killed."

"Yes, possibly."

"What are your orders? From the Spymaster?"

"I'm not at liberty to say."

"How are you going to escape?"

Theil gave him a sour look, disappointed in him. "I'm not at liberty to say."

Donovan threw his hands in the air and paced angrily away and back. "I almost have all the pieces, dammit!"

"I'm on your team, Donovan," Theil said softly. "But I'm not playing the same game. Make sure you cipher your words to our mutual friend."

"Is anyone else going to come try to kill me?" Donovan asked, exasperated.

Theil shrugged. "I would expect so, but I imagine you're safer in the building than outside of it. Probably. Possibly. A bit, anyway — it's really hard to judge."

Donovan hung his head, suddenly tired, and ran a hand down his face. "Thank you."

"You're welcome. Best of luck. And I'm sorry I didn't have more for you. We'll speak again soon."

Donovan walked back to the entrance and knocked. Major Kelick unlocked it and let him back through.

"You look ill. Are you all right?" She frowned with concern.

"I'm fine, Major. Just thinking." Donovan managed a thin smile.

"Did he tell you anything, then?"

"No, I'm sorry. I wish I could help." He stepped toward the exit.

"Oh sir?"

He turned to her.

"I'd like the flask back when you finish it."

Donovan touched the metal in his pocket and, for a moment, considered keeping it. Quickly enough, though, he handed it back, full, and unopened. "Thank you. I'm sorry I didn't learn anything for you."

"I'm sure we'll come to answers eventually, sir." The major locked the door behind him.

"We can hope." Donovan started his walk out of the prison.

At the entrance, he looked up and across the courtyard to see Beal shuffling angrily toward him. Donovan shoved his hands in his pockets and waited.

The steward was fuming and didn't bother trying to hide it. "You were told the prisons were out of bounds." He was angry enough that he appeared to have forgotten to pretend Donovan didn't exist. Their eyes met for the first time since Donovan arrived.

"The general said I could visit the prisoner after he'd been interrogated. He'd been interrogated, so I went to speak with him."

"What did you learn?"

"Nothing."

"Don't lie to me."

"Watch your tone, steward. I am a guest here, and I don't think the general would appreciate this treatment. And *stay out of my head.*"

Beal's fists were clenched at his sides.

"If that's all?" Donovan began his walk away.

"It is not."

Donovan stopped and turned to face him again.

"There are rules here and, guest or no, you are expected to obey them."

"Gladly. When I receive a list of these rules, I will follow them to the letter."

"The general ordered you to stay in the keep and you deliberately disobeyed. I know you went to the training grounds this afternoon. That is *unacceptable.*"

"I'm not a soldier. I'm not obligated to obey a military command."

"You act above the station of your birth."

Donovan felt his cheeks grow warm. "I wasn't born to money, but that doesn't make me less of a man."

Beal sneered disdainfully. "The general is on his way. You are to meet with him in his study before dinner."

"I'm happy to do so. This way, right?" He turned on his heel and strode quickly past, relying on the map in his mind to keep him on course. The door was locked when he arrived, and there was no answer when he knocked.

"Wrong door," Beal panted, coming up behind him. His face was red, but with rage or exertion, Donovan didn't know.

"This is the one you said was the general's study," Donovan said confidently.

"There are two. He wants you in his private study. This way."

Donovan threw his hands up and rolled his eyes. Why a man would need more than one study was behind him. He thought he heard the door open and glanced back, but there was no one looking out.

He followed Beal down another corridor, to a set of stairs that led down to the general's quarters. The steward knocked in a neat pattern and, at the word from within, admitted his charge with a withering glare.

Donovan's own temper hadn't cooled much on the short walk, but he managed not to respond in kind.

General Ost's study was exactly as Donovan expected it to be: the floor was covered in a thick, soft green carpet, with a lounging area in the middle of the room, a desk at the far end and the rest of the walls covered with alternating war and hunting trophies and book shelves of what Donovan could only assume was more military knowledge. The trophies consisted of a mixture of maps, weapons, animal hides and the like. Glassed lightning encircled the room with an interesting choice of yellow glass — it made a much softer light.

Seated behind his desk, Ost stood and beamed as Donovan entered.

"Rudd!" he boomed. "We meet again. Beal seeing to your needs?"

Donovan nodded, "Well enough, thank you. He doesn't seem to like me much, I have to say."

They shook hands and Donovan sat in the proffered chair.

"Pah!" Ost waved the comment away. "He comes across prickly, but softens with time. How do you like my castle?" Ost leaned back in his seat, which creaked beneath him.

Donovan replied honestly. "I haven't been exposed to many castles, but it seems to suit your interests."

Ost laughed. "Spoken like a man on his way to being a politician. Don't let the Lady Kraemer turn you too far to her side; I know the kind of politician she is, and they're a dangerous breed. Did she tell you our family lands are near one another?"

"She mentioned that you'd met as children."

"I'm nearly a decade older, of course, and it mattered more then. Our fathers were friends, and when mine gained favor, we spent much of our time in court. Her sister was always Braun's favorite, though we never got on — she's not much for fighting, and that's all I talked about, I'm sure. Annette and I were better friends, but we've little in common these days, except speaking of years past."

"She's been a good friend to me." Donovan smiled as well. Then, sensing an awkward pause in the conversation, he quickly asked, "How are your graduates settling in? And your daughter?"

"Well! She's always doing well — I can barely keep up with her on a good day. My officers know how to keep the recruits busy and the rest of the soldiers know how to go about their duties. I don't like to leave it, but, to be truthful, I'm not wholly needed here. My people know how to run things and Camila will no doubt be taking over in the next twenty years."

"That's the duty of a good leader," Donovan pointed out. "To leave his works in such a state that they are uninterrupted when he leaves."

"True," the general agreed.

The silence began again, but this time, Donovan didn't know how to fill it. Ost looked to be searching for words.

After a long moment, he said, "Beal said you spoke to the assassin? I wasn't expecting you to make your way there so soon."

Donovan licked his lips. "I'm sorry if I broke some rule. You said I could speak with him when you'd finished interrogations, and no one said I couldn't when I got there."

"No, no, that's fine," Ost said, waving the words away again. "I was hoping to have my own crack at him, but I'm sure you can share what you learned?"

Donovan hesitated, but he liked Ost, and it didn't seem like there would be any harm. "He said there are two factions of blood mages, and one is trying to kill the other."

"Factions." Ost tasted the word. "Interesting. And what do the factions lack for commonalities?"

"As he put it, Faction A would like us all dead, and Faction B would like us as allies."

"Ah. What do you think of that?"

Donovan shrugged. "If we can find common ground and negotiate fairly, I ... don't see why not. If they're the kind of people who want peace, surely that means we can keep any ... abhorrent behavior at bay? After all, we do the same with nearly all magic: there are consequences to improper use, just like if you wield an axe, or something equally dangerous."

"And he said they were blood mages, these two factions?"

Donovan cocked his head and realized, "He didn't specify, really."

Ost smiled wanly.

"Of course, it means that you can find them all in one place," Donovan added. "If they're fighting each other."

"That would be a blessing! Did he say anything else?" The general didn't look surprised by any of the information.

Donovan shook his head. He'd already learned the etiquette about sharing another's status as a spy, allies or not. He'd also learned to trust his instincts and currently the back of his mind was ringing a distant bell.

"Do you mind?" Donovan stood and gestured to the shelves around the room.

Ost waved permission and Donovan scanned the titles as he gained more time to think.

"I'm not sure if you know," he told the general, "but I've been trying to learn what I can about the blood mages — find a weakness and all that."

"Have you?" Ost sounded surprised and turned in his chair to follow Donovan's progress through the shelves.

"I thought: if I wasn't a good fighter, I could at least try my hand at research. There's not a lot to offer, unfortunately, but when the assassin mentioned the two factions, it got me thinking. Are you familiar with the idea of life magic?"

The general's eyebrows shot to his hairline. "I can't say I am ..."

"The texts that I've read are mostly mythologies and distant histories, but they mention 'life magic' in a few places. It has me wondering if that's what these factions are: blood magic and life magic."

"You have texts?"

"Some. Mostly vague histories." Donovan silently cursed himself. "Mythologies, like I said."

"Do the histories say much about it? This new magic?"

"Not with any certainty. But I imagine life magic would have been the start, and then people are corrupted, as people are, and they develop blood magic."

"That seems a reasonable conclusion ..." The general sounded hesitant, but didn't offer anything to fill the conversation.

Donovan wondered about that. Why invite him here to talk with no topic in mind? He perused the next shelf, barely seeing what he was looking at.

Ost asked suddenly, "What do you think the difference might be?"

"Well." Donovan trailed a finger over a book spine, "I would liken it to a village family minding their own business in their daily lives, or a deranged murderer, drunk on power."

"You believe these life mages might be worth negotiation, then?"

Donovan was having a hard time reading Ost's tone. Was he interested in the idea? Disgusted by it?

"I think anyone might be worth negotiating with, if it means avoiding war and saving our people from horrible deaths."

Ost nodded. "I am in the trade of war, but I do not believe in unnecessary loss of life. My soldiers are the children of my country, and it is my duty to see to it that they serve to the best of their ability, beyond what they know themselves to be capable of, and then return home. A loss on the battlefield only aids the enemy."

"'Sacrifice may be necessary, but it is not to be sought'," Donovan quoted. He wasn't sure what he was quoting, but he remembered it distinctly.

Ost's eyes widened for a moment as he recognized the quote, but he didn't acknowledge it otherwise.

Donovan approached the desk to read the titles there. "I heard some rumors while I was amongst your soldiers today."

"Did you? Soldiers are prone to exaggeration when they've time to laze about."

Donovan nodded, still looking at titles, his neck craned to the side.

"What did these rumors say?" Ost prompted.

"Other than talk of the deserters, they said you have spies in your army."

"Really."

"They said your deserters are not deserters at all, but still loyal."

The big man laughed boldly. "That seems unlikely."

"I thought it was interesting, though. If there are spies, and these few learned about them, they might consider it safer to step outside of the normal procedures and handle it in their own way."

"Soldiers must have discipline. The group is stronger together. If there are spies, how do we fight them if half of our number is not following orders?"

"Half?" Donovan looked at him.

Ost waved flippantly. "I'm prone to occasional exaggeration myself. Too much time to laze." He smiled, but it was more of a grimace.

"Did you still want me to track down these defectors, then?"

The general nodded. "If you're willing, I'll use you to greatest effect."

"I want to be of assistance. In any way I can."

Ost smiled again, truly this time. "I'm glad to hear that."

The tension lessened and Donovan said, "I'm quite impressed with your collection."

"I enjoy reading — my father always encouraged it. It relaxes me in a way that the interests of my peers do not. Do you collect?"

"No. I do spend most of my time surrounded by books, however, and I am always impressed to see the assemblages of others. I grew up with only three or four in my home at any time."

"The Order must have been something of a shock to you," Ost chuckled. "I trained there, though my parents wished for me to have stayed at the palace. They have more military-minded works on the palace shelves, but I'd read nearly all of them by the time I left, already clear on the path I wanted to take."

"I expect your Seeking assignments of map studying weren't so much a trial?"

"Not at all. I excelled!" Ost stood and came around the desk to draw Donovan's attention to a map across the room, framed behind glass. "I helped finish out those borders," he boasted. "Couldn't find anything with consistent edges, and decided I'd have to do it myself. King Braun came as well, of course — prince, then."

Donovan looked around. "Are these other prizes from your youth?"

"Yes! I wanted to have my boots on the ground as much as I could," Ost explained excitedly. "I knew once I took command, I would have a hard time getting away. I've been all over, including a brief visit to Manazia — they don't like us there."

"So I've been told. My first partner was Manazian. Odd, but he was a brother to me." Donovan smiled to remember.

"I have them in my ranks. Their ruler is always telling King Braun he should send the people back, refuse them haven, but our borders are open to civilians, and always have been — as long as they keep the peace, of course. We have to keep a sizable force on the border, in case their military thinks that invitation extends to them." He wandered down the row of his other trophies.

"I wouldn't want to be forced into military service and priesthood, either. I can't blame them," Donovan said.

"Perhaps not for your whole life, but I think mandatory service would benefit our people. Just for a few years, of course."

"You don't have enough people to keep track of, General?" Donovan asked.

Ost laughed again.

Donovan turned to the shelf behind the general's desk.

Across the room, Ost drew Donovan's attention again, "Ah, you said you've never fought in the military."

"Right."

"Why is that?"

Donovan shrugged and stood to face the general. "It was never for me. I didn't ever have much desire to leave my small town, patrol the kingdom, fight villains."

"And now you seem to have done all of those."

"And more," Donovan chuckled. He looked at the shelf once more and scanned those titles nearest the ground.

"My highest ranking officers will be joining us at dinner." Ost approached the desk and politely intercepted Donovan, who stepped back around to the front. He avoided Ost's outstretched arm. "One of them is Manazian. I'm sure you'll like her. She's easy to spot."

Donovan cleared his throat and focused on the general once more. He pushed the urgent realizations from his mind. "Oh?" he asked. "Head tattoos?"

"Just so."

"I'm sure it would be more popular here if religion was as prevalent amongst our people."

"I think religion is prevalent enough," Ost said, "if you know where to look." He encouraged Donovan back to the seats in the center of the room.

"My late partner and his family follow the Elements. My family was never so godly, but I like the culture — there's a sense of family, even among strangers."

"Finding belief in something so late in life can be difficult, but certainly rewarding. To see my daughter find strength and peace through the faith we share is beautiful. Do you think you could ever adopt a religion for yourself?" Ost asked.

Donovan put out his palms. "Probably not. I have a hard time believing in anything I can't see for myself."

"That does make things difficult." Ost smiled thinly. "What about a cause? Could you follow such a thing?"

"Perhaps." Donovan cocked his head. He was sure the general would hear his heart race. "Did you have one in mind?"

Ost laughed again, but it wasn't as sincere as the others had been. "I find people are strongest when they believe in something, that's all."

"What do you believe in, General?"

Ost twined his fingers in a practiced pattern as he thought about his answer. "I believe in the future. I believe in loyalty. I believe in compassion. I believe in honesty with oneself."

"That's quite a list."

"An important one. Do you think you're a good person?"

Donovan's eyebrows jumped at the sudden question. "I think I try to be one."

"But you aren't yet?"

"I think I have done good, and I continue to try to do good."

Ost laughed. "You are dodging the question."

"It's an unexpected one."

"I speak as I think, forgive me."

"Certainly."

The conversation lulled again.

Donovan gestured vaguely. "I might have to borrow a few titles if I get the time to read them."

"What are you hoping to learn from your study of blood magic? You said you're determined to find a weakness. Anything else?" Ost crossed a leg over his knee.

"Anything to provide an edge in the war. I'm a bit long in the tooth to be fighting on the front lines, but our enemies have Ruben, and I will do anything I can to get him back."

Ost nodded. "That's very good of you. Many others would let the difficulty of the task daunt them."

"It is daunting," Donovan agreed. "But ..." he shook his head, looking Ost in the eye. "You have a child."

"I do. And I would go to the ends of the earth for her."

"Yes."

A gentle tap sounded at the door.

"Shall we?" Ost smiled politely and motioned toward the door.

Beal waited in the hall and looked to the general as they exited the study.

Ost pulled a ring of keys from his pocket to lock the door and said, "I hope you'll enjoy the meal. It's simple fare, but my cook enjoys the opportunity to feed more than the usual crowd."

"I'm sure it will be delicious. I rarely meet a meal I can't stomach." Donovan thought Annette would be proud — he wasn't sure how he was doing, but neither Beal nor Ost seemed suspicious.

The general gestured for Beal to lead the way. Donovan followed behind, thoughts spinning so fast he thought he might trip. On the shelf behind the general's desk, low on the bottom shelf, Ost had half a dozen of the books Donovan had been studying over the last several months: books on blood magic, life magic. If they were all shelved together, the general could have a dozen more that Donovan didn't recognize, that the Order didn't possess.

He wanted to speak to Annette, to Whitman, but if Ost was a sympathizer — supporter, perhaps — Donovan didn't want to arouse more suspicion than he might have already. The alarm bell in the back of his mind was deafening.

"Would sir like to dress for dinner?" Beal asked over his shoulder as they walked.

Donovan shook his head. "I'm already wearing my best shirt."

Beal didn't answer, but Donovan heard him sniff in distaste.

Ost didn't say anything.

It wasn't far to the dining room. When they arrived, young men and women, dressed in military finery instead of servant's attire, were putting the finishing touches on the table. They seated each of the officers as they arrived. Donovan gave everyone his best political smile and wondered what was going to happen next. The hairs on his neck wouldn't lie down.

"Master Rudd, it's a pleasure to meet you."

"It's so good to meet you."

"Welcome."

"Gracious of you to join us."

"We've heard good things about you."

"Welcome. We're glad you made the trip."

"How are the roads? I haven't left in ages."

"It's a pleasure."

"An honor."

"Welcome."

A parade of names and ranks and faces flew by him; his hand was nearly numb from all the strong grips he endured. His mind was elsewhere, so he was a bit surprised to find himself in front of a chair, one of the serving soldiers nearby to assist him.

Donovan was still analyzing the conversation in the study. Every sentence was tainted with suspicion now. Had he given too much away? What had he missed?

The first course was served. He was pretty sure it was delicious: some kind of soup. Ost and the other officers were discussing various topics, but Donovan's mind kept wandering. He paid enough attention to laugh when it was expected, or nod, or "*hmm*" appropriately.

Could Ost be a sympathizer to the blood mages? Or at least the life mages? Factions A and B ... The man was a life-long soldier, but his words on not sacrificing lives needlessly did sound sincere. As did the rest, really, but what kind of judge was Donovan? Was Ost giving information to the enemy? How far did his loyalties extend?

"What?" Donovan looked up from his roasted quail and vegetables and stared around the table. All eyes were on him. He coughed and blushed. "I'm so sorry, I was far away — I missed something?"

"They were hoping for a demonstration of your Seeking abilities," Ost supplied.

Donovan wiped his mouth with his napkin and stood. "Um, all right. Was there a specific question?"

An officer near the opposite end said, "I can understand the uses of increased sight and hearing, but surely smell and taste and touch cannot be nearly so useful?"

Donovan nodded, the question a common one in his classes. "Hearing and sight are clear favorites of many of my students, but we train thoroughly in each sense. Let's see ... as a fighting man, consider your sense of touch. Hands on the table, if I tap my end, you can barely feel it, yes?"

He nodded.

"Now if I increase my sense of touch and you tap a quiet rhythm?" Donovan closed his eyes and accessed his magic. It was inaudible, but he felt the sensation clearly and repeated it for everyone to hear.

The officer looked impressed and nodded at the correct repetition.

Donovan continued, "I have used this technique at distance to signal a friend when speaking would give us away, or even if a location was too loud to make it plausible. Touch ... I have had minor injuries, inconveniences, and removed the sensation of pain from them. It doesn't stop the bleeding, and risks further damage, but it got me to safety much more easily than I might otherwise have done. I hesitate to suggest that one, as I haven't received clearance of safety from the Healers and surgeons yet — we're not sure of the limitations, so please be careful."

This stopped all of the soldiers, including the servers. He could see the possibilities start to unfold behind their eyes. The value of Seekers was on the rise.

"As for taste, it is far more useful as a precaution — knowing the tastes of poisons, if you fear assassination. Of course, it would still require you to have ingested the poison enough to memorize it, but if you know your antidotes ... Smell is more useful, I find. For example," he brought his sense of smell to increase tenfold, wrinkling his face as the scents in the room grew nearly overwhelming. "It takes practice and focus, but I know that the sergeant here has been riding recently, and could locate the horse she rode, though I don't want to spend long in the stables, trust me. I know that you prefer extra garlic in your food, sir, and that the general spends lots of time in the library or at least around books and ink."

Donovan inhaled the clear scent of paper and ink, but something else caught his attention. He glued his smile in place and increased his smell to be painfully sharp, hunting the scent again.

"I hope that answers your questions!" He dropped into his seat and took the glass a server provided, laden with herbs for the inevitable illness following his use of magic, and used it to cover his shock.

He'd smelled that scent before: outside the Order months ago, just before the Smiling Man had kidnapped Ruben. He recognized it easily since their last encounter, and it set his heart jumping painfully.

His eyes darted around the table, taking in the faces once more, and then across the servers.

Where was he hiding?

Donovan knew the Smiling Man wasn't nearby, or the smell would be stronger. Someone, Ost it seemed, had met with him recently. How recently? He hadn't been sniffing around all day. He should have been, but he hadn't suspected Ost until now, either.

"I'm so sorry." Donovan set the glass down. "I tend to need a moment of recovery. What was the question?"

"How long did it take to hone your skills?" the officer across from him asked. She was the Manazian Ost had mentioned, judging by her slight accent, shaved head, and braided vine tattoos along her scalp.

"Um. A few months, but it was fairly constant training with a motivated partner, and we were determined to learn as much as we could, as quickly as possible. I'm still learning. My students teach me every day."

He smiled and she returned it.

"How was this lost for so long?" a lieutenant asked further down the row.

Donovan shrugged one shoulder. "I expect it was taken for granted, and all focus was put on the Seeking we knew of, because of the dangers and more difficult aspects. And its usefulness in war."

"Wait," the soldier who'd asked for a demonstration said, "if the main trouble with Seeking is that your body gets overwhelmed with sensation, why not numb yourself before you go? That would give you plenty more time, right?"

"That was our thought as well," Donovan agreed. "Assuming you are in a safe place with people you trust, that is the newly recommended method, but that's not the only danger. In our research, and with the assistance of Healers, we've found very old studies in the records where Seekers stayed outside of their body for more than the normal few minutes and suffered mental damage and death, even while numbing their senses. The body can't live for long without a ... spirit to keep it alive. Your aspect, the magic that you bear, fuels your body beyond what we yet understand."

"The body might die before the spirit does," the general stated, clarifying.

Donovan looked at him. "That is our understanding. You see why we're loath to attempt more experiments on the subject. This whole avenue of study has led to an incredible increase of questions. We can no longer take our knowledge for granted."

The table was contemplative as the next course was brought out. Donovan picked at the salad, trying to stay more focused on the conversation this time. If the Smiling Man was here, Donovan needed to leave. He didn't know why the man wanted to kill him, but he'd made the attempt twice. Most likely, he wasn't used to people surviving; he wasn't the kind to leave survivors on purpose and somehow Donovan kept managing it.

He realized he was rubbing his chest, the scar from his arrow wound still visible beneath his shirt. Sometimes he woke up in the night, chest heaving as he tried to breathe through his own blood. Other times he saw the Smiling Man standing over him while electrical shocks shuddered through him. Or he heard the guardsman Robert's screams as the flesh melted from his face and hands.

Donovan released his utensils from white and shaking hands. He cleared his throat and sipped his water again. No, if the Smiling Man was here, Donovan needed to run, and quickly. He'd been lucky so far, but was sure he wouldn't survive another encounter.

Thankfully, everyone had duties to attend to, and there was no cheese plate to prolong the meal. The last course came from the kitchen in the form of a beautiful baked apple filled with cream. It was too rich for Donovan's preferences, but most everyone else tucked in with a will, making appreciative sounds and discussing its creation.

It was late when they were dismissed. Ost didn't try to take him aside, but instead stayed in the dining room to supervise the cleanup, giving Donovan only a polite nod of farewell.

In the hall, one of the officers shook his hand again as the rest moved away. "Thank you for what you've done," he said earnestly.

Donovan gripped his hand warmly. "You're welcome."

"As soon as I learned you were coming here, I wrote home — my whole family, nearly, is Seekers and this is such an amazing time to live through."

Donovan waved after him, smiling ruefully at the sincerity.

Something in the man's words struck him. If this young man had written home, how many others had as well? How many recruits and soldiers had seen him in this place? Some of them were passing information to the deserters and whatever spies there were, too, so surely many of them would know ... Donovan realized with a pang that he was safer here than he would be anywhere else. Theil had been right.

"Is there something further you require?" Beal asked from the doorway.

Donovan turned slowly to face him, feeling the familiar brush across his mind. Unthinking, he responded as he would to another Seeker, with the mental pinch of a vise. The questing brush faded abruptly and Beal grimaced.

"Don't do that," Donovan warned softly. "Does the general have other guests?"

"It isn't my place to speak on the general's guests to those who have no need to know." Beal turned away.

Donovan walked back into the dining hall. The steward turned to address him, but Ost's voice rang out, "Beal. Thank you. That will be all."

He bowed and walked past Donovan with a glare, closing the doors behind him. Donovan and Ost were alone now. The faint sound of clinking dishes and splashing water came through a second set of doors.

"To what do I owe the continued pleasure?" Ost's eyes bored into him. His tone was much less jovial this time; he sounded heavy with fatigue.

"Are you a life mage?" Donovan voiced the question he'd been debating all through dinner. He felt stupid asking it, but that was a familiar sensation these days and didn't scare him as it once had.

Ost didn't answer right away, didn't feign outrage or confusion. He took a heavy inhale and let it out before saying, "I have studied it."

"Do you follow their teachings?"

"Do you even know what that means?" Ost countered.

"No," Donovan admitted easily.

"So if I said yes, you would ...?"

"I would ask for definition, as none of my research has been entirely revealing on the subject."

Ost laughed and wiped his thick hands across the table a few times. Donovan stared at them and wondered ... the sounds and motions from the primer flashed through his mind, and he remembered the motions Ost had made in the study as well.

"Are you afraid I'll bite?" Ost asked.

"Yes. Running away is more easily accomplished near a door."

"Assuming no one's behind it."

"Life magic?" Donovan prompted. He wasn't entirely sure of his safety, but he knew he had little defense anyway, especially now.

"Do not take more than can be spared. Do not cause harm. Do not destroy. Do not endanger. Seek others who strive to preserve and build community with them. Accept no one who seeks only to conquer and challenge. Do not make war unless all other options have been attempted." Ost spoke by rote, repeating something he'd said a thousand times.

"Those are the rules of your faith?" Donovan asked.

"Mine and thousands of others — truly, we are a terrifying people." The sarcasm was thick.

"Then where do the blood mages come from?"

"Where do any evil people come from?" Ost's impatience and irritation were clear now. "You had the right of it earlier: anyone can turn from the path, and power is a lantern in the swamp. It takes control not to abuse it. Plenty of criminals in this kingdom have no magic, or use Talents to achieve their goals. How are my people expected to be different?"

"Your people ..." Donovan couldn't get the words out.

"My people are at war with the blood mages. Your people are at war with everybody. Over the centuries, the Order has put thousands of peaceful, innocent people to death because they *might* be performing blood magic. Almost all of them were fighting *against* the blood mages. You've been systematically destroying potential allies for decades."

"Where is Ruben?"

Ost's eyebrows rose and then dropped quickly. "Why do you think I would know?"

"You do, don't you? How does kidnapping a child fit into your 'do no harm'? 'Do not endanger'?"

Ost turned red and stood suddenly. "You don't know what you're talking about. Tools are used for the betterment of a community. Tools that are turned into weapons are not quickly restored to their original purpose."

"You think he's a weapon?"

"I know the Order sees him as one."

"He's a little boy!"

"He's more than that: he's dangerous."

"In your hands, yes! *Where is he?!*" Donovan took several steps forward with fury propelling him.

"Oh, do continue. I'd like to see where this is going."

Donovan spun toward the kitchen door, his fury morphing to fear and back at the sight of the Smiling Man leaning nonchalantly in the doorway.

"Ah, well, I thought it might progress thusly. No greeting for an old friend?" He considered his words and then shrugged. "Old being relative — our relationship is aged near to a year."

"You're here to kill me?" Donovan remembered Theil's words about assassins. His hands clenched.

"I've actually been given clear instructions not to, which, I'll admit, I find rather frustrating." The man came further into the room, his tread the confident stride of a large cat. "Apparently it would 'draw too much attention'."

"What do you want?"

"With you? Nothing. Surprising, I know. Your presence here has nothing to do with mine. A happy coincidence."

Donovan looked back at Ost and saw a look of mild distaste of his features. He didn't like the Smiling Man either. "You have strange allies, Ost."

"Don't think to lecture me," the general snapped.

"How far does your betrayal extend?" Donovan asked. "How many of the king's soldiers have you turned to your cause?"

Ost only glared in response.

The Smiling Man strode casually forward. Donovan backed away.

"Run along to your room, Donny-boy. There's nothing for you here."

Donovan's eyes darted to Ost's face. The general was glaring at the Smiling Man, but his look didn't change when their eyes met.

Fear had his hands trembling, but Donovan turned his back. His steps were quick on the way to his room. Where else could he go?

The door to his room was open and Beal exited as he arrived. The steward looked smug as he left without comment.

Donovan saw his bag on the bed, clearly searched. The primer he'd brought was partially unwrapped. Donovan slammed the door closed and paced around the room, angry and afraid by turns.

Now what?

9

"LONG AGO, BEYOND LIVING MEMORY, two magics were born and lived as one: twins, alike, but so very different. Together, it was a living thing, untainted with the desires and ugliness of mankind. One of the magics was lazy, and angry; the other was strong and bright. When man came about, magic decided that it would imbue these human creatures with itself. The lazy magic decided it would be born into people and they would learn to wield it with little effort, but the cost would be pain, so that the gift would not be abused.

"The bright magic relished in the chase, and decided that any human could learn to wield it if they worked hard, but the cost would be devastation, so that the gift would not be abused.

"Humans are oh-so-unpredictable, but it didn't matter because everyone lived in harmony then, exploring magic and learning what there was to know about the world.

"One day, the first magus was born. This was a mage who was born to magic, and could wield the bright magic. It was too powerful a creature, and so the magics worked together to give it a powerful

cost. No matter, because these magi were rare things, and the cost was dreadful indeed, made to keep it in check.

"As time went on, humans grew bored with their gifts and they grew violent as humans do. They fought, the slight differences between them enough to war over. Centuries passed in war and peace, war and peace, and this time when the magus was born, it was into a time of such violent bloodshed that the two magics thought their humans would never recover.

"But the magus was a smart one, and he remembered his teachings about the costs, and he learned and studied what his magic could do, and he formed a plan."

"Are you making this up as you tell it?" she asked wearily.

"Yes," he replied with a laugh. "But now comes your part."

* * *

While this wasn't the first time Whitman had found himself detained, suspected of something, it was the first time it had happened within the Order. This was the most comfortable by far. He was under suspicion, but no one had charged him with anything. Kept in paper and ink, and with guards coming and going overhead, it was easy enough to send a message out with his first meal.

The message had put into action a series of events that ultimately lead to a guard in his employ taking up one of the positions above him at the last post change. He was now able to send and receive direction and information. It was nearly like being back at his own desk. Nearly.

He closed his eyes and wished for patience. His memory was incredible, but not infallible, and he needed access to his files to conduct his work properly. Most of what he'd discovered was in the medical field: Elliott had been poisoned with foxbane — a common enough herb, purchasable at any apothecary and carried by most midwives. Beyond that, if you knew what you were looking for, you could find it out in the fields surrounding the Order. Most children were taught what it looked like so as to avoid it.

Bitter unless it was ground down into a powder, it dissolved fast, killed faster in a large enough dose. The poison was easily flushed from the body with a mixture of alcohol and various other plants, which would do more damage than the poison alone if they did not mix with the foxbane, but it was such with so many remedies. If the poison didn't kill you, then certainly would the cure ...

He rubbed a rough hand up and down his leg and frowned at the floor of his cell, wishing he could better recall Elliott's schedules going back several months. No doubt Captain Gant was doing so already, but Whitman preferred to be more than one step ahead: it kept his reputation lively.

Better news indicated that the Mentalists and Healers were finally making progress with Kina — or at least they were trying something new. The door to her room had been closed for several hours after admitting nearly a dozen people. If she had any updates, he wanted to hear it, so he'd placed a servant nearby ready to bring him what she learned.

Lady Pennison had visited several hours earlier to assure him that Oslan was comfortably tucked away in her office with a pile of work and books to read. He understood the need for it all, but Whitman still regretted the position his work put his husband in. Anything to keep him safe, however.

He wondered how many of his contacts had tried to deliver reports or requests — he couldn't be missing for too much longer before his network would be in trouble. Remove the spider and too many flies could bring the web down. He'd considered telling Gant what the man already suspected, but had decided against it. Let him suspect, but keep the truth hidden for now — it might be safer for both of them at the moment.

The distant sound of metal doors opening and closing rang out, indicating someone's arrival. He waited, curiosity piqued, until Captain Robert Gant came into view to check on his favorite prisoner.

"Hello, Captain!" Whitman spoke cheerfully from behind the small desk he'd been allowed. It was already covered with pages upon pages of notes, his inkwell an eighth used. "What brings you to my humble, and temporary, abode?"

Gant smiled crookedly. "Doing well, then, are you?"

"Of course! It is like unto a vacation, but with a bit less sun than I prefer."

"I imagine."

"Fret not so, my dear man." Whitman smiled pompously. "I'm sure your culprit will be captured soon."

"Oh aye?" Gant asked.

"Certainly. You have a limited number of people able to access the Head's office, and a large number of them are already scrutinized by the Mentalists on a thrice-weekly basis — sometimes more. That limits your list considerably. To such a degree, that one wonders if the murderer was meant to escape at all."

"... True."

"Any child may know about foxbane, but how many of them in his service have the ability to administer it? The cooks? Servants? His food was randomly tasted, and his rooms were guarded, so even shorter runs your list."

Robert leaned against his cell bars with one shoulder.

"Against the rules, that," Whitman said airily.

"Be honest. Do you know who did it?" Gant asked.

"I have strong suspicions, but you're far more capable of confirming them than I. Especially from here."

"It is your duty to report any —"

"Dear man, can you tell me who is currently running the Order in the absence of an agreed upon Head?" Whitman interrupted.

Robert's eyes narrowed. "The council, of course."

"Which consists of how many people?"

"Nearly fifty, right?"

"Forty-four, you will recall. The head of every department and a second, voted into position by 'the people'. How long have they been in a closed session?"

Robert shrugged. "About two hours now. Took a bit to get everyone gathered."

"No doubt. Vale of the Retrievers likely being last — she always hates those things."

Robert's eyebrows rose, but he didn't reply.

Whitman continued, "I hope you will excuse my suspicious mind, but how many of your guards do you have in that room?"

"None of mine. Commander's there with two votes —"

"Because Ost is unavailable for an emergency session, yes, and ...?"

"Just her."

"Right. If we can assume that Elliott's death was, as it appears, an assassination, why would we not have the other heads under guard to prevent the majority loss of our leadership?"

"They're capable of defending themselves," Robert said slowly.

"Certainly. That in mind, and with traditional weapons not allowed, how many do you think would need to be under the influence of the Hunters to perform a coup?"

Robert blinked at him. "Devious."

"I thought so."

"You've already arranged soldiers in the room, then?"

"Yes, but I thought you'd like to know your guards believe they are acting with your authority. There will be some tweaked noses, I imagine. Your signature was not hard to forge."

"Closed session is closed session."

"Yes, but generally speaking, most guards are trusted to keep their mouths shut or risk their careers. When the council is not afraid of murder and can decide to stop lurking in shadows, their sessions are allowed to be viewed by any of the public interested in attending, especially in selecting a new Head, who is generally chosen from their already voted-upon ranks. It would be very bad for us if that person was working for the enemy."

"I could agree."

"Why do you not like the Commander?" Whitman asked suddenly.

Robert frowned. "I don't mind her."

"She is your superior officer."

"One of them, aye."

"But when you mentioned her, your face twitched a bit, like you were trying not to roll your eyes. Full of herself, is she?"

Robert chuckled, shaking his head. "Nah, just grates on me is all."

"Why?"

"Because we're all soldiers and sometimes we don't get along. It's called discipline, not happy-family-time."

"As eloquent as ever, my dear man. Always do I treasure your words."

"Need anything?"

"If you were going to break into the prison, when would you do it?"

Robert stood away from the bars and crossed his arms. "Really?"

"Humor me."

"No."

"No?"

"You're under guard, not on holiday."

"Ah, but I am innocent until proven guilty, and as I cannot be proven guilty, being that I am innocent, I am under guard *protection*, not simply 'under guard'. Call me suspicious if you must, but I would very much value your view."

Gant rolled his eyes and turned away. "Enjoy your puzzles, bard."

"When my husband arrives, could you send him right in, please?"

He heard Robert snort before the door closed behind him. Whitman grinned, pleased with himself.

It didn't take long before light footsteps carried his love to his cage. Whitman stood and limped to the cell door and put out his arms to embrace Oslan as warmly as he could through the cold metal.

"I miss you," Whitman said tightly.

"I miss you," Oslan replied the same way.

"I was so worried."

"I know."

"Are you all right?"

"Yes, of course."

"Lady Pennison took you in."

"Yes."

"Treating you well?"

"Of course."

"This will be over soon."

"I know."

"I love you."

Oslan smiled. "I love you, too, you handsome badger. What happened?"

"I left Elliott's office to tell Gant to order raids through the city and he got a note a few minutes after, saying I was the prime suspect in the Head's death. That is all I know."

"Foxbane?"

Whitman raised an interested eyebrow.

"Lady Pennison left reports on her desk and I helped myself when she was out of the room. I'm a quick study," Oslan replied.

"Cheeky. Used enough to make it common — I have people out looking for the shop that sold it."

"Assuming our assassin didn't simply pick it on their way into the city."

"Yes."

"Your mail is backing up."

"I expect so." Whitman gritted his teeth with frustration. "I am not a prisoner, but neither am I free to go about my business."

"Anyone I can speak to on your behalf?"

"I have friends on the council, but none know me as myself except Vale, and she is hardly subtle; Elliott was my scalpel there. It would complicate matters if I directed them to have me freed."

"True."

"I hope this blows over quickly."

"No Mentalist to free you, of course, with all the trouble in that mind of yours."

"Unfortunately."

Oslan ran a finger down Whitman's cheek. "I might say I wish I could join you, but I fear they'd be too happy to oblige, and I prefer to remain outside of your little bird cage."

"Sweetly trilling my wish to fly. Maybe I should request my lute ..."

"What happens next?"

"Another assassination attempt. This time of the murderer, if my guess is right."

"Will they come here?"

"I expect so. Gant will locate and bring them in. The assassin will have to follow."

Oslan nodded thoughtfully. "I'll come back when the commotion starts."

Whitman grimaced. "Take this." He handed Oslan his cane.

They kissed as deeply as the bars would allow. Whitman felt an ache in his chest. He wanted so badly to hold his man close and pretend as though none of this was happening. He'd considered retirement many times already, despite his youth, just to be able to keep Oslan safe. Still, he knew Oslan would never forgive him for taking such action when he had so much left to do.

Oslan left and Whitman watched until he was gone from sight before he sat behind his desk and stared up at the grating that made his ceiling. His mind revolved with theories and ideas and worries. He closed his eyes again and watched the weaving threads, waiting for the connections to make themselves known.

* * *

The sound of scraping metal woke Whitman from his meditation. He blinked a few times and yawned, stretching and bending to touch the ground. Upright, his fingers barely brushed the ceiling grating, even on his toes. After a short time, a new prisoner was brought in and shown to the cell across from Whitman's. He wasn't surprised to see that it was Bruno, Elliott's secretary. The elderly man looked nervous, shaken, as he was placed inside and the door locked behind him. The escorting soldier left the way he'd come without comment.

Bruno wrung his hands and spun about, looking in every direction other than toward Whitman, except for a few furtive glances. As patient as the day was long — at least on the surface — Whitman watched him for a time. Internally, he churned with impatience.

Bruno finally completed his tour of the small space and could no longer help but look across the aisle at his prison-mate.

Whitman said, "I thought I would be seeing you."

"Oh?" Bruno made a timid attempt at amusement.

"The messengers and pages all get examined by Mentalists weekly, and you simply have too much private information in that head of yours to allow a Mentalist to go poking about it."

"Right." Bruno swallowed hard. "Same for you, I see?"

"Naturally."

Whitman leaned against the bars and felt the chill of them against his cheeks as he peered through. "Curious, what happened."

"Very curious," Bruno agreed readily.

"Sad, too."

The older man nodded quickly.

"That is shame I see on your features, friend."

"Sh-shame?"

"Come now, Bruno. It is only us. And our nearby friends." Whitman glanced upward at the guards pacing through their rounds. "You can talk to me."

The man only continued to wring his hands and step from foot to foot.

"All right, then. I expect we have a couple of hours before anything ... exciting occurs. You should get some rest."

Whitman sat at his desk and dipped his pen, scratching it across the parchment. Half of what he wrote was nonsense, but the look of the thing was far more important for now. He referred to other pages and was soon doing actual work, making lists and rewriting some of his previous thoughts more concisely as he waited for Bruno to crack.

It took longer than Whitman expected, but after about an hour and a half the man said quietly, "He was a good leader."

"Yes, he was." Whitman didn't look up. "He tried hard, had goals and worked to achieve them. Better than some this Order has seen."

Bruno paced his cell.

"Why did you do it?"

Bruno shook his head as though to deny the claim, but seemed unable to put voice to the lie.

"Did the Hunters threaten you?"

"Stop," Bruno whispered as tears welled in his eyes.

"I cannot help you if you do not tell me." Whitman kept his voice low and soft.

"I know." Bruno sat on the edge of his cot and stared at the back row of bars to the empty cells beyond.

They heard footsteps above them as the guards jogged away toward an unseen emergency. Whitman's stomach sank to see them go. It was starting.

He crossed to the bars again. "What did you do?"

"They had my family," Bruno whispered.

"Why did you not tell anyone?"

"*They had my family.* They knew, and they threatened to tell the Order. Elliott never would have tolerated it."

Whitman felt dizzy. "Your family is blood mages?" he asked, incredulously. The implications of that hit him hard. "*How dare you?*"

Bruno waved an impatient hand in his direction. "You're all fools. You have no idea what this war is going to do to the people on *both* sides."

"Then tell me, Bruno. Tell me so I can help you."

"It's too late for me."

They heard the prison door open and boots hurried their way. A petite woman rounded the corner clutching her arm. She looked pale and sickly but held a crossbow haphazardly in her injured arm, a quarrel in her teeth. She spared a tired glance toward Whitman but turned her attention to Bruno in his pen.

"Excuse me, miss," Whitman said politely.

She didn't answer, but loaded her weapon.

"What possible purpose can this serve? We already know he did the poisoning."

She looked at him then, contempt and sadness warring across her features. She winced as she balanced the crossbow on the crossbar of Bruno's cell.

He was staring at the bolt wide-eyed while terror shook his body.

"Hey!" Whitman snarled. "The guards will return at any moment. You were expected."

The assassin nodded as her grip tightened on the crossbow. Her injured arm was held tight to her side.

He realized then, "You are not expected to escape ..." She looked familiar and it took his memory a moment to supply him with her face. "You are the Elementalist. One that failed to kidnap Ruben — you escaped." He shook his cell door, rattling the bars loudly, impotently. Letting Gant lock him in had been a mistake.

The Elementalist lined up her target.

Bruno backed away, mumbling to himself, eyes wide.

The bolt fired.

And stuck.

The assassin and Whitman stared at the crossbow bolt suspended in midair, just in front of Bruno's chest.

Bruno himself was sweating now as he mumbled and stared down at the thing determined to take his life.

The assassin cursed violently and threw the crossbow to the ground with a loud clatter. She backed away from the cell and took several deep, shuddering breaths, then put out a hand that shook with fatigue and fear.

Before she could bring her magic to bear, Oslan sprinted around the corner with Whitman's cane held over his shoulder, prepared to do violence. The Elementalist was too tired to react with speed. Oslan smashed the cane across the side of her head and she fell like a stone.

Whitman let out the breath he was holding. "My love, please tell me you have keys to Bruno's cell."

"Not yet." Oslan sprinted away again without pause.

"Hold, Bruno ..." Whitman encouraged him.

The secretary still mumbled, but his words came slower. Sweat poured off of him as he stood frozen in place. Physically helpless where he was, Whitman's academic mind strained to hear the words Bruno was mumbling. They mostly seemed to be gibberish, but the strain of maintaining the unknown power was taking its toll.

Whitman scanned through his meager belongings to find something to help him pick the lock, but knew it was fruitless. Meaningless. Gibberish.

"Bruno, if all you need is words, speak on the merchant contracts that Elliott signed in the last five years."

He watched for a result.

After a moment, Bruno's words changed to the subject Whitman suggested. His voice became stronger and more confident.

The bolt in the air before him wiggled warningly when he shifted his weight. Something about his position kept it steady.

The spymaster took a moment to study the unconscious assassin on the floor. Her breathing was shallow and while the head wound wasn't bleeding, a blue welt grew under her hair. Her eyes twitched occasionally, but she had yet to move with purpose.

Bruno was growing breathless by the time boots echoed above them, though Whitman knew only minutes had passed.

He called out, "I need keys to unlock this cell, on the double!"

A soldier appeared above him, hair sticking out in all directions, uniform disheveled. "What's going on?" he asked. "What happened?"

"A man's life is in danger! Let me out of this damn cell! Drop the keys! I'm in protective custody, not a prisoner!"

The soldier hurried to comply, Whitman's tone convincing him if nothing else. He opened a hatch above Whitman's cell and jumped down, rushing to the door to unlock it. As soon as it opened, Whitman charged past in a skipping hop with the guard's keys already in his dexterous hands. He threw open Bruno's cell door and grabbed the man's blanket off of his cot, throwing it over the bolt.

The murderous thing buzzed and flailed violently under the wool, like a wasp, but more deranged and hateful than usual.

Bruno, freed, collapsed against the bars and sank to the ground, gasping for breath and holding his heaving chest.

Whitman leaned against the bars beside him and put a hand on his shoulder. "Are you all right?"

Bruno nodded wearily. Thundering boots indicated the approach of more soldiers with Oslan in the lead.

The guard from above was examining the unconscious Elementalist. "What struck this woman?" He indicated the welt on the side of her head.

Oslan, catching his breath, held out Whitman's cane.

The soldier took it and his eyes widened with surprise.

"It's custom made," Whitman explained. "A bit heavier than normal."

"This is wholly filled with lead," the soldier argued.

"As I said."

Two more soldiers entered Bruno's cell and lifted him onto the cot. They tried to question him, but Whitman angrily waved them away. Bruno was still fighting for breath after his ordeal in self-preservation. Besides which, Whitman desperately wanted to question the man himself.

Gant and another officer of equal rank joined them a moment later to survey the scene. The Elementalist-assassin was still unconscious, but a soldier with Healing Talent was giving her an examination, kneeling with a hand on her forehead and wrist.

Whitman still leaned against the bars, arms crossed, eyeing his cane in the hands of the first soldier. He saw Gant look his way, but they said nothing to each other.

Captain Gant barked, "Listen up! I want reports from everyone, on my desk, in one hour." He pointed at the first soldier and the Healer. "You stay." He pointed at the two guarding Whitman and Bruno. "You go. I want to know how she got in and incapacitated so many of our people."

They left and the second captain beckoned Whitman out of Bruno's cell. He eyed her suspiciously as she started an examination of her own, but appeared competent.

He held out a hand for his cane. The soldier hesitated until Whitman threatened him with a slowly arched eyebrow.

Oslan put his arm around Whitman's back.

"Well?" Gant asked.

Whitman pulled Oslan close. "Quite. I believe I am on the road to answers, Captain. There is a signpost ahead, but it is out too far to read at present. I can see the tread of increased traffic guiding me to my goal, however. Any word from Lady Pennison or the Mentalists regarding the condition of Kina?"

Gant blinked at the rapid play of words and subject change. "No."

"I shall need to travel in that direction then, with Bruno, who is in need of rest and some nourishment. He had something of an ordeal whilst in your prison and needs to recover before being questioned. I am happy to present my own report of these events, but I fear it may take longer than an hour to have it on your desk; I have quite a few other things to attend to at the same time."

Robert nodded slowly. "Andrea."

The Captain in Bruno's cell glanced up and then stood to dole out orders. "You two, fetch two stretchers, on the double." The remaining soldiers trotted off to do as ordered. Andrea followed in their wake after quietly conveying information into Robert's ear.

"Anything else to say?" Robert asked.

Whitman gestured to Bruno. "He really does need to recover. He performed some kind of magic about which I need to question, before your people start demanding answers of him." Whitman pointed at the still-unconscious assassin. "The work of my husband in our defense. She will need containment and questioning as well, which I am also happy to perform. Likely a Healer will be needed to ensure the damage is not permanent. She was sent to kill Bruno, and was not expected to escape. I imagine she managed to hide on the grounds after the botched attempt to kidnap Ruben, and I am curious to know how she received new orders for this plan. She has few options now."

Gant nodded slowly, absorbing the information.

"How goes the election session?"

The soldier inhaled deeply. "Peacefully. Dully. Politics have never been my forte, despite how often I find myself drawn into them with recent promotions. The council members are still in session."

"Still? Interesting. I will need to learn what I can about that, as well, then. Our enemies are still among us, clearly."

"I'll go," Oslan interjected. "I'll catch up and keep you informed." He gave Whitman a peck on the lips and left.

Gant turned to watch him leave. "Trouble does find you, aye?"

Whitman sighed. "Every day, it seems." He glanced back at Bruno. "I expect I am free to go? Or have you yet to confirm that Bruno is your killer?"

"I'm swayed by the attempt on his life, but we will need to confirm his involvement before you're entirely free. He'll need to confess before you have a private chat, of course."

"My thanks. Do not expect me to be quick about letting myself be caged again in the future."

The soldiers returned with stretchers and more hands to carry them.

Whitman sent for a page to gather his sheets of notes and take them to his room and followed the soldiers to the Medical Wing. He felt simultaneously drained and invigorated, in need of a nap, and excited to discover the next piece of information.

*   *   *

Whitman approached Kina's door but, before he could knock, a strict-looking gentleman came out to shush him with a silent finger to his lips, and lead them a distance from the room.

"Any progress?" Whitman asked.

The gentleman quirked a small smile. "Some, but it is difficult to describe. We're moving gently."

"I think that is wise," Whitman agreed.

"Please don't approach the door. We've asked the same of the nursing staff — some of our efforts result in unpredictable Mentalist effects and we prefer not to have unexpected minds joining our conferences."

Whitman bowed his head. "I will wait for your contact. If possible, please give her my regards."

"Certainly." The gentleman nodded curtly and headed back to the room, visibly steeling himself before stepping inside.

Whitman next visited the office of Lady Pennison. She often did rounds throughout the day to check on patients and staff alike, but he had not yet seen her. Sure enough, he found her behind a desk with stacks of paperwork threatening to overwhelm the space.

Wielding a quill with practiced efficiency, she made a few notes and put a thick stack of documents in a tray. She smiled to see him in the doorway.

"Proven innocent, I assume?"

"I have been assured that my innocence is not yet proven, but that another is a favorite for the crime. He has been brought in for rest and recuperation."

"Bruno Clarke, to be kept under guard. You've also brought me a Hunter assassin."

"Mmm." Whitman took the seat in front of her desk and sighed with relief to be off his feet.

"What else can I assist you with, Bard Acres? Your husband was a dear, by the way, assisting me with certain paperwork more suited to a clerk's skills than my own."

"Yes, he hates to be bored," Whitman smiled. "I wondered, my lady, if we could discuss the continued Healing of my leg."

"A moment." She cleared a space and went to a large cabinet to withdraw an embarrassingly thick file with his name. She opened it to the most recent injury, scanned the details and nodded to herself. "All right. What are your thoughts?"

"I was thinking it is time that this injury cleared up, do you not?"

"Repeated Healings, especially on joints, can cause future issues and, while this is not a repeat injury, any allowed weakness can result in something more permanent. We Healed some initial damage alongside a surgery, and it was decided best to let natural healing continue until the muscles had strengthened."

"Yes. And now I would like that to be revisited. My knee has gained strength. I continue to exercise in all of the suggested ways, monitor my walking, stretching, etcetera."

Lady Pennison nodded. "A secondary Healing could very well be considered, after an updated assessment."

Whitman smiled lightly and wondered at the game being played. "I'm glad. I look forward to your permission to schedule that."

"Feel free to book a Healing with the front desk. You prefer Parel, yes?"

"Yes. He's done all of my Healings in the past."

"I saw that. He's free to perform your Healing as he chooses. Unfortunately, until I know what command structure has his priority, I've had to place certain restrictions on his movements through my office and other records."

Ah-ha. "Command structure?" Whitman leaned back in his chair.

"Loyalties have been under constant scrutiny since the recent upheavals."

"Certainly, you have found no sign that Parel works for the Hunters ..."

"No. Only that he works for you, which can be damning enough."

"And why is that?" As Spymaster, Whitman had certain liberties, and protecting his position was one of them. He didn't have anything to fear from Lady Pennison, but she was incredibly skilled, and her relocation would be a loss for the Order.

She took a steeling breath. "I don't like you, Bard Whitman Acres. I find it better to express that directly than dance around it. Professionally, our relationship has not changed. I will always make sure that you are provided with the best care that we can provide. Personally, however, I feel you carry too many secrets that could harm those outside yourself. I cannot trust you. I cannot put trust in you. I realize that you must play an important role here, else authorities would have displaced you long before now, but I can certainly chalk some of the chaos that surrounds your person to your effortless and limitless charms. You know everyone, you are everywhere, and where you go, trouble follows."

He smiled kindly. "You are not the first to say that. Today."

"I don't doubt it."

Whitman pursed his lips in thought. "My lady, I wish I could assuage your fears. I do carry secrets, some of them very dangerous, as any bard can claim. I certainly do not wish to challenge you in any way. Your position is one I do not envy, but that you perform excellently, beyond measure. Let me assure you, for what my assurances are worth, that I have only the best intentions for this Order and the people in it. I have never and will never directly harm your patients or staff."

"Of course," Lady Pennison smiled thinly. "However, intention of harm is a relative thing. I believe that you believe your words. In the meantime, my restrictions will remain on Parel and any others I discover to be in your employ. We shall see how that develops as time continues."

He gave her a long look and then bowed his head. "As you wish."

"I will agree to whomever you request to operate on your knee, and will consult to ensure that you can be safely Healed without undue future worry."

Whitman stood. "Illuminating, as always." He bowed. "And thank you."

He left her office and walked a few steps down the hall before he leaned his back against a wall. Too much was happening, had been happening for weeks now, and he felt a painful headache building.

"Whitman!"

He looked up from the mounting pressure in his skull to see a familiar face hurrying toward him.

"Annette!" He grinned and felt his burdens fall from his shoulders at the sight of her. "Oh, it is so good to see you. I was worried my letter did not reach you, but so much has happened."

"Of course I did, you duck — I had to hurry to session before it ended — I've called a recess, hopefully to gain my footing before the vote. Cara is making friends and taking notes."

"Can they vote without a Royal Liaison?" he asked. "I might need to brush up on Order laws ..."

"Certainly not, but they can decide on anything before I arrive so that my vote means very little in the end. Minds made, and all that. How are you? What have I missed?"

He let out a mirthless chuckle. "We should share news. How long is your recess?"

"Two hours."

"Come with me. You can absorb as we go."

"Lead the way."

"Who is Cara?"

"Donovan's former wife."

"Ah, *that* Cara. Intriguing. I am sure that is a story to hear."

"Oh yes." She smiled to herself while they traversed the wing to the first room on Whitman's short list.

"You look to be somewhat recovered, Bruno." Whitman took a seat by the former secretary's bedside. Annette stood unobtrusively in the back of the room.

Bruno eyed her and nodded cautiously.

"You are under guard here," Whitman explained. "You confessed to killing Elliott, but under duress, correct?"

Bruno nodded again, with urgency.

"Help me understand. I will speak in your defense if there is anything to it. They cannot sentence a man so severely if his actions were not of his own motivation."

Bruno stared at the ceiling for a long moment as though seeking inspiration, or courage. Whitman let him. He knew when a person was ready to speak; sometimes they just needed to gather their thoughts.

"My sister," Bruno said at last, "believes in the life of magic. Her husband is the same, and they've raised their children to it as well. She knows my position and has never pushed. But children ... they learn you don't know something and they share everything. And I love my nieces and nephews. They've grown now — families of their own. I'm outnumbered and love every moment with them. I learn bits and pieces, just how it works, but practice ... that's something else. I can't condemn them for blood-magic — that isn't who they are. Those are a different people, but the Order can't see that. One magic can prevail and it must be theirs." He looked sharply at Whitman. "Not that I disagree with that, you understand."

"Of course."

"But they feel the same."

"Why is that?"

Bruno waved a tired hand. "It's all theology and interpretation."

"I would be interested in whatever you know," Whitman pressed.

"Yes, I thought you might." Bruno sighed and closed his eyes. He licked his lips and continued, "Consider that all living things produce what we know as magic, and to perform feats of magic, you draw on their life power. Some aspects are more powerful than others. Motion, breath," he met Whitman's eye, "blood. A river would supply more than a tree, a mammal more than an insect, and so on. They have quite an interesting hierarchy listed — I saw it at holiday once when the children were young."

"Speaking words, making gestures, these all contribute to the power of this life magic," Whitman confirmed.

"Yes. Some people believe that specific words and gestures assist in greater ways, but that is far beyond me. Otherwise, it is merely will, just as I'm told Order Talents are — the magic is still part of everyone."

"Why can the mages not use your blood until there's been an injury?" Annette asked. "If every living thing produces magic, as you said, then surely they'd be able to access it more readily." She touched the scars on her arms.

Bruno frowned, hands up in supplication. "I don't know. Boundaries are an aspect of both magics. You can access your own essence, but have to break the boundary of another? They break the leaves of plants, cut roots, that sort of thing. My brother-in-law spoke of dueling techniques to break boundaries in a fight, but my sister wanted nothing to do with any of it, and forbid her children from discussing it. I expect that's where the blood magic started from."

"What about the addiction?" Whitman asked. "Just about everyone knows that blood magic is addicting."

"I expect it is," Bruno shrugged. "Blood is a powerful force to draw on, but no one I've met and befriended bothers to use it. Daily household tasks can be accomplished with breath and gestures and the occasional plant. And they're strict about not over-using the essence of anything: you don't want to kill it. Children are constantly monitored until they understand control."

"Do you know why they hate born mages so much?" Whitman filed everything away in his mental storage.

"My sister's family has no quarrel with the born Talented, but her husband and his friends have said enough: those born with magic don't consider the cost. They upset some kind of balance. I haven't learned enough to have details for you — like I said, I never asked, they never pressed, and I only picked up bits and pieces over the years."

"You say the Hunters discovered that your family performs this life magic, and was threatening to turn them over to the Order?"

Bruno nodded. "I would be removed from my position, sentenced for harboring mages, and my sister's family would be tried and likely sentenced to death. The children would be put into foster and forced not to practice until they forgot everything about their teachings. I couldn't have that. Elliott was not a man of gray. He saw the world in black and white, and I knew I had few options. If we ran, both sides would hunt us, and we'd have to leave the kingdom entirely to escape persecution."

"You could join the Hunters ..."

Bruno turned away distastefully. "This is my life. I love the Order, and what it stands for. I can't just run off and join a group of people who will hate me for where I came from."

"You will be sentenced for killing Elliott." Whitman ran a hand through his curls. "But I will do what I can to speak in your defense."

Tears fell down Bruno's face, their directions altered by his wrinkles and scrunched expression. He looked to be in pain as he whispered, "I didn't want to. He trusted me, and I —" he buried his face in his hands and turned his body away as he shook with grief.

Whitman stood and motioned to Annette. They left quietly, leaving him to his guilt, neither with words of comfort to offer.

The second room was smaller than the first and in a guarded hall. Whitman held up the note of passage from Gant and the nurses and surgeons at the desk allowed him through.

"One more," Whitman told Annette. He rolled his neck and put his shoulders back to stand taller than he felt. Annette gripped his hand for a moment, lending him strength. He thanked the guards at the door and entered, Annette once more in his wake.

Dull canvas covered the padded walls. A small cot stood against a wall, a ceramic chamber pot beneath it. The prisoner, now wearing ceramic manacles, had been changed from her own clothing into a set of Medical clothes. Thin and boring, they were also guaranteed not to be hiding pockets with anything dangerous. Whitman didn't doubt that there was also, somewhere, a Healer with this woman's memories of how to use her Talent in his mind, taken from her for the safety of others. It was a drastic measure, but occasionally necessary.

No chairs or stools in this room, so Whitman stood by the cot where the Elementalist sat, her back against the wall. Annette took position in a back corner, though the small size of the room made her seem to loom more than before. The assassin wore an apathetic expression and gazed at the wall, not bothering to make eye contact.

"How are you?" Whitman asked politely.

She blinked slowly.

"Concussions are never fun. I have had a few of my own."

Blink.

"I am sorry your mission failed. I am glad, of course, but, having experienced failure with severe consequences, I am sincerely sympathetic. I certainly do not expect you to be glad of your current situation, but I imagine it could be worse —your side does not yet know of your failure, and we are more interested in the information with which you might be able to part than your immediate execution."

Blink.

"You were sent earlier in the year to kidnap our magus, Ruben. The rest of your troupe was captured or killed, of course. Did you make physical contact for your updated instructions, were they left as a message, conveyed to you in some other way?"

Blink.

"Who is the leader of your army?"

Blink.

"Where is your army located?"

Blink.

"How many people fight with you?"

Blink.

"Why did you turn to life magic when you were born with a Talent?"

Blink. Eye contact.

Ah-ha ... "Were you raised in life magic?"

Blink. Nod.

"Forgive my lack of knowledge about your beliefs, but was your family disappointed or upset when you developed a Talent?"

The Elementalist sneered and growled, "Don't pretend to care. Just ask your damn questions."

Whitman leaned against the wall. "I do care, actually. I am a bard. Life is about stories — otherwise what is the point?"

Blink.

He sighed. "What will happen to you now?"

She seemed surprised, confused by his question. "What?"

"If we let you go, what will happen?"

"Not sure. Might depend on who finds me."

"Us or them?"

"You've already found me."

Whitman frowned. "You have me confused."

She rolled her eyes and turned away again. "Your lot knows nothing."

"Then enlighten me."

"Why?"

"Because someone should have a single clue as to what is going on and it might as well be me."

A ghost of a smirk played about her lips.

"Do you have a name, at least? I am Whitman. Whit, if you like. She is Annette."

"… Jasmin."

"Jasmin, thank you. Please tell me what I am missing."

"What do you think you're missing?"

"I believe I have just finally grasped onto the existence of life magic, and perhaps what it is, how it works, and possibly the beliefs that accompany it. You seem to be implying that we are fighting two groups when I was convinced for the last thirty years that it was only one. Everyone has been telling me how little the Order knows. I am a scholar. I live for knowledge and crave it like air."

"I live for …?" Jasmin glanced around the little room and gave him a pointed look.

"If your information assists me, which I can almost guarantee it will, I will make sure that you escape execution. That does not mean you will not spend life in prison, of course, but I am willing to hear any deal you can produce."

"What sway does a bard have around here?"

He pointed to Annette. "She is the Royal Liaison and has votes in council meetings. She pulls more strings than I can reach. Besides, what can a bard *fail* to do when his mind is tuned to a task?" He winked.

"I want a big cell, nowhere near others, and all the books I can read. And some other things, but that to start. I'll think of the rest when I have a chance."

"Easily done. You have to help me, though."

"What do you want to know?"

"Who are we fighting?"

"Blood mages and life mages."

"What is the difference? The main difference — the difference of beliefs."

Jasmin took a deep breath and winced as it shifted her injuries. "Think of it this way: your blood mages want all Order mages dead, the whole line wiped out, and your people enslaved."

"Drastic."

"The life mages want *them* wiped out, completely, and want your Order to train all magic users, correctly, and balance everything like it once was."

"You belong to the life mages."

She nodded.

"Like it once was ...?"

Jasmin quirked an eyebrow. "You don't know this place used to teach life magic?"

Whitman filed that under Very Important Research. "What changed?"

"The Cataclysm, of course. People died, blamed it on magic, and the born mages decided that they were better than everyone else and tried to wipe out everyone who'd trained and wasn't them. Here we are now."

"How do you know that?"

"It's taught to everyone I know, *Whit*. My mother explained it to me just as her mother did to her. It's common knowledge, except here, where that ancient mistake has been plaqued like an achievement. Except that you don't know. Maybe it's one of those trophies that gets tossed in a closet and forgotten about because it's embarrassing."

"I expect so." Whitman was already mentally cataloging the books he would gather from the library.

"The war is about to happen. We'll wipe them out for sure." She laughed dryly. "And you're going to help, know or not."

"What do you mean by that?" Annette took a step forward as she asked.

Jasmin shook her head. "I've answered your questions. I need demonstrations that you can actually help me."

"You did not answer all of them," Whitman pointed out.

"I don't know who's leading the army — that's above my head. As for where the army is, well." She grimaced. "I don't know exactly. And I really can't tell you how many people fight for our side — it wouldn't be right."

He couldn't argue.

"And my mother was proud when I got my Talent. She's an Elementalist, too. Trained me herself. In both magics."

Whitman smiled. "Thank you, Jasmin. I hope you recover quickly, and I am quite sure we will speak again."

They left the room and Whitman spoke to the guards, "She is assisting us with information about their military and is not to be harmed in any way. No one gets through that door unless they are cleared specifically by Captain Gant or Lady Pennison. Let us not lose the one advantage we have, please?"

The soldiers nodded curtly. Whitman rejoined Annette, who had moved further down the hall.

"She still didn't say where the army is and that's been our first question since the war became official," Annette griped.

"I have gained more knowledge in the last hour than the last year. Everything is coming to bear, I know it. I just need more time. I have *nearly* all the pieces." He closed his eyes to better sort through his mental space.

"I have to return to session. They're going to vote on the new Head," Annette reminded him.

"Try to stall them again. Failing that, have someone installed that we both know."

"I only have two votes, Whit."

"Who are the candidates, again?"

"You're not even listening."

"No, I need to figure out this life magic situation."

"It matters who gets elected."

"Only if they support blood mages, yes? We cannot have that."

"If they support life mages, then the leader of the Hunters will have major control over the only safe place for born mages."

"But they do not *want* to destroy the born mages. You heard Jasmin. They want to even the field, bring life mages back into the Order, what could be wrong with that?"

"What's wrong with that? Can you be serious for a moment? We don't even know what they believe! She could have been lying!"

"She was not lying," Whitman said confidently.

"Braun won't like any of this."

"The king does not have to like it. The Order stands apart from royal ruling and always has. It is the only way to ensure that we keep ourselves from becoming like the Manazians, after all." He took her hands. "Annette. We know these life mages allegedly do not want to kill us. We know they want some kind of equality. We know they are committing themselves to a war with our enemy without our guaranteed support. Jasmin said it is happening soon. How soon? Where? I need to get this information to Donovan."

"He's on Ost's lands, helping the general."

"Ost might know something, perhaps."

"Why would he know?" Her eyes widened. "*He* has the army. Their army."

"What?" Whitman asked, puzzled.

Annette shook her head. "Our army is on his land right now doing training exercises. He's had them there for weeks, months. If these life mages managed to herd blood mages nearby, Ost would be forced to commit his troops, because they would be forced to engage him. The life mages would simply have to stay out of the way and let us destroy the blood mages for them."

"Low risk, high reward." Whitman stared at her. "Annette, this is it. We know where their army is: right next to ours."

A bell overhead rang the hour and Annette grimaced. "I have to go."

"When is the vote?"

"Soon. I can't stall it."

"Get Hector installed."

"I sincerely doubt the whole council will agree to promote the Dean of Students into the position of Head of the Order."

"He is a reasonable fellow, and clearly able to control chaos."

"Yes. And he's too competent in his current position."

"Gant does not like the Commander. Why?"

"Because he is a mistrusting person? How should I know?"

"Have you met her?"

"Of course. She's friends with my sister."

"Go sit next to her. See why she is so disliked by our friends."

"One friend."

"Shoo. I have to pack."

"Donovan is days away."

"Then it is time we joined forces again, no?"

"I thought you were going to try to have your knee Healed."

Whitman's momentum sputtered to a halt. "All right, fine. But we are leaving as soon as we can. I will have Jasmin transferred to a cell with trusted guards around her. We do not want my protective custody situation to repeat itself. Better yet, maybe I will recruit her. She can come with us."

Annette rolled her eyes. "Don't leave without me. I'm warning you."

"Right. Go to session. We will talk after."

Annette hurried off and Whitman went to the front desk of the Medical Wing to ask for Parel. Things were in motion once more.

10

HE LOOKED DOWN INTO HER EYES and she saw again that flame of madness roaring and popping for all to see. He grinned with a sadist's charm. "I want you to kill me." She didn't move and he assured her, "No, not today, not tomorrow; don't cheapen it by wasting your chances and forcing my hand in response, but know that one day, I will expect to die, and I expect it be by your hand, little Beast."

"Why me?" She was exhausted, and this felt like one burden too many.

"Because you impress me, despite your youth. You already have proved difficult, and willful, and powerful. If anyone can do it, it's you."

"Why not let me kill you now?"

"Where is the challenge?" He was immediately enraged, insulted. "What creature willingly seeks its own death, puts itself on the sacrificial altar without fighting with all his worth? No, I expect subterfuge, cleverness, strength. Promise me you'll try."

She didn't hesitate. "I will."

"Good." He grinned again, temper cooled. "Now to work." He set her upright to walk on her own feet. They ached, but she could tolerate a few more miles, perhaps.

"What are we doing?" She looked around the crowded and depressing not-quite-a-town.

"I think it's a worthwhile task for a person of your abilities." He gestured. "Fix this. Make it what it wants to be, and when you've done that," he clasped his hands in front of his perfect teeth, "put the magics back together, like you said you could."

She stared at him, mind working to wrap itself around the idea as reality and no longer theory and boast. "How long do I have?"

"Until the next magus can best me. If I die by any hand but yours, I will do everything I can to take you with me." His face split into another familiar grin. "This is the challenge, the game, of a lifetime."

* * *

"Good morning!"

The door bounced off the wall behind. Ruben sat up so quickly he tweaked his neck. The sun hadn't yet risen and a chilly breeze blew through the open window. He shivered. A cloth bundle smelling of ham and strong cheese landed on the foot of his bed.

"Relieve yourself and get dressed. Eat. We're going outside." Travis lounged in the doorway, his eyes bright.

Ruben jumped to do as he was bidden and returned to find the gray-haired man looking through the books on the shelf. Ruben dressed, wincing as the stitches tugged on his arm, but carefully avoided numbing it with his Seeking. He knew the pain was the price of his choice.

"You keep cold walls," Travis noted with a shiver.

Ruben looked at the window. "Spend some time in a dark cell and tell me you wouldn't leave the window open."

"Fairly thrown. Set?" Travis led the way outside.

Ruben dug into the cloth package and withdrew the two hot and fresh rolls stuffed with meat and cheese and vegetables. Travis tucked the cloth into his back pocket. They passed the hall where Ruben had attacked Oats and came down the ornate, curved staircase into a large entrance hall with a tall ceiling. A statue of some nude warrior wielding a sword greeted guests as they entered. The doors were large and paned with expensive, tinted glass, which Travis didn't seem to notice as he pushed through them.

Ruben's heart pounded, and he had to force his shoulders down from their hunch around his ears — it had been so long since he'd been without a roof overhead. A path led to a road, but they ignored it for the grass. Dew froze his toes, but he loved it. He inhaled deeply and trembled with the heady rush of freshness it brought to his body. He stretched his arms out and turned in a slow circle, opening his eyes to see Travis doing much the same, but he'd kicked aside his boots in favor of wet feet.

"Beautiful, isn't it?" Travis asked in a reverent tone.

Ruben couldn't agree more. The field sparkled with diamond droplets as the sun rose, painting the clouds with the skill of a master and the abandonment of a beginner — bright, unsubtle colors merged and mingled across the sky as the flaming eye rose second by second. Ruben shivered again and raised his hands.

"Hold," Travis warned him. "Man's magic doesn't reign the now."

They watched until the sun was too bright to look at, standing in silent companionship.

When the spell was broken, Travis picked up his boots. "I love sunrise."

"Me, too."

"Wren said I'm to teach." Travis walked further into the field with his boots knotted together and slung over his shoulder. His hem was wet and clung to his ankles. "We'll teach as I taught my daughter, but bite your opinions about my faith between your teeth. Speak your questions — I'll answer them fairly, but naught of that murder binning until you know what you're talking of."

They went to the fence to lean against it to bask in the new sunlight. Ruben's feet felt thoroughly frozen, but he dug his toes into the dirt with relish.

"You can braze if you lack the warmth," Travis permitted. "Sunrise weren't time of it."

"Why not?" Ruben let heat flow through his body until he was comfortable again.

"Moments for consideration, when earth speaks honestly, we listen our best. When we speak too much, listen too little, she'll take more profitable ways and bite it into your ear. She wants to share, so for all you grab, choose caution, be polite. What's the due of magic?"

"It depends, right? Dizziness, nausea —"

Travis interrupted, "To born folk, sure. In discussion to life magic, no. The due of magic is life. Even trade, just like any market."

"Not my market," Ruben joked carefully.

Travis smirked, winked, and continued, "When death comes due, the body decays to earth as flesh, turns to dirt, or dung, or ash." He crouched and took a handful of damp soil, rolling it around between his palms and staining them like any farmer Ruben had known. "The soil turns you to family, eats you up into grass, is eaten by the bunnies and they're hooked by the hawk and ever on so. Eventually, all is mixed with all and you'll find no familiarity or difference in your granther and his roses.

"All that fee, that cost, is named potential. Grow as a blackberry bramble instead of grass and mayhap it's not the bunny but the bear that takes a bite, or the hog, or the beetle. Every chance that ever was in this and any lifetime is only potential and *that* is where magic comes from."

Travis formed the dirt into a long, thin worm. He held it to his face and blew a gentle breath across it. Ruben watched in wide-eyed fascination as the worm wiggled as though alive, bending and twisting in Travis's palm until his breath stopped.

Travis dropped it and stood with a groan as he stretched his back. "A tool like any other, an aid to those who practice, and you must learn the perils. What trade suited you?"

Ruben smiled. "I sold horses. Indentured."

"Indentured — aye, me, too, in my time. Regularly sold to farming, which suited me. You hurt yourself being a fool at trade? Burned or bit?"

Ruben glanced at his stitches. "Yes."

"Magic bites worse than any horse you've minded. A powerful force, full of possibility, and it stings if you don't pay focus. Are you paying focus?"

"Yessir."

Travis ruffled his hair affectionately. "Good. Hop here."

They walked again, enjoying the air. Ruben felt energized by the perceived freedom. He looked past the fence, hardly a barrier, to the fields and foothills covered with groves and growing things.

"If magic is in everything, then why not use more of it?" Ruben asked. "I mean, seems like there's so much life about — plants, animals — that you could do anything."

Travis cast a loving gaze across the landscape. "How long, to your mind, would a grove last? Use up a tree every day for floating about from place to palace? How quick would the grass grow if it knew it lived to die? If you thieved its promise so as to light fires every eve?"

"Not long, I suppose, if everyone was doing it."

"Aye. Respect and a strong measure of communal sense sees a worldly good. Plant living things for your children to nourish, for your grandchildren to feast."

"So ..." Ruben considered.

"Aye, on way," Travis prompted.

"Blood mages ..."

Travis sighed and tugged on an earlobe. "She said you'd badger. Skipping ahead, mind, but if you have the bit in your teeth ... Sit."

Ruben sat and Travis tossed a dozen stones in his direction. Ruben flinched, but realized quickly that they weren't targeted at him. Travis settled with a grunt and set the first stone in front of him. "As magic is potential, what measure of potential has this stone?"

Ruben shrugged. "Not much."

"Not much," Travis agreed. "But some." He balanced a second stone on the first. "What measure has grass? Or tree?" He balanced a third stone on the pile.

"More."

"Much more. They grow, they nourish, they feed. The tree becomes a thousand, thousand trees; the grass a million's million blades." Another rock added to the stack. "What of a creature? A rabbit, squirrel? Stag?"

Ruben watched the growing pile, impressed.

Travis balanced a fifth stone for a moment before the pile fell over. He shrugged. "What measure of potential has a man?"

"Compared to a tree?" Ruben looked across the field and thought about the Order, and the hands that had built it. He considered how many people there were, planting those trees and harvesting fields ... "A lot," he said at last.

"An incredible lot, yes," Travis agreed. "How many ancestors lived before you? How many could you bring to live after? What can a man change in his world? Aye, now what material might you use from a man to pay for that potential?"

"Blood?" Ruben offered.

Travis *tsk*ed through his teeth. "Start small."

"Um." Ruben shook his head. "Hair?"

"Aye, hair. Or breath?"

"Oh, right, the worm!" Ruben smiled.

Travis smiled back. "First thing a child does in her life is take a breath. How powerful must it be to bring such potential into the world?"

Ruben tried to grasp the nuance of such thinking. "So, breath, then ... spit?"

Travis grinned. "Unquestionably. And snot, and all manner of sticky horrors that children are. All parts of every life and, lacking, you'd struggle. There lies the danger." He started stacking stones again, as though to work his thoughts through his hands. "Blood is common because violence sees it easily taken. It's why women are the stronger, though plenty argue wrongly. Blood. And sperm also, aye, don't think it avoided."

Ruben blushed.

Travis sighed sadly. "Violence is easy and man is easily killed, but man is rarely willing to die. As easily taken as a man's expulsion, but why seduce a lover when you can put an arrow through them, or hack off a limb, aye?" Travis rubbed his nose with agitation and left behind a small line of dirt. "That take of power is like rotweed — fast into your head, it makes you *feel* stronger, *believe* you to be stronger than you've ever been, and when fading ... the weakness and hunger are heavy. You crave it again and it becomes habit. You start a need within yourself and are forever altered." His eyes were sad without their twinkle.

"That doesn't happen with breath and spit and the like?" Ruben asked.

"Aye, just as all else is aligned, people need *discipline*, strong hands, tenderness, good teachers, to remind the community that magic isn't a fix. A tool, like any axe or hammer. And magic will hurt you when abused. Hammer's no good if you haven't a nail."

"So blood mages are those who abuse life magic."

"Aye."

"Has anyone stopped being a blood mage?"

"I reckon fewer than those who mishandle the drink and return to clarity. Always tempting, once you have the crave for it, and maybe your people worry a bit more — keep an eye on you."

The stone pile fell over again at seven.

"How do you use it, then?" Ruben asked.

"Hasty," Travis admonished. "Tell me another danger of the magic. We learn the spread of fire before we light the fire." Travis didn't seem to be in any hurry, but Wren had been. She wanted Ruben to learn this, and he'd promised to try.

He looked at the dirt. If magic was potential, and the danger was using too much ... He was ashamed to realize it, but his few lessons with the Smiling Man had helped him expand his thinking.

It didn't take him long to answer, "You can shorten your life."

Travis nodded, pleased. "Yes. Focus is what you need. Get carried away and you'll borrow from the largest source around, which is you." He snapped his fingers suddenly, a shockingly loud sound, and Ruben jumped.

"Repeat that," Travis ordered.

Ruben did so, stuttering, and Travis made him do it again.

"Focus. Don't draw from your friends; don't pull too much from yourself. Might be tempting, but it'll kill you sure as time, and double as quick."

They sat in companionable silence for a few minutes while Travis stacked rocks and Ruben stared through the grass. His mind was pleasantly blank as he took in the surroundings. He liked being outside.

"What's the feel, when you use magic?" Travis cocked his head to the side.

"I'm not sure," Ruben said honestly.

"Never turned a thought to it?"

"I guess I didn't." He turned his palms up and brought fire to them, focusing on the sensation before he switched to lightning. He Displaced one of Travis's rocks, and raised and lowered his smell.

Travis sat patiently while Ruben experimented.

He tried to explain, “It's like … reaching out a hand? I reach, and it's there.”

“Moving a muscle?”

“Yeah, like that.”

“Mm. My magic is that way. I set it aside for a while and it goes a bit stiff and tough to move about, like a bad joint. I expect you'll find the ease to my magic soon enough.”

“Why does the cook say ‘pah’ when she's cleaning dishes?” Ruben asked.

Travis quirked an eyebrow. “Which cook?”

“I don't know her name.”

“Scouring's hard work. Remy has a bad elbow from a new break. I expect she turns to breath to ease the chore.”

Ruben nodded. “Whistling might do it, then, yeah?”

Travis chuckled, delighted. “I knew well a fellow who would dance streamers to whistles. Rare to see, and I cheered at the cleverness.”

A memory stirred. “After, um, Oats and I …”

“Aye.”

“After that, when the Smiling Man walked away, Beth was mad about him and she just made a lot of ‘k’ sounds. Was that another trick of it?”

Travis nodded soberly. “There's two paths of thought for sound: one instructs any noise you like, and the other educates to a precision. They see our language as developed to a purpose. Hard sounds, hard forms. ‘K’ is a very hard sound, seen as stronger, aggressive. ‘Pah’ is soft; gentle, but firm. Make sense?

“I never thought to need specific words and sounds for my magic, but some swear by it. They develop poems and chants and songs, easier to remember, I suppose, but put a lot of store by it. Write it all down and act as they've the only things to have a chance. Which makes it so, in a way.”

At Ruben's confused look, Travis winked. “Brought me around to your earlier question easily enough. Keen to know how magic works? As a muscle: stretch it, practice the use of it. But will makes magic so. Potential is everywhere. And who says the stone's never wanted to fly?”

He snapped his fingers again and the rock on the top of his pile wobbled into the air, swinging back and forth as though on a string. Ruben grinned and felt a desire unfold in his chest. He wanted to learn to do that.

"Believe that rocks want to fly and maybe they will. So begins lesson the first. Truly, were it in my schedule, you wouldn't dream of touching magic for another few weeks. I want you listing for me the potentials in dozens of lives, but Wren wants you pushed. Do you hear my risk and my trust? Best not see it abused."

"I won't," Ruben promised earnestly.

Travis gave him a sad smile. "I know you'll try not. Youth is always eager, and elders ever cautious. Find our balance and maybe you won't kill us all."

* * *

Ruben turned another page, his eyes itching with fatigue. The sun was coming up again. He hadn't slept at all, trying to get through as much of the book Wren had given him as he could before the Smiling Man returned. He'd practiced locking away his memories, too, and thought he had the knack of it.

Travis had pushed him to identify potentials in living things, even as he explained the need of focused willpower, having a clear idea in your mind for the magic to take form, otherwise it could be unpredictable. He spoke of the dangers a lot, sprinkling warnings through his lessons all day, and even while they ate, giving him not a moment's break. It took Ruben six and a half hours to make a rock wiggle, but Travis had clapped him on the back and congratulated him all the same.

The book from Wren was interesting. Full of stories, but not for children. Some were tales of murder, or betrayal. Some were love, and regret; none of them were more than twenty pages, and often they stopped before the ending was clear, forcing him to decide what happened in the end.

This last he read was the tale of a rich boy, heir to his barony, suspected of murder. Sent away to a school for magic, the boy learned what it meant to lose everything when his father disowned him, his peers abused him for the loss of status, and he had to work to pay for his place at the school, turning to poorer classmates in unexpected friendship, and having to decide between the school he'd grown to love or the life of a merchant that he'd always dreamed of.

With half a page left, and the story nowhere near concluded, Ruben had resigned himself to another ending-less tale. He could see why Wren wanted him to read it, though: all of the stories had to do with misuse of power in various forms.

As the first rays of sun cleared his window and crept across his floor, someone knocked. Ruben growled with frustration and rolled off of the bed, rubbing at his sand-filled eyes.

"Yes?" He opened the door.

The woman from his first day out of his cell was there, her hair in its silver bun, a pinched look on her face. She looked down her axe-like nose at him from her lofty height and stated, "The Lady has summoned you."

Ruben thanked her and glanced back at his book. He let out a long-suffering sigh and walked to Wren's office, knocked, and entered. Nothing had changed in a day, but he couldn't help but peek at the stacks to see if any had collapsed.

"You look brighter." Wren came from a back room. She was already dressed for the day: her hair was tied back in a bundle, and she wore riding clothes.

"Brighter?"

"Not as scared," she elaborated. "Enjoying the book?"

"I think so." After so long in his own company, with no entertainment but his memories and magic, the stories had been plenty exciting, even when they lacked action.

"Read all night?"

"Yes."

"He's coming back soon."

Ruben felt his jaw tighten and his chest tense.

"You've stowed our conversation where he can't find it? Assuming he doesn't look too hard — nothing is secret forever."

"I've stored it. And my lessons with Travis."

"Good. Keep practicing. Practice everything and practice it right. He'll know immediately that you've picked up life magic, but there's no need for him to know how much if you can help it."

"I'll do my best."

Wren smiled thinly. "Now that you have our secrets, what do you plan to do?"

Ruben blinked. "Um ..."

"Think about it. Now, do you know how to ride?"

Ruben dared to hope. "I — I love to ride."

"Been a while, I expect. Come on, then."

Wren led him outside and around the mansion, past the kitchen gardens full of herbs and spices. At first sight of the stable, Ruben nearly cried. The smell of horse was thick in his nose, and it was all he could do not to sprint ahead of Wren and throw himself into the nearest pile of hay, used or not.

"Take a mare and get her saddled. We won't be out long, but I like to clear my mind first thing in the morning."

Ruben did as he was bid. The stable wasn't large; it had half a dozen stalls, all full of older beasts, like the mansion tenants, with calm dispositions and bored or friendly gazes. He picked out a pretty brown creature and laid down her blanket and saddle, and slid the bit past her teeth. He was ready faster than Wren, who took her time and hummed a tune he vaguely recognized, but couldn't place.

Nearly dancing with impatience, Ruben followed as Wren led them out to mount and set off at a trot. The clear fields around the mansion were perfect for riding. Too close for planting, they'd been designed flat and kept clear of rabbits and moles by the various dogs and cats he'd seen about.

Wren gave her horse its head and Ruben followed suit, whooping as the beasts eased into a canter. They rode for half an hour before Wren waved at him to come to her side again. He did so, unable to stop grinning, and she smiled toothily at his expression.

"Having a good time?" she asked.

"Yes!"

"You can ride whenever you like."

"Thank you!" He tried to flatten his windswept hair, suddenly embarrassed by the gift she had given him.

She pointed. "Do you see that tree?"

Ruben turned to see a lonely tree atop a hill only a few miles away. Part of the trunk leaned away from the mansion at a drastic angle before it came back upright, probably pushed over by an ancient storm.

Wren continued, "The bend in that tree is pointed directly toward your Order."

Ruben stared.

"I won't say how far, of course, but if you decide to leave, that is the direction in which you would travel."

Ruben blinked sudden tears from his eyes. "Why are you telling me this?" Fear gnawed at him. It turned his earlier excitement sour.

Wren was silent for a long while and the horses stomped impatiently. "I haven't seen my home in decades. There are some things about it that I miss, and many things I do not. I'm not ungrateful to be where I am; I worked hard for this position, this responsibility and I don't know if I would have gone home if given the chance long ago. I was always a curious child, and it's made me a motivated adult. But I do know that I wish I'd had the option, just to know what I would have done. It doesn't matter now, after all."

She shifted in her saddle to look him in the eye. "There are a lot of things about this world to learn. It's easier if your attention is on the work, not split between it and escape. If you want to leave, I won't stop you. No one will stop you. I can't speak for *him*, of course." She looked irritated at these words. "Your friends are looking for you. I don't doubt they'll find you eventually. Do you know what will happen when they do?"

Ruben turned back to the tree.

Wren brushed an errant curl behind her ear. "I don't either. But I bet they won't let a fourteen-year-old fight in the front lines with them. It will come down to fighting, Ruben, and not long from now. Spies are useful things, but eventually their work is accomplished and the heavy machines move. I could be wrong, of course." She laughed. "Maybe they will let you fight, but if I were them, I'd send you back to the Order, and I'd keep you there with guards and schedules."

"I liked the Order."

"Of course you did; it's beautiful, and full of almost everything you could want. Almost. That's why I'm still here." She put her arms out to encompass everything they could see. Her horse pawed the grass for a mouthful.

"The problem is I don't care if you live or die. I have my preferences, but I'll use the tool at hand until I no longer have it, and then I'll make do as I did before. I will leave soon to join my army before it engages to destroy the largest and last blood mage threat we've seen in a long time. I'd like to bring you along. I can't promise I won't aim you at all of my enemies, some of whom are your allies, but I can't force you to use your magic, so that's something you have in hand."

"You want me to fight for you?"

"I want to make use of a valuable resource in which I have invested. Don't decide yet. Mull it over. Bring your thoughts to Travis — he's got a good head on his shoulders, even if it does spew that country-accented babble." She smiled briefly to soften the insult. "Either way, the choice is yours."

Wren turned her horse to trot back the way they'd come.

Ruben sat.

He stared at the crooked tree for a long time and finally urged his horse toward it, cresting the hill until he could touch the bark. He studied the bend and pushed his vision to the limits of his ability, but saw nothing except green and brown and the ever-lightening blue.

The mansion was waking: people were going to breakfast, going about their day. He could hear an increase in the noises the building produced. It grew warmer as the sun rose and filled the stones with heat. He thought about the last page of his book and started back down the hill.

He could stay one more day.

What was one more day?

11

"WHO ARE YOU?"

The bearded man was the epitome of fatigue, every bit of him dropping. His wife stood beside him with keen and wary eyes.

"We're here to help." Forest bowed politely. Wren did the best she could, exhausted as she was.

"What kind of help can you offer?" The would-be king was clearly skeptical, but hopeful.

"Advice. And effect. Your people need guidance, and you have no idea what you are doing. At this rate, you'll all be dead by winter."

The man sat forward on his would-be throne — affronted fury lent him energy. His wife laid a placating hand on his arm.

"What kind of advice *can you offer?" he spat through gritted teeth.*

"I can help your people flourish. You will live in any town, work any job, exist wherever you like. It will take patience, and a lifetime to bring to fruition, but your people will see themselves in their proper place once more."

The would-be king let out an exhausted chuckle, riddled with disbelief. "Is that all?" He looked at his wife, who did not share his façade of mirth.

"Certainly not," Forest continued. "To do this, my young friend here must inherit your rule."

"Don't be ridiculous," the wife snapped.

"Is it ridiculous?" Forest asked calmly. "She's young, very smart, very capable. You could do so much worse. Who would you have inherit instead? You haven't any children, and won't, if I'm to judge."

"How dare you!"

"Starve, then." Forest shrugged carelessly and turned on his heel. He strode out without a backward glance.

Wren tried to keep up, but fell quickly behind.

"Girl," the wife called. Wren swayed to a stop and half-turned. "Who are you?"

She sagged. "He'll do it. He'll do what he says. If you don't accept his help, he'll take your throne by force, and then you'll have nothing."

"That is an outrageous assumption. Impossible!" the life-king snarled.

"More impossible than war? You aren't well-hidden, you have no fields planted, and you won't harvest enough to feed everyone when you do finally plant. You'll be found in less than a year — closer to seven months, I think — and once you are, the army will come, and they will kill you. They will kill everyone."

"And you think you can lead?" the life-king asked scornfully.

"I know I can." Wren didn't bother haggling with him. She knew it as fact, and she could see his wife held the real power.

"If this is life or death as you claim ... and so soon ..." The life-queen struggled with her words.

"I haven't failed yet."

* * *

Donovan sat in the guest room with his head in his hands. He was tired and didn't know what to do. Only a couple of hours had passed since he'd confronted Ost, and the idea that the Smiling Man could come through his door at any moment to kill him was all he could think about. He nearly jumped out of his skin when the door opened — he knocked the chair askew in his haste to back away. But it was not the Smiling Man who had come for him.

"Theil?"

"The one and only. Let's go. You don't want to be here any longer."

Donovan didn't hesitate. He grabbed his bag and threw it across his shoulders, following close on the spy's heels. The keep appeared to be asleep: all of the daily sounds had quieted, and their footsteps seemed loud on the stone.

Thiel whispered, "We should be able to reach the stables and get away. No one saw me leave and it was luck I learned that our 'friend' is here. I didn't think that was part of your plan, so I came to get you."

"You're right. And thank you."

"Are you quick at saddling? I don't want to linger —" They stopped short.

Beal stood blocking the wall. "Master Rudd, tell me who …" His eyes narrowed. "You're the prisoner."

"Am I?" Theil held up his wrists. "No shackles. I think I make a compelling argument." He shuddered and his shoulders tensed. "Get out of my head."

He tried to quickly close the distance between them, but Beal backed away a few steps, clearly unwilling to physically engage. His magical attack grew stronger. Theil staggered to a stop and pressed his hands to his head. He fell against the wall and curled on the floor with a moan.

Donovan felt the wave of pressure now. He winced and backed away. Seeker tricks wouldn't help him against a determined Mentalist.

Beal hissed, "Master Rudd, I do have orders not to harm you, but if you insist on leaving your room, I will be forced to take measures to ensure your safety. After all, we have an escaped prisoner on the loose."

Donovan growled and marched forward. The pressure redoubled and he gasped at the blinding pain. Then he choked out a laugh. It wasn't unlike Seeking, this agony.

Beal was startled by his laughter, and he missed Theil's kick to his legs. The Mentalist hit the ground hard. His magic stopped as his concentration was broken. Donovan caught himself against the stone and gasped for breath. His head throbbed.

Theil crawled to the steward's side and wrenched his keys from a pocket. "What do the gate guards know?"

Beal spat in his face.

Theil wiped it calmly away. "Not the worst critique I've received." He held up a fist threateningly. "If you ever want to use your magic again, you'll tell me the quickest way out of here."

Beal's eyes narrowed again. "I've seen you before."

"Oh?"

His eyes widened. "You!"

The steward lunged forward and they grappled, each fighting for a choke hold or other advantage. Donovan skipped away to avoid tripping over them, and stayed out of the way until he could see how to help.

"You followed me! On the rooftop! I swore I'd find you, and here you are, delivered!"

"You murdered a child! Blood mage trash!"

They rolled across the floor, but it was no contest: Theil was the younger man and had muscle from training. He got free of Beal's zealous grip and twisted behind the steward to put a forearm across his throat.

The Mentalist attacked them again, clearly trying now to kill them both before his own demise.

Theil cried out, but did not loosen his hold. He squeezed tighter across Beal's throat. Donovan's head pounded. He tried to compress his skull and release the poison. There wasn't enough air in his lungs. He wheezed and tears poured down his face as it worsened.

It stopped just as suddenly as before.

Donovan hit the wall and then the floor with bruising force. The hall was silent. He felt lightheaded, dizzy.

Theil came into blurry view. His mouth was moving, and he looked concerned.

It took Donovan a moment to realize what he must have done. He increased his hearing slowly. "What?" He panted.

"Are you all right?" Theil repeated. He put out a hand to help Donovan to his feet.

"I think so." Donovan raised his sense of touch, having dampened it unconsciously. Seeking was easier to do without thinking now — he'd need to be careful of that.

"We have to go." Theil turned about to regain his bearings.

"It's that way," Donovan pointed.

He straightened his back and winced as his knees and spine protested their recent treatment. He'd done something to his elbow, too. They stepped over Beal's prone body. His face looked puffy and pale, tinged in blue. Donovan tried not to think about it — he'd killed people when needed, but he could never feel glad for the need.

Theil put up a hand for Donovan to wait as he snuck further ahead to look in the stables. He came back quickly, shaking his head and looking murderous.

"They have extra guards posted," he whispered. "Someone was expecting one of us to look for a ride out of here." He gave Donovan a disappointed glance.

"It's not like I told them I would try to escape!" he retorted.

Theil grinned at his indignation and led the way further on. He seemed to have almost as good a mental map of the place as Donovan did.

They came to a side gate and waited around the corner. The guard was alert and armed. And young. Theil took deep breaths and Donovan could see he was prepared to do harm to the young man, but Donovan put a hand out to stop him.

He took his own deep breath and stepped into view. Theil cursed quietly behind him, but didn't follow or try to stop him.

The guard saw him immediately and his stance was wary. "Good evening, sir. It's very late."

Donovan nodded. "I'm sorry, but I need to leave."

Private Nathaniel Oats hesitated. "I have orders. I'll be in serious trouble if I disobey."

"Oats, I'll be dead if I stay here."

The young man's eyes widened. "Why?"

"There are conspiracies and plots in motion that I cannot even begin to explain — I don't understand half of them myself. But I need to leave, right now, with my friend. If we don't get away, I don't know what will happen to us, but I do know it won't be pleasant."

"What will I say?" The boy looked to be on the verge of tears.

"I'm very persuasive?" Donovan suggested helplessly. "I'm sorry to put you in this position, Oats, I really am. I'm so sorry, but please. Please let us through, son."

The private hesitated a moment longer, a hand on his sword pommel. Then he turned away muttering quietly to himself. When his back was to them, Theil ran forward, Beal's keys in hand. He jammed the first three into the lock with no result before coming to the correct one. He left the bundle in the lock and they ran for the tree line.

It was dark and chilly. They saved their breath for jogging and had only gone half a mile when they heard shouting. Oats was covering himself by giving them a head start, but still calling their escape.

"I can't blame the boy," Theil said as they sped to a run.

"Where are we going?" Donovan panted after another mile. "I don't think I'll be welcome with your blood mage friends."

Theil looked at him incredulously. "No jest. I wasn't going to suggest that one, but thank you for the laugh. We need to get back to the Order. I have a feeling the spymaster has new orders for me."

Donovan changed directions. "That's the wrong way. We need to go further east."

"I was heading for the river," Theil explained. "Easier to follow it for the first bit."

"Sure, if you want to travel half again the distance."

"Fine, fine. Lead on, Seeker."

*　　*　　*

Donovan crouched with Theil close beside him. They scanned for sentries and saw no one. That didn't mean much, considering how often he'd hidden in trees or other positions to watch without being seen. The fire was banked low with burning embers safe in a pit neatly circled by stones. Four horses stood staked close by, serene in slumber. They could make out two lumpy, sleeping shapes. One tossed restlessly.

"Worth it?" Theil whispered into Donovan's ear.

Donovan shook his head and replied in kind, "We can walk. Why risk it?"

"We can get there by morning if we ride. Otherwise, it'll be another day."

Donovan shook his head again. "I don't like it. What if they're Hunters? We're not well-equipped to deal with them."

"Let's get closer."

"So they can spring a trap? No. We're going." Donovan started to back away.

Theil followed more reluctantly. They tried to be quiet through the leaves and debris found on any forest floor, and made a wide circle, aiming to pass the group unnoticed.

Exhaustion laid heavy on Donovan's shoulders. The two of them had walked for nearly twelve hours since he had last slept — three hours of sleep, at that, and all of it after Seeking to check their trail. No sign of pursuit, thankfully, but he longed for a horse.

Theil caught him as he stumbled over a root.

"All right." Donovan's shoulders slumped. "I won't make it much further. We'll take the horses."

They returned to the sleeping campers. Theil went ahead. Donovan increased his hearing and touch enough to give him, hopefully, enough warning of danger. They found themselves amongst the horses with little trouble. Theil pulled up a stake and gathered the rope to a sleepy horse. Donovan did the same a moment behind him.

Lightning crackled through the little clearing. Donovan winced and dimmed his vision by instinct before forcing it back to normal to wait for the light to settle. He crouched in a protective position.

"Think to make off with what's not yours, eh?" a woman's voice snarled. The camp was waking, and quickly. Bodies rose and converged on them.

Donovan released the horse and readied himself for what was sure to be a very short fight.

An Elementalist advanced from his right, lightning in hand.

Theil was already mounted and gazed about strategically as he steeled himself for heroics.

"Wait, *wait* stop!" someone shouted.

A large form ran forward to put a hand on the Elementalist, who immediately dropped her magic. Flooded in darkness again, the clearing was twice as confusing.

"Be quiet!" the voice shouted.

Everyone froze.

Donovan cocked his head. That voice was far too familiar.

"Don?"

"Whit?"

Laughter cackled out of the bard's throat as the Elementalist raised her hands to light the clearing once more. Whitman grabbed Donovan in a bear hug, nearly crushing him.

"I missed you!"

"And I, you!" Donovan answered sincerely. He didn't realize how worried he'd been about the young bard until now, seeing him alive.

"Who else is with you?" Donovan looked around. "Annette! And — Cara! What are you doing here?"

"Jasmin, can you get that fire up? Annette! Donovan was stealing our horses!"

"So I see." She came forward for her own embrace. He returned the hug warmly. It had only been a couple of days, but Annette was a friend, and he'd missed her. Cara didn't come forward, but smiled warmly at him. His stomach turned over, but he smiled back.

"Who's your friend?" Donovan asked as they staked the horses back down and gathered around the fire.

Whitman answered, "Jasmin."

Annette made a face.

"She was one of the people who came to kidnap Ruben the first time, but she is now assisting us with finding the Hunters."

Donovan looked at Jasmin, taking in her face. She did the same and both realized at once that she'd been the one to torture Donovan into unconsciousness before Vale had arrived to chase her team off and save him. They held eye contact until Jasmin looked away. She took a few steps back and threw furtive glances his way until she turned to disappear amongst the horses.

"I thought there'd be hard feelings," Whitman admitted. "I respect that. I only hope they will not keep us from working together as best we can."

"So you're the bard. Whitman Acres." Theil had been watching Whitman the entire time, and Whitman had seemed to ignore him.

"I am!" Whitman said brightly.

Theil stared a moment longer and then ran a hand across his growing beard. "I was going back for orders, but I guess now's as good a time as any."

Whitman's face fell. "I'm sorry you figured it out."

"I'm an actor, sir. I can recognize the voice that produces an accent."

"That was a concern. Oh well, it cannot be helped now. I will need your report as soon as you can deliver it."

They stepped away to speak privately.

"What happened?" Annette asked. "We were coming to meet you with Ost."

"That's no longer an option," Donovan massaged a cramp in his calf. "Ost is a sympathizer. He was meeting with the Smiling Man before we left. We can't trust him."

Annette looked devastated, then took a deliberate breath. "That's ... disappointing."

"I'm sorry."

"He's a backer for the blood mages or life mages?" Cara asked.

Donovan blinked at her. "Life, I think."

"So does that mean the Smiling Man is on the side of the life mages, or the blood mages?"

Donovan shrugged helplessly. "I want to say the blood mages, but it ... doesn't look that way. Somehow."

"And you're saying those are the *good* ones?"

"My enemy's enemy is my ally," Jasmin said softly. She'd returned silently to join them. Everyone stared at her, but she kept her eyes on the fire.

Whitman and Theil returned but Donovan kept the Elementalist in his view.

"Whit, your knee," Donovan realized suddenly.

Whitman stretched it out with a grin. There was no sign of a cane or brace.

"It was Healed?" Donovan asked excitedly.

"Yes! Finally! I can run again, Don! And jump, and *fight!* Oh, you have no idea how I have missed this!" He jumped to his feet and jogged around the circle, turning a cartwheel and pushing off one hand into a flip. He landed imperfectly and stumbled. "I still need some practice, but that is more than I have done in *months!*" Nearly everyone was drawn into his enthusiasm.

"So what brings you away from the Order?" Donovan asked Cara, looking to Annette and Whitman for information.

"The vote went through," Annette said. "Paola Rosales is now Head of the Order."

"I've heard of her. She was in charge of Order agriculture for a while, and then transferred to finance, right? Manazian family long ago, but I haven't heard a word against her," Donovan said.

"She has been head of various departments, quietly gaining favor here and there," Whitman replied. "I am not surprised, honestly. I have watched her for some time, but I expect they could have done worse."

"That's why you left?" Donovan looked at each of them in turn.

"No, we found out that Bruno was blackmailed to kill Elliott because his family practices life magic — did you know there was a difference between life magic and blood magic? — and Jasmin here was sent to assassinate Bruno to keep it all quiet, but through her we found out about these two separate factions of mages, one of which is *not* blood mages, and do not necessarily want us all dead, and they are going to fight —"

"Whit, *Whit,* we know. That's why we were coming back: to tell you all the same," Donovan interrupted.

The bard pursed his lips and glared. "I hate when people know more than me."

"It's a feeling I've grown accustomed to." Donovan looked around. "Where's Oslan?"

"He stayed to scribe and keep an ear to the floor for me, both." Whitman's reply was too casual.

Donovan looked to Annette again, who nodded. "He's fine, but decided it was best if he stayed. Jasmin," Annette said distastefully, an eye on the woman, "gave us information that makes us think the Hunter army is near to Ost's lands. If he is a sympathizer, then he already knows, and has a plan in place to kick off this jolly war in earnest."

"Well," Whitman stretched and jumped a few times. "No time like the present. We can double up on the horses and walk them as needed — should still make good time."

"We're heading back to Ost's keep?" Donovan stood and stretched as well. His elbow made a disconcerting pop, loud enough that they all stared at it for a moment.

He was still exhausted, but the relief of being back amongst friends made it easier to bear. And the promise of a horse.

"Of course not," Whitman said. "You said we cannot trust him. No, we are going to find the life mages and see if we can get the final piece to his puzzle."

"Ah. Of course. The insane choice is your favorite one." Donovan looked imploringly at Annette and Cara, but they mirrored his expression.

"It certainly brings the most excitement." Whitman rubbed his hands together and smiled wolfishly. "Shall we?"

ABOUT THE AUTHOR

Morgan Chalut (she/they) has been writing since she learned that anyone was allowed to do that; it wasn't illegal or anything! While it didn't slow down her talking, it at least gave her parents and six older siblings (and her poor, poor teachers) a break once in a while. She hopes to continue to discover characters and worlds she can plot and explore and share.

Morgan lives in Dallas, Texas with her delightfully handsome and silly, charming, supportive, and lovely husband, Philip. They have two dogs together: Caramel, who absolutely wants to be your friend, and Sammie, who very definitely does not.

You can find out more about the world and works of Morgan Chalut at *morganchalut.com*.

ALSO IN THIS SERIES

SEEKER

BOOK ONE OF "THE UNWOVEN TAPESTRY" SERIES

There is a war brewing, centuries old. The Hunters, blood mages and child-snatchers fight the born mages, people of the Order, the school of magic and scholarly pursuit.

Available from Water Dragon Publishing in
hardcover, trade paperback, and digital editions
waterdragonpublishing.com

YOU MIGHT ALSO ENJOY

GRIMAULKIN

BOOK ONE OF THE "GRIMAULKIN" SERIES

by L. A. Jacob

Treading the straight and narrow is not natural to one who summons demons.

JUST A BIT OF MAGIC

by Barb Bissonette

Every morning, Jenny Smith stares into her magic mirror, searching for glimpses of two girls. Today, she is joyful with anticipation, knowing that this is the day they will materialize in her village.

MERMAID STEEL

by Jay Hartlove

The power of love over hate.

SKY CHASE

BOOK ONE OF "THE FLIGHT OF SHIPS" TRILOGY

by Lauren Massuda

Travel to a vast world of airborne ships and floating islands.

CPSIA information can be obtained
at www.ICGtesting.com
Printed in the USA
LVHW040417110522
718423LV00001B/38

9 781957 146423